THEY CONTINUED TO WALK on hand in hand through the growing darkness. The music from the saloons blared down Front Street, but everything around them seemed strangely serene and quiet. Karen asked coyly, "Am I soft and pink like a nursery?"

Joe stopped, turned to face her. He took her other hand and, holding the two up close to his chest, said, "Yes, ma'am, you are at that. And I'm here to tell you that I could have no fonder dream of a woman than I'm seeing right now."

Karen blinked back a tear, afraid to speak. Afraid if she did, the moment would spin off into the darkness never to be retrieved again. It was like a flash of magic, a wink of time that each wanted to savor forever.

Joe swallowed hard. "Since I already stepped out on a limb here, would you permit me to go ahead and make a complete fool of myself?"

"Why don't you let me be the judge of that?"

He swallowed hard once more. "Well, you're a woman of means now, and I'm just a no-count cowboy. There's no cause for a pretty lady like you to settle for someone like me." H

"Ar

His that means, an other v

BOOKS BY JAMES WALKER

Husbands Who Won't Lead and Wives Who Won't Follow

THE WELLS FARGO TRAIL
  The Dreamgivers
  The Nightriders
  The Rail Kings
  The Rawhiders

THE RAWHIDERS

+ + + + + + + + + +

JIM WALKER

BETHANY HOUSE PUBLISHERS
MINNEAPOLIS, MINNESOTA 55438

Published by Bethany House Publishers
A Ministry of Bethany Fellowship, Inc.
11300 Hampshire Avenue South
Minneapolis, Minnesota 55438

Printed in the United States of America.

Library of Congress Cataloging-in-Publication Data
Walker, James.
    The rawhiders / Jim Walker.
        p. cm. — (The Wells Fargo trail ; bk. 4)

    I. Title. II. Series: Walker, James. Wells Fargo trail ;
bk. 4
PS3573.A425334R4   1995
813'.54—dc20   94–476
ISBN 1–55661–431–4   CIP

This book is dedicated to a young woman with spiritual fire, the kind of person who has made a radical difference in my life and who makes all who come to know her a better person—my daughter, Julie.

JIM WALKER is a staff member with the Navigators and has written *Husbands Who Won't Lead and Wives Who Won't Follow*. He received an M.Div. from Talbot Theological Seminary and has been a pastor with an Evangelical Free Church. He was a survival training instructor in the United States Air Force and is a member of the Western Writers of America and the Western Outlaw-Lawman History Association. Jim, his wife, Joyce, and their three children, Joel, Jennifer, and Julie, live in Colorado Springs, Colorado.

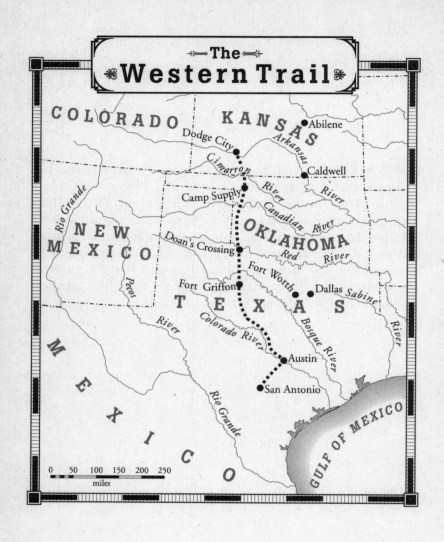

The Western Trail

CHARACTERS

+ + + + + + +

Barbara Reddiger—Oldest daughter of the Reddiger family. Barb feels a motherly instinct toward her sisters and is protective of them. She wants desperately to continue her family's heritage and preserve the ranch.

Karen Reddiger—Blond spitfire who can ride, rope, and shoot with the best of men. She considers herself the black sheep of the family. Called Car on the trail.

Dorothy Reddiger—Outspoken and headstrong third daughter. She doesn't know how much she still needs to learn about men and life.

Vonnie Reddiger—At fourteen, she's the youngest of the Reddiger girls. She is contemplative, but adventurous.

Frank Emmy—Local banker who holds the note to the Reddiger ranch. He is smitten with the attractive Barbara Reddiger, but pulled along by the forces that seek to control the Reddiger property.

Joe Cobb—Ex-Confederate soldier, now a cowboy. Joe is savvy in the ways of the West and handles horses well. Older brother of Zac.

Poor Soul—Ex-slave of the Cobb household. He is good-natured, literate, extremely quick with a gun, and fearless.

Zac Cobb—An agent for Wells Fargo using the alias of Ian Adams, he is a soldier of fortune on assignment. Zac doesn't know if any of his brothers have survived the war.

Skip—Zac's adopted son. He fears the loss of anyone who gets close enough to love him.

Pete Hammond—Trail boss hired by the banker, and a man without scruples.

Wolf Macrae—Gunslinging ramrod, assistant to Pete Hammond.

Yanni—The son of a circuit-riding preacher who has strayed far from his parents' teaching.

Jim Crossy—Talkative, fun-loving Irish cowboy who can be depended on to show his experience while making light of the world around him.

Lance Randolph—Yale graduate, former Philadelphia lawyer, the son of a powerful Eastern family. He has gone west to escape the designs of his father.

Frank Green—Nicknamed Greener, Frank is a young man who needs a job to provide for his young wife and expected baby.

Tipper—Young fifteen-year-old runaway, branded "bad" by his drunken father after his mother died giving birth to him.

Earl Richards—Lord Edward Richards, Earl of Northumberland, sent to the American West by his father in order to prove his mettle as a man.

Bobby Pera—Italian trail cook who wants to start a restaurant.

Dr. Marvin—Local traveling salesman. An older man, he's a former minister who, after the death of his family, has chosen a life of providing for other people's needs.

Quirt Muldoon—Three-hundred-pound albino. He seeks to corner the Kansas cattle market by any means necessary and takes special delight in manipulating people.

Nat Black—Muldoon's devious, mean-spirited lieutenant who demonstrates his skills with a bull-whip on any man who opposes him.

Rass Bodine—Muldoon's hot-headed assistant who is fast with his guns.

Jock O'Connor—Huge Irish red-haired fellow, the brute strength segundo to Muldoon's operation.

CHAPTER 1

+ + + + + + +

LIKE AN INVISIBLE RIVER, the wind lapped against the mourners. The warm Texas sun shone brightly and birds flitted across the tops of waving bluebonnets. It was a beautiful day for a funeral.

Twenty-two people stood beside Will Reddiger's casket in the family burial plot. Eight years earlier the three sisters had buried their mother here; now it was time to bury their father. Barbara, the oldest, was twenty-five and towered over the other two. According to local custom she should have been married by now. Even Dorothy was old enough to be married, at the tender age of sixteen. She had fair skin and auburn hair. La-Vonne, called Vonnie by the family, was an impish and gangly fourteen-year-old just beginning to bud into womanhood. Karen, a fourth sister, wasn't present at the funeral, at least not in close proximity. At twenty-two, she was the wild beauty of the bunch. Their father always said that no man would ever get close to her a second time. When he told her that, the other girls would all laugh. Karen would purely shame the men who came around her, she would. No matter what they were doing—riding, roping, shooting, or just playing checkers—Karen always seemed to do it better. All that, and she played the piano too.

Maybe her father loved her so much because in some way she reminded him of what he had been like in his young, wild days, when Texas was growing up. He had killed Comanches and built the ranch into a place that everyone envied. People liked the ranch, and they admired the water rights even more.

The grass on the Circle R was greener, and there were pecan trees scattered along the lowlands. Vonnie loved to climb them and shake the nuts down. She'd bounce on the limbs, all the while shaking them with her arms, listening to the fat pecans hit the ground.

The sisters held hands tightly. Being the youngest, Vonnie was always between her sisters in church; this was no different, a sort of outdoor church service.

As the group sang "Shall We Gather at the River," Vonnie looked up the boulder-strewn hill to where Karen was watching. No one else saw her. She sat on her favorite mare, the one with the white stockings. Karen had told them all that she didn't want to remember her father as a hole in the ground. Barb had tried to shame her into coming, but whenever Karen made up her mind about a thing, that was that. She said she didn't want to stand around listening to a bunch of hypocrites spout off about how much they all admired her father when none of them had lifted a finger to help him when he was alive, and few had tried to find his killer.

Vonnie clenched her jaw as she thought of the upcoming auction of her family's property. Her father had gotten the bank to agree to hold off, but now it would go on as scheduled. All these people were saying such nice things now, but Vonnie knew they'd be there on Wednesday, be there to buy everything she'd ever known. They finished the songs and listened to the preacher pray, then one by one, each put a spadeful of dirt over Will's box.

The parson held his Bible and looked up into the sky. Vonnie followed his gaze and imagined her papa and momma looking down on them all. "The Lord giveth and the Lord taketh away, blessed be the name of the Lord," the parson drawled.

Vonnie heard the preacher's voice clear enough, but still didn't understand much of what he was saying. She had always been thankful for what the Lord gave, but hated Him for what He had taken away. Blessing Him for it would be a long time coming.

"By golly, I'm so sorry about your papa, Vonnie," the storekeeper said. Vonnie hated it when grown-ups put their hands on her head. It always made her feel small. Mr. Bickerstaff was a nice enough man, but Vonnie couldn't fight shy of the feeling that maybe he was owed money. He and his wife moved on down the line, talking to each of the sisters. As every other merchant walked by, Vonnie couldn't get over the feeling that maybe they were looking to collect from what was left of the Reddiger family. Will would have wanted them paid, if they were owed, but still, the thought made Vonnie feel uncomfortable.

One by one, the mourners filed past the girls, and each said something. Many of the women had brought food. Some of the ladies had brought apple and berry pies and set them in the back of the buggy. At least it was still their buggy for a short time yet. Karen would never want to give up the horses, but the buggy and tack would have to go, along with the ranch. In a few days, somebody else would own the place where they had been raised, and somebody else would own the land where the graves were dug. Vonnie had already made plans to ride back in the morning with flowers and her Bible. She wanted to be alone with the two of them—just them and her.

Frank Emmy, the banker, held his hat in his hand. "Barbara, I know this here is a bad time to bring this up, but I'll be out to your place on Tuesday to make arrangements. I hope that'll give you girls a chance to pack your things."

Barb wiped her eyes and stood up straight and tall. "That'll be fine," she said. "It has to be done. What about the stock?"

He scratched his head and rubbed his smooth chin. "Well, Barbara, the bank doesn't have a lien on your stock, or on the herd for that matter. The bank will give y'all a fair price for them, though. I believe I can promise you a dollar a head. Cattle aren't worth much these days in Texas."

"Karen tells me we have around four-thousand head of cattle, Mr. Emmy. We have over a hundred horses too. Like Papa told you, we were planning to drive them north to market."

"Barbara, your father might have been able to do that, but for you girls, I'm afraid that notion would be nonsense thinkin'.

Four girls and whatever scalawags you can talk into goin' with you ain't gonna get far with all them cattle. Besides, four thousand dollars is a lot of money. That's plenty enough to see you girls settled in town. I can find you a house to rent. Now, the horses will bring more, of course. Most of them are mustangs, but I think y'all will find buyers for them at the auction." He paused and looked over the girls. "We can find jobs for you too, something that will make use of your talents." He smiled. "I didn't see Karen."

"I doubt you will," Dorothy said. "She's not much one for funerals."

"Even her own father's?"

"Especially Father's."

"Well," he stretched the words out and directed them past Dorothy and toward Barb, "I'm not exactly sure how to find employment for her. Your sister has something of a reputation 'round here. I wouldn't 'zackly call her the dependable type."

Barb lifted her chin. "Mr. Emmy, Karen can be depended on to do exactly what she wants to do."

He put his hat on and cocked it to one side. "I can only hope, then, that for your sake, she decides to do something useful." Patting her shoulder, he smiled. He walked briskly to his surrey. Bouncing the springs hard when he got in, he slapped the reins on the backs of his well-matched team.

The hands had all been standing there in the sun with their heads bare. There were only three of them left, and they hadn't been paid in two months. Doug was the foreman. He'd been with the Circle R for ten years. "I reckon me and the boys will clear our things out of the bunkhouse and go," he said.

Barb reached into her pocket and brought out her papa's gold watch. "Here, Doug, you take this and sell it. It's all I've got to give and I know Father would have wanted you boys to have it. Lord knows you've earned it."

"No, ma'am. I won't a be a takin' your daddy's watch. You'll be needin' that. You just feed us and send us on our way. We can all find us another job. You can't get another watch that was carried by your daddy."

She looked at the watch. It was solid gold and inside the lid was a picture of her mother. "You would think whoever shot him would have taken his watch," she said.

She placed it back in her pocket and spoke to the men. "All right, we won't be keeping you men any longer. We haven't made up our minds about a drive, and I'm not sure the bank will wait. You need to be looking for other jobs. You've all served my father well, but I guess we won't be needing anyone after Wednesday. When we get back to the house, we can all eat in the dining room. We can at least do that for you all."

Doug hung back as the other men mounted. "Miss Barbara, I'm a gonna be driftin' on. I know some of the boys will more'n likely go to work for the Bar-H, but you won't see me wearing that brand."

The sheriff was the last to leave. He led his horse toward the girls and pushed his mustache up from his lips. "I'll be along on Wednesday. I just wanta be sure there's no trouble."

"Then bring money, Sheriff," Barb said. "And while you're at it, bring our father's killer."

"Now, you girls know I've gone and done my best on that score. Your father was well-liked around here."

"Our water rights were well-liked," Dorothy shot back.

Barb put her hand on Dorothy's arm.

"Are you suggesting that someone from somewheres 'round here killed your father?"

Barb spoke up. "Sheriff, you know as well as we do that our father would have found some way to pay off our note. He was planning on a cattle drive north, and if it weren't for the thought that we girls couldn't carry out his plans, the bank wouldn't have called our note." Barb's back was ramrod straight. She was always one to be proper, but when she was pushed, she could be a real scrapper. "The prospect of us losing the place and the water seems to be reason enough, I would think. That, combined with the fact that whoever wanted our father dead wasn't man enough to take him on face-to-face. He had to shoot him in the back with a rifle. That ought to show it was somebody who knew my father could handle a six-gun."

The man shook his head slowly and looked at the ground. "I think, Miss Barbara, that whoever done this thing was somebody passin' through—probably didn't even know your daddy." With that, he tipped his hat and turned his horse around.

The girls stood beside their buggy and watched him ride off.

Before the dust was settled, Karen galloped her mare down the rocky hill and skidded her to a stop. Taking out the rope, she swung it over her head, built a loop, and threw it over the little fence around her father's grave.

"What are you doing?" Barb asked, incredulous. She grabbed the reins of the mare, but Karen jerked them free.

Taking a dally around the saddle horn, she backed the horse up and pulled down the fence. "There ain't no way I'm gonna leave no fence around his grave. He hated fences. Said fences were the death of Texas. He'd a wanted cows, horses, and antelope moving over him, not some durn fence keepin' 'em out."

Barb moved in front of the mare, waving her arms to keep the animal back. "This is sacred ground, Karen. You can't do that!"

Karen jerked the horse around her and, taking in the rope, swung it free, building another loop. "This whole place is sacred. There's no part of it that's more sanctified than all the rest. These two people gave their lives for this ranch, not these two little spots that bank will leave them."

With that, she threw the rope around the other half of the white picket fence and jerked it out of the ground. "I won't see it come to this. They worked too hard to give this all to the Bar-H."

Dorothy held Barb back. "Let her do as she likes. She's right."

Karen pranced the mare forward. She curled the rope and tied it to her saddle horn. "You want to ride back with me, Vonnie?" she asked.

Smiling, Vonnie scooted up behind Karen and clamped her arms around her sister's slim waist. Karen's flowing blond hair hung down beneath her hat and fell between her shoulder blades. Vonnie pressed her cheek onto it.

The horse pranced and stamped as Karen turned her around. "One thing's for sure," Karen said. "Whoever killed him will be at that auction on Wednesday. He'll be there to claim his prize; this ranch, and our water rights."

Barb and Dorothy looked up at her. There was no disputing what Karen said. Few people ever disagreed with her for long, even if they were right. But this time she was right, and they all knew it.

"And if that rattlesnake of a sheriff is there with his saddle gun, or the sidewinder he's covering up for, then we'll have the murderer that done it. Everybody knows that man's bought and paid for by the Bar-H. He ain't no sheriff. He's just a drifter, a hired killer with a star on his chest."

The mare continued to stamp at the ground, impatient to move on. "You aren't planning to do anything foolish, are you?" Barb asked.

"Who, me? What can I do? I'm just a girl. What can a girl do in Texas?"

"You're liable to do anything. But violence is not the way Father and Mother would have wanted it. Remember, you're Mennonite."

"I do shoot rattlesnakes that crawl out from under rocks."

Barb reached up and grabbed the mare's mane. "They'll hang you in Texas for that, just the same as they would a man."

"That would be something, at least. If I can ride, rope, and shoot like a man, then I guess I can die like one."

"And then we'd leave three graves here instead of two," Barb said. "We'd have three graves, but the land would still belong to the Bar-H, and it would be their cattle stomping your grave down. The three of us would have to leave, but you could stay here with Mother and Father. Is that what you want?"

Vonnie tightened her grip on Karen.

"The best we can do," Barb went on, "is to keep all we can and do what Father would have wanted us to do—beat these people."

"And how do we do that?" Karen asked. She spit out the words, more out of anger than curiosity.

"I don't know. But all the same, we've got to find a way. We've got to stay together and find a way."

Dorothy took off her bonnet and shook her reddish hair free. "Daddy used to call us his female machine," she said. "Do you remember that? He used to say that he had no need for boys, that a boy would be like throwing a spool of barbed wire into a well-oiled machine."

The girls smiled, remembering. Will had a way of making them feel needed and wanted when anybody else would only have looked on them with pity. He'd never been a man to see the end of a thing, only the beginning. He marched them proudly into church, insisting on sitting all of them in the front row. He used to say, "I want everybody to see how beautiful you all are, and I don't want one person to miss the sight." He embarrassed them and made them proud all at the same time. There was never any room in him for pity. For Will, his four daughters were a matter of pride.

Dorothy went on. "I wouldn't want to see any one of us do anything that would shame him, or Mother for that matter."

"That's right," Barb said. "We're all we've got right now. And I don't want to see us lose one fourth of what we've got because of some hot-headed foolish plan for revenge."

Karen pulled up on the reins. "You just keep that man out of my sights, then. I wouldn't do like he did. I wouldn't shoot him in the back. I would draw down on him, though. I'd stitch a line of slugs down his belly too quick to talk about, and don't think I wouldn't."

She slapped her spurs to the side of the mare and bolted toward the hill. Gripping her sister's waist tightly as they galloped, Vonnie said nothing. The two had always been close, in spite of their difference in age, and Vonnie knew Karen didn't want to talk.

Riding over the grass, they sent a bevy of quail flying in all directions, but Karen had the mare so well trained, the animal never missed a beat.

When they slowed down and trotted down the hill, Vonnie spoke. "There's something wild about you, Karen. You scare me a little. When are you just gonna be a woman?"

"I don't like woman's work. That's something I just ain't ready for, and I doubt if I ever will be. I ride, rope, dig fence holes, swing an ax with the best of them, and never refuse to do anything—except cook."

"I seen you kicked, stomped, gored, thrown, but I ain't never seen you cry. You know, Karen, I admire you something powerful, but being like you is a cross can't none of us carry. Still, I just admire watching you all the same. You're like a wild stallion that won't be broke, like some mustang that ain't worth nothin' 'cept the pleasure a body feels in watching it run. Your wildness plumb scares me from time to time, but I love to watch it."

Karen laughed. "Then hang on, gal. We step into some chuck hole, we're gonna fly, so you just better hang on and pray." With that, she once again sent the mare into a wild gallop as Vonnie hung on.

When they cleared the ridge, Karen slowed down. "How you 'spect to take that man if it comes to it?" Vonnie asked.

"You've seen me. I can always outdraw and outshoot the hands in the bunkhouse. They've never even been close. They walk away muttering to themselves, scratching their heads."

"I know. You ride like any man, shoot better than any man, and then sit down at Mother's piano not ten minutes later and play a piece from Handel. You're a wonder. But you're a woman too."

She was also a beauty. Her long blond hair set off her hazel eyes. And her figure in a dress was enough to catch any man's eye. Of course, they seldom were brave enough to come close to her. Karen had a way of making a man feel like he wanted to be a man, and then showing him how small he was at the same time. It was the one thing that had irritated Will about her, irritated him and made him smile at the same time. He had been proud of her, and Vonnie was proud of her too. They were sisters, but Vonnie belonged to Karen in a special way. There was an attachment between the two sisters that made it so that only Vonnie could ask her the things she asked, and it also allowed Karen to tell her the truth, to conceal nothing.

CHAPTER 2

+ + + + + + · +

KAREN WAS UP EARLY. She had saddled the mare before the rest of the girls started breakfast and rode off toward the brakes, the rough country, to find unbranded cattle. The sisters watched her ride away. "Why do we need to go into War Eagle?" Dorothy asked.

"I thought you girls liked going into town."

"It all depends."

"Depends on what?"

Vonnie busied herself with drying and putting away the dishes while Dorothy washed, and seemed to be driving the questioning. Vonnie had always been content to watch the other girls before picking sides. Dorothy put down the dish and stared out the window at Karen riding off in the distance. "We always went into town with Papa," she said.

"That can't happen anymore." Barb's tone was sharp.

"I just don't want to be stared at and talked about," Dorothy continued. "I feel like some kinda spectacle. I ain't never been an orphan before."

"All right, then stay here. I'll take Vonnie and we'll go. Do you want to go, LaVonne?"

The girl nodded her head and continued putting the dishes away.

Dorothy swung around and placed her hands on her hips. "I don't understand. Can't figure out what you need to go into that place for."

"We talked about the drive north and I just want to make

sure that if we do that and manage to sell the herd, we'll have a place to come home to."

"Now, how do you plan on goin' about that? You heard that man at the bank say he didn't think women moving a bunch of cows was worth a risk—why would he change his mind?"

Barb wiped her hands on the towel. "If I can show we have the means to do it—the hands, the equipment, the cattle—then I think Mr. Emmy can be persuaded to give us Father's original terms. If we had that six months, we could make the drive and pay off the ranch."

"Now how you gonna persuade him to do that?" Dorothy asked.

Vonnie had seated herself at the table and continued to watch her sisters spar. "Mr. Emmy likes the looks of Barb," she said with deliberate sweetness. "I've seen him watch her."

"That old letch!" Dorothy shot back. "You can't be serious. I wouldn't let that man come within ten feet of me."

Barb carefully took off her apron and hung it up. She straightened her hair. "This is our place now. Father and Mother spent their lives building it, and I won't stand by and see it taken. Frankly, I hope Vonnie's right. I didn't say anything about what I'm thinking, but I don't mind using whatever's on his mind to save this ranch. Right now, that may be all we have to work with."

The girls blinked at her as she took soap in hand and rubbed her face. She splashed herself with water, then gently patted her features dry before pinching her cheeks to produce a rosy hue. "There now, let's change into town clothes and get about the business of saving this ranch. Just because we buried Daddy doesn't mean we buried his dreams."

In less than an hour Barb had changed into her prettiest blue dress and hitched the team to the buggy. She slapped the backs of the animals with the reins, and the rig bolted down the road toward War Eagle.

"Vonnie, we'll go to Bickerstaff first. I'll see him with my list and leave you there to look around while I go to the bank."

The girls rode quietly all the way to town, each lost in her own thoughts. Barb stopped the team in front of Bickerstaff's store, tied them to the rail, and straightened her dress. Vonnie followed her inside.

"By golly, it's good to see you girls." Bickerstaff rounded the counter and wiped his hands. "I am so sorry about what's happened to your papa."

Barb cleared her throat. "I wanted to see what my father's bill might be, Mr. Bickerstaff."

"Your papa's bill?" He waved his arms. "If it weren't for dat papa of yours, den none of dis vould be here. He saved me when Harrod and Emmy moved their store into dis town. Why, if dat papa of yours hadn't stepped his own self into de mess and had some of dem ranchers keep buyin' from me, den I don't know where me and my missus would be. Now, how can I serve you?"

Barb watched as the dark, curly-haired man behind the shopkeeper stopped his sweeping and leaned over on his broom. "We are planning on a drive north to sell our cattle. I don't have any money, but if you can help with the food and supplies we need, then I can promise payment when we get the cattle to market."

The balding man grinned broadly. "I vould love to give you anything I got. Take it all if you like. I know you'll pay me when you kin. De apple don't fall far from de tree and dem folks of yours raised people to be counted on." He hurried his pace around the room and pointed out items that might be needed. "I kin give you beans and bacon, salt pork, tomatoes, flour, anything you need. You vill be needing coffee, lotsa coffee."

The man on the broom spoke up. "How 'bout that wagon we got?"

"Durn shootin' right!" the shopkeeper exclaimed. "Ve got us one of dem dere chuck wagons dat Charlie Goodnight come up with. It's cleaner'n a whistle. Come on out back, I'll show you."

The three of them walked through the store and out the back door. Parked outside was a large wagon, the likes of which Barb had never seen. The walls of the wagon were high, and Bickerstaff took her around to the rear, where he showed her the bracket of shelves and drawers that held everything from spices to pots and pans. "Dis here is the very latest thing. You'll be happy with it and it kin carry 'nuff grub to feed yer whole durn crew fer quite a spell."

"I don't think we can afford one of these, Mr. Bickerstaff."

"Pshaw! Like I done told you. Der ain't nuthin' a mine you can't afford." He paused and scratched his whiskered chin. "But you vill be needin' a cook. You little gals can't 'spect to care for a passel of trail hands all by yer lonesome. Your papa vould turn over if he knew you vas doin' such a thing. You gots to have you a man you kin trust out dere."

"I'd be happy to go along with you gals." The other man had laid aside his broom and spoke up. "And Mr. Bickerstaff here can speak for my cooking."

Bickerstaff laughed and held his ample belly as it shook. "Dat's fer durn sure. Bobby Pera here is a vonder. He's von of dem Italians. Puts olives into everything. He's been dryin' and stringin' pasta all over de place 'round here. He come into town to start a eatin' place, but ain't had no luck yet." Bickerstaff put his arm around the man. "And by golly, dis boy can bake bread like you ain't never seen before."

"Well, I had planned on cooking myself," Barb said, "but it sounds like I could use you. You'd have to take a dollar a day and a one-hundred-dollar bonus if you finish the drive, same as any other man. Of course, I won't have any money until we finish the drive."

"Sure, that'll be justa fine with me. I'ma happy just to be gettin' outta Texas." He held out his hands and counted on his fingers. He skinned a broad smile. "Holy Saints and prophets, that mighta be three hundred dollars. I ain'ta seen that much money all at one time. With all that, I mighta be able to open up a place to cook for folks."

Barb smiled. "I think a man who has ambitions to cook full-time is just the sort of person we ought to have."

"By golly," Bickerstaff slapped Pera's back, "den Bobby's yer man. He's even got his own pile a fixin's and such. Got a barrel with more of dat olive oil den I ever seen before."

"All right, I'll get Karen to bring some mules into town to-morrow. If you can load that wagon with supplies between now and then, that would be wonderful. I'll make sure we have her bring another wagon. We'll probably have to take more supplies than this can carry all by itself. Meanwhile, I'm leaving Vonnie here with a list that we have."

"Okey-dokey," Bickerstaff said. "You leave it all to me—me, Bobby Pera here, and the missus."

"Mr. Bickerstaff, I sure do appreciate all that you're doing for us. We will be back."

He put his hand on her shoulder. "I have no quibbles about dat, girl. You belong to dat papa and momma of yours. Dey had sand, and so do you."

The gray boards squeaked beneath Barbara's feet as she walked down the boardwalk from the store. The bank would be a different story, she knew that. It made her all the more pleased that she had started with Bickerstaff. Somehow, any degree of success made it easier to make a case with Emmy. As she crossed the street, she straightened her dress and once again pinched her cheeks.

"Is Mr. Emmy in?" she asked. The clerk blinked his eyes from behind his thick glasses. "Could you tell him that Barbara Reddiger is here to see him?"

In a matter of moments, the small man emerged from the corner office and held the door open for her.

"What an unexpected pleasure it is to see y'all. And I might add, you are looking exceptionally beautiful today, if I might be so bold as to say so. Please be seated."

Barb scooted the chair closer to the man's desk, but he walked toward the corner of the desk and sat on it, hovering close to her. His steely gaze made her feel uneasy.

"To what do I owe the pleasure of this unexpected visit?"

"Well, Mr. Emmy, to come right to the point, I would like to talk to you about arranging the same terms with me that you had with my father. Originally, we had another six months on the bank's note, and I would like the same option."

"Now, Miss Barbara, we've had this discussion before, it seems to me. Your father had what I believed to be the capability of paying off that note, but I wouldn't say your prospects are nearly the same."

"But, Mr. Emmy, our plans are the same as his, nothing has changed. We've talked this over among ourselves and have decided to drive the cattle to market and return with your payment. That ranch is just too important to our family. My parents died on that place and for that place."

"I understand your desire to preserve your folks' stake there, but there's no man now, and I . . . er . . . the bank just doesn't think you young women are capable of doing what your dear daddy might have done."

"We are very capable, Mr. Emmy. We have supplies, more than enough cattle, and shortly I will hire some men."

"Why, aren't you the industrious thing." He smiled slyly. "Somehow, I feared this idea might still be rattling around this pretty little head of yours." He placed his hand on Barbara's hair. "You know, Barbara, there are other ways to keep that ranch. Since my dear wife died, I've looked quite fondly on you."

"I don't understand," she lied.

"Oh, I think you do. I believe any man would view you as a fine prospect for marriage, and certainly I am among them."

"What are you saying, Mr. Emmy?"

"Call me Frank, Barbara." He pushed her hair back. "I believe you would make a wonderful second wife, Barbara. You're industrious. You have what appears to me to be a fine figure for bearing many children, and you are one of the most attractive women in this humble town of ours, in my estimation."

"I'm not sure of what to say to that," she murmured, stifling her feelings.

"It's all quite simple. Just say that you will wed me, and the ranch will be yours as a wedding gift. My gift to you."

"Well . . . Frank . . . if you have such feelings and confidence in me, then why won't you merely extend our note, like you promised to do with my father? I was always taught that a man's word was his bond, and if I knew you could be trusted to keep your word, then I might be persuaded to trust you even more."

Emmy crossed his arms and grunted. "It seems you have me

at a terrible disadvantage, Barbara. It would seem that my heart is at cross-purposes with my business sense."

"That would appear to be the case," she said.

"And if I give you the extension and you fail to deliver the cattle, then where does that leave us?"

Barbara batted her eyes. Everything inside her churned at what she was about to say, but she smiled on the outside. "If we fail, it appears you will have a second wife, Frank." She saw his eyes widen at the suggestion.

"And if you succeed?"

"Should we succeed, you will be in an even more advantageous position."

"How so?"

"I will be here with the money for the property and you stand to gain not only a wife, but one that has financial wherewithal. You underestimate yourself, Frank. Any woman would be proud to be called Mrs. Emmy."

Beaming, he reached out and took her hand. "Then let's forget all this foolish cattle-drive talk. Say you'll be mine and I can make the arrangements now."

She left her hand nestled in his and smiled. "Frank, I think you're forgetting something. I do place a great deal of stock in a man's word, and your agreement with my father makes all the difference with me. That, and my desire to leave a fair share of the proceeds to my sisters. I'm afraid I can't be persuaded to stop our plans. The only difference you can make is to validate my opinion of you and make me want to return. Otherwise, I and my sisters will have no reason to stay in Texas. I'm afraid without the ranch to come back to, we would be tempted to simply sell the cattle and start again somewhere else."

Emmy dropped her hand and walked to the window. He crossed his arms and stared out into the street. Turning back, a sly smile crossed his lips. "All right, Barbara, we'll do things your way, but only on one condition."

"What would that be?"

"I will draw up papers to the effect that you have agreed to marriage, should you fail to sell the herd. That way, I can justify this action to my board of directors. Only then can I excuse the bank from this impending auction. Do you agree?"

Barb nodded her head. "I should be going," she said. "I still must find men for the drive."

"And where do you propose to do that?"

She stammered. "I . . . I was planning to go to several saloons and ask for men who might be needing work."

"I can't let you do that. I won't have any wife of mine traipsing in and out of saloons." He grabbed his hat. "You'd better let me come along. I know a man who can help you in selecting good men. He's been a trail boss, and he'll serve you well." He stopped at the door and, reaching out, took her chin in his hand. "You've made me a happy man, Barbara." Leaning down, he gave her an icy kiss.

"We'd better go," she said. "Vonnie is waiting for me."

+ + + + +

The Silver Dollar Saloon was swarming with out-of-work men. The drought had caused many of the ranches to operate shorthanded, and men who came looking for work found little to be had. Emmy marched Barb directly to a darkly dressed man who sat beside a poker table, bottle in hand. "This is Pete Hammond, Barbara. As fine a trail boss as ever drew breath."

The large man slowly rose to his feet. He wore his six-gun thonged to his hip. His features were dark and his brown eyes dulled with liquor. His lip curled; he drawled, "Pleased to meet you, ma'am."

"Miss Reddiger here is the one I told you about, the one who might be outfitting for a drive." He turned to her. "Somehow I figured you might plan on something like this."

Barbara cast a glance at the banker, and several of the men at the poker table put down their cards and gave their full attention.

"I've told her you might be able to find enough men to help her."

"Well now, I'd love to help the pretty lady," Hammond said. "This here is Wolf Macrae. He's my ramrod, knows men and knows cattle. How many head you got?"

Barbara cleared her throat. "Between three and four thousand."

"Gonna be a big job, then. Been my experience that you'll need about one man for every two hundred fifty to three hundred cattle."

"I'm prepared to pay a dollar a day and food, along with a hundred-dollar bonus for every man who finishes the drive."

"Ma'am," a young man seated at the table interrupted. "My friend and I'd surely take kindly to a job like that. Times are mighty lean 'round here. A body'd as soon work for vittles as little else."

The man who spoke was thin, with sandy hair and brown eyes. His clean-shaven lantern jaw was set and he looked Barbara directly in the eye. Sparkling on his midsection was a brass buckle with the letters CSA stamped on it.

"Name's Joe Cobb," he went on, "and I hail from Georgia. My friend here calls himself Poor Soul. It ain't his real name, mind you, jes' the one he answers to."

"We hire our own men," Macrae barked. "And we don't hire no rebel tramps passin' through." He brushed back his black beard, and his brown eyes sparkled as he looked Poor Soul over carefully. "We don't hire no buffalo skins, neither."

"I was speaking to the lady," Cobb said. "Sounds to me like she's the one with the say-so. As for Poor Soul here, he may be blacker'n the ace of spades, but he's the best durn cowboy I ever laid my eyes on. And he can take down a running rabbit with one shot of that .45 he carries, so I wouldn't rile him." The ramrod's lip curled. "I don't rile my lessers, I bury them." Macrae dropped his hand to his side, but before he had it wrapped around the handle of his revolver, he was staring down the barrel of Poor Soul's .45.

The black cowboy smiled widely. "Is this a dagger which I see before me?" he sighed.

"Shoulda told you," Joe cut the silence of the moment and smiled. "He's the fastest man with a shooter I ever saw too." Joe paused. "And he surely does love Shakespeare, even though he pains me with it. That line's from *Macbeth*. My mother read old Will to us almost every night."

"So you two have known each other for some time, then?" Barb asked.

"Yes, my daddy owned him and his folks. Guess you could say we've grown up together. S'pose we're more like brothers than friends."

Poor Soul set the hammer of the ivory-handled gun gently down on the chamber and slowly holstered it. Macrae relaxed back into his chair, his jaw tightening.

"Nowadays a man needs a brother," Joe went on. "Had three of them who went into the war with me, but when I came back, only Poor Soul here was alive and standing. My folks died during the war."

"Then you've worked with cattle before, Mr. Cobb?" Barb was feeling very uncomfortable with the tension, but she knew men; she knew they spent a great deal of effort in sizing each other up. The fact that Hammond was apparently a friend of Emmy worried her a mite. Just now, she found any man who would be able to stand up to him especially appealing.

"Yes, ma'am, we've worked more'n our share of cattle. We're no green pistols. Poor Soul and I have made two drives up the Goodnight-Loving Trail and one to Dodge City in the past five years. We've jingled horses quite a bit to boot, and we've got our own rigs."

"Then you'll do," Barb said, "both of you." She nodded at his belt buckle. "I admire a man who fights for what he believes in. I just might need you to believe in me."

"Oh, you can count us in on that, ma'am." Joe picked up his battered jacket and sloughed it over his shoulders. "Ma'am, we'll just follow you out there. Poor Soul and I ain't got no good-byes to say 'round here."

Emmy nudged Hammond's arm. The man took his cue and spoke up. "You can leave the rest of the trail crew to me, miss." He waved his arm toward the men milling about the saloon. "I know everybody around here there is to know, and I'll get a crew to your place pronto."

"Be assured of that, Barbara," Emmy broke in. "I'll make sure, along with Mr. Hammond here, that you have the best men possible." He walked her to the door and gently squeezed her arm. "I want you to be successful. Any bride of mine deserves the best." He paused at the door and looked her in the eye. "By the way, I'll have those papers drawn up and take them out to the ranch for you to sign. You and I are gonna make a name for ourselves in Texas. Your father woulda been proud."

CHAPTER 3

+ + + + + + +

THE SUN WAS BLAZING HOT when Jeff Bridger rode up to the Cobb hacienda. Chickens lazily clucked across the cobbled courtyard and the flowering vine that clung to the side of the adobe building blushed a bright magenta.

"S-sh-sheriff, Sheriff Bridger, k-k-kinda hot for a ride, ain't it?"

Bridger looked down at the towheaded boy and then, glancing up, squinted into the sun. "Hotter'n the door on that fiery furnace in the Bible, I'd say."

A large spotted dog trotted out and stood next to the boy, trailing a litter of pups.

"I see your dog had herself a mighty fine bunch."

"Yes, sir. Meg's had nine of them, but one died."

"I suppose with all that's left, she ain't frettin' over the one."

The boy reached down and scratched the big dog's ear. "I don't reckon a body ever forgets the one, even if you got a bunch more."

"I guess not."

Bridger swung his massive frame down to the ground, took off his large black hat, and wiped his brow. Squashing it back on his blond head, he bent down to the boy's level and placed his hands on his knees. "It's plenty hot, but what my missus sent for you, Skipper, just couldn't wait for a cloudy day."

"Really?"

"Yeah, really." He stepped back to his oversized horse and opened the saddlebags. "I do believe that woman of mine knows what a boy that don't get into town very often needs the most."

Reaching into the saddlebags, he produced a bag the size of two of his own huge fists. Smiling, he bounced it in his hands and pulled the drawstring to open it. "Let's see if it made it through this heat." He held the open bag down to the boy, who eagerly slid his hand into the bag and grabbed hold of one of its contents. Skip's face lit up when he pulled one of the soft white balls of sugary confectionery out of the bag.

"Divinity!" the boy said.

"That's right, divinity, yours and my favorite." He held the bag lower. "You can see she stuck nuts into some of 'em, and pushed a few cherries into some of the others."

"Here, Sheriff." The boy held the prize he had pulled from the bag out to the man. "You carried it. Only r-r-right you get the fust one."

Bridger laughed and tousled the boy's hair. "No, Skip, these are all for you. I got the lady at home waiting for me that done cooked them. All you got is that mean old German stirrin' stew for you and Cobb." He handed the boy the bag. "You take this, and try not to make yerself sick, ya hear?"

"Yes, sir," the boy nodded. "Tell Mrs. Bridger thank you for me, will you?"

"I shore will now. My kids are lookin' forward to doing some swimmin' with you too, especially on a hot day like this one."

"Zac promised to take me down to Morro Bay to swim some later on today, but I guess he's waitin' till it k-k-k-kinda cools down."

"Sounds mighty nice. Those two cranky old men you live with in the shade yonder?"

"Hans is out back in the c-c-cook shack, but Zac's in the library, reading. Least he was when I left him. He's been reading *Ivanhoe* to me of late."

Suddenly, the sound of violin music came through the open door. "Well, I do believe he's put his book down and picked up that fiddle of his. You go and enjoy your candy, but save some room for supper. Doesn't pay to get that old German down on you for not eatin' what he fixes. I'll just wander on in and listen up close."

The boy scooped up one of the puppies and held it up to Bridger. "I'd be much obliged, Sheriff, if you'd take one of Maggie's puppies home with you. I'm sure your kids would like this one."

"I'm sure they would, Skip. You don't think Maggie's gonna grieve over losing another one, though, do you?"

"No. Giving something away to be loved is different than having one just die."

"I reckon you're right there, Skipper." He held the squirming pup in his hand and scratched the animal's muzzle. "He's mighty cute, son. My young'uns will love him. First thing you know, they'll be askin' me to bring you some more divinity."

"That'll be just fine."

He stepped onto the cool tile floor. The shade of the house was a welcome relief from the summer sun. Bridger moved past the dining room and stood at the doorway of the great room, watching Zac Cobb play the violin nested beneath his chin. Cobb slowly pulled the bow over the stings and stared out the back window. To the side of the room, the stoop-shouldered cook also watched and listened.

"Don't believe I recollect that one," Bridger said.

Cobb stopped the music and lowered the instrument. "Don't imagine you would. That's Beethoven's "Ode to Joy." Wouldn't 'zackly think you'd have run across it before."

"I suppose you're right to think that. Saloon music played by women of easy virtue is mostly what I get in my line of work."

"There's something about music and poetry that stirs the soul up to be better than it already is."

"I s'pose you're right. I guess I got myself a ways to go before I can spend my hot afternoons appreciatin' either one of them things."

Cobb put the violin and bow down on a polished oak table and signaled to the cook. "Bring our lawman here some coffee,

Hans. He's had a long ride and still has a ways to go to get back home."

"I'd just as soon take some cold water, Hans."

Zac signaled toward a chair opposite the table and then took his own seat facing the lawman. "We've been up 'round here long before daylight. With the weather like it is, we got to do most of the work before noon."

"Right smart plan, when a body can set his own hours."

While Hans poured a tall earthenware goblet of water for the sheriff, Bridger took the envelope out of his pocket and pushed it across the table to Zac. It was a routine they had been through before. Hans put the pitcher of water on the table, pushed his glasses down the bridge of his pudgy nose, and placed his hands on his hips. "You vill be the death of dis place with all dat gallabantin' around the country every time dem folks holler. Why can't dey just find somebody else to do der dirty vork?"

Without answering, Zac got up and walked over and took a pot of coffee from the fire. Taking a cup from the mantel, he poured the steaming liquid.

"How can you be drinkin' that stuff on a day like today?" Bridger asked.

"Hot coffee just makes the day seem cooler to me."

Bridger sat the puppy on the table and began to rub the back of the animal's head.

Zac took a table knife and slit open the brown envelope while Bridger sipped his water. Zac ignored the old German cook more out of habit than deliberation. He'd learned long ago never to argue with the man who did the cooking, especially a Prussian. It was an argument that couldn't be won.

Undeterred, Hans went on, "And you can't just sashay off and leave dat boy again. You're de vun adoptin' him, not me. Every time you saunter off someplace, dat boy pines and moons by dat vindow over yonder. Why he should care, I'm sure I don't know."

Zac paused over the folded paper he pulled out from the envelope, refusing to open it while Hans continued to look over his shoulder. "Hans, you're gonna know about this soon enough without standing over my shoulder." As the cook ambled off, murmuring, he unfolded and read the message.

Bridger finished his water and poured another glass. "Horse ride, or train ride?" he asked.

Zac reread the message and folded it. "They want me to guard the payouts for cattle drives along the railheads in Kansas."

"Seems like a simple job local people can handle. Why you?"

Zac looked at the note again. "Whole herds are being stolen, along with the money it takes to buy them. I guess the people who insure the buyers are screaming bloody murder, and now Wells Fargo is guaranteeing 'em. The company has lost one man already, and they want to put a stop to it."

"And they want you to be the stopper." Bridger brushed his heavy blond mustache aside. "What I'd like to know is when are you gonna stop?"

"When the devil stops telling people to take what don't belong to them."

"Been my experience, the devil doesn't have to go far to convince people to steal."

"No, you're right. The love of money is the root of all evil. Combined with an evil nature, it'll take many a man to the gallows." He sipped his coffee and smiled. "I suppose it'll take me on this assignment too. The pay is good, more money than my calf crop this year and my daily rate to boot. It's been four months since I've said yes to them, and I reckon if I keep saying no, they'll soon find out they can be in business without me."

"And you think that'd be a bad thing?"

"Right now it would be. I can use that money, and I don't mind the work."

"I thought you said money was the root of all evil."

"I didn't say it, the Bible says it. Besides, it's the love of money, not money itself."

"And I suppose you don't love it."

"No, I don't, but right now, I do appreciate what it can do. This weather's been hard on the ranch and we could use it just now."

"Cobb, somehow the money never works out to be enough with you, and the job those people send you to do never seems to be as simple as they make it out to be." He took off his hat and continued to play with the puppy as he placed it in the hat. "Plus, I just don't believe you do anything for just the money. If you ask me, with all that sense of right and wrong you got swimming around inside of you, you'd be just as happy being a preacher."

"Thanks," Zac snarled sarcastically.

"What you gonna do about the place 'round here?" Bridger asked. "You might be gone for a spell."

"This place can do all right for a while without me. I'll hire out what work needs to be done while I'm gone. The only thing I worry about is Jenny and the boy."

"You got that right. You can't exactly hire out everything you do. She ain't gonna take too kindly to seeing you ride off again."

Zac curled his fingers around the cup of coffee. The steam spiraled around his black mustache as he pressed it to his lips and drank the hot black liquid without changing his deadpan expression. "You know, these last months have taught me a lot about my feelings for that lady, but I don't quite think she's made up her mind about me. In fact, I'm not so sure she'd bat an eye at seeing me ride off. Jenny's old enough to know what she's bought into where I'm concerned."

"But the boy ain't."

"No, he ain't. And just now, I can see him turning into somebody that has a bright trail in front of him."

"And these are days with that boy that you'll never get again. I've watched my own go through that age. They need to talk, and when you're not around to do the talkin' with them, some things just don't ever get said."

Zac drew out his pipe and stuffed it with tobacco. "I know. I can't keep this up much longer. I s'pose my mind drifts back to my own father. At times I wonder what he'd do if he was in my place. Duty was important to him, but not more important than us kids. I s'pose the Mexican War taking that leg of his off was a blessing in disguise. He always saw himself as useless after that, but I never did."

"I don't think I'd ever wish for something like that to happen in order to keep me close to home."

"No, I guess there's easier ways to learn that lesson."

"I've seen that boy change you, Cobb."

Zac struck a match and lit the pipe. "How so?"

Bridger smiled and pointed at the pipe. "Last time you were in town, I saw you in the cafe swishing your pipe smoke away from him. Next thing you know, you'll be puttin' the thing away."

Zac blew smoke into the air. "You don't know what you're talkin' about and y'all don't know me. I'm mighty set in my ways."

"Don't I? You think about that boy a lot, and for one, I sorta like the changes I see. Besides, sometimes things do happen that change a man's ways. For one, I don't think I'd ever hire my gun out if it took me away from the family."

"Jeff, that badge hires your gun out."

"Maybe so, but it don't put me on no train. I don't think I'd go anywhere I couldn't take my children. Maybe you should take the boy with you. You could build some things into his life while you travel, if you gotta travel."

Zac grunted at the comment. "The last thing I want is to put that boy in harm's way."

"He just might keep you out of harm's way, might make you think first before you get yerself into a scrape. Besides, you'll need some cover for that job. You can't expect to ride in with that special agent badge, kick the door in, and do what you need to do."

"I got plenty to think on when I'm doing my job. Having somebody I got to look after just makes things all the worse."

"Maybe you're right there. But don't expect that just because you take a train clear cross the country, that you've looked after him. Been my experience that once a man becomes a father, he's a father full-time. Distance don't make no difference."

"I'm keepin' the boy. That don't make me his father."

Bridger scratched the puppy's ears. "Partner, when God gives you something to care for, it's just as much yours as if you'd given birth to the thing, and saying it ain't so don't make it no different."

Zac lifted the cup to his lips once again. This was a decision he wasn't about to make in a hurry. He knew full well that no matter what anybody said and no matter what he did, he'd carry with him the notion that he was doing something wrong.

CHAPTER 4

+ + + + + + +

"QUIRT, I'D SAY THERE ARE about five hundred head of prime two-year-olds or better." The dark-haired, olive-skinned man with the black leather pants squinted once again through the tubular telescope. The sunlight flashed off the brass-covered apparatus, the row of silver conches that studded the sides of his pants, and the silver grips of the two six-guns tied down to his hips. "I only count five riders," he commented as he handed the telescope to the white-skinned man towering beside him.

"I'd say this group will be real easy, Mr. Muldoon." The heavyset, freckled-faced Irishman grinned and cracked his knuckles as he spoke. "They'll fetch a pretty penny in Dodge."

Muldoon slid the telescope back into his carrying case and, without looking at the men, walked toward the surrey. He continued to stare down at the moving cattle. His shoulder-length hair was the color of fresh-fallen snow, and his eyes, blinking against the glare of the sunlight caroming off the golden grass, were a bright red.

Reaching into his inside duster pocket, he pulled out a pair of gold-framed, dark-tinted glasses. He wound the wires around his ears and squinted his eyes, adjusting them to the sudden shade the dark lenses created.

He hoisted his massive weight and six-foot-five-inch frame into the surrey. As he sat down on the heavily stuffed leather seat, the springs of the rig sank in his direction and then righted themselves. He motioned to a third man, who had been stand-

41

ing beside the surrey. The man's curly black hair and beard shone like the wings of a raven. Around his shoulder, he proudly displayed the instrument of his power; a black bullwhip with small jagged pieces of metal attached to the ends of the rawhide fringe. He dropped the deadly device into his hand and stepped toward the surrey.

The large, white-skinned man spoke to the man with the whip with a hint of a Scottish brogue rattling deep within his throat. "Nat, you and the boys will haf to swing them around Dodge and move them on to Ogallala. There's only so many herds we can sell in one season before someone gets himself too wise."

Nat smiled slyly at the other two men who had moved over to the surrey. "Ramrodding a crew all the way to Ogallala—by all rights, that should mean an extra share."

"It will mean a thousand dollars for you. Will that satisfy you?"

Nat Black's eyes brightened, and he nodded slightly.

Quirt Muldoon had always been a man to keep his chief henchmen guessing—to keep them in the position of several dogs waiting for only one bone so they'd watch each other. That way, each of them would be his eyes and ears, even when his head was turned. He had no pigmentation to his skin and the sun was hard on his eyes, so he stayed indoors during most of the daylight hours.

As hard as it was for him to move about, he needed men he could trust to do what each of them did best. Since the men who worked for him were by nature men who could only be trusted to be ruthless, he had to find ways to get them to use the lower parts of their natures to hold each other at bay.

He pointed his stubby finger down the hill toward the milling cattle. "Kill them quickly and then fill their bodies so full of arrows they look like pincushions." He leaned forward. "Take their scalps, too. I want everyone to figure their loss on the Kiowa. Kill a few of the cattle with arrows as well. It will make the picture even more convincing. Besides," he grinned, "it'll send up a cloud of buzzards that will make them all the easier to find."

The men turned away to mount their horses, but Quirt called Nat Black up short. "Black, you leave that bullsnake whip coiled up. I know you love to use it, but I haven't heard so much as a single story about a Kiowa ever using a whip on a man. Is that understood?"

"Yeah, I understand."

+ + + + +

Two teenage boys, the sons of one of the men on the drive, were riding drag. The bawling cattle kicked up a small cloud as they dragged their feet through the Kansas dirt, and the boys wore bandannas to keep out some of the billowing dust. One of the teenagers tugged on a lead rope attached to two tethered mules loaded down with cooking equipment.

Two other young but weather-beaten cowboys rode the flanks of the herd, turning back bunch-quitters and keeping the stream of beef moving north. Slightly ahead of the group, an older man with shotgun chaps and an olive-drab hat rode with a small group of horses. He was the first to see the surrey and the band of a dozen or more riders that rode down the grassy knoll in their direction.

He removed his hat, rode to the front of the small horse herd, and slapped at the lead horse, turning the mustangs back in the direction of the cattle. The two swing riders had now spotted the uninvited guests and rode up toward where the trail boss sat his horse. Each of them unloosed the thong that held their six-guns secure at their sides. The boys at the rear of the herd maintained the formation of cattle and began to move forward to keep the bunch together.

The three lean Texas cowboys sat their horses and watched the surrey and the surrounding horsemen ride up. The appearance of the man riding under the covered rig frightened even people who knew Quirt Muldoon, but to someone who had never laid their eyes on the man, the sight was unnerving.

Muldoon pulled the reins up on his team of bays and stopped

in front of the three cowboys. The men riding aside his rig fanned out around the three mounted Texans. Muldoon squinted at the men from behind his dark eyeglasses. "Welcome to Kansas, gentlemen. Where are ye bringing these cattle from?"

"We're up from Texas way," the older man spoke up. "My name's Burns. We're aiming to sell the herd in Dodge City."

"Texas, you say?"

"That's right. We come up from a place south a the Red River, near Vernon."

"Well, I'm afraid this is as far as we'll allow you to go with those cattle. This is my land. Your Longhorns carry Texas tics on them."

The three cowboys looked nervously at each other. Again the older trail boss spoke. "Well, mister, you just tell us how to get off'n your place and we'll swing this bunch around. I know how important a man's land is to him, and I ain't got no intention of abusing yourn."

Muldoon spread his hand over the horizon. "My land stretches as far around here as you'll ever draw another breath." He dropped his reins and placed his fists on his hips. "Now, I think you had better turn this bunch back to Texas."

"Well, I can't rightly do that."

Muldoon reached into a box that sat on the floorboard of the surrey and produced a wad of greenbacks. "You won't be able to drive those cattle of yours a mile farther north, but I will do you a favor and buy them from you." He paused and smiled. "I'll pay you fifty cents a head."

The three cowboys looked stunned at the suggestion of so low a price. "Mister, I coulda sold 'em where I come from fer a dollar a head, and in Dodge I hear they're payin' thirty to thirty-four dollars fer each one of these," Burns said.

"I'd advise you to take my offer," Muldoon smiled. "It may not seem like it now, but it's the best offer you've ever had."

One of the cowboys spoke up. "Mr. Burns, these men ain't ranchers no way. They ain't nuthin' but a mangy bunch of rawhiders—a bunch of low-down, no-count jawhawks."

The older man extended his arm to stabilize the young cowboy, but it was too late. The boy dropped his hand to his holster, but before he could draw, Muldoon's man, Rass Bodine, drew one of his silver-handled guns and fired. The cowboy dropped to the ground, but Bodine continued to thumb back the hammer on his .45.

At Muldoon's signal, the men on either side of the rig slowly drew their revolvers. "You see," he said, "it was my best an' my only offer."

Burns held up his hands along with the remaining rider. "Don't kill my boys back there. They're my oldest, but they're only twelve and fourteen."

Muldoon removed his dark glasses. His red eyes shone on the two Texans like a stare from the devil himself.

+   +   +   +   +

The Reddiger girls rode back to the ranch, talking to the two men from Georgia. Vonnie listened with interest.

"You were in the war? Did you fight with General Lee?" Vonnie asked.

"The whole country was in the war, only some of us were shot at."

"Was it exciting?"

"Vonnie, why don't you find another subject," Barb said. "I'm sure the war is one Mr. Cobb would rather not revisit."

"Oh, it's all right, Miss Barbara. There's only a natural curiosity there. To tell you the truth, Vonnie, life in the army can be boring—gathering wood, cooking what little food there is, caring for horses, cleaning weapons, washing clothes, washing dishes."

"That sounds like what I do every day," Vonnie said.

"Yep. Only in war, sometimes the monotony is overtaken by a few days of fear and a few minutes of terror."

"And what did you do during the war?" Barb directed the comment to Poor Soul, who had been listening, expressionless.

"I helped with the farm and cared after the Cobb folks. Mostly though, I just kept up with my education as a man, a free man."

"And how does one do that as a slave?"

"Poor Soul was never a slave," Joe corrected. "Folks 'round about our place may have called him and his folks that, but we considered them family. My daddy bought Soul's folks when he came back from the Mexican War, but they were never slaves."

"My education as a free man started on the knee of Joe's mama," Poor Soul continued. "She'd wash my face and read the Bible to me. That woman was an angel on this here earth."

"At night, we children would all gather and she'd teach us to read and play musical instruments too," Joe added.

"Did she teach you to read music?"

Poor Soul smiled. "Lordy, yes! All us kids could read the notes on a sheet of music before we learned to read words. And she spent no less time with the black children than she did with her own."

"She sounds like a fine woman. I'm curious," Barb said. "Why do you call yourself Poor Soul?"

He laughed. "Because I want to be a king someday."

"A king?"

"Why, yes, ma'am. One of the first things Mama Cobb taught me from the Bible was, 'Blessed are the poor in spirit, for theirs is the kingdom of God.' I ain't got no kingdom down here on this earth, but what I have got I'm tradin' off for that one up there."

"It sounds like your home was a very loving place, Mr. Cobb. Like a school of love."

"That it was. There was plenty of work to do early in the day, then playtime for the kids, music to be played after supper, and then the reading." He shook his head. "The reading, the reading, and the reading."

"Don't forget the poetry and the playacting," Poor Soul added.

"Playacting?"

Joe smiled. "Yes, a body could never forget that. Ma and Daddy had a costume barrel beside the dinner table. If you were a guest, you might just find yourself acting out Shakespeare after the meal, like as not. Daddy would pick the play and we'd take our parts. Sooner or later, we'd be rolling on the floor, holding our sides laughing at our poor attempts."

"The laughin'," Poor Soul joined in. "That place was sure 'nuff a laughin' place. The laughin' and the prayin' were the things I remember most about it."

As the foursome reached the rise in the road and the ranch house came into full view, an unexpected sight greeted them. Two young men stood beside the railing of the front porch. A third, someone Vonnie and Barb recognized but wouldn't want to admit they knew, stood on the steps. Karen looked like a man. She had cut her hair off and parted it down the middle, donned batwing chaps and spurs, a blue drover shirt, and a red bandanna. A six-gun was tied low on her hip. Dorothy stood beside her with a smirk on her face. They pulled the team to a halt in front of the house.

"Well, are we going or not?" Dorothy asked.

"Yes, we are going," Barb said. "We have a wagon and some supplies, and the bank has given us the extension. These two gentlemen have signed on to help. Mr. Joe Cobb here." Joe took off his hat. "And his friend, who calls himself, Poor Soul."

"Pleased to meet you, gentlemen." Dorothy stepped toward the men on horseback with outstretched hand. Joe shook her hand and cast a glance at the stranger on the steps.

"And who are these men?" Barb asked.

One of the men, who looked to be about nineteen, walked toward the wagon. "Name's Frank Green, ma'am, and I sure do need the job."

"Is that right? Have you ever cowboyed before?"

"Yes'm, a might. Jes' got myself married six months ago, and my wife's in a family way, expectin' our first in about six months. We just can't be makin' it unless I bring in some cash money."

"And who is this other young man?" Barb looked at the boy who stood sheepishly by the rail. Dorothy motioned him over. "This here is Tipper. Come over here, Tipper."

The boy moved cautiously forward. "He doesn't look any older than Vonnie," Barb said.

"He ain't," Karen spoke out from the stairway in a deliberately lowered voice, "but he's a man all the same."

Barb narrowed her eyes and shot Karen a glance, then turned to the young blond boy with freckles across his nose. "How old are you?"

"Almost fifteen," he replied. "I don't know straight up about a cow, but I ride well, and I works hard enough."

"I think a boy like you should be home with his mother."

"My ma's in the ground now, and my pap's in the bottle all the time. You don't have to pay me much. Just give me some vittles and get me outta Texas is all I'm expectin'. I'll work hard fer you, that's fer durn sure."

Vonnie peeked at the boy from around Barb, and his face flushed.

"We'll have to see," Barb said. "What is that you have on your forehead?"

The boy lowered his head. "My pap says I have to wear it till I prove otherwise."

"Come over here and let me see." She brushed the boy's hair back, revealing a three-letter word painted in red across his forehead—B-A-D. "Your father did this to you?"

"Yes'm. He said folks needed to know what I was."

Barb swallowed hard and brushed the boy's hair aside. "Dorothy, take this boy out back and wash this paint off." She looked up at Karen on the stairs. "But first, introduce me to this third young man."

"Kare—" Dorothy caught herself. "Car. He calls himself Car."

Barb got down from the wagon along with Vonnie. "Why don't you men put your things away in the bunkhouse over yonder while we go in the house and talk with Car here."

The men dismounted, and Barb led the women into the house. Closing the door behind them, she stood with her back to it. "Now, just what do you think you're doing?"

Karen took off her hat and scrambled what was left of her blond hair with both hands. Straightening up, she explained, "I'm going on this drive, but I ain't about to do no woman's work. I'm goin' as a drover, same as the rest."

"You'll do no such thing."

"Yes I will, and you won't stop me. Besides, with all these strangers you're hiring, you're gonna need someone to tell you what they're really thinking. You're women alone, traveling with everything our family has ever worked for."

"She's got a point," Dorothy said. "We talked it through while you were gone to town. And if any woman could ever pull it off, Karen can."

"And how do you expect to fool the men? They'll see you're a woman."

Karen unbuttoned the flap on her drover shirt, showing a tightly woven wrap around her chest. "This here will hold me in, and I won't be taking no baths with them."

CHAPTER 5

+ + + + + + +

HOURS LATER, Hammond rode in with the men he had chosen, accompanied by Frank Emmy in his carriage. Barb walked out on the porch and brushed her hair back.

"Barbara, I believe Mr. Hammond here has picked out some very good men, and I brought the agreement we discussed for you to sign."

Barb ignored him and walked over to the men, who were dismounting. They were a varied lot, some looking rough and others with an odd refinement to them. One of them, a man with black hair and shining eyes, bowed low and swept his hat to the side.

"These here men are the most dependable ones I could find. That's the Englishman, but he does work. There ain't many who'd want to work with a bunch of women, ma'am. You understand that."

"I understand." She studied the men.

"My name's Jim Crossy, ma'am," a second cowboy spoke up. "I've ridden over all the hills of Texas, Kansas, the Indian territory, Nebraska, and most of the Dakotas. I been everwheres, done everthing. I fight Injuns, bears, lions, and most any varmint a body could name." He removed his hat and smoothed his black hair backward. "I done things that would make a man's blood run cold." His eyes twinkled. "And a bunch a things that would make a man's blood run powerful hot."

"Madam, I am Edward Richards," the Englishman spoke up. "Very pleased to meet you." He once again bowed low at the waist.

51

"The boys call him Earl," Hammond said. "He says he's some kind of English nobleman whose daddy sent him west to grow up. Weren't exactly my best choice, but he don't need the money and he promised half his share to me if I brung him along."

Emmy edged his way to Barb's side. "Barbara, if we don't get these papers signed, I can't get the bank's approval."

"You mean to say you can't get Blev Henry's blessing from the Bar-H?"

"Well, he is a major investor. He does have an interest in our loans."

"I'll tend to the men first, Mr. Emmy, then you and I can conclude our business. Mr. Hammond, please introduce me to the rest of the men you've chosen."

"You've met Wolf, ma'am, my segundo."

"Yes, I remember Mr. Macrae from the saloon."

"This over here is Randolph, Lance Randolph. He's too edgycaded for his own good, but a good man with a rope."

The man removed his hat, exposing sandy brown hair with a touch of gray showing around the temples. He nodded an acknowledgment.

"And that over there is Yanni."

Barb saw that the young, clean-shaven man Hammond was trying to introduce had made his way to Dorothy's side and begun flirting with her. His hat was in his hand, revealing long, curly blond locks that fell to his shoulders. At the mention of his name, he whirled around and flashed a crooked smile.

"I got three other men I used before who are riding out here in the morning."

"Those men will not be necessary, Mr. Hammond. Besides Mr. Cobb and his friend, I've employed three other riders to go with us."

Emmy interjected, "Barbara, Pete Hammond here is the trail boss. It's up to him to hire the men he wants to work with. The men who are coming are men who, unlike most of these, Mr. Hammond has worked closely with. After all, the bank is financing you on this venture and I have my confidence in him."

Barb's eyes narrowed. "It may be your note we're trying to pay, but it's our ranch, our cattle, and my sisters. It's a long way to Kansas, and I believe I have every right to hire men that I am comfortable with."

Hammond had been eyeing the men who sat on the porch. "Miss Reddiger, you done gone and signed on a Reb drifter, his darky, a coupla green kids from what I can see, and a little boy fresh outta diapers. I wouldn't call them people trail hands. The men I got showin' up tomorrow are tough hombres that I can count on. Now, if you 'spect me to get these cattle to market, you gotta let me bring men along who can do the job. These boys comin' are some a my best men."

There was a strong undercurrent of mistrust in her face, and when she decided to dig her heels in, Barb could be a hard woman to move. She bit her lower lip. "They won't be needed, Mr. Hammond. And if you're as good as you say you are, then you'll be able to work with anybody I choose. When Mr. Emmy gets back to town, he can tell those men to simply find another job."

"I'm hesitant to do that," Emmy said. "Hammond here is right. I've met the men he's selected and they are first rate. I believe the bank would have every confidence in his choice."

Barb's face softened. Reaching out to Emmy, she took his arm and drew him close. She lowered her voice and led him a few steps from the rest. "Frank, please have faith in my woman's intuition on this matter. I would feel so much more comfortable with the men I have chosen. And when I sign those papers you've brought, you will have nothing to lose by trusting me." She batted her eyes at him and watched his resolve crumble. "How could you not trust the woman you intend to marry?"

She had played her high card, and they both knew it. "Well, I suppose. I'll talk to Hammond about this."

"Good, Frank, you do that, and I'll show the men where to put their things."

Sometime later, after she had signed the papers and Emmy had talked to Hammond, Barb waved goodbye to the banker. As he whipped his horses and bolted down the road toward War

Eagle, he passed the chuck wagon coming over the rise.

"I see Mr. Pera is here with the cook wagon," Barb said. "He can fix the meal for tonight and we'll all get a chance to taste his form of cooking."

"That will be wonderful," Dorothy said.

"Does that mean we still have to do the dishes?" Vonnie asked.

"Yes, this is no free ride for us. We all have work to do, same as the men."

Pete Hammond had washed his face and combed back his hair before he walked over to the girls. "Miss Barbara, Mr. Emmy and I have an understanding here, and I think I should make it clear to you."

"Of course."

"You folks own the cattle, but I am the trail boss. If I take these cattle out and find you crossing me at every turn, I'm just gonna take my men and ride off. Now, I don't want to seem unfriendly like, but you gotta let me do my job, even if you do feel contrary."

"Mr. Hammond, how you operate on the trail will be strictly your decision."

"Good. I decide who does what. I don't want any of these people you hired to feel they can go to you and whine whenever there's something to do they don't hanker to."

"I understand perfectly."

"Fine." He started to walk off, but then turned around once again to make his point. "I do mean what I say. If I ain't allowed to do my job, you're gonna find yerself with nearly four-thousand mangy steers in the middle of Injun country, with nuthin' but a Reb, a darky, and a bunch a kids to nurse you along."

"You will be allowed to do your job, Mr. Hammond. And I'm sure you'll do fine. I only ask for one consideration."

"What's that?"

"I've heard some of the language used by your men. My sisters and I are Mennonite. We are Christian young women and we would ask you to speak to the men about guarding their tongues. Lightning will be a serious enough problem on this trip without you or your men calling down more of it."

Hammond turned on his heel and grumbled to himself as he stalked off.

Only a short time later, Bobby Pera beat on a tin pot with his large spoon to call everyone to supper. The line began to form beside the wagon, and Karen had taken her place at the front of the line when Barb pulled her aside.

"Listen, this is the most foolish thing I've ever seen you do. Why you insist on it is beyond me—it's against nature."

"People being against nature is what built Texas."

"All the same, why you insist on refusing to be a woman is more than I can understand."

"Now get this straight, Barb. I am not refusing to be a woman, but I will not spend the rest of my life tied into a corset and bloomers. I want to do more than that. I want to be treated like an equal, not kowtowed to and sat on a shelf for some man to admire."

"All right then, but you can't have it both ways. If you're going to be a man, you'll have to act like one. You can no longer have first place in line with the women. You better start thinking like a man, whatever that is."

Karen pulled her sleeve away from Barb and took her place in line with the men. Barb had been worried about her when she saw Hammond's attitude toward the men she had hired, and the look of the men he had brought with him did little to calm her fears. It was plain to see that Hammond's men were determined to prove themselves against the men Barb had selected. They elbowed their way to the front of the line.

"What is this slop?" Crossy bellowed. "Worms?"

"It's pasta," Pera shot back. "And you'da better like it."

The men sheepishly held out their plates as Pera piled it on. "It's my mother's special dish from the old country, and it's far too good for the likes of trail hands."

Barb could see that mixing with cowboys was bringing out the fight in the man. It was bound to do that with a man who had been sweeping out a store and waiting to open a restaurant. She smiled slightly.

"If it's worms," Crossy said, "it's more'n likely what kilt her."

As the men came through the line, Yanni stuck out his foot, sending Karen sprawling to the ground, face down in her food. The laughter sent her springing to her feet, and Yanni rose to meet her. "Stop this!" Barb cried out.

Hammond grinned. "Men need to work these things out on their own, Miss Barbara. Let 'em get it out of their craws before we get on the trail."

There was something about the tension between the two groups that made Barb aware that something had been said in private to put the men on the prod. She knew Hammond wanted no part of the men she had hired, and she knew the division that was evident would be considered her fault.

Yanni stepped forward and smirked at Karen. "Boy, if you can't walk, you durn sure can't ride." Karen swung her fist from her waist and landed a solid blow to the tall cowboy's middle. His face reddened and he stumbled backward. Straightening himself, he paused and rolled up his sleeves. "Youngster, you may think you're a man, but we're about to see just how far you got to grow yet."

He feinted a punch that drew Karen's fist up to her face, and then suddenly swept her feet out from under her with a kick to her ankles.

She landed hard on her backside and sprung once again to her feet. Her sisters were turning white. Barb stuck out her arm and blocked Dorothy from stepping forward. "It's a lesson that has to be learned," she whispered.

"Boy, you do have some kind of difficulty staying up, don't you? Now, why don't you just pack your stuff and ride on outta here?"

She took several wild swings at the man's face, and he jerked his head backward to avoid the blows. Pushing his hand into her face, he held her at bay, staying slightly beyond the barrage of wild swings she flung in his direction. Looking at the men who were watching, he laughed.

Dropping her hands to her side, Karen seemed to be ready to

quit. Suddenly, she exploded with a savage kick directly into his groin. He doubled over, the wind taken out of his sails.

Bracing himself, he stretched himself up against the chuck wagon. His face was red. The look in his eyes frightened the girls. He had quit playing at the fight. It was time to end it. He launched himself forward, but suddenly found himself jerked backward and slammed into the chuck wagon. Joe had reached his hand out and caught Yanni's collar. Momentarily stunned, he dropped his hand to his holster, but Joe slammed a knee into his thigh, dropping him to his knees. "Let the feller eat his food in peace," Joe said. "You just sit down and be a gentleman in front of these ladies here, you understand?"

Hammond had been eating his food quietly, and Yanni shot him a glance. Hammond nodded. Yanni quickly turned his attention to Dorothy, then slowly got to his feet. "All right. I was just funnin' the boy, that's all." He dusted off his chaps with his hat and then pointed directly at Karen. "We ain't done, boy. You and me is gonna have us a go 'round when your Rebel big brother ain't here to defend you." Turning abruptly, he put his face up next to Cobb's. "Reb, you ain't got the best a me by a long shot. You just better count your fingers and toes before this is over."

"I'll be watchin' my backside." Joe gave him a gentle push. "Now you just go and eat your vittles and leave the boy alone. Besides, looks like to me he can take care of himself."

"You got that right." Karen lowered her voice in the most menacing way she could muster. Keeping her eyes on the man, she picked up her plate. She continued eyeing her nemesis as she slowly walked back to the pot of food for another helping.

Joe had seated himself on the steps and made room for her when she returned with a fresh plate. "Men are sorta like a pack a dogs," he said. "Everybody has to show what they're made of before they can be comfortable. They'll settle down before long, each one deciding where he belongs in the pack."

"Well, that dog with the long blond hair had just better keep his distance from me," she croaked.

"I don't think it likely he's gonna do that. He'll find some way to prod you till he thinks he's got yer measure." He spooned the pasta into his mouth and wiped it with his sleeve. "You'll have to handle him yer own self next time. You'll do right well, I 'spect."

"Well, I won't be sleeping in the bunkhouse tonight. I'm going to pitch my bedroll outside." She'd been looking for an excuse to separate herself from the rest of the men, and this was probably as good a reason as she was going to get.

"Suit yerself," he said, "but that there Yanni feller strikes me as the type that don't let up. He's the kind of man that's been proving himself at the expense of others for years. Kinda keeps a ledger in his head, wins on one side and losses on the other."

"I don't give up either. When I set out to do something, I do it."

Joe smiled. "You'll do, son. You'll do."

Karen watched Joe eat his food. This was a man that had more to his thinking than he gave off at first glance. There was a manliness about him she admired, and yet a boyish quality and a sparkle in his eye that attracted her. She bit her lip softly. It had been years since she'd felt drawn to a man, and this was no time to start.

CHAPTER 6

✦ ✦ ✦ ✦ ✦ ✦ ✦

FOR DAYS, THE SUN had seemed to reach out from the sky and hammer each man into the dust. Vonnie and Dorothy carried water out to the cowboys branding the herd. Vonnie winced as she watched men kicked by steers and calves large enough to be ridden. She lingered with the bucket, watching Karen work with a rope and horse. No one would have ever guessed she was a woman. Vonnie took her some water.

Karen pulled her hat down and clamped the piggin' strings in her teeth. Spurring her horse into an instant gallop, she swung her lariat and built a loop. Twisting her wrist over her head, she took aim at the large yearling and let the rope fly, dropping the loop over the animal and taking a dally over the saddle horn. The sudden jerk on the line sent the calf to the ground, and Karen bolted from the saddle and straddled the animal, tying his rear legs as he kicked wildly.

Putting her boot on the beast's front leg, she stretched him out and pulled out a knife. She made several quick strokes. Putting the knife back in its sheath, she held out her gloved hand for the hot iron. Vonnie took her the branding iron from the steel box of red coals and watched her clamp the glowing metal to the hide of the newly castrated animal.

Vonnie took the branding iron back and brought back a ladle of water for Karen. "You all right?" she asked, holding out the ladle.

"I been kicked, stomped on, nearly hooked, and thrown twice, but I'll make it. The drive can't be any worse than this."

"Yanni says the drive is the worst thing of all. Heard him tell Dorothy that just yesterday."

Karen's jaw tightened. "Tell her to keep away from that woolly-legged snake. He's no good."

"Can't nobody tell Dorothy, you know that."

Karen removed her hat and shook her short hair. Picking up the bucket Vonnie carried, she poured half of it on her head and down her back. "You tell her for me, she never had any sense when it came to pickin' a feller."

"You picked a feller?"

Karen removed her bandanna, plunged it into the bucket, and draped it over her neck, allowing the water to trickle down her shirt. "Don't talk nonsense. All I'm thinkin' about now is cows."

"Is that so?" Vonnie smiled.

Macrae rode his horse up to the two of them. He glared at Karen. "You thinkin' about working today?"

Karen turned and went back to her horse and rope.

"You best be moving on quick, little girl," he said to Vonnie. "I wouldn't want them tender ears of yours pickin' up what these boys say when they get popped by some hoof."

+ + + + +

Bobby Pera served the supper early. Normally, the men would have taken the evening off, but not today. Hammond gathered the men around the horse corral. Barb, Dorothy, and Vonnie watched carefully as he addressed them.

"Tomorrow will be time for you men to pick out your mounts. I'll tell you when you can go in and choose. Every man will get six, and we'll have some spares left over for the herd. The Reb, the darky, and the blond kid, Car, over there, you three will herd the horses on the drive. You'll need to keep a fresh mount ready from every man's string."

The fact that Hammond was keeping the herd for the men he had brought along was one not lost on Barb, nor on the three he had singled out. He pointed over to Tipper. "You're gonna be little Mary. Keep you outta my hair and keep away from the animals."

Vonnie leaned over to Lance Randolph, who was smoking a rolled cigarette next to her. "What's 'little Mary' mean?"

"By all rights it's a job you girls should have. Cook's helper. Fetchin' firewood and peeling potatoes is what they do mostly. S'pose he don't think the kid belongs here at all." He flicked the stub of his cigarette out into the coral and leaned on the fence.

Vonnie watched the glow of the stub in the dust. "Will tomorrow be hard?"

"Yes, it will be difficult. Snapping broncs is bad business, and those mustangs you got there haven't had much of the rough taken off them. It'll be a show."

Vonnie watched the man. He seemed so self-assured, and yet didn't appear to brag like many of the cowboys she had seen come and go. "Is it true what they say about you?"

"What's that?"

"That you're a lawyer."

"That's true enough."

"Why would a lawyer come to Texas and be a cowboy?"

"My father comes from a long line of lawyers in Philadelphia, and I was living my life just being another one. I guess I decided I was getting tired of living out his dream for me, that's all."

Vonnie leaned on the fence, just like the man. "My father's dream for me was always to be a Christian woman just like my mother."

Lance studied her, and her innocence made him smile. "Things are much simpler for a girl, I guess."

Vonnie straightened her back. "They might be simpler on the outside, but not on the inside."

+   +   +   +   +

When the next morning broke across the Texas sky, there were still no signs of rain. The sky was as blue as the dress that Barb wore when she stepped out onto the porch with a large pot of fresh coffee. She passed out cups of the steaming liquid as each man in turn took his place at the chuck line.

Everyone watched the show as each man threw his loop over a string of horses. Hammond made sure each of his men went first. Dorothy watched Yanni rope his string of horses. One by one, he saddled and broke the string, jerking on the halter as each beast in turn did its best to unseat the man. She then stood beside him, petting the animals and talking. Occasionally, she would glance over at Karen and catch her painful glares.

By the time Frank Green entered the arena, the pickin's were getting slim. But for a reason none of the women knew, one large beautiful white mare remained. Green built a loop and went after her. The men looked at each other in a way that made Dorothy curious. "What's wrong with the white one?" she whispered.

Yanni watched Green build his loop. "No smart cowboy will ride a white horse."

Joe Cobb held his string next to them. He joined in. "In the war a man would have to be a plumb fool to ride one. They drew cannon fire like you wouldn't believe. I think some of a cowboy's thinkin' on the matter is left over from the war—different reasons though, mostly superstition."

Green threw his loop over the animal and held him steady, winding his end of the rope around a pole in the middle of the coral. "So why don't cowboys like them? No cannons out there."

"Lightning," Yanni said. "They draw lightning like a pretty woman draws a lonely man." He leaned over at Dorothy and chuckled, smiling with his eyes.

She drew back slightly, ignoring the come-on. "That doesn't make any sense."

"It's true enough," Yanni said. "Even if a body's got one, no man will ride night herd with an animal like that. The white of the horse attracts the white of the lightning." He watched the white mare bounce on the end of the tethered rope. "'Sides, even in full daylight, them horses all seem like shadow jumpers. The least bit sends 'em into a fury. And a bad horse can beat a man plumb to death."

Jim Crossy had overheard the comments. "White horses all once had wings. I bet you didn't know that, little lady."

"What?" Dorothy said.

"Yeah, sure." He tried not to smile. "You check a white horse's withers and you can feel the bone joints the wings came from. Most cowboys feel that's mainly what attracts the lightning to 'em. You know—heaven's fire striking down one of its own. Some say they is fallen angels."

"That's crazy."

"It's gospel, ma'am. You go over and feel that horse's withers and you'll see for yourself."

Dorothy looked at the man and then looked for someone around who might confirm her suspicions, but no one offered any disagreement. She'd always been a bit naive when it came to believing what men told her. She marched over to where Green was cinching up the white mare and rubbed her hand over the horse's neck and down to its withers.

When she turned back, laughter rippled among the men. Crossy was rolling over on the ground, not even trying to keep it all in. Dorothy dropped her hands and, whirling around, marched off toward the house.

+ + + + +

The day had been a long one when the girls gathered around the piano. It might be some time before they could sit down again to the instrument their mother prized so highly, and they were determined to make the most of their last evening at home. They had been playing for some time before they noticed Joe and Poor Soul standing outside the open door, listening. Barb stopped playing.

"Go ahead, ma'am, we're just listening. Poor Soul and I are jest drawn to music like a lost man to light in the darkness."

"You're welcome to come in," Vonnie said.

"Yes," Barb agreed, "don't just stand out there."

The men walked through the door and stood at the entrance to the parlor. Barb turned and continued to play. As she finished, she swiveled around and faced the two men. "Music was important to our mother. She said that what we did around the piano and what went on during prayers at the dinner table was what made us a family and not just people sharing a last name."

"Yes, ma'am," Joe said. "A body's name ought to be a collection of what he does, what he takes pride in."

"From what I've learned about you, it sounds like your home had some wonderful values as well. You must have been very proud."

"There was never a place where my daddy walked that wasn't better for having him pass by. And my mother spent her time making us the kind of people that anybody would be pleased to call a friend, making us someone that'd come a running when there was trouble, and be the last to leave. I'm rightly proud of being a Cobb, but that's only 'cause I was proud of the people who wore the name."

"And have you no relatives now?" Dorothy asked.

"Dorothy, don't ask such a thing," Barb said. "You know what Papa would have said. Here in the West men go their own way. What they don't say, shouldn't be asked."

"Oh, it's all right, Miss Barbara. Poor Soul and me ain't running from anything or anybody. Womenfolk are naturally curious. I think men wait to see a man prove himself, but women need to know about folks early on. I may have family yet, but I'm not sure. I had brothers and sisters that died as young'uns. Nothin' sadder than that. But here now, I said enough. Poor Soul and I ought to be gettin' on to bed."

"No, please go on," Vonnie said.

"Yes, please do, Joe," Barb joined in. "My sisters and I will be traveling for more than three months with men we don't know, and all that we own is riding on it. It would give us great comfort to know the men we're with."

"Tell about your momma and the children," Vonnie said.

"Well, I'm not sure how Momma bore up under it. I asked her one day if she ever thought on those children that had passed on. She told me there wasn't one day that went by that she didn't think on 'em."

"Sadness is one of the strongest bonds in a family," Poor Soul said. "And it reminds us of how little we can hope for when we are all alone in the world."

"That is so true," Barb said. "Our father's death is the one thing that makes us determined to make this drive. We'd stay together no matter what, but the sadness has given us strength. Did you say you have brothers and sisters alive today, Mr. Cobb?"

"I'm not rightly sure. My oldest brother Julian was shot up bad at Gettysburg, so I stayed with him. He lost an arm and his left eye. When the war ended, we split up from the camp where we was being kept. I went home, and he went to Mexico to keep on with the war. Ain't heard from him in some time. That's part of what keeps me in Texas, hoping he'll turn up."

"Why would he want to continue the war?"

"You'd have to know Julian to know that. Once he feels like he's been wronged, he never makes peace with an enemy. Him and my brother Zac were the toughest of us boys to deal with, but Julian, mostly. I heard from some relatives that James was building bridges and had gone off to college, but I ain't never heard from Zac. Figure he died during the war."

Poor Soul smiled. "Julian was the hard one, took everything personal like. James had the head for figures. Zac was always the one with the thoughts for books, pretending to be a knight of the Round Table lost in the South. And Joe here," he smiled, "he was the steady one among all the young'uns. Played his music, did his work, and came when he was called."

Joe put an arm around Poor Soul. "Now, I suppose, Poor Soul and I are all that's left of family, but it sure takes us back to listen."

"I had forgotten you men were raised with music too," Barb said. "Do you play piano?"

"Joe here sure does," Poor Soul responded. "I was learned in the ways of stringed instruments my ownself."

"You must not get many opportunities to practice," Barb said.

"Oh, I play from time to time."

"Where does a cowboy find a piano?" Dorothy asked.

65

Joe blushed slightly. "There are places."

The girls blinked. They had no familiarity with saloons. They were places their own father hadn't visited, except to talk to the men who frequented them.

"Well, please play for us, Mr. Cobb."

"Joe, ma'am. You can call me Joe."

"All right, Joe. Please play a song of yours for us."

She rose and stepped aside, allowing Joe to take his seat behind the set of gleaming ivory keys. He tested several notes and then began a beautiful and smooth rendering of "Greensleeves." Amazed, the women watched his fingers fly over the keys. There was a feeling to his music. Expressing feeling was something that they had been coached in for years, but without much success. Without the feeling, all a person heard was the proper notes; with it, one could hear music as it was meant to be played. The movement of his hands over the keys seemed to take them off to another place and time. When he played the last of the song, his hands lingered on the keys and the girls applauded.

"That's so good," Vonnie said. "It was beautiful. You play as good as Karen."

"Karen?" Joe asked.

The girls were flustered. "She's our other sister."

"Where is she?"

"She's gone her own way," Barb said.

Joe rose from the seat. He knew enough about women in the West who had gone their own way to know that further questions on the matter were out of line. It embarrassed him to think that perhaps he'd uncovered something the girls didn't want known.

"We'd best be going off now."

"To sleep, perchance to dream," Poor Soul chimed in. He bowed to the girls. "Yes, we generally like to read before going to sleep. An educated man's dreams are sweeter."

Vonnie clapped her hands. "Goody! Do you both have books? We will take along some books of our own and would love to swap with you."

A smug smile crossed Poor Soul's face. "Why, yes. I carry the works of Shakespeare, and a collection of English poetry. I also enjoy Mr. Walt Whitman, the Yankee poet."

"There's a number of the boys out there that have books," Joe said. "The Earl has a few with him, and Lance Randolph's a lawyer. He carries Blackstone."

"And you, Joe?" Barb asked.

"I get by with my mother's Bible and Sir Walter Scott's *Ivanhoe*."

"Well, then," Barb said. "We will leave you tonight in good hands."

The two men turned and walked leisurely back toward the bunkhouse while the sisters stood at the door and watched.

"You like Joe, don't you, Barb?" Vonnie asked.

Barb continued to watch him walk away. "I would just like to spend about an hour talking to his mother," she said.

CHAPTER 7

+ + + + + + +

THE DAY BEGAN long before the sun was up. Pera had started banging pots and repacking supplies into the chuck wagon and the extra supply wagon in a way that was hard to ignore. Several days earlier, he and Tipper had pitched the wagon bottoms with caulk and fixed them so that they would float. He'd already heard about how deep the rivers were that they would cross, and he didn't want to take any chances on getting his supplies ruined. Tipper would drive the extra wagon, and Pera had made sure he and the lad knew how to handle the mules.

The girls had limited themselves to one large carpetbag apiece—any more would be to single themselves out as pets who carried more weight than they were worth.

"Dorothy, you ride with Pera today," Barb said. "Vonnie and I will be in Tipper's wagon." Vonnie shot her a look and a sly smile.

Hammond and the men had moved out to the cattle and sat in their saddles in position around the herd. In the distance, the girls could see that Joe, Poor Soul, and Karen had already left with the horses. They would be riding ahead to look for water.

Pete Hammond rode his spotted gelding to the front of the herd. The men had tagged an old red Longhorn steer with a bell around his neck. The huge animal had a span of horns that measured over seven feet. The cattle would follow the leader, but everybody knew that keeping them together would be difficult for a few days, until they got worn out and trail-wise.

69

As the first lip of the sun bulged up from the east, Hammond let out a blood-curdling yell, and the rest of the men began to yell and wave their hats in the air. The drive was underway and everyone—from the oldest man to the youngest calf—knew it. The bell on the red steer began to clang as the beast moved off to the north.

"We'll be pushin' 'em hard for a week or so till they find their place." Hammond continued to ride the line of steers as the mob meandered northward, shouting out orders. The girls would take their turns riding drag, "where the women and children belonged," to hear the cowboys tell it. The dust would be something fierce and the women might just as well forget about their hair, as it would become dusty and brittle with the hot sun and swirling dirt.

Often during the first morning the women watched in amazement while the cowboys gave herd quitters the "rough treatment." The animal would break off from the herd on a dead run for parts unknown and one of the "swing" or "flank" men would take out after him. Building a loop, the cowboy dropped a head catch over the animal's horns. He would then flip a section of rope over the steer's flank and ride almost parallel to the fleeing beast. Suddenly, the rider would take off at a forty-five-degree angle, twisting the steer's head while lifting its hind legs. The results were always the same: a violent corkscrew and a crashing cloud of dust.

"That must hurt something fierce," Vonnie said.

Tipper gave out a boyish grin. "Hurts worse when they don't get up. Hurts the cow and hurts the owner."

"I s'pose it has to be done, though."

"It does, unless you want them to get the idea they can just run off. My pap's done it. Them cows don't talk English, ya know."

Hammond had positioned Macrae and Yanni near the point with him. Earl and Crossy rode the swing position, and Randolph and Green, whom the men were calling "Greener," rode the flanks. That left the women taking turns with Tipper to ride drag and push the herd along. Pera rode in the chuck wagon with

Dorothy. He had refused to put the chuck wagon in the rear where the dust would settle on the food, so Tipper, Barb, and Vonnie in the supply wagon took their turns in the swirling dust and baking sun.

For most of the day, the flank riders were breaking down runaways, while the men near the front circulated toward the rear to pick up the slack. The system worked well, Barb could see that, but it would be a hard first week of chasing cattle and wearing out horses until things settled down. The point riders might get through a day on only three of their horses, but those men on the flank and swing positions would go through all six of theirs, and maybe more.

In the distance, they could see the horse herd, or the "remuda," as the men called it. Joe, Poor Soul, and Car were keeping them bunched and close to the main group. It was plain to see the day was going to take a toll on everybody and the animals. It was just not a job for the weak-kneed or faint of heart. Almost four thousand cattle and a hundred-plus horses made a ranch a body could take pride in. But moving all the stock together and all at the same time was a task that put fright into the heart of any greenhorn.

Tipper moved the team of mules back and forth at the rear of the herd. Even though he wasn't on horseback, he had the instincts of a natural-born cowboy, at least in Vonnie's estimation.

"Did you keep cattle on your place?" she asked.

"For a while. To hear tell it was a nice spread too, till Ma died and Pap went to seed."

"How did your mother die?"

He slapped the backs of the mules with the reins. "She cashed out when I come into the world. That's why Pap says I'm less than worthless, I'm bad. I carry a picture of her with me."

"Can I see it?"

"Sure." He reached his hand down the front of his shirt and produced a dog-eared photograph. It showed a woman with curly hair and what appeared to be a contented smile. "Pretty, weren't she?" Vonnie passed the photograph to Barb.

"Tipper," Barb said, "your mother's death was not your fault. When our mother died, the only thing Father would say was, 'It was God's will.' That's all he would say, and I guess it was all that needed to be said."

"Pap never had no use for God. Never had no use for me neither. Guess all he ever had any use for died when Ma died."

Barb handed the photograph back to the boy. "Everyone dies, Tipper. When we've done all that God intended for us to do, it's our time to go. Perhaps in your mother's case, the thing God had most in mind was to give birth to you. I would say that makes you pretty special, not worthless, and certainly not bad."

The boy stared through the blowing dust at the backs of the mules. The thought was brand new to him, and Barb knew it would take many such thoughts to begin to erase fifteen years of hearing the wrong words.

"Maybe tonight after things settle down, Vonnie and I can read you some of the Bible. Would you like that?"

"Yes, ma'am, I'd like that a powerful lot."

The evening couldn't come soon enough to suit everyone. Pera had driven the chuck wagon on ahead and already had dinner ready when the herd pulled into a narrow cut that was still running a muddy stream. Any other time of the year the place would have been a swampy marsh, but what was there made the cattle fan out and begin to drink. The men swung out of their saddles and gathered around the chuck wagon.

"Form your line," Pera said. "I have cowboy favorites tonight—red beans, bread, and red bean pie. I'm saving my good stuff for when you've done some work."

There were few murmurs from the men as they formed their line, each shuffling forward with worn but eager faces. Yanni had taken two plates and circled around to where Karen had taken her place in line. "Here, kid, take this. Call it a peace offering. If we're gonna let greenhorns on this drive, guess we oughta find a way to get along."

Karen took the plate and the piece of bread he held out to her. She blinked her eyes at the man in disbelief, but put her spoon into the red mess and walked to a place to sit down. Several minutes later, her yell broke the men's concentrated eating.

"What's in this stuff?" Karen had directed her screech at Pera, but Yanni smiled and continued to spoon down his beans.

The curly-headed Italian walked over to where she sat. "It appears to be some kind of beetle," he said. "But don't look at me, I didn't a cook it thataway."

"It's a tick," Yanni offered. "Figured you'd be needin' some meat with them there beans."

The men roared in laughter.

She moved toward the grinning cowboy, but Hammond stepped in front of her. "Hold!" he said. "I won't have it in my camp."

She tried to lunge past the man, but he spun her around. "Listen here, kid, I didn't hire you—that was Miss Reddiger's doin'—but I won't put up with any trouble from you. You go to scrappin' and I'm sending you back to wherever it is you come from."

The sisters sat in stone-cold silence, and Barb bit her lower lip.

"Car over there just needs a little trail savvy," Yanni said. "He's mighty scrappy fer a scrawny feller."

"You'd do best to keep your funnin' to yerself," Hammond shot back. "We got work to do here."

"Aw, Pete, didn't mean the boy no harm. He's just a slip anyways."

The idea of not being taken seriously cut Karen to the quick—all of her sisters could see it in her face. But as long as she wanted to keep this masquerade up, they knew they had best go along. Karen was the type who didn't want to be told anything. What she learned had to be grasped in her own way.

The time around the campfire talking, smoking, and drinking coffee passed all too quickly. The women did the dishes, and the sun had been down only minutes before Hammond called the men around him to give out his nighttime orders.

"We're gonna have to watch 'em close for the first week or so. That's gonna mean three riding night herd each go-around. You can call it or draw lots, I don't rightly care. You men on the remuda will have to take yer turn like the rest." He pointed over to Tipper. "And you, boy, will have to ride like any man."

"Yes, sir."

"Now don't be out there telling no ghost stories 'bout haunts, witches, and the like. Them animals ain't got the run near outta them yet. Watch out for the quitters and keep 'em quiet."

"I say there, Hammond," Earl said, "which shift do you prefer?"

Grunting out a mixture of curses at the Englishman, Hammond made his choice clear, "The trail boss sleeps."

Greener, Poor Soul, and the Englishman drew the short straws and won the luck of the first shift. It would last from 8:00 till 11:00. The second group of riders would be awakened to take their places from 11:00 to 2:00, and the last bunch would be in the saddle till daybreak.

The three lucky men rode out grinning. They approached the herd and paused. "I do say, they don't appear prepared to sleep just yet."

"No, Earl, I don't believe they are," Poor Soul replied. "They're still milling about. You head off yonder, and Greener will circle to the north. I'll wait here about twenty minutes and make my own circle. It helps if you sing to them."

"What shall we sing?"

"Anything, just so it ain't no blood-raising song. I've always found a hymn to go best with cattle. The biblical blood is the best to raise on a night when they're not of the mind to sleep. But any old cow song will do. Hum if you must, but don't go to whistling."

"How will we know when it's time to go back to camp?" Greener asked. "Can't rightly see my watch in the dark, and I don't reckon them fellers will take too kindly to being roused when it ain't their time yet."

"You see the North Star there?" Poor Soul said. "Well, it stays planted right where it lays, but when the old earth here turns over on its belly at night, them cover sheets of heaven, the stars, they seem to move about. You see that Big Dipper yonder? When it drops down to where the lip of the cup is about ready to spill out, that'll be our time. The next bunch gets off when the cup is low enough to keep the milk from spilling, and that dawn group will know from there."

Joe had taken a shovelful of hot coals over to the remuda after he and Karen had picketed a string of horses for the night riders. He had a small fire going when Karen walked up and sat down hard on her bedroll. "Horses like a bit of a fire," he said. "They won't go far tonight. Grass and water are right here. But they will drift some."

"I'd say they're plenty wore out after today," she said.

"First and last months are always the hardest on a remuda."

"That doesn't leave much in between."

"No, it doesn't."

"How will we know when it's our turn to ride night herd?"

"Poor Soul will rouse us gentle like."

"Just so I don't have to ride with that long hair."

"Car, I'd say every man has to figure out how to kill his own snakes, and you have a ways to go with that one. It won't do to ignore him, though. That kind just never learns on his own."

"I do have an advantage. I take care of his string of mounts."

"That you do," Joe laughed, "that you do. I'm sure before this here drive is over, you'll find a way to make sure he fights shy of you."

"That white mare Greener picked out is a troublemaker," she said. "I'd best go and hobble her to keep the others from going very far."

"You show good horse sense for a green-broke kid."

"I'll take that as a compliment."

Some time later, when Karen returned, she could see Joe nestled on his bedroll next to the fire, catching the light to read his Bible. She sat down quietly, not wanting to disturb him, a practice she had learned with her father. When he closed the book, she spoke. "You seem to be quite an unusual man to be a cowboy."

"Every man is unusual in his own way, I reckon."

"Why are you doing this? Why not settle down with a house and a home?"

"I suppose before I make a home, I've got to find somebody to share it with. Just a man living in a house seems to be a mighty lonely picture to me."

"A man like you must have had plenty of girls on the string from time to time."

"Few that interested me much, and none at all that challenged me."

"Challenged you? Why would a man want that?"

"Well, most men just want a woman who does her chores and has his kids, but my sights are set a little higher, I reckon. Probably just the molding I had back home."

"What more are you looking for?"

"I suppose I'm looking for a friend first, someone who sees me as her most important chore, and let's me look on her thataway too. Now you best get some sleep. Poor Soul will be slidin' into camp before you know it."

Karen moved her bedroll away from the fire and off into the darkness. She held the edge of the bag between her and the fire, and unbuttoning the shirt, she loosened the wrap around her chest. It felt good to breathe free again. She laid her head to the ground and fell asleep to the sound of the horses clipping grass.

CHAPTER 8

✦ ✦ ✦ ✦ ✦ ✦ ✦

MORE THAN A WEEK of dry ground and sandy grass had passed before the herd settled into a rhythm. It was easy to see when it happened—the cattle all knew their places in line. In the morning, each would take its place along the march north. The man who rode flank or swing made sure the look of the steers was one of moving contentment. When things were going well, the steer might half close his eyes on the march, partly to keep the flies away, and partly on account of sheer fatigue. It was the sight the cowboys all longed for. Tired cattle seldom ran. When it happened, a cowboy could swing a leg over the horn and roll a smoke in the saddle.

Poor Soul, Joe, and Karen had begun to spend some of their time breaking the horses that hadn't been ridden. When Poor Soul left the remuda with a fresh string of horses for the men on the herd, Joe surveyed what remained. "Here, bring me that bay gelding," Joe said. "That's a fine piece of horseflesh, if we could get him scrubbed down."

Karen built a loop, threw a rope on the bay, and walked him over to where Joe had dismounted.

"What are you going to do?" she asked.

"Don't think we've had a saddle on him yet." He held out a hackamore. "We might as well start to snapping the rough offa some of these horses. In a couple of weeks those with the herd will be needing more horses. Cattle tends to get a horse played out before long. Now, hold on tight."

He slipped the braided leather on the animal while the gelding fought hard against the coil of hemp around his neck. Reaching into his belt, he pulled out a hobble. "Whoa . . . whoa." He rubbed his hand down the horse's neck and felt along the animal's still-braced leg. Wrapping one end of the hobble just above the hoof, he pulled it tight.

He looked back at Karen. "So far, so good." Continuing to talk to her and the horse as well, he reached for the other hoof. "Reminds me of the feller in Saint Lou. He jumped out of a seven-story building. Every floor he passed, folks heard him say plain as day, 'So far, so good.' "

With that, he cinched the other side of the hobble on and backed away. Grabbing the rope from Karen's hand, he pointed to the gear beside his own horse. "Bring me the saddle blanket over yonder and tote over the saddle. We'll see how he stands up to the blanket all by itself first."

The sound of someone giving out orders pricked Karen's spine. She wasn't used to men ordering her about. Of course, since she was pretending to be a common cowboy, she had to change her normal reactions to orders. It wasn't that she didn't want to work—she was a worker, sure enough. It was just that if she had her druthers, she'd rather be the one to see the need and do it and not have to be told.

She picked up the saddle and slung it over her shoulder. Walking over to the man, she watched him. He was sure about the things he did, she could see that. She also knew that when he asked somebody to do something, it had little to do with him trying to be the better man. He wasn't like most men she had seen. There seemed little he tried to prove, and she couldn't catch even the faintest scent of Joe's ego.

He dropped the rope and held on to the hackamore. Taking the blanket from Karen, he began swinging it in front of the horse's face. Even though the animal was hobbled and bridled, he still had plenty of fight in him.

Bracing himself, the horse backed up and fought the bit. Joe jerked on the reins and, coming around, laid the saddle blanket gently on the animal's back. Slipping off the rope, Joe quickly cross-hobbled the animal, cinching it from the front of the tethers to one of the rear legs. He pulled it tight. He patted the bay's neck and, leaning back around, spoke to Karen: "Now the fun starts. Hand me that there saddle."

Holding the saddle up, he spoke softly to the bay and then flung the saddle over its back. The horse immediately kicked out its hind legs, and then bounced and pawed with its hobbled front hooves. "Boy, you best not fight me. You may be bigger and stronger, but I'm an ornery cuss, and a whole lot smarter to boot."

Turning to Karen, he smiled. "Some would say that was open to argue on."

After steadying the horse, he drew up on the rope that wove underneath him and tightened the cinch. Having cinched the saddle down, he released the rope from the hind legs and took a firm hold on the reins. In what seemed to be less than a second, the gelding burst into the air and, in spite of the hobbles that held his front legs, tried to throw the saddle off his back. It was quite a show, even with an empty saddle.

"There's the hard way, and there's the easy way," he said to Karen. "Just between me and you, I'd much rather have it the hard way for him, and the easy way for me."

"You've done this before, I can see."

"Yep. Jingled horses many a time. I love 'em to death, though. I suppose if I had things my way, I'd just as soon go to raisin' 'em my ownself. When I break a horse, he's still got the fire, but it's under control. I sorta think that's the way things should be with people, too."

"People under control?"

"Yep, some folks are so headstrong, they're no earthly good. They gotta have things go their own way all the time. But we all need to be under control somewhere. 'Blessed are the meek' means just what it says."

"Well, I don't want any part of being controlled. To have somebody control you is just to admit that person's a better man."

"Maybe fer some"—he pulled down hard on the reins, stretching them out in front of the horse—"but many's the time it just shows you to be the smarter man. If you are the better man, time and what you do will bear it out, not just something you say."

He continued to put his weight on the reins as the horse bucked against the saddle. "To love an animal like they should be loved and not break them is a sheer pity. I'd say that was that feller Yanni's problem. He ain't never been broken. He's more'n likely been loved, but that ain't no good without the breaking."

"I suppose that's what my father did to me," Karen said. "I was a favorite of his for some reason. I never doubted he loved me, but at times I guess he let me go my own way too much. I always seemed to be saying, 'If you love me, you'll let me do it my way.' I guess I'm learning, though, that not every way I thought of as a child was the right way."

"Well, a young feller like you has got a few years and a few miles to go."

Karen had mixed feelings at being called a feller by Joe. On the one hand, it was what she had wanted, to be acknowledged for the work she did as an equal. On the other hand, when she was with Joe, she wanted to be thought of as a woman—by herself and by him.

"Time seems to do the breaking with some folks," he went on. "My own daddy was a fine Christian man. He come back from the war with the Mexicans with only one leg, and I guess that was what it took to break him. He used to say that everybody needed to be under God's control. He said if that was the case, then there was more freedom to be had than a body could use in one lifetime."

"Sounds to me like that older brother of yours never got broke."

"You got that right. I guess Julian's way was pretty set by the time Daddy learned his own lessons. Don't get me wrong, though, Julian's not a bad sort."

He jerked on the reins to steady the horse. " 'Course, on second thought, he might be bad, but he ain't evil. He'd go out of his way to do you a good turn, but if you crossed him, he'd go halfway 'round the earth to bring you down. He was just about as determined a cuss as I ever laid eyes on. 'Course, Zac weren't much better in that regard. He wasn't mean like Julian, but he sure was determined. And even though he was young when I knew him, crossing that boy was like cutting open a sackful a wildcats."

The gelding had quieted down, and Joe slipped up to him and removed the hobbles. "I suppose living with those brothers of mine taught me a little something about dealing with green broke horses. Now, watch careful like."

He gently placed one foot in the hanging stirrup and took hold of one of the gelding's ears and twisted it. "A little pain takes their mind off of what you're really doing." With that, he swung into the saddle and the big bay began to stomp and buck. With each launch, Joe slapped the animal across his flanks with a leather strap that dangled around his wrist. In a matter of minutes, the gelding settled down and allowed Joe to ride around Karen and their two horses freely. Joe rode up to her and stopped.

"Good work," she said.

"Ain't quite over. Hand me that slicker of mine."

She quickly found the oil-skinned garment and handed it up to him.

"Horses that spook too easy ain't much good with cattle. Don't pay to ride a shadow jumper in the middle of a herd of angry steers." With that, he began to wave the slicker in front of the bay's face and the jumping and bucking started all over again.

Several times, he brought the animal to a standstill, only to once again flag the slicker in front of the horse's face. It was after Poor Soul came back to the remuda with the played-out horses from the herd that Joe thought he had finally done his job.

"He is surely something, isn't he," Poor Soul said.

Karen looked up at him and then off to Joe, who was putting the horse through a series of sharp turns. Her face beamed as she watched him work the big bay. "Yes, he's something, all right."

Hours later, in the midafternoon, Hammond spotted the

dust up ahead from a rider bent on getting back in a hurry. It would be Macrae. The rider pulled his winded horse up next to Hammond. "No water, not for miles yet, and that ain't the worst of it. They got fences up, and we'll have to take 'em through San Antonio."

Hammond grimaced.

"Thirsty as these animals are," Macrae went on, "that won't be no easy task."

Without a word, Hammond rode his spotted gelding over to the chuck wagon. "You go on up ahead. We're gonna make a dry camp tonight. I'll send Yanni with you. Find us some shade if you can, a draw if you can't find shade. In fact, if you men can find us a deep draw, we might be able to get by with two riders at a time."

Pera slapped the reins to the mules, and Hammond waved for Yanni to go along. Today would be a long walk. The cattle would be thirsty and sniffing the air for any sign of water. Without it, they would mill around anxiously through the night.

"It'sa gonna make things plenty tough on them cowboys tonight. The cattle will be edgy, as well as the men," Pera said.

"Should we break out the barrel of dried apples tonight?" Dorothy asked. "We could make some apple pies, do something really special for them. My papa always said that men who worked hard ought to be fed well."

"By golly, that's a good idea. It'll get their bellies full and take their mind offa the night ahead. 'Sides, if we go through San Antonio, I can get some more. I'll use the dried tomatoes too, and the peppers."

Yanni rode up beside the big wagon and flashed a smile at Dorothy. "Looks like I'm riding with you for a spell. The boss man wants me to pick out a spot. What with no water, he don't plan on stopping till it gets dark. Figures to burn the critters out and make 'em think of sleep instead of water."

"That'll give me plenty of time to cook, then. We'll have us a wingding tonight."

Yanni leaned over on his horse to get a little closer to Dorothy. "Maybe the missy and I will have us a wingding of our own before they get up on us. By the time we get to where we're going, it'll be hours before the rest of 'em catches up to us." He cracked a wide smile that made his teeth shine and his eyes sparkle.

"Then you better ride on and go about your business," Pera said. "Sooner you find us a spot, the sooner I can get to cooking."

"Then you foller me, Mr. I-talian, and hurry on with them mules." With that, he used a leather strap he carried around his wrist to slap the rump of the lead mule, and then rode off in a big hurry.

Two hours later, Pera and Dorothy in the chuck wagon spotted Yanni under a tree. It was a perfect location, overlooking a good-sized draw that would suit for the cattle to stay fairly close together during the night. Pera drove the team ahead and pulled the wagon up next to the napping cowboy.

He sprung to his feet and held his hand out for Dorothy. Taking hold of her waist, he helped her to the ground, but once there, he pulled her closer. "Why don't I show you some sights tonight?"

"I don't know. I shouldn't."

"You and me'd never be missed. I don't ride night herd till the last shift. We'd look up at the stars. We'd see something real pretty, and you'd come back a different woman." He stroked her hair and, leaning down, gently kissed her ear.

Dorothy didn't fight the kiss. The attention flattered her. "Barb would skin me."

"Is she your momma or something? You seem like a grown-up woman to me, but I could be wrong."

She pulled away from him and straightened her dress. "I'm grown-up enough. I make my own decisions."

"Good, then that's settled." He led the horse to the back of the wagon where Pera was unloading supplies. "I'm going into town with the lady. You want me to get something set aside for you?"

Pera held out his hand and began to count on his fingers.

"Tomatoes if they got them, dried apples, coffee, flour, beans, chilies, and onions."

Yanni grinned. "I got it. We'll put the stuff aside so as to pick it up first thing." With that he booted himself in the saddle and, grabbing Dorothy's hand, pulled her up behind him. With a clap of his spurs, they rode down the draw and over the rise.

A short while later, he pulled the horse up on a grassy hill overlooking San Antonio. "Why don't we just stop here for a spell. It'll be dark pretty quick and the stars and the lights of town both coming on together will make a mighty fine sight to see."

He slid her off of the saddle and, stepping down, loosened the cinch.

"We aren't planning on being here long, are we?" Dorothy asked.

"Well now, that all depends on you."

CHAPTER

+ + + + + + +

IT HAD BEEN TWO WEEKS since Zac had gotten the telegram. The train ground to a halt, its wheels screeching, the steam billowing up clouds in front of the windows. Skip tried hard to keep his head facing forward. Acting calm, like Zac, was important to him, even if he did have to scoot forward to touch the floor.

When Zac had wired Wells Fargo, accepting the job, they had sent an advance payment, along with expense money and the name of a woman who ran a boardinghouse. Along with that, they'd given him another name, a man that he'd have to find later.

Getting directions from the stationmaster, he and the boy made their way down the street. They were careful to avoid the rowdy part of town. Dodge was famous for its gunfights, and for the Texas cowboys that fandangoed the town with great regularity. Zac knew he'd be spending a great deal of time there, starting tonight, but there was no sense in starting it now.

"Now, you remember our story," he said.

"Yes, sir. You're Ian Adams, a cattle b-b-b-buyer, and I'm your son, Skip. You sure I caen't have another name?"

"No, I don't think so, Skip. Simpleminded as I am, I'm liable to call you Skip anyhow. We best go with what you're really called."

"And I have to go to school?"

"You bet you do. 'Fraid there ain't much else for you, if you don't get your book-learning done. Besides, what would you do all day?"

The boy looked up and down the tree-shaded street. "Oh, I'd f-f-f-find something to do."

"Yes, I'm sure you would. But if it's all the same with you, I'd just as soon know where you are when I'm not with you."

Zac checked the address once again, and the two of them walked up to the large red-and-white house. The outside door was something Skip had never seen before—a large oak frame held smoky glass panes, and a brass doorknob stared out at them in the shape of a cherub. Zac twisted it open, ringing a set of bells that were attached to the inside of the door.

They both stood in the large foyer of the house and gazed up at the crystal chandelier that hung above them. When they heard a woman's shrill voice, they set down their bags.

"Just a moment." The woman sang the sentence in a high-pitched melody, as if she were trying out for a part in the opera. "We are coming just as fast as we can." She continued to sing out the words, but they could both tell that she was getting closer.

The buxom woman, properly attired, rounded the dining room and smiled. She held a finger in the air. "Now don't tell me, let me guess." She placed the finger beside her rosy, carefully rouged cheek and tapped it lightly. "You must be Mr. Adams, the cattle buyer, and his son."

Zac nodded.

She clapped her hands. "Mercy me, aren't I the wonder now. I do declare." She held out her hand. "Please call me Laura, Miss Laura."

"Pleased to meet you, Miss Laura. This is my son, Skip."

Skip bowed slightly at the waist, just as he had been taught.

"Mercy me, young man, aren't you the proper gentleman." She pinched his cheek. "And so very handsome, too." Looking up at Zac, she added, "Like your daddy." She paused to let the compliment sink in. "Is Mrs. Adams with you?"

"There is no Mrs. Adams." Zac tugged at the white paper collar that was pinching his neck something fierce. He had dressed the part of the cattle buyer: dark suit, white shirt, black tie. The only thing that seemed the least out of place was the gray cavalry hat that he still couldn't part with. He held it in his hand.

"We don't get ourselves many visitors who wire ahead with payment, now do we, darling."

"We?" Zac asked.

"Oh yes, my dear departed husband, Wilbur, and I. He built this house when he was president of the bank. He passed on five years ago and"—taking out a handkerchief, she patted her eyes—"I had to turn the place into a guest house. But still, I feel his presence here as my partner, don't you?" She blew her nose.

"Yes, I feel some sorta presence here, now that you mention it."

She patted Skip's head. "You both must be quite tired. I'll show you to your room and show you where you can bathe before supper."

"That would be nice." Before Zac could say more, the woman had begun to ascend the carpeted staircase. The ornate mahogany wood made the house seem dark, even in broad daylight. Zac and Skip picked up their suitcases and tried to follow as best they could.

The woman pranced up the stairs, marshaling instructions over her shoulder with every step. "I have placed towels on your beds, but extra ones are in the cupboard here. The privy is behind the house, but with the warm weather, I shouldn't think you would mind the short walk." Whirling around, she placed her hands on her hips and confided, "I hear there are people these days that are actually building privies inside their houses! Can you imagine that?"

Zac and Skip continued to watch her, dumbfounded.

Turning around, she paced down the long hallway. "If you place your laundry outside your door, I will see to it. Leave your boots and shoes in the hall each night. I have a man that shines them." Twisting the doorknob to the last room on the left, she turned and smiled. "Supper is at five. You must be prompt so as to not miss prayers. And by five-o-five, most of the food is gone."

They followed the woman into the room and watched her

light the pink-shaded glass lamp. Small, carefully carved shards of glass hung from the edges of the lamp. She ran her fingers under them, stirring them and causing shadows to dance on the walls. Walking to the large, ornate mahogany bed, she turned down the quilt. "This was Wilbur's bed." She smiled. "I can assure you of its comfort. If it's less than you should desire, please let me know." She placed her hand on Zac's sleeve. "I always try to please my gentleman visitors."

"I'm sure we'll be fine without any further attention," Zac replied.

"I've prepared a palette in the corner over here for the young boy. But if you desire, I'm sure I could find another location for him." She smiled and softly batted her eyes. "You might want your privacy."

Zac tossed his hat onto the bed. "No, I brought Skip with me to keep me company."

"I see." She moved to the door. "Well, now that you see what our fair city has to offer, should you change your mind, please let me know."

"Thank you. I will."

"Your tub is directly across the hall. If given notice, I can make certain you have hot water."

"I'm sure you will," Zac said. He closed the door behind her, just as it appeared she would say more. Turning back to Skip, his eyebrows arched. "Stick close by me, Skipper. That there is the kind of woman I'd like to teach you to avoid."

"W-w-why is that?"

"Oh, some folks fill up the emptiness of their lives with things—more land, more cattle, more pretty stuff. But there's others that try to fill it up with people. They need love and they don't care where it comes from or how they get it. My folks filled my life up with love from the get-go, and I want to make sure I do that for you, just like I'm sure your folks intended."

"Is that why you brung me?"

"I suppose it is. Being away from you all the time don't rightly seem like the best way to teach you what you need to learn as a man. Tomorrow, we'll go and find you a school."

They had put their things away and managed to scrub their faces before they walked down the stairs. They were ten minutes early. Zac turned to the boy and said, "Better ten minutes early than two minutes late."

"Good evening, gentlemen." Laura was busying herself with setting the table when they arrived. She motioned to the two other early arrivals. "This is Mr. Charlie Harrow. He's a cattle buyer too."

Immediately Zac's heart skipped a beat, but he remained calm on the outside. The tall man with the gray mustache rose to greet him. To use a cover was one thing, but it wouldn't pay to try and make small talk about a subject he knew only partly about. "Pleased to meet you."

"And this fine gentleman is Doctor Marvin. He produces the most marvelous elixir and sells whatever a body needs in that wagon of his out there."

"Designed to make your eyes shine." The man extended his hand. He wore a checkered suit fronted by a bright red tie. "Yes, I can do it all, but only with help from above." He pointed to the ceiling and his eyes rolled upward. Skip's gaze followed the man's finger, as if he might really see where the man got his help.

Zac pumped on the man's hand. "Name's Ian Adams," he said, "and this here's my son, Skip."

The other men had begun filing into the dining room and hurriedly took seats. At a nod from Laura, the salesman rose and said grace. He had no more than said "Amen " than some of the men around the table grabbed for the bread, while others launched into spooning a weak-looking porridge from a large white serving dish. Zac managed to scoop some of the contents into both his and Skip's waiting bowls.

"I've made chicken and dumplings tonight," she said. "The biscuits are fresh too. Mixed them up this morning."

The men said little. They were absorbed in the process of finishing their first go around before diving in for more."

Skip continued to rake his spoon in the bowl. He looked up at Zac and said in a voice that was all too clear, "I f-f-f-found me the dumplings, but I ain't f-found no chicken yet."

Zac was quick to see the remark had registered with Laura.

"You keep looking, darling, there's chicken in there," she said.

"Same chicken we been eatin' on all week, I'll wager." One of the rough-looking men shot out the words, and laughter erupted at the end of the table.

"I see the boy has a slight speech impediment," Marvin said.

"Yes, but it's getting better all the time."

"I'd like to help the lad, if you'd allow me."

"Why, Doctor Marvin, I do declare," Laura joined in, "I believe you can do just about anything."

"Why no, madam. I can do very little on my own." He held up his hands. "But the Lord works His will through these fingers." He leaned across the table. "I do believe I can help the boy, Mr. Adams, if you'll allow it."

"Well, Doctor, Skip and I will talk it over. When the boy finishes his schoolwork, and if you have the time . . . I'm sure it would be fine."

"Splendid!"

"So I gather you're a buyer too, then, Mr. Adams." Zac could see Harrow looking him over. "I work for the Illinois Central Meat Company. Who did you say you are with?"

Zac had chosen the profession of meat buyer to get him as close to the payrolls as possible, but it was something he didn't want to be pressed on, especially by a man in a position to know.

"I didn't say." The remark was sharp, but in the West a man seldom pressed a question about another man's private affairs.

"Don't mean to intrude," Harrow went on, "but I see you're carrying a holster under your arm there, and we've had quite a stir in these parts." Several of the men stopped chewing to listen. The remark was pointed, and not lost on anyone. He went on. "'Course, don't rightly know of no bandit that travels with his son."

"I always come ready," Zac shot back. "I buy cattle, I don't steal them."

"Then you've heard about our difficulties out here?"

"I've heard."

"And we get little help from the law, and none from the army."

"Well, I'm sure if you sold to the army, you'd get plenty of help." Zac knew enough about prices to know that the army paid substantially less than the market rate. Saying what little he knew seemed to show he had some knowledge about the matter. The man smiled.

"I'm afraid I leave that market to other folks, Adams. I got hungry people to feed back East."

After finishing dinner, Zac made sure Skip was comfortably settled in his own bed with a good book. "I believe you'll enjoy Sir Walter Scott. The tales of knights and such were always good company for me."

"W-w-will you be gone long?"

"No, I'll just be at the tables a short while. I got to get my face seen a little and learn what I can."

The street was buzzing with the sound of piano music when Zac turned the corner. There was so much to chose from, but he walked straight into the Longbranch. Coming through the doors, he recognized one of the owners, Luke Short, not a man to trifle with. He didn't know if Short would remember him or not—they'd never crossed each other. He stood with his back toward the man next to a poker table only half full. "Mind if I join you men?"

"'Course not. Pull up a chair. We need somebody with money to lose. Most of us are beginning to feel like we're winning our own money back."

Over an hour and many hands later, Zac saw a sight he'd never seen before. Striding into the Longbranch was a man who appeared to fill up the doorway, a man with pure white skin and shoulder-length snowy hair. Even though it was completely dark outside, the man wore gold-wired spectacles with dark-colored lenses. He held the doors open momentarily, and then walked to the bar with another equally unsavory-looking character. Zac didn't know who he was looking at, but he knew the type. He watched him and continued to play.

Some time passed before the men looked up from their bottle at the bar and surveyed the room. They quickly spied Zac's table and the two empty chairs beside him. After a few words between them, the two men sauntered over. "These seats open?"

The man across the table spat out, "Only to folks sportin' the coin of the realm."

The two men smiled. Zac noticed the white-skinned man's companion had all the looks of a gunny who fancied himself fast. He wore his silver-handled revolvers slung low and tied down at the thigh. He spoke. "We got money, but we don't plan on losing." They both sat down, the large man at Zac's elbow. "Deal 'em up," he said. As the cards were flipped face down around the table, the men all introduced themselves. "Name's Quirt Muldoon," the big man said.

The winning hands seesawed around the table, each man winning an occasional draw. Zac wasn't much for gambling, but he'd learned enough about the West to know that around a poker table was the place a man picked up most of his information if he was new to town, and in most of these cow towns, everybody was new.

The man across from him had the deal. He called himself Matt Barbour. "That feller to yer left, Quirt Muldoon, is a cattle buyer," Barbour said. "You two ought to get yerselves better acquainted." Then to Quirt, "He calls hisself Ian Adams."

"Aye, I've heard of you," Muldoon spoke in his Scottish brogue, and nodded.

Zac knew the man was lying. Ian Adams was a fictitious name. He hadn't heard of the name himself before yesterday. The other thing that bothered him was the fact that Barbour had called Quirt by name. Zac knew enough about cheating in poker to know that a typical "cold-deck" scheme required a man to deal cards to someone he appeared *not* to know. The man who dealt would lose like everybody else, but he'd make sure that the other pigeons in the game lost more. And Zac knew he'd opened himself up for it with his suit and tie, and the cover of being a cattle buyer. They'd set him up to get his confidence level sky high, and then they'd take him down like a child.

The third time Barbour dealt, Zac could see the confidence builder being played out. Down fifteen dollars at that point, Zac got two jacks on the first draw. Barbour himself was the first to raise. "I'll kick in ten, I'm feeling lucky."

Several of the men, including Zac, matched the bet. He discarded three of his cards and sure enough, in the three new cards given to him was one of the missing jacks. Zac thought he spotted a curt smile on Barbour's face as the card was dealt. There were several raises and Muldoon went in another twenty dollars. At the showdown, Zac found himself raking in close to a hundred and fifty dollars of other people's money, not enough for a man to quit, but just enough for him to lose all common sense.

"Gentlemen," Muldoon said right on cue. "Why don't we just play a man's game. Time's a wasting. I'd suggest a twenty-dollar minimum bet, instead of the two-dollar one we're fussin' with."

The men all agreed and the deck was passed to the hard case that sat beside Muldoon. Zac knew full well that the next time the deck went to Barbour was the time slated for the kill. He'd be given good enough cards to flush out the pot, but Muldoon was slated to win. It was time to decide. It would be hard to quit, having just won a big pot. When the good cards were dealt to him when it got around to Barbour, he could fold, but that would arouse suspicion.

Muldoon won one hand as the deck got circulated around the table. Zac won a hand, and Barbour won another. Two more men shared the winnings until the deck once again passed to Barbour.

Barbour shuffled the deck. The man was good at this business. What would seem like a friendly hand of poker would soon turn out to be high-stakes robbery, and Zac was to be the victim.

When he picked up the five cards in front of him, Zac could see the trap sprung. He was holding three kings, the makings of an almost unbeatable hand—almost. When the man dealt him another king, only four aces would take the pot, and Zac knew full well where the four aces would go. It was time for a decision.

CHAPTER 10

+ + + + + + +

ZAC DREW OUT HIS PIPE and stuffed it with tobacco.
Raking a match under the table, he lit the pipe and smiled. From
the corner of his eye he saw Muldoon lean back and gaze at his
cards. For a man who knew what was coming, this Quirt Muldoon was a cool customer. Reaching his hand under his black
coat, Zac wrapped it around the butt of his little Shopkeeper .45.
"Now, why don't you just lay the deck face down on the table,"
he said. "And don't you go to moving those hands around any
place but the top of the table."

Barbour froze and the men at the table looked spellbound,
except for the surly gunslinger who sat beside Muldoon. He
dropped his hand to his side, but was surprised at how quickly
he was looking down the barrel of Zac's little .45. "I wouldn't
do that," Zac said. "This don't concern you, least not directly."

The man put both hands on the table and Barbour slowly
lowered the deck, face down. "What do you think you're doing?" Barbour asked. "You've been winning, as far as I can see."

"I may be new to this place," Zac said, "but I ain't no greenhorn. Now you just deal yourself three cards from the top of the
deck. Deal yourself first, just like you been doing."

Barbour deliberately shifted three cards from the top of the
deck to the pile of cards in front of him, just as he had been instructed.

"Now, you deal me the two cards on top, face up. One of
them will be a king, more'n likely the first one up."

Barbour swallowed and slowly flipped the two cards across

95

the table face up. The men blinked as the first one that flashed across the table was the king of diamonds.

Zac turned his cards over, showing the other kings. "How 'bout that," he said, "four kings. Now, I want you to reach under the deck like you been doing the last two go-'rounds and deal the bottom three cards over to Mr. Muldoon here, face up."

Muldoon sat up straight. His pale white skin took on a rosy hue. "I don't need your money, Adams."

"He's right," Barbour chimed in nervously. "Quirt Muldoon owns a big ranch north of town."

"I own everything north of town," Muldoon corrected.

"Well, then, just maybe this little friend of yours was trying to do you a favor without your knowing; I'll give you that. 'Course, for some men, everything is never enough. Some folks take pleasure in the taking, never in the having." Zac turned his icy stare to Barbour. "Deal those bottom three cards over to our rancher friend here."

The tension of the game had drawn a number of passersby. Others left what they were doing to stand beside the table and watch, among them Luke Short. Zac could see that he was being studied by the gunslinger saloon owner, as if the man were searching his mind, trying to place him.

Barbour's hand trembled as he slid the bottom three cards out from under the deck and flashed them across the table to Muldoon's pile. Two of the cards were the aces of spades and clubs.

"Let's just see what kind of a mind reader I am," Zac said. "I'd be willin' to bet that pot yonder along with another hundred dollars in my purse that Muldoon's hand here has the ace of diamonds and the ace of hearts."

With that, he reached over with his free hand and turned over the pile of cards in front of the big man. The men murmured as they saw the two aces. "That just about cashes you folks outta this here game, I'd say."

Once again the gunny sitting beside Muldoon dropped his hand to his side. Zac's only response was to cock the little .45. The man froze at the sound of the hammer.

"You say you're a cattle buyer, Adams," Muldoon said.

"I deal with cattle, that's right."

Muldoon slowly got to his feet. He removed his darkened glasses. His red eyes flashed in the glow of the lamplight. "Then you and I are going to be seeing each other again. You've embarrassed me, and I don't care to be embarrassed." Picking up his straw hat, he planted it on his white head.

Zac looked the man directly in the eye. "I enjoy doing business with a man who knows where he and I both stand. I like a game with all the cards on the table, and I look forward to offering you a fair price for your cattle, just like this never happened."

Muldoon placed both hands on the table. They were huge, like the paws of a polar bear. He leaned forward, directly into Zac's face. "But it did happen. You've accused me of cheating, and in an establishment that I frequent."

"I just showed everybody here what Mr. Barbour over there already knew."

"Adams, right now I'd say you were out of business in Dodge City. No one that knows me will sell you one single scrawny cow, no matter what you have to offer."

Zac sat in silence as the man turned and slowly walked to the door. Standing with one hand on one of the batwing doors, he discussed the situation with the gunslinger at his side. The look of the two men was one that would have chilled most men down to the bone.

Zac laid his revolver on the table and turned to the other men, who were still sitting in stone-cold silence. "You men can divide the pot, 'cept for Barbour here."

With that, the men eagerly began to rake the bills and gold coins piled in the middle of the table, while Barbour quietly left the table and walked out the door on the heels of Muldoon and his henchman.

"Mr. Adams, that took a hundred pounds a guts to do what you just did." Luke Short had edged his way to Zac's side. "I've never seen it done before, and I've seen a whole lot here in Dodge City. You appear to have a mighty keen eye. If you look cattle over like you watch those pasteboard cards, I'd say those employers of yours are mighty happy people." He held out his hand to shake. "I'm Luke Short and I own the Longbranch."

Zac took it and gave him a strong grip. The man was short of stature, just as his name implied, but his eyes were sharp and penetrating.

"I don't think I'd go walking out that door for a while yet," Short added.

Zac raked his winnings into his hat. The gray officer's hat with its gold braid was distinctive. It didn't match anything in his outfit, but Zac was never without it. What he'd been through wearing it during the war just seemed to be something he couldn't set aside. He saw Short catch sight of it.

"You do remind me of someone, Adams, but I just can't place you. You carry yerself like a man who's not to be trifled with."

"I'm just here on business with my son. This is my first trip to Dodge City."

"Well, you sure know how to make a lasting impression, I must say. Muldoon's right, though. If he says nobody will sell to you, then I'm afraid that's it. The man's a menace, but he does bring money into town, lots of money. Knows everybody and everything there is to know around here. When he steps out on the street, everybody hides and shakes."

"Well maybe a full night's sleep will be enough to put his mind on business," Zac replied.

Short chuckled. "You don't know him. If you live through the night, you're gonna find that there's not one man in this town that doesn't know what happened at the table here tonight. They'll all know what's expected of them as far as you're concerned too. If you take my advice, I'd say you best go on to Ellsworth or Abilene to buy cattle—you ain't about to get a whole lot done here, not anymore."

"You'll find that where I'm concerned, I always get done what I came to do. But I'm a careful man. Do you have a back door to this place?"

"Follow me."

Short led him past the tables of the gambling room where

even in the short span of a few minutes, he was turning heads. Everyone wanted to get a look at the man who had faced down Quirt Muldoon and was still breathing. He didn't look the part of a desperado, but it was plain to see he was well built. And because he was only using a shoulder holster, he didn't even give the appearance of being armed.

"Here it is." Short paused at the door. "It comes out on the alley, but I'd be careful. Wherever you're staying, those folks will know about it come morning. You best take my word on the matter and ride off to greener ground. You won't get nary a nibble at the stock pens."

"If I have to, I'll ride out and buy the cattle before they come in. Those herds from Texas know nothing about this here Quirt Muldoon."

"Don't bet on it. 'Sides, the area south of us is not too healthy for a man riding alone. Rawhiders and Injuns been crawling all over out there. If you do go, you better take a long gun with you, that and a fast horse."

"I appreciate the advice. It's mighty friendly of you, me being a stranger and all."

Zac touched the tip of his hat and scooted out into the dark alley. It took him a few seconds to adjust his eyes to the near darkness. Made him wonder about Muldoon, the whiteness of the man. He'd heard of such a condition before, but he'd never seen it. The man reminded him of a white rabbit he'd seen once in a store in San Francisco, the red eyes and all. It made him wonder if Muldoon could see well in the dark. It was just a wives' tale that rabbits could see better in the dark. Still, it gave him pause. The man's eyes had been haunting. He wondered if Muldoon was watching him. If he was, he'd be in plain view just about now.

He edged his way along the rear of the building, gliding his feet so they wouldn't step on and break any debris that might be lying about. The music from the Longbranch poured out into the street, mixing with the tinny sound of other honky-tonks competing for the passerby's attention.

Coming to the corner, he stopped. Peering his head around

the edge of the noisy building, he could see a man standing in the shadows. The man looked to be about the size of the gunman who had sat next to Muldoon. He was standing in an area of the darkened alleyway that gave a good view of the street, standing and watching, his back to Zac.

Zac pulled out the little .45. A fistful of little was better than a handful of nothing.

Quickening his pace, he walked straight toward the figure. At the last moment the man caught wind of the movement behind him and whirled a shotgun around to meet the intruder. It was too late.

Zac smashed the handgun into the man's face, sending his hat flying. The shotgun dropped to the ground and Zac scooped it up. As the man groaned and got to his knees, Zac holstered the .45, gripped the scatter-gun, and slammed the butt of it directly into the man's forehead. The sharp concussion sent him spinning backward into the building. Moaning softly, he slumped to the darkened dirt of the alley and lay still.

Zac broke open the weapon and slammed it against the corner of the building, sending the shotgun flying into pieces. Wheeling around, he quickly returned to the rear alley and made his way to the back street.

Minutes later, he hurried into the boardinghouse and bounded up the steps two at a time. What he had done was foolish. It was just the sort of thing that had gotten him into trouble before. When was he going to learn? It might have made it easier to ignore if the mark those men had in mind had been somebody else, but he was to have been the pigeon of the evening. His mother had always told him that his need to be the knight in shining armor was going to get him into a peck of trouble. He should have listened to her.

He reached his door at the end of the hallway and listened to the closed door. All was silent. He turned the knob and slowly pushed open the door. Quietly, he removed his jacket and hung it on a chair, then took off his shoulder holster, removed the .45, and shoved it under his pillow.

It was one thing to try to set things right that didn't concern him when he was alone, but now he had Skip to think about. He did have a last will and testament prepared. If anything happened to him, the boy would be well cared for. But if anything happened to that boy, nothing in this world or the next would allow him to forgive himself. He should put the boy on the train headed west tomorrow. Only then could he sleep.

Skip slept soundly on the pallet the woman had set out for him. The light still burned beside him, and on his chest lay the open volume of *Ivanhoe* that Zac had given him. Zac picked up the book, carefully marked the place, and set it on the table beside his bed. Kneeling down beside the boy, Zac watched him sleep. He knew he could never change the kind of world the boy would grow up in. But he knew it was his sacred duty to shape the boy, to make him ready for that world. If he didn't, who would? He reached over and blew out the light.

Sometime later, in the wee hours of the morning, Rass Bodine limped into Quirt Muldoon's study at the ranch. The caked blood on his forehead told all there was to tell. His legs were weak, and he wanted like all the world to sit down, but he knew better. He stood in front of the massive desk and watched Muldoon scribble figures in his ledger. "That man's no cattle buyer," Bodine croaked.

Muldoon lifted his red eyes, surveying the damage done to one of his best men. "You try to face him down?"

"No, that's what I'll do next time. He come up behind me in the dark. Next time I'll be in the daylight, just him and me."

"And just what makes ye think ye'll come out of that alive? This man has an edge, man. He knows something. A cattle buyer you could shoot without much fuss, but what if he is something else, like you say?"

"I'll ask around. If he's known at all, somebody will be able to tell us something."

Muldoon rose up from the oversized leather chair and paced toward the window, squinting into the darkness. The big Scotsman, above anything else, was a thinker. He always had an edge in that department. The man had never dealt himself into an honest game in his life. "Now why would a known man come to Dodge City? What could he hope to gain? Everybody knows we have the city and all the surrounding area sewed up. Gunslingers and road agents either work for me or they lie in the bone yard."

"He's good. The man is smart. I watched him at that table. He never even broke a sweat. He's not an Earp—I know most of them—'cept I ain't never seen Warren, or Morgan."

"Did you see that hat?" Muldoon asked. "The Earps are all Yankee Republicans. They wouldn't be caught dead in a Rebel hat."

"Maybe not, but he's somebody all the same. The way he acted, it was like somebody that's got a lot of guns backing him up, only he was all alone. He was cold like a snake, and he come up on me like a ghost."

Muldoon walked back to his desk and leaned on it. "Aye, this man has seen action before. Fighting for the South, he knows what it means to be outnumbered."

"It's more than that, Quirt. He handled himself like a man that wasn't outgunned at all." Bodine shook his head. "I've never seen anything like him. I tell you, he ain't no cattle buyer."

"We'll know soon enough. I'm sending out wires to people I know in the meat business. They'll tell me if he is who he says he is. And besides, if he is a cattle buyer, then he'll find out soon enough that there aren't any beefs to be had by him in Dodge City, not at any price. When he learns that and decides to move on, then you can have him your way. It does appear to me," he added, looking the man up and down, "that you'll be wanting that."

"And if he isn't?"

"Then I want him to stay in Dodge. My father back in the highlands used to say, 'Keep your friends close, and your enemies closer.' I want that man close, to see what he's about. Then we can pick and choose what happens to him."

Muldoon sat back in his chair, and Bodine turned to leave. "Rass, I want ye to stay on the ranch for a while." He reached over, took a decanter of whiskey, and poured it into a cut crystal goblet. The big man always enjoyed toying with the minds of the men who worked for him. To outthink a man was to maintain power over him, and power was the thing that consumed Quirk Muldoon. "That face of yours will take some healing before you can be seen. Besides, it will give me time to see just what or who we're up against."

He slurped the contents of the crystal goblet. "Send some of the boys angling back south. We'll catch a few herds that are alone. I want to make sure that all the loose cattle in Kansas have my brand on them. What we're doing is too important to go off half-cocked. There's too much money to be made. One day this whole territory will belong to me."

CHAPTER II

+ + + + + + +

HER SISTERS HAD ALWAYS told her she was naive about men, and now Dorothy understood why. She drew back against the tree, her face drawn. "I think we ought to go, if you're gonna get those supplies you promised."

Yanni dropped the reins on his horse, allowing it to wander off and begin to clip tufts of grass. "Listen, darling, you and I could stay under this here tree for hours yet, afore they miss us. I've got some ideas how we could pass the time."

She sprang to her feet. "Well, I have no intention of doing what you have in mind." She held her back firmly against the rough bark of the tree.

He moved forward and, planting both hands on either side of her, leaned into her face. "All women want Yanni, given the time to think about it."

Her lips trembled and she said lamely, "I'm . . . saving myself for my husband."

"Fine, that's real fine," he smiled. "You a religious gal, are you?"

"Yes . . . Yes, I'm a Mennonite."

"I was religious once." His lips pouted out the words. "My pa is a circuit rider."

"Your father? A minister of the gospel?"

"Yeah, but I don't want no part of it now. Guess he's even stopped prayin' for me." Yanni pressed his lips against Dorothy's as she froze. "All I want is you."

She pulled away. "Why don't you want any part of religion?"

"'Cause my pa was so busy with them churches of his, he never had any time for his kids, that's why," he said evenly. "Only thing he had time for was readin' his Bible and prayin'. Said he prayed for us, but he beat us too. Couldn't bring himself to play with us. Said frivolity was the devil's device." He lightly brushed her cheek with another kiss. "I guess I belong to the devil," he laughed.

He pulled her closer, held her tightly as she struggled to free herself. Behind him, she could see the lights flicker from the town. Under normal circumstances, a romantic setting. But she'd never imagined the kind of terror she felt now to go with it. Barb had been right.

He kissed her repeatedly on the lips, then on her chin. "Now, ain't that nice?"

She knew she had to do something to get his mind on something else. "Why would your father stop praying for you?"

He lifted his head away. "Said once I belonged to hell and the devil. I figure if that's the case, I might as well make sure he's right. He hates to be wrong." He smiled. "Might as well enjoy myself, too, while I'm at it."

She moved her head aside as he kissed her again. "Please . . . please don't do this. Let's . . . get back to camp."

He pulled back, and his teeth sparkled as he grinned. "Why, miss, I thought you were enjoying this. Fact is, I don't think you have much to say about it. This is Yanni here you're dealing with. Womenfolk don't fight me for long." He wrapped his arms around her and pulled her close again.

Please, Lord, help me!

In the same instant the horse began to whinny and stomp nearby. The certain whir of a rattlesnake broke the ensuing silence. Yanni's head jerked up, he dropped his arms to his sides, and drew his revolver.

The horse reared, its hooves flashing in the twilight. Jerking aside, it spurted across the hill and was gone before Yanni could reach for the reins. Yanni spotted the snake and took aim, then turned his head to catch the direction the horse had taken.

Seeing her chance, Dorothy grabbed her skirts and ran down

the hill without a backward glance. Behind her, several shots rang out, accompanied by the sound of Yanni's cursing.

+ + + + +

Miles away, the hands had finished supper and were pawing at the remains of the apple pie. They lingered around the camp-fire and sipped their coffee as they ate. They hadn't seen a cloud in days, but spotting one in the night sky brought on some wish-ful thinking. "I sure hope it rains afore tomorrow comes," Greener said.

"I shouldn't believe that to be a likely occurrence," Earl joined in. "Those clouds in the distance do not appear to be rain-bearing in nature."

"We get so much as one clap of thunder," Randolph inter-jected, "and the way that herd is now, thirsty and all, they'll be gone every which way."

Crossy put down his plate and spread his hands in front of the fire, not so much for warmth, but for visual effect. "I was out near the staked plains once. Flat salt plains with tumble-weed scattered ever which way. We had a herd a yearlings." He dipped his head and arched his eyebrows. "Well, all of a sud-den"—he gestured broadly with his hands—"a norther come up. We had thunder, lightning, wind, and rain. And not ten minutes earlier there weren't no kind a weather at all."

The women appeared interested, causing him to become more animated in his description. "That wind scattered them tumbleweeds in every sort a direction, and them yearlings, well, I tell you, they didn't rightly know where to run." His eyes wid-ened. "So they run off in every direction a body could imagine. Didn't run as a bunch. All thousand head stampeded off, chased by them flying tumbleweeds."

He got to his feet. "Well, old Panhandle Corkey went to chasing a bunch down. He rode for miles trying to turn the lead-ers, before he found out he was trying to turn a bunch a tum-bleweed."

The men around the campfire laughed, and Vonnie clapped.

"Stampedes are queer things in how they start," Randolph

said. "Saw one commence when a cow stepped into a tomato can."

"Snakes will do it, too," Crossy added. "And Lord knows there be a passel of 'em here in Texas. We're not too far from where I saw the biggest snake ever seen by mortal man without the aid of liquor."

The men laughed.

"I went through a spot up near the Red," he said, "where they was so thick, a body had to parade around on stilts to keep from being bit."

Macrae grunted and crushed out his cigarette. "Crossy, that squaw talk of yours is as shy of the truth as a goat is of feathers."

* * * * *

Dorothy felt as if she'd been stumbling over rocks and brush for hours. She was exhausted, and leaned against a rock in a darkened hollow. She had heard Yanni's voice several times behind her. She thought she'd rather be dead, with honor, than alive in his hands.

"Oh, Miss Dorothy! Don't be wanderin' alone out here in the dark. Come to me. I'll take care of you."

She could see him on the rise above, silhouetted on his horse against the night sky. *How in the world did he catch that horse?* she thought.

"Come to Yanni now, darling. You know that's what you want. I won't be hurtin' you. Just want to give you a little comfort, stroke that pretty red hair of yours."

Her heart began to pound and she held her breath to control the panic.

"I'll take you into town and show you the sights," he crooned. Then, slowly, he began to move his horse down the grade, in her direction. She thought it was dark enough that he couldn't see her, but she couldn't be sure.

"Leaning, leaning"—incredulously, he began to sing a hymn, one of her favorites—"leaning on the everlasting arms. Leaning, leaning, leaning on the everlasting arms. What a fellowship, what a joy divine, leaning on the everlasting arms. What a blessedness, what a peace is mine, leaning on the everlasting arms."

He moved closer, his voice strong and strangely comforting. She could tell it was a song he had sung many times before—he knew it well. The thought of him in a church on a Sunday morning was hard to imagine. *What a crazy, mixed-up character*, she thought. *With all the potentially good background, why the twisted result?*

The idea that a human being could violate his conscience so completely was foreign to her. She knew men who had no faith, plenty of them. But she'd always had the idea that the only thing such men needed was a clear knowledge of the Bible. They could be taught that easily enough. Given time. . . .

"Leaning, leaning . . ."

She could hear him coming closer . . . and closer. The moon was low, but its outline glowed clearly. She inched to her right, and her dress snagged on a thorny twig. She froze.

"Safe and secure from all alarms . . ."

But this man knew the same things Dorothy knew. He knew she wanted to stay pure, and he knew why. Was he truly beyond God's reach? It was a thought Dorothy couldn't bring herself to believe.

He stopped his horse not ten feet from where she was hiding, and the song stopped. "If you think I can't see you, you're wrong."

She inched backward, hoping he was just talking to the darkness. She held her breath, placing her hands on the smooth rock behind her.

Yanni dismounted his horse and hitched it to some brush. "I can't believe you'd turn me down."

He *had* seen her. She lifted her skirts and scrambled along the bottom of the hollow, her heart thumping in her chest like a squirrel in a rain barrel. She heard his spurs behind her, the tiny bells clinking a steady beat. Then he was wrestling her to the ground.

"Now we'll see what kind of a woman you really are," he said in a low rumble.

"Why are you doing this to me?" She thought she detected a faint smile on his face.

"Maybe it's because you're the kind of person I don't like very much. You should have stayed with your own kind. My pa always said I was bad, and when I'm with you religious types, I'm really bad."

She struggled beneath his weight. "Please. You're hurting me."

He pulled her to her feet and pinned her against a large boulder. "If you cooperate, I won't hurt you. . . ."

The distinct sound of a pistol cocking stopped him cold. "Just leave her be, white boy." Poor Soul's voice was the sweetest sound Dorothy had heard in a long time.

Yanni swung around to face the man. "Where'd you come from?"

"My pa always said I could find a hair on a frog. I heard the hymn you was singing, and just followed the sound of your voice." He paused. "Mighty fine singing it was, too. Every note perfect."

Yanni lowered his hands to his sides.

"I wouldn't even think it if I was you. You wouldn't be the first white man I shot and killed." He smiled widely, showing a row of pearly white teeth in the moonlight. "'Sides, I ken see you a far sight better than you ken see me. We're close to San Antonio. I think we could find someone to take yer place tomorrow, right after we say some words over you. Now, you jes' use your left hand there and unbuckle that gun belt. Let it drop nice an' easy."

Yanni paused. Slowly, he unbuckled his gun rig; it landed in a heap at his feet.

"You're pretty smart fer a white boy. Now, you jes' get on that pony of yours and ride on outta here. You so much as look a second time at Miss Dorothy here, and I will kill you flat out."

As Yanni turned to leave, Poor Soul sent a swift but powerful kick into the seat of the man's pants, sending him sprawling forward on all fours. "That's somethin' I been wantin' to do since the first time I laid eyes on you. Don't make me do what else I been wantin' to do."

Yanni got to his feet and gingerly walked over to his horse, unhitched the animal, and swung up on his back. Without a word, he slapped his spurs to the horse's sides and bolted up the hill in the direction of the herd.

"Why'd you kick him?" Dorothy asked.

"Shame is a powerful motivator, ma'am. You all right now?" He held out his hand and helped her to her feet.

"Y-Yes . . . I think I'll be fine."

"Then we'll go back to the herd and have a talk with Hammond. I don't want that man nowhere near here come morning."

"No, please don't. This was all my fault . . . really."

"That's nonsense. Nothing about this was your doing."

"Please, say nothing about it, as a favor to me."

"But why?"

"I have to live with my sisters. If they find out, I won't hear the end of it."

"I don't want that man anywheres near you."

She swallowed. "Maybe he won't be there by the time we get back to camp."

"If he has an ounce of pride, he won't."

"Well, then, it'll be done with. There will be no need to discuss it with anyone."

Pour Soul walked her up the hill to where he had his horse picketed. He helped her onto the animal, then jumped up behind her.

"I am deeply grateful to you," she said. "You were an angel of the Lord tonight, and I won't forget it."

CHAPTER 12

+ + + + + + +

ZAC WAS UP and dressed before the sun rose. Strange beds always made sleeping difficult. He looked at Skip, still asleep on his pallet, and had a fleeting thought of envy. Maybe the boy would trade places with him tonight.

Breakfast was about to be served, and from the way the men at the table the night before mauled the food in front of them, Zac knew they couldn't afford to be late. He bent down and shook Skip.

"Time to get up, partner. We're burning daylight." As soon as the words were out, he remembered his own father saying the same thing to him. Fathering required a pattern. And being unfamiliar ground to him, the natural thing was to repeat how he'd been spoken to and treated.

The boy roused, rubbing the sleep from his eyes. Zac poured water from the pitcher into a bowl on the large dresser. "You can wash up here, then we better be getting on downstairs."

Minutes later, they were seated at their places, with Skip next to Dr. Marvin, and Zac pouring himself a cup of steaming coffee. He warmed his hands on the cup, then held it up to his lips with both hands.

"You men look rested," Laura said, carrying a large iron pot to the table. "I have hot porridge here, and will bring biscuits and honey out in a spell."

"You have honey?" Skip asked.

"Yes, little man, we certainly do." She pinched his cheek slightly and smiled. "Right from our own bees. And next to kisses, it's the sweetest stuff found in all of Kansas."

"Whereabouts would we find the schoolhouse?" Zac asked.

"I'll be happy to show you after breakfast. Miss Joy runs the school. Sweet woman." Laura smiled slyly.

Zac raised his eyebrows.

"I'll be taking my wagon out that way," the doctor said. "You can ride Doctor Marvin's marvelous chariot of the plains." He placed his arm around Skip and squeezed. "I might even break the boy here into the medicinal remedy business."

"Fine, fine. Be much obliged for the lift."

After breakfast the three rode down the main street toward the edge of town. On a side street, they found the school and several outbuildings. A woman who looked to be the school-teacher was sweeping off the porch.

Zac removed his hat. "Good morning, ma'am. Name's Ian Adams, and this is my son, Skip. I'm a cattle buyer and was looking for a place for Skip's book-learning while I'm away at work."

Dr. Marvin had already climbed down and was tying the team to the hitching rail as Zac finished his introduction. The woman's blond hair was swept up behind her head in a bun. Her blue eyes twinkled as she pushed at the coiffure.

"And I, madam"—the doctor removed his hat and swept it low—"am Doctor Marvin. I am known from Saint Louis to Den-ver as the miracle worker of the plains. My elixir has been known to cure gout, rheumatism, punies, flea bites, and the dropsy, the infamous disease of the Bible only the healing touch of Jesus could affect—until now, thanks to his wayward but humble child."

With those words, the good doctor placed his hat on his heart and bowed his head. He then lifted his eyes and broke into a broad smile. "I can also show you vanities direct from Saint Louis—corsets, tortoise-shell combs, and beautiful bonnets from Paris, the plumes of which were plucked from savage os-triches in the heart of Africa, not more than one year ago today."

The teacher had placed her broom at the edge of the door, and in spite of everything Dr. Marvin had been saying, she hadn't taken her eyes off Zac. She extended her hand as he got down from the van. "And I am Miss Joy. It is a pleasure to meet you." She nodded at the doctor, "Both of you. I will be delighted to show you our facilities."

She picked up her skirts and started up the stairs. "And have you a wife to care for the boy when he is not in school, Mr. Adams?"

"No, ma'am, I'm afraid Skip's mother has passed on. It's just the two of us."

A faint smile crossed her face, and she turned again quickly and headed up the steps. Dr. Marvin stuffed several fancy combs into his pocket and a bottle of his elixir, then followed them into the schoolroom. It was Saturday, so the place was quiet. Miss Joy took her time showing them the desks and supplies, the selection of books that lined a shelf on the wall.

"If you're going to be traveling about, Mr. Adams, you may need somewhere to leave the boy. I have a guest room in my home, and I have often lodged the children of traveling men."

Skip looked up at Zac, who could see the boy wanted no part of the teacher's plan but knew enough to hold his tongue.

Zac patted his shoulder. "Thank you. We'll have a look, but right now we're pretty well fixed up. We're staying at Miss Laura's house in town."

"Oh . . . I see." The four of them walked out of the school and through the woman's house at the back, making an unexplained stop at her own ornately decorated bedroom. "Having the boy here with·me would make things very convenient, and unlike the place where you're lodging, I can feed him well. I could even be persuaded to prepare a very fine breakfast for the two of you."

It was a line of reasoning Zac didn't care to pursue.

"Madam," the doctor interjected, "let me take you out to my wagon and show you those hats. A splendid figure of a woman such as yourself should wear a headdress that does her justice."

Her eyebrows wrinkled, and a slight frown crossed her mouth.

"You go ahead," Zac said. "It'll give Skip and me a chance to talk over your offer."

The notion made her frown disappear. "All right. I'm sure you two will come to the best decision."

Zac and Skip stood in the dining room, watching the doctor escort Miss Joy out to the waiting van. "You ain't about to leave me here, are you?"

"I'm not sure. I had a bit of difficulty last night I didn't tell you about, and it made me a mite fearful about you being with me. You know the work I do, the scrapes I sometimes get into, often without warning."

"I c-c-can take c-c-care of myself, I done it b-before."

"I know you can, Skip. You handle yerself pretty well. It's just that the people I'm up against here strike me as the type of men who will stop at nothing. They wouldn't hesitate to use you to get to me, and I know you wouldn't want that. Besides, gunfire can't tell the difference between me and a ten-year-old."

The boy's eyes shone, and his lip quivered. "It's just, I feel like I b-b-been left b-b-behind all my life. I'm much more scared a seein' you go than anything else. I w-wouldn't know where you are, and what's gonna happen to me."

"I'm afraid I don't 'zackly know how you feel, Skip. See, I was born after my pa got back from fightin' in the Mexican War. Julian was about your age when Pa left, but he never talked about it much. Guess he got good at keeping everything all bottled up inside."

He placed his hand under the boy's chin and lifted it slightly. "Right now, partner, I reckon you and me feel about the same way. We're all the family we got. You're scared of losing me, and I'm plumb petrified of losing you."

The boy reached out and held Zac's hand, then squeezed it gently. "I promise I w-w-won't be no trouble. I'll stay outta your way. I'll run when you tell me to, and stay close to the ground if I have to."

"All right, Skipper. You do just as I say, and right when I say it. I trust you." He smiled. "In fact, you're the only man I do trust."

It took more than half an hour for the two to make their apologies and head for the wagon. The doctor coaxed his team forward and waved goodbye to the schoolteacher standing somberly on the steps. She wore the new blue bonnet well, even with the ostrich feather swooped low over her brow.

"I'd say that gal cut quite a fancy to you two boys," the doctor commented.

Skip smiled, while Zac kept his gaze fixed on the road ahead.

"You fellers mind if I make a swing around to the north of town to see if there might be some ailing folks in need of my medicines?"

Over an hour later, they rode to the crest of the butte that overlooked the large ranch. They had been traveling the fence line that seemed to stretch on forever, stopping occasionally to make a sale at the squatters' places that dotted their side of the fence.

"Whew-eee. That there is about the biggest place I've seen in these parts," Dr. Marvin declared. "I'd take that to be the Muldoon spread. Look at them logs. He must have hauled them things all the way from Colorado. That house goes on forever and ever, set down in that draw like it is. I tell you what, boys, if'n I could interest them in some a what I'm carryin', I'd just about be set for the week."

"I'd like to see that place myself," Zac said. "But I can't be seen right now. Skip and I'll climb into the back of the wagon till you get close, then I'll see if I can slip out the back and have a look."

"I figured you was up to something. I don't see any riders down there. But I can talk to the ladies in the house about my wares. I'll leave you to figure our your own plan."

Zac and Skip climbed from the front seat to the back of the wagon. From the outside, the brightly painted vehicle gave the appearance of a circus calliope. Inside, the items hung from the ceiling, swaying and bouncing with every movement, and boxes and barrels were stacked on the floor. Zac and Skip crouched low beside the rear door.

Inside the massive house, Muldoon stood beside a window

with his brass telescope, watching the colored wagon descend the hill. Taking the scope away from his eye, he closed it and smiled.

+ + + + +

The cattle had been fanned out and the men began pressing the march close together. Shortly after serving the last meal, Pera took Dorothy into town to pick up the supplies he needed. He thought she was strangely silent, but took it as the unpredictable temperament of women, knowing better than to question her mood.

"We'll get our supplies and wait for the herd on the other side of town. I don't think I want to be anywhere around when those boys take them steers through that place."

They had finished their shopping and were pulling the chuck wagon down the street when they heard the bell on the red steer clang behind them. The cowboys were shouting, and men and women were clearing the streets in every direction. Pera gave the mules a slap, and the wagon bolted ahead.

The cattle streamed down the street, the scent of water ahead of them—a herd dangerous to be in front of even on the open plains. The men were nervous, and Hammond quietly spoke his orders. "Keep 'em moving. The quicker we get past here, the better. Keep the leaders walking though, no faster."

All along the street, people gathered to watch the parade. It was a sight to behold. The shops began to empty as the cattle surged past the historic Alamo.

A cattle drive was bound to be unpredictable. Some things just couldn't be controlled no matter how skilled the people in charge. Lack of water on the trail was bad enough, but controlling crowds of people was the worst. They couldn't be counted on to do the right thing, no matter how carefully they were coached.

Hammond could not have missed seeing the woman run out of her house, or the white sheets drying on the line as he walked his spotted gelding by in front of the leaders. Oblivious, he lit a cigar and began to puff it to life. Then the woman began screaming, and Hammond swung the gelding around.

She had decided to gather her sheets before the cattle knocked down her line. She was using the first sheet in hand as a flag to steer the cattle away from her precious laundry. "Get away!" she cried.

As if on cue, the herd began to stampede down the dusty street, erupting the crowd in a pandemonium of noise and confusion.

The cowboys rode beside, scrambling to keep the damage to a minimum. People who moments before stood on the sidewalks to see the sight were diving for open doors. The street and the boardwalks belonged to the herd, and nothing could stand in its way.

Hammond rode at a gallop beside Macrae. "We'll pay for this!" he yelled. "Keep 'em goin'. We can't stop 'em now till we get to water."

Crossy galloped his mount abreast of the cattle, waving his hat to try to keep them in the street. Up ahead, he spotted a little girl, no more than a baby, that had crawled out on the boardwalk and sat unattended, bawling a cry that only she could hear.

He pulled his hat tight around his ears and sprinted his horse toward the child. There would be time for only one pass. Grabbing the apple on the front of the saddle, he swung his body low and stuck out his hand. Leaning back in his saddle, he snatched the garments of the baby and jerked the screaming child up into his arm. His horse danced forward into the milling stream of cattle.

Righting himself in the saddle, he pulled the reins sharply to the left. No time was a good time for the maneuver, but to avoid catching a horn and spilling both of them into the streaming mass of hooves meant performing the best move of his life. One way or another, he was going to have a wreck. With split-second timing, he dug his spurs into the horse and once again jerked the reins, sending them crashing into a white picket fence. He whirled the animal around, keeping it on its feet, and made for the only open door he could see. Lowering his head, he danced the horse through the opening and into the house, tearing the door off its hinges in the process.

+ + + + + + +

CHAPTER 13

CROSSY FOUND HIMSELF smack dab in the middle of somebody's dining room, with the family cowering in the corner and food still steaming on the table.

"Sorry 'bout the interruption. Hadn't figured on inviting myself for lunch."

The child he held continued to cry as he swung his horse around in the suddenly crowded room. "Ma'am," he said, his eyes pleading with the woman who had pressed her back in the corner, "could you take this child? She belongs to some folks up the street."

The woman cautiously approached the horse and took the frantic baby from his arms. Crossy tipped his hat. "Thank you, ma'am."

Without further fanfare, he spurred his horse back out through the smashed door and into the street, where the rear of the herd was continuing to run without letup.

Up ahead, the leaders had slowed beside the river and begun to fan out and slurp at the slow-moving stream.

"Let 'em drink," Hammond yelled. "Then we're gonna move 'em outta here real quicklike. What happened in that town back there ain't gonna sit right with some folks. We'll be plumb lucky not to get our necks hitched up to some tree."

He began to count the hands as they rode in with the rest of the herd. Satisfied everyone was accounted for, he circled the milling cattle and continued to bark out his orders.

"What are we going to do?" Barb asked him. She turned her

head around and watched the smoke and dust that continued to swirl in the street behind them. "I know there'll be damages to settle. But what little money we have was intended for supplies."

"Ma'am, I'll be greatly surprised if we haven't bought the last of our supplies back there. If they come for us, we'll have to settle up best we can."

The remuda had come through earlier, and Joe watched the herd continue to drink from the slope where he, Karen, and Poor Soul had decided to let the horses graze. "There's going to be the devil to pay for that mess," he said.

Poor Soul nodded.

"We had best get these horses out of sight," Karen said. "They're probably the most valuable thing we've got just about now."

✦　✦　✦　✦　✦

Dr. Marvin pulled the wagon to a halt in front of the two massive doors that led to the log hacienda. Reaching up to the bell suspended from the wall of the wagon beside the driver's seat, he grabbed the line and sent out a series of rhythmic clangs.

Several Mexican women and a dark-haired housekeeper assembled in front of the wagon. The doctor leaned back and spoke softly to Zac. "I'll go on with my sales, and you can slip out the back. I'll watch the boy. Seems to be only womenfolk about." He chuckled at the notion of being in on something dangerous.

Stepping down from the wagon, the doctor removed his hat and swept it low. "Ladies," he called. "I am Doctor Marvin, known from Saint Louis to Denver as the miracle worker of the plains. My elixir has been known to cure gout, rheumatism, punies, flea bites, and the dropsy, the infamous disease of the Bible that only the healing touch of Jesus could affect—until now, thanks to his wayward but humble child." He bowed low and smiled broadly.

Reaching up under the seat, he removed a banjo. He began

to strum a tune and sing a melody. The tune was familiar, but the words advertised his wares. He paraded the women around like the Pied Piper of Hamelin and in moments had their backs turned toward the colorful wagon.

Zac got out the back door and ran for the side of the house. He skimmed the side of the log structure until he found what he was looking for, a back door. Opening the door, he stepped inside. The kitchen was laid out with preparations for the evening meal. Plucked chickens and a variety of vegetables covered a huge oak table. Large strings of big red peppers hung on every side.

He walked into a darkened hallway that led through an enormous dining room with antler candelabras suspended from a lofty ceiling. The walls were matted with intricately woven tapestries and paintings. Wrought iron sconces hung on the walls, each holding a burning candle.

He turned the corner and walked down a large hallway lined with books, many with ornately designed leather covers. Ahead of him was a large room with a massive stone fireplace. French doors with panes of carved glass were open, and over the doorway hung a Scottish coat of arms with crossed swords above it.

He stepped lightly through the door and surveyed the room. An ornate desk stood in its center with a large leather chair behind it. Framing the scene was the biggest window he had ever seen outside of a fancy saloon. Its curtains were slightly parted, the gold trappings and cords hanging almost to the floor.

Moving to the desk, Zac spotted the large ledger books at once. He skirted the desk and began to turn the pages on the book that lay before him, glancing occasionally up through the doorway and listening to the sound of the good doctor's singing.

Then he spotted some pages that interested him: line upon line of brands of cattle. Beside each brand were numbers, counts of each brand. And underneath each line was a sale price. The totals were enormous. Turning other pages, he saw the names of men. Beside each name was listed a sum of money, followed by a date. If there was massive theft of cattle and payrolls, then it was plain to see by some of the names in the book why the thefts had gone unsolved.

"Well, well, Mr. Adams. How nice it is to see you again."

Muldoon stood in the corner of the room, an open door behind him. He had a smile on his plaster-white face that set off his red eyes. He also had a shotgun clutched in his oversized hands.

Zac froze behind the desk and dropped his hands to his sides.

"It appears to me, Mr. Adams—if that is your name—that you've drawn into a busted hand." He held out the shotgun and walked toward the desk.

"Everything I've heard about you, Muldoon, is that you're one of the most successful ranchers in several states. Given the way you play poker, I just couldn't bring myself to believe that your success was due to any hard work on your part."

"Aye, but my success is brought about by wisdom, something which seems to be lacking on your part. Honesty has never been a virtue of mine, but ruthlessness is, as you will soon discover."

"If you're going to kill me, you better have at it. You won't get a second chance."

"You do disappoint me, Adams. You have saved me the trouble of hunting you down, but do you think I'd want to splatter your blood all over these old world tapestries? My treasures are too important to me. They've taken too long to acquire. Besides, I don't kill a man unless I know who he is. You might have friends. Your death might arouse curiosities among people that I would rather not provoke."

He reached for a silver bell on the corner of the desk. "I'm going to allow some of my men to savor this moment with me. Then we'll send you on your way, a better man for having known the hospitality of Quirt Muldoon." The tycoon grew men's hatred like so many daisies. It would give him pleasure to know that before they were through, Adams would be fully conscious of the power he held over him. Death would be too easy.

Responding to the sound of the bell, six insipid-looking men walked through the doors on either side of the desk. One of them, a massive brute with red hair, had brass knuckles looped around his fist. From the direction of the front door, Zac recognized the man he had seen the night before. The fresh scars on his face told him at a glance that it was the same man he had dispatched in the alley. He carried a coiled black bullwhip in his hand. Zac could see the metal pieces dangling from the end of the bitter weapon.

"Gentlemen," Muldoon addressed the group. "Let's see to Mr. Adams here. I don't want him killed, but I do want him to remember his visit here as they cart him out of Dodge City."

The men grabbed him and wrestled him to a standstill, then hustled him out a side door.

"Goodbye, Mr. Adams. The day you see me again will be the day you die."

Zac felt like an unwelcome guest being pushed out the door of a bar, a man who couldn't pay his tab. With the men pressing him closely on every side, he couldn't move, much less fight back. He was being rushed down the hall toward the kitchen, where he had entered.

Suddenly, as he was thrust out the door, he felt the red-haired man's forearm around his neck, choking the air out of his lungs. For a fleeting, dizzy moment he was back in California. The wind was being forced from his throat and his ears buzzed as the world swirled around him and turned black. He was on the beach—in his mind—in the powerful surf, the wind and the waves in his ears, the blackness of the water beneath dragging him deeper toward his death.

Then the big man loosened his grasp, and for a split second Zac hung suspended, as if frozen in the air. Now the man grabbed him by the coat and held him up as blow after blow rained down upon him. Through the buzz in his brain brought on by the lack of air, he could feel the deadened blows of the men's bare fists, punctuated by the cold sheering of the brass knuckles. His head snapped back and forth with the force of each blow.

Dropping to the ground as the big man released him, he lay

numb, his mind spinning. Several kicks thudded into his ribs, sending shooting pains through his whole body. Quietly, his mind began to tiptoe away. He longed for the blackness of unconsciousness, the last escape of a dying man. There was a sense of surreal peace that flooded his soul.

The words of his mother were seared in his mind and came to him now. "Jesus will help you, son, if you ask Him." The words were simple; all her words had been simple. She had a way of getting to the truth of a matter.

Then he felt the sharp bite of the whip on his back, jarring any thoughts of home far from him. The fire from the end of the whip lifted him off the ground. Again and again, he felt the tearing of the flesh right through his jacket and shirt, the metal strips removing his clothing along with his skin.

If he had a way of controlling the involuntary jerking, he might be able to appear as a dead man. Maybe then the wolves would remember Muldoon's instructions to leave him alive. But the man with the whip bore the scars Zac had planted on him the night before. Mercy was unlikely.

Through two more slaps of the spiked leather thongs, he did his best to remain motionless, to still the muscles that screamed with pain.

"All right, that be enough of that." The Irish brogue made no impression on the man with the whip. He coiled his arm to strike again, but the big man grabbed it. "You heard Quirt. We're not about the business of killing this man, not just yet. Here, men, pick the feller up and carry him around to that peddler's wagon. We've given him plenty to think about."

At last, when the men lifted him, he blacked out. The next thing he felt was the motion of the wagon. He heard the whip as the doctor applied it to the mules, mixed with the sound of pans banging together and Skip's soft cry.

The wagon careened along the open road, each jarring motion sending new shivers up Zac's spine. His ribs ached, but his mind was beyond caring. Blinking in and out of consciousness was a mixed blessing. He took comfort in knowing he was still alive, but the pain tore into his brain. At times he swam the deep waters of nothingness, and then a bump in the road would send him back into the world of pain.

The sudden stop of the wagon brought once again the mindlessness of deep sleep. The next time he came to was in the arms of Doctor Marvin and several men who were carrying him up the stairs and toward his room. "Don't you worry, son. We sent for a doctor. He ought to be here directly."

The men stripped back the blankets and placed him on the cool sheets. Zac felt his boots being gently pulled from his feet and then he heard Miss Laura's voice.

"I brought some soap and hot water. Get him settled and leave the rest to me. This is women's work."

Only faint sounds came from his lips—the words stayed in his brain. He closed his eyes and dropped back into the dark safety of his mind. The next thoughts that came to the surface were accompanied by the feel of the warm cloth massaging his body and the feel of the doctor's hand moving over his wounds as he inspected them. Then he felt a cold stethoscope on his chest.

"Can't say for sure if the man's lungs are punctured. He's breathing mighty ragged in there. Wash the blood from his mouth and nose."

The woman did as instructed, and then Zac felt the small hand of a boy holding his. "Don't die, Zac, please say you won't die."

Zac struggled to open his eyes and looked directly at Skip. "Don't you worry, son. I'm gonna make it."

CHAPTER 14

✦ ✦ ✦ ✦ ✦ ✦ ✦

THE MORNING CAME AND WENT, and it was well into the evening when Zac opened his eyes again. Skip was fast asleep beside his bed in a chair. The boy reminded him of a puppy that refused to leave home. Zac felt his forehead; he found a careful line of sutures, another series of stitches crossed his cheek.

It was bad business for a man with something to live for. Up till now, Zac felt he had to find an excuse to lay down his role as a knight in full armor, but looking at Skip made him see he already had a real reason to do so. The boy was young, and he needed a father. Zac felt himself getting older by the minute—not just in body, but in his thinking. Maybe that long-awaited corner in his life, the one he knew he'd turn someday, was right here and now. He knew that if indeed he were to become a man like his father, he needed a son. A man not only had to have something to leave behind him in the world, he had to have someone to leave it to.

Glancing over to the dresser, he saw an envelope propped up against the mirror. And even though he couldn't make out what it said, he knew it came from Jenny. He recognized her carefully slanted handwriting immediately. She must have gotten the telegram about his new name and where her letters could find him. The woman was amazing. The letter must have come today. It was almost as if she knew what he needed when he needed it.

He rested his head back on the pillow and closed his eyes. It wasn't many men who got to be in the same room with everything he loved most on earth. He breathed deeply. He was just that man right now. The things he wanted most on this earth were the boy that slept beside him and the woman whose letter rested on his dresser. For so many years, what he wanted most in life was to be the kind of man who did his job like no one else ever could, but now he wondered how important that really was. To be a man who could look himself in the mirror with pride was one thing, but to do it while losing the things he loved best was another.

He coughed. At first it was a slight cough, and it made his ribs ache, but then a series of coughs sent his skull reeling and shivers of pain rippling through his entire body.

"Are you okay?" The boy sat up in his chair and put his hand on Zac's chest.

The cough subsided.

Skip wrung out a washcloth and placed the cool compress over his head. "You are k-k-kinda hot. The doc said to watch that. Said you might have some infection, that might b-b-bring on a fever."

Zac croaked out the words, "I'd like some water."

"Sure." Moving to a nearby table, the boy poured a glass of the clear, cool liquid. He held it up to Zac's lips and let the water slide down his throat. "You want me to read something to you?"

"I'd like that. You can read that book I gave you."

The boy reached for the novel *Ivanhoe* and held it up to the light. "W-w-where would you like me to start?"

"Any place you've a mind to. I like all of it."

Skip read a couple of chapters, then put down the book to change the cold compress. He laid it gingerly on Zac's forehead, then asked, "What's a Jewess?"

"An outsider . . . I guess. In those days, somebody people didn't much care for. But God loved the Jews."

"You mean folks like us, outsiders like we are?"

✦   ✦   ✦   ✦   ✦

As Zac drifted in and out of sleep during the night, Skip continued to change the cold compress. Every time Zac opened his eyes, Skip dipped a spoon into the glass of water for Zac to sip. When daybreak came, Zac awoke to find the boy slumped in his chair beside the bed, sound asleep. The door was gently pushed open, and there stood Dr. Marvin, the remedy man, with a tray of steaming food.

"I thought you might be needing some substance. Miss Laura will be up in a few minutes with your doctor."

"Good," Zac said. "Skip's out. Nursed me all night."

"Bless his heart." Placing the tray of food on the bedside table, Marvin said, "Got some applesauce here for you, good for the system and what ails you."

Zac continued to look at the boy. "He read to me from his book, kept cold compresses on my head, spooned cool water down my throat. The kid's worked hard all night."

"I'd like to take him with me today, show him around, get him out of this house."

"Great idea. Mighty kind of you."

"I'd also like to do something about that stutter of his. I think I can help him."

"Whatever you can do, I'd sure appreciate it. The boy's been through a lot in his short life. Lost everything in the world. Reckon I'm all he's got left."

Marvin tucked a napkin under Zac's chin. "You can trust me; miracles are my business. As long as I'm helping people, I feel I'm doing the Lord's work." He spooned the applesauce into Zac's mouth. "Speaking of work, these people 'round here don't seem very hospitable to cattle buyers. I'd have thought men who have cattle would've greeted you with a brass band, not beat you half to death."

"I think you and I both know I'm not a cattle buyer."

"What you are isn't any of my business. But I'll carry what I saw around with me till the day I die."

Zac's eyes narrowed. "I wasn't prepared when I entered that place. Normally, I make sure I have more to offer than the people I'm after can take, but I only had my short gun on me yesterday, and I was kinda outnumbered."

"That you were, son, that you were. Well, whatever your se-

cret is, it's safe with me. Now, you may not think that a man
of my profession has much to prove by keeping his word, but
before I took to the road, I was a man of the cloth."

Zac smiled. "With what I've seen of some of them folks, that
don't put you too far ahead of being a drummer."

"I suppose. But a man shows himself by what he does, not
by his outward trappings. Like you—you dress and arm yourself
like a cattle buyer, but you said yourself . . ."

Zac laughed till he could feel it from his head to his toes,
bringing a grimace of pain to his face.

Skip woke up just as Miss Laura and the doctor arrived. Zac
placed his hand on the boy's head. "Skipper, why don't you go
with Dr. Marvin today. Have a good time. You worked hard last
night and I appreciate it."

Less than an hour later, Skip was in the front seat of the
wagon, craning his neck around to watch the front door of the
big house in the distance.

"Don't you worry none about him, boy. That man is pure
spring steel and rawhide. He won't die until the Lord himself
decides it's his time."

Minutes passed in silence until Skip responded: "D-d-do you
think everybody has a time?"

The mules walked lazily on. "Yes, boy, God has His time and
we're all included in His plan. He has work for us to do, and we
don't get to leave this world until our job is done."

"G-g-get to leave?"

"That's right. If you know the Lord, the place you're going
to when you leave here is so wonderful, the Bible says words
can't describe it."

"That's w-w-where my momma and d-d-daddy are now."

They rode on in silence for a time. "I'm sorry about your
folks, boy. Somehow, I didn't think Mr. Adams was your real
father, but I didn't know for sure. I'll tell you one thing, though,
that man loves you just like you were his own flesh and blood."

"D-d-do you think so?"

"Never been more sure of a thing in my life. And I know
what love is, boy. In my time I've performed hundreds of wed-
dings. Been married myself once, but my wife passed on long

ago. And my four sons all died in the great strife between the North and the South. I suppose that was what put me on the road." He paused, and looked the boy over carefully. "Yes, that man loves you sure enough. He'll take good care of you too, and I know you'll take care of him."

The boy bobbed his head in a subtle nod, kept his head bowed low. Then his eyes began to fill with silent tears. As the two of them rolled down the dusty road, the great ball of fire that was the Kansas sun beat down on them, but it didn't seem hot. The breeze blowing in from the north created waves upon the golden grass, and it made the sun seem to be just heaven's way of warming them.

"How long you been talking like you do, lad?"

When the boy lifted his head, his eyes were dry. "I-I guess since my momma died. Just my c-c-curse, I reckon."

"It's been quite some time since I've seen a boy of ten with a curse on him. How you reckon it got there?"

"I guess it's God's w-w-way a warning folks to steer clear."

"Steer clear of what?"

"Of m-m-me, I reckon. Everybody that b-b-belongs to me up and dies."

"Oh, I get it. And you think your loving that man back yonder is gonna kill him too?"

The boy nodded silently, his eyes again filling with tears.

"Well, boy, now that just isn't so." He pulled up on the reins, stopping the wagon in the middle of the road. "Now, before Dr. Marvin here can put some good things into your head, he's gonna have to take some bad things out."

The boy looked up at him.

"People's problems in this life all stem from one thing— from the way they see God. He's plain enough to see; just look around. But people see, and they don't see. It's been my experience that folks either believe that God doesn't love them, or that He's powerless to do anything for them even if He had a mind to. Now, which of these is your problem, lad?"

"W-w-well, I know He's powerful. My daddy taught me that."

"Then He just doesn't love you? Doesn't care fiddlesticks about what happens to little Skip?"

The boy blinked back tears and bowed his head.

"You know that isn't true. Fact is, He came down here in human form and died for us. And do you know that even if you'd been the only one here, He'd a done it just the same? Now, you just stick out your tongue."

"W-w-what?"

"Just do like I say. Never mind how silly it seems."

Skip hesitated, then stuck out his tongue.

The old man grabbed it between his thumb and two fingers and pinched hard. "Who made this tongue, boy?" He released his grip, and the boy swallowed.

"God, I reckon."

"That's right. And everything God makes is good."

"I-I reckon so."

"Boy, reckoning won't do, you gotta *know* it's so. Now this is what I want you to do. Say mm-m-m for me."

"Mm-m-m."

"Good, good, that's right. Now you say a whole sentence, but before you start the first word, say mm-m-m."

The boy hesitated and then began. "Mm-m-m . . . do you think that will make me talk better?"

"It did, didn't it?"

"I guess so."

"No. Say, mm-m-m, I guess so."

His face brightened. "Mm-m-m . . . I get it."

"There. Now, that's what I want you to do every time you speak. After a while, you can just think it. It will help you to get the sound coming out before you form the words you want to say. Take it from me, boy, I owe everything I have to the mouth that God gave me. I sing, I preach, and I sell. Now stick out your tongue again."

The old man grabbed the boy's tongue again and, pinching it, lifted his eyes and prayed for God's help. "There, boy, put that back in your mouth now and use it for God's glory."

"Mm-m-m . . . yes, sir, I will."

"Good, good boy. Now, today we're going to sell a lot of clocks to folks out here."

"Mm-m-m . . . clocks? Why would folks out here need a clock?"

"A clock, my good man, is a sign that civilization has come to the prairie. They might not think they need one, but in two weeks they won't be able to live without one."

"Mm-m-m . . . how's that?"

The old man cocked his head with a mischievous smile. "I show them how to wind it up, place it in some prominent location in the house, and then tell them I will come back for it in two weeks." He chuckled. "Folks get used to the ticking sound—regular things are comfortable to the soul of man. They hear the clock, they see the clock, and before long, they need the clock. The same thing happens to us, boy. That stutter of yours was your clock. It's been ticking for so many years, and you've heard it for so long, you began to think you needed it."

"Mm-m-m . . . but I don't need it no more."

"No, boy, you can live without it just fine."

Hours later, after they had made six or seven stops at farms along the way, placing clocks at each homestead, they turned their team around and headed back to Dodge City. Dr. Marvin used the occasion to do what he liked best, sing at the top of his lungs.

The two of them heard the sound of the horses approaching from the rear before they saw the men. The horsemen separated, and rounding the wagon, one of them grabbed the reins of one of the mules. "Now you just hold up here." The others circled around the front of the wagon and stopped. Among the rough-looking men was the large red-haired fellow both Marvin and Skip had seen the day before.

"Good evening, gentlemen. I am Doctor Marvin. I am known from Saint Louis to Denver as the miracle worker of the plains. My elixir has been known to cure gout, rheumatism, punies, flea bites, and the dropsy, the infamous disease of the Bible that only the healing touch of Jesus himself could affect—until now, thanks to His wayward but humble child. Besides all that, I sell notions and clocks. Here, allow me to give you a sample of my miracle elixir."

Marvin reached under the seat and removed several sample

bottles. Handing them down to the men, he forced a smile. "Now don't go to drinking it all down, gentlemen. I wouldn't want you getting too healthy all of a sudden. The body takes its health in small doses."

A small, bearded man began to gulp, then coughed and spit out the amber liquid.

"You see? You, sir, are a sick man, and that body of yours requires healing more slowly."

The men laughed. The smallish man threw the bottle into the air, drew his revolver, and with one shot broke the glass container, showering the men with what had remained inside. "You're trying to poison us."

The red-haired fellow rode his big red roan closer. "No, this fellow here ain't about to poison us, but he has meddled with us, snooping around and bothering about in places where he don't belong. We done taught his friend what it means to stick his nose in other people's concerns, but we haven't begun to teach this fellow here."

Skip blurted out the words. "Mm-m-m . . . you fellers leave him alone. You ain't so much. You're just all right when yer up against an old man and a boy, or when you gots a feller outnumbered." He paused and glared at the men, his eyes dancing with passion. "Mm-m-m . . . I bet your mommas would be really proud of all of you."

The words of the boy cut the men to the bone. The man who held the reins on the mule dropped them and tugged on the big Irishman's sleeve. "Come on, O'Connor, let's ride outta here and get drunk like we planned."

The rest of the men pulled their horses back. Finally, the big Irishman joined them. With one last look, he swung the roan around and put the animal into a gallop up the road.

Marvin and the boy sat quietly on their seat and watched the dust rise on the road from the hooves of the running horses. The doctor put his arm around Skip. "Boy, what you said was pure glory. You opened your mouth and did the Lord's work today. You keep that up, and you may preach yet."

Skip beamed.

CHAPTER 15

+ + + + + + +

THE WEEKS ON THE TRAIL seemed to move by like clockwork.

Iron spiders crouched over the blazing fires before the break of day, each one bearing a coffeepot beneath it, or a Dutch oven with hot biscuits. The old red steer waddled over to the chuck wagon and waited his turn at a biscuit, just like any other drover. Everybody knew full well the animal was as valuable as another cowboy. And if he did his job right, he'd be led back to Texas along with some of the horses, escaping the train back East and the butchery of the stockyards.

"Here, old boy." Vonnie held out the biscuit and fed the beast from her hand. Reaching under his neck, she untied the bell they had muffled the night before, a task they performed every night. She held out a second biscuit.

"I say there, you make sure that brute beast doesn't keep eating all the way to your elbow," Earl said.

"No, me and Big Red here are friends." Vonnie patted him. "I practically got him coming to me like a big dog now."

"You be careful. That big dog, as you call him, has a set of seven-foot horns."

Randolph sipped his morning coffee. "Longhorns are perfectly fashioned for this kinda trip. They can go many a mile between water and grazing, while the bones of one of them shorthorn's would be bleaching in the sun. Their hooves are harder than normal, and a system the tic fever just can't get through to."

137

Barb walked up and handed a cup of coffee to Earl.

He sipped it and frowned. "I say, I'll never get used to the things you Yanks eat and drink. Right now, I'd kill for a pot of Earl Grey tea."

Randolph gave a sly half-smile. Turning back to Barb, he sipped his coffee. "Ma'am, that pa of yours had the timing for this drive figured out about right."

"How is that, Mr. Randolph?"

"The pace we're going, we might not get out of Texas before the snow flies. Those Longhorns carry tics that'd make those northern English brands mighty sick. The Shorthorns carry a lot of meat on them, but they don't do well with things that don't even phase the Longhorns. The cold kills the tics, and that'll save us a lot a trouble when we get to Kansas."

"The Yank barrister has it absolutely correct, Miss Barbara. The law, and ranchers in Kansas, inspect incoming cattle. I've been through there before. Of course, there's times when it's rawhiders intent on stealing your cattle that're masquerading as inspectors."

"We seem to have picked up some extra cattle," Barb said.

Randolph threw what remained of his coffee into the fire and dropped the cup into the wash bucket. "Kinda funny, ain't it." He stepped into his stirrups and straightened himself in the saddle. " 'Bout the time that snow flies, you'll be having some calving and we'll lose some along with the calves we gain. A stampede tends to thin out the cattle too. But anybody who drives a herd through picks up strays. And people coming through here months from now will be pickin' up Circle R stock."

"I guess it's the Lord's way of balancing things out," Barb replied.

"Maybe so, but I've never seen anyone who's been satisfied with their end of the scales by the time they get to market and money. Folks always want more than they got."

Hammond rode along the line of cattle and swatted the big leader, trotting him back into position. "Yo!" he roared. "We're burnin' daylight."

As soon as the old lead steer was back in position, the line of cattle began to fall into place. Barb watched, fascinated by the way each animal knew his own spot in line. Even lame cattle who could no longer set the pace at the front found their place again eventually. They'd retreat to the rear of the herd for a spell, walk along with the yearlings and calves, then when they had their step back, find a way to work back into their old position. A cowboy riding at the same spot in the march might as well take to naming the animals that walked beside him.

Barb turned to the girls. "Let's get to these dishes so we can catch up to them." Tipper had been saddled and riding drag for several days. Turning in the saddle, he tipped his hat to the women and Pera as he rode away. Wolf galloped his black mustang back to them. The animal seemed to suit him.

"You hurry along and go around us. We'll get to the Brazos today. You'll need to be there and across by the time we get there."

"You jesta tend to those cows of yours," Pera shot back. "You got my little Mary, but the women and I will do jest fine here. I'll be on the other side cooking son-of-a-gun stew before you can even see the river." The old Italian was feeling his oats. Any cook on the trail, before long, had to assert himself in order to survive.

The black-bearded ramrod wheeled his horse around, but not before Pera shouted further orders in his direction. "You jesta make sure them scalawags of yours bring some more scrub wood back for my possum belly. Get them coming back with some right away."

The "possum belly" was a sheet of canvas designed to carry loose firewood, strapped to the bottom of the chuck wagon. The area was sparse of burnable material, so everyone depended on cowboys hauling in scrub wood to keep the possum belly full.

Macrae galloped back along the line, passing out the order. Far to the front, Yanni positioned himself as far away from Dorothy as possible. He'd found he couldn't look her in the eye, and he didn't even want to breathe the same air as Poor Soul.

The sun was high when Hammond saw the two boys on horseback ahead of him in the distance. They watched the cattle with interest, and then rode their horses down the hill in his direction.

"Howdy. Our pa done sent us out here to look for strays. Mind if we cut your herd?" The boys looked to be barely fourteen, lean as rails, and scruffy. Their hats appeared to have suffered many a winter rain, topped off with summer sun and the dust and hoof of many a cow. "We'd sure 'preciate it if'n we could find some XL cows 'mongst yers."

"I don't let nobody cut my herd," Hammond shot back. "Any cows you got in here are used-to-be's, far as I'm concerned. Now, you ride back and tell yer pa that fer me."

The boys blinked their eyes at each other and their mouths dropped open. "This here is XL range, mister."

"Right now, it's our stompin' space. Tomorrow it'll be XL range."

The boys turned their horses around and spurred them back up the hill. Hammond and Macrae watched them stop at the top, taking one more look at the herd, and then disappear. "I let every scurvy bunch a riders come cuttin' through this herd, and pretty soon they'll be finding unbranded steers that they just think look like theirs. No sir. Anything walking with us, eatin' with us, sleepin' with us, belongs to us. You ride back there. If you find one of them XLs, you take it back to that cook and tell him it's what's fer dinner."

+ + + + +

Hours later, the remuda came to the Brazos River. Joe dismounted and allowed his horse to drink. "We'll cool 'em here," he said, "then find a safe place to cross."

"That river's mighty low," Karen said. "There ought to be some easy places to ford it."

Joe removed his hat and held it out in front of his face to shield his eyes and watch the slow-moving stream.

"That's just the problem," Poor Soul said. "It's been dry and there ain't as much flowing as normal. Makes it dangerous for quicksand and bogs. We don't want to lose any horses."

Joe walked over to several scrub trees that dotted the banks of the river and broke off a number of branches. "We'll use these to stake out a place to cross. I'll ride downstream a bit while the horses drink and see what I can find. When I let out a whistle, y'all come a runnin' with the horses." He mounted his green-broke mustang and trotted it downstream.

"I guess there's a lot to learn," Karen said.

"You got that right, Car. You keep your ears and eyes open and stick close to us, and you'll be a regular fella by the time we get ourselves to Dodge."

She swallowed hard and continued to watch Joe, now walking his horse slowly downstream. She lowered her voice. "That man just doesn't quit, does he?"

Poor Soul's teeth shone brightly through his smile. "He quits when he's finished. Always been like that. He's a pretty responsible hombre. It's almost like if he knows there's something standing in front of him that needs to be done yet, he just can't sit down and wait for it to come to him. He waits for trouble, but he goes out and gets work."

In the distance, Joe bent down and began to push the stakes into the muddy bottom of the river. Working his way to the other side, he turned and rode his horse back through the stream and staked out the other edge of the clearly marked path. Back on their side, he whistled and began to wave his hat.

"Let's get up and go," Poor Soul said. "That man would say, time's a wasting."

"I guess he would."

The two of them mounted and began to push the horses toward the spot where Joe had staked out his path.

"Car," Joe said. "Why don't you take the next string of ponies back to the herd soze the men can have some fresh mounts. Then bring the played-out ones back here. We'll get these across and have 'em feedin' over yonder; help you cut 'em out first."

In a short time, Karen was driving the fresh mounts back to the herd. She came up on the two wagons; an XL steer trotted along, tied behind the chuck wagon. She noticed the foreign brand. "Whose is that?"

141

"Macrae brought us this one. He said it would taste better than any of ours."

"I suppose it would at that." She turned around in the saddle and looked back in the direction of the river. "Joe's got a crossing staked out for us. With the water so low, you shouldn't have any trouble crossing. There's quicksand back there, so you better be careful. Just stay between the stakes."

"We'll do it." With that, he clucked at the mules and they launched the big wagon forward. Barb was driving the freight wagon. She stopped it next to Karen.

"Is your secret still safe?" she asked.

Karen dropped her chin. "I suppose it is."

"You don't sound very happy about it."

Karen jerked her head up. "Well, I am. I'm being treated like a man and working like a man. If I was wearing a dress, I'd be doing dishes and riding in that wagon with you."

"Yes, but at least he'd be looking at you like a woman."

"What do you mean by that?"

"You know exactly what I mean. I've seen the way you look at Joe. Don't think that just because you're wearing britches, you can stop the feelings of the woman you are."

"You callin' me a mare in a mule's harness?" She kicked her spurs into her horse's sides and bolted away from the wagon. Barb had spoken plainly, and she didn't like it. She swung her hat at the string of horses and galloped full speed toward the herd.

In the late afternoon, the herd reached the Brazos and began to fan out to drink. "Bunch 'em back up and get 'em on across," Hammond yelled. "They can drink, and then bed down on the other side."

Randolph and Crossy held their horses. "You seen them three men who've been shadowing us?" Crossy asked. "You reckon they'ze with the XL?"

"No, don't think so. They've been with us for better'n a week now. I've seen their fires from time to time while I've ridden night hawk."

"A week! They can't be in no hurry, then."

"I suppose not. I can see someone keeping close to a herd for protection against the Comanches, but not for that long. There must be something here they want."

"A job, you reckon?"

"Maybe, but it ain't likely. More often than not, I'd say it's the horses. There's not enough of 'em to take the herd."

With the orders given, the cowboys began to yell and wave their hats in the air, stirring the herd. The big red steer with the bell was the first to cross, followed by a growing stream of the other cattle. Minutes later, they heard a faint yell from above the braying of the swimming cattle. Randolph turned his horse around midstream and headed back in the direction of the cries.

On the edge of the herd, near the bank, Greener had run his horse belly-deep in the quicksand. He had slipped off the animal and now found himself pulled into the buckskin-colored muck.

"Help! Help me!" The young man's panic was evident. He continued to yell as Randolph built him a loop.

"Kid, this may sound crazy, but lie down if you can. You'll sink faster if you try to stand up. Lie down flat in it, and don't struggle."

But in spite of the orders, the frantic man continued to churn and fight the gooey mire. And the more he fought it, the deeper he sunk.

Randolph caught his eye. "Do what I say, kid, or you ain't about to get this rope. I'll just stand here and watch you go under."

With such a threat in his ears, the kid lay on his side but continued to hold out his hands. His descent slowed and Randolph threw the lariat. It landed not four feet from the boy and lay there on the top of the quicksand.

"Greener, reach over there and grab that thing. Keep flat. Make like you're swimming and you'll get it." Randolph swung his head around and yelled for several men on the other side. "Got a horse and rider in quicksand. Bring out some rope and large pieces a wood."

Some of the men began to search the trees on the side of the river for wood while Earl and Crossy dashed back across the muddy stream. Greener had managed to grab hold of the lariat.

"Now, put that thing under your arms, boy, and I'll pull you free."

Greener tugged on the riata and looped it around him. Scooting his arms underneath it, he grabbed the line.

Randolph turned his horse around midstream and began to pull, sending the boy slithering out of the muck, minus one boot. The other two men began to do what they could to save the horse, which continued to struggle against the slime. Sometime after Greener found himself lying on the bank gasping for breath. The six men working to save the horse managed to pry the animal loose. Greener looked up at Hammond, seated on his gelding beside him. "Boy, you almost cost me a good horse."

"Kid, you are greener'n a gourd," Yanni joined in. "You done got us plumb wore out."

"I'm sorry." Green shook. The dying sun was still warm, but fear still had its grip on him.

Hours later, the men sat silently around the campfire. They spooned the stew and broke the fresh bread to mop it up. "You boys like my son-of-a-gun stew?" Pera asked.

The men nodded.

"It has everything in it, but da hair, horns, and holler, and it'll fixa you boys right up." He proudly proceeded to name the ingredients—leftovers from the steer he had slaughtered that afternoon. "I been boiling it up for hours now. We'll have the lean meat tomorrow. You got brain, heart, liver, kidneys, lungs, tongue, gut parts in dere—along with a few special ingredients of mine own."

Poor Soul looked across Karen at Joe. "What it needs to go with it is some grits."

Joe chuckled softly.

Pera walked back from the chuck wagon and tossed Green a boot. "Here, boy, I hada myself a spare back there." He watched the boy try the boot on. "It'sa not too much, but at least you can hang one of them spurs off the back of it." The boot was larger than his foot, which was good, because now he had two left boots.

The men's chuckling evolved into laughter.

Green turned to Barb. "I guess Greener is a good name for me, after what I done."

"It could have happened to anyone," Barb said. "Just be thankful you're still alive."

The man hung his head. "Yeah, I suppose. But it happened to me. I guess I'm not cut out for this work. I'm a farmer, and should have left it at that."

"Don't take it so hard."

"I had to do what I could to bring in some money for April and the baby we're gonna have. Promise me something, will you, Miss Barbara?"

"Of course."

"Promise me that if anything does happen to me, and if I don't make it back home, that you'll see that April and my baby gets what's comin' to me."

"Nothing will happen to you. You'll make out just fine."

"Just promise me anyway. I don't get these notions too often. Had one 'bout marryin' April, though. I'll sleep a whole lot better knowin' they'll get my share. Folks said we wuz too young to marry, said kids shouldn't be havin' kids. But when I met April, I knew I wasn't no kid no more."

"You're not a kid. You're a husband, soon to be a father."

The boy lifted his chin, as if soaking in the notion of fatherhood for the very first time. "Doggone straight. I guess I am at that. Well, a man's got to take care of his." He looked her in the eye. "You promise me now, Miss Barbara."

"I promise, if it will help you to sleep."

CHAPTER 16

+ + + + + + +

THE DAYS THAT PASSED were filled with dust and tedious chores that knew no boundaries or hours. One morning before the sun rose, Barbara was stirring the coals under the iron spider that held the coffeepot. Randolph and Earl, who had drawn the duty for the last watch, came riding into camp to change mounts. As they stepped down from their saddles, Barbara poured each of them a hot cup. This time Earl didn't complain. It was hot and it was black, even if it wasn't tea.

Barb watched them blow the steam away and slurp their first sips. "Of all the men on this drive, you two are the most unlikely."

Earl gave off a slight laugh. "We were recently discussing that ourselves. However, there is a significant difference as to our rationale. You see, my own father back in England sent me here to come of age."

Randolph cocked a slight smile. "And mine, when I gave up the law and came West, said I'd never grow up."

"You see the humor in our circumstances. Two men quite alike in many ways, separated by a mere ocean, have come to the same place, to do the same work, for what their fathers see as opposite denouements. I say, is that rich?"

"But, you, Mr. Randolph—"

"Call me Lance, ma'am."

"You, Lance—you came West and left a profession, abandoned responsibilities."

"I left other people holding me accountable for their responsibilities. I sure didn't escape mine. In some ways, I'd just as soon be responsible for cows. The poor dumb creatures don't know any better. But in the legal profession, you find yourself protecting people from their own mistaken thinking, or defending them when they've lost all sense of God and man's accountability. Just between us, I think I prefer the responsibilities of raising other people's cattle and horses."

The other men began to smell the coffee and roll out of their bedrolls. Stumbling to their feet, they approached the fire with outstretched cups. Hammond was pouring himself a cup, when suddenly Poor Soul and Joe came riding into camp with four Mexican vaqueros at the head of forty-some-odd mustang horses. The Mexican riders gave the rugged appearance of men on the dodge, dirty and rough-looking. The saddles they sat were of the expensive California variety, but everything else about them said "rustler."

Joe sat his horse and made introductions. "These men here are selling horses. They appear to be a likely lot, and we just might need 'em before we're all done."

Hammond took a look at the animals and walked back to the fire. "I see you got some with brands, and some that appear to be free of any claim."

"Sí, señor. I sell them for five dollar each."

Hammond sipped his coffee. "We're cash poor here, but I'll give you two dollars a head."

The man in charge, who could speak English, translated for the other riders with him. They murmured back in Spanish.

"Is not enough, señor, five dollar."

"Now, we might have someone come riding in here and claim the horses you stole. Then we'd be out the money we spent. I'll give you one dollar for each one with a brand, and three for the horses with no brand."

Sipping his coffee, Hammond watched the man translate. Barb listened carefully. She frowned. The notion of doing business with this kind was something that didn't meet with her approval. She noticed several other men wagging their heads. She wasn't going to correct Hammond in front of the others, however. She knew enough about dealing to know that was bad business.

"Four dollar each, señor. Is a good *caballada*. Plenty fire in dese horses."

"Let's shuck these greasers," Yanni chimed in. "We don't need to buy trouble."

One look from Hammond was enough to tell the hot-headed cowboy that he'd said too much. Hammond sipped his coffee and once again stared up at the Mexican lead man. "You can try to sell these broomtails off onto somebody else, if'n you've a mind. But it appears to me you boys are throwing a long rope. You stick around here, and the next people who come to make you an offer just might be some Texas Rangers. Suit yerself."

Joe straightened himself in his saddle. "Mr. Hammond, it's your drive. But if we buy these animals, I won't be able to mix 'em in with the remuda just yet. I'll have to have the boys take turns mustanging 'em first. It can be done, but it'll make us a mite shorthanded."

"Well, there you are." Hammond looked back up at the Mexican. "We buy these animals, we're buying into trouble, but we're paying no more than three for the unbranded and a dollar for the ones with the sticky rope marks on 'em."

The lead man jerked his reins and conferred with the men who rode with him. Turning back, he threw his sombrero to the ground. "You can put ze money in ze hat, señor. We sell."

Hammond walked over to Barb, who began counting out a portion of what little money remained. "I don't like this," she said.

He lowered his voice. "That may be, but in Kansas we can sell these animals for over forty dollars a head, especially with these men we got working with the remuda. They're snappin' these mounts into some fine cow ponies."

"Do you mean to tell me, Mr. Hammond, that I made some good choices in the men I hired?"

"Well, those three are earnin' their keep, but we're draggin' the other two boys along."

She counted the money out. "And you may have made a good

THE WELLS FARGO TRAIL

bargain, but money doesn't make things right."

"It does in my book. I don't do nothing 'cept for the dollar. Nowadays, a man's gotta be crazy to be moved by anything else. You keep that in mind."

"And I think you should keep something in mind, Mr. Hammond. There may come a day when you need more than money—a day when you need loyalty and friendship. I trust when that day does arrive, you'll find more than money in your pocket."

+   +   +   +   +

The day in the saddle seemed to drag by. Earlier, Joe explained the situation about the new horses to Karen and Poor Soul. "Those mustangs are gonna run. You gotta keep followin'. All horse herds turn around and double back. They'll see you and run again. Stay after 'em. It may take several days, but after that, they settle down. Then we put 'em in with the remuda. I can't chance havin' 'em spook the horses we gotta have for the men riding herd."

They nodded and Karen took the first shift and rode off behind the new horses. Joe called out after her. "Car, watch out for them fellers who brung them in. They just might decide to circle round, take 'em back, and sell them somewheres else."

She waved her hand as she rode off.

"You be careful," he yelled. "Fire that long gun in the air if you see anything."

The Chisholm Trail was well traveled. At times, herds had to wait beside river crossings for days while other herds crossed. The drives had become big business for everyone from rustlers and thieves to drummers. The drummers they could handle. The pots and cookware they sold often came in handy. Occasionally, a drive would come across a rustler hanging high from a cottonwood. They were left as a warning that stealing cattle and horses was a bad business to be involved in.

It was midday when the men in the front of the herd spotted the Indian. The man wore a full headdress that trailed feathers down his back, and a broadcloth and leggings with buckskin fringe. Long dark braids trailed down his beaded shirt. He sat his white horse regally, and everyone knew this was a Comanche warrior, part of the tribe that had held Texas hostage for generations. The man was alone, but everyone knew there could be a group of warriors over the next hill. He rode up to Hammond with a piece of paper clutched in his hand. Hammond took it and read it.

Turning to Macrae, Hammond barked, "Note from Shanghai Pierce. Says this feller here is a chief. Says if we give him a 'wohaw,' we won't be pestered none."

"What's a 'wohaw'?" Yanni asked.

"One cow," Macrae responded.

"When the first settlers pulled into Texas behind oxen," Hammond added, "these devils heard the wagon drivers holler *whoa* when they wanted them to stop, and *haw* when they wanted them to go. It stuck."

"Typical for any Texan, I'd say," Earl added.

Hammond ignored the jab. "The man wants payment to pass by. Cheap, at any price."

"Go cut out one of them XL cows," Hammond said. "Won't hurt us none, but these people could."

Yanni drove off one of the XL strays, and they watched the Indian herd it up the hill. Hammond signaled the herd ahead. "Getting to be busy 'round here," Hammond said. "But it's late in the season. Since we killed or drove off most of the buffalo, more'n likely them folks would go hungry without them 'wohaws.' We don't need their trouble, not now."

"You reckon they spotted our horses?" Yanni asked.

"You can bet they got their eyes peeled on 'em right now."

+ + + + +

Karen rode behind the new group of horses. Mares were something the remuda was short on, and for good reason. In heat, they tended to distract most of the herd, making them skittish and full of romp. This new group had a black mare that was making them run with abandon. Near as Karen could figure, she had put about five to six miles between her and the rest of the remuda. The horses had circled, just as Joe had predicted, and now they grazed on some fresh grass as she approached them. She walked her gelding up to the animals cautiously.

Once again, the mare picked up her head and bolted away, followed by the rest of the new herd. Karen screwed her face up and put her hands on her hips. She'd save herself a lot of trouble if she just shot the thing, but she knew she couldn't do that. She clapped her spurs to the gelding, and once again began the chase. She'd try to circle them now. Maybe she could drive them back toward the remuda. She had no desire to drift too far away.

As she cantered over the rise, she spotted the horses still on the run. Moving in on the herd, she also saw the four Mexicans who had sold them. She straightened up in the saddle and continued to ride, casually lifting the rawhide loop from the hammer of her .45.

The four men turned the running horses and brought them to a halt just as Karen rode up to them.

"Gracias," she said. "I'll take them now."

The leader of the group gave a slight smile. "Amigo, you can't take these horses. We just found dem."

Karen pushed back her hat. "And I appreciate it," she said. "Now, I'll just be thanking you and take them back to the herd."

Once again, the man smiled. She noticed two of the others begin to circle, one on either side of her. "No, amigo. These horses belong to us. They are lost and we find dem. What we find, we keep. Those hombres are too far behind to help you now. I think it best for you to just turn around and ride back."

One of the other men began to speak Spanish to the English-speaking leader.

"My amigo, here, he say he like the look of the animal you are riding, and the saddle too. He say it best for you to get off and walk back. We take care of your horse. That's a man's horse. You are just a boy."

This was one of the times Karen was glad she wasn't suspected of being a woman. Normally, she kept her pretty face smeared with dirt, but this morning she had made the mistake of washing it. She didn't like the way one of the men was looking at her. Then he began to rattle off Spanish to the leader. Some of the words she recognized. One of them was *señorita*.

The leader cocked his head at her. A smile skimmed his teeth. "Maybe, amigo, you are not a boy at all." He dismounted. "Why don't we take a look, see for ourselves."

Karen tugged on her reins and backed the gelding up. "You take one more step, and I'll plant you right where you stand."

"Señorita, you speak with the fire. Me and my amigos here like the fire." He held his hands high and stepped forward.

"Don't come any closer. I'll send you to the fire."

He spoke Spanish to the other men, then turned back to her. "Maybe, señorita, the point of a gun will make you more agreeable?"

With that, Karen saw the one on his mount reach for his revolver. She slapped her holster leather and jerked the .45 clean in a split second. As the man lifted his gun, she fired. The shot took him in the breast pocket and spun him out of the saddle. She cocked the hammer on her gun, backed the gelding, and the herd stampeded.

The men dropped to the ground to assess the damage. Her victim was dead—shot through the heart.

Karen's hand shook slightly, but she swept the .45 between the three who remained. "I got four more where that came from. There's three of you, and I don't miss."

The leader slowly dropped his hands to his sides.

"Don't even think about it," she said. "Whoever draws gets my next bullet."

The man talked in rapid Spanish to the other two, holding his hands up as he spoke.

"Now," Karen said. "You put your friend there on his saddle and clear out of here, comprende?"

The men looked past Karen, up the hill, then quickly loaded the fallen rustler onto his saddle. As they rode off, Karen realized who had distracted them. Joe Cobb was galloping his horse down the hill in her direction. She stepped down from her saddle, turning as she did so, and grabbed a handful of dirt and rubbed it into her face.

"I was trying to find you and spell you some," Cobb said as he rode up. "I saw what happened. I guess I got here too late."

Karen looked up at him. She was still shaking, but stuck out her lower lip. "I t-t-took care of 'em. You g-got here just in time." Her eyes were tearing, and she mopped them with the back of her hand. "Don't say anything about this to anybody."

Joe stepped out of the saddle and picked up her reins. "Look, kid, you don't have to be that way with me. You got plenty of guts." He handed the reins to her. "You better get back to Pera and have him dip you some sugar. Ain't nothing to be ashamed of. I killed my first man up close at Shiloh. I still see the boy looking at me at night from time to time."

When Karen rode up to the chuck wagon, she stepped out of her saddle and unbuckled her gun belt. Rolling it up, she put it in the wagon and picked up a cup. Her hands shook as she poured the coffee. Pera and Dorothy watched her unsteady hand raise the cup to her lips.

"Are you sick?" Pera asked.

"No." She raised the cup again.

Pera walked away and continued to make bread.

"You do look sick," Dorothy said.

"Well, I'm not." She lowered her head. "I just killed one of those men who sold us the horses, but don't say anything about this to Barb, do you understand?"

Dorothy covered her mouth with her hand as if she would be sick. "Oh . . . you must feel awful. What happened?"

Karen's eyes remained riveted on the ground. "I can't talk about it. It's not like I ever thought it would be. Oh, Dorothy, I feel terrible."

Dorothy's hand moved to Karen's shoulder and she gave her a quick squeeze.

"Where's Vonnie?" Karen asked.

"We spotted a pond. Her and Tipper went fishing."

CHAPTER 17

+ + + + + + +

"I AIN'T HAD FISH fer over a year," Vonnie said.

Tipper uncoiled a ball of line with a hook on the end of it, obviously a kit he'd used many times before. They had dug out a number of worms from near the bank. Tipper baited the hook and threw it into the pond. "Mosta these old water holes ain't nuthin' but rain, but whilst I wuz riding by I spotted this one." His eyes widened. "I saw some rising out there, and yessiree, I wanted to put a line in this thing so fast."

"When did you get so much time to fish?"

He pushed his hat back and sat on the ground. "T'weren't too healthy 'round my place when Pap was in the bottle, which was mosta the time. Fishin' was my chance to get away."

"That must have been hard."

"Weren't so easy on my backside, I can tell you that. Some folks 'round our place told me my pap used to be a fine man." He scratched the back of his head. "Wonder what gets into folks to make a 'em go to the devil? You reckon somethin' like that could happen to anybody?"

Lifting her skirts to her knees, Vonnie continued to dig in the mud for worms. "Maybe it could happen to anybody, but I don't reckon it's likely for some."

"You think it could happen to me?"

Vonnie squinted at him. "If you was to go into the bottle, I s'pose you could come out that way."

The boy shuddered, his shoulders wagging. "Lordy mercy, I never want to even taste it. Why would a body even want the stuff?"

Vonnie pulled out a few fresh grubs. "I s'pose 'cause it makes a man feel different on the inside."

"'Course afterward," Tipper said, "everthin's just the same as always, and worse."

"My family're teetotalers. We're Mennonites."

"Yer lucky in that way."

"My father used to say there ain't no such thing as luck, there's just the grace of God, and hard work."

"The grace of God? What's that?"

"You don't know? Well, it's God giving you something you don't deserve. Like mercy and forgiveness."

"That's mighty befuddling. Why you s'pose, then, I ain't never had Him pay no nevermind to me?"

"Maybe He has. Maybe you just ain't never seen it before. It's like the angels around us—we can't see them, 'cept for sometimes folks in the Bible saw them. They're all around us, maybe even right now, it's just that we can't see them with our human eyes."

The boy swung his head from side to side. "Well, I can't see any, that's for sure."

"'Course you can't, but that don't mean they're not there. My father used to say that God had all His children staked out with a guardian angel. They follow us, makin' sure we don't come to harm before our time."

"And what happens when a feller gets to be my age?"

"I don't know. Maybe since you had such a hard time of it, yours might still be around."

She found another worm and held it up. "Here, take this thing."

He put it in his torn pocket and pulled his line from the water. "Maybe in my case, my angel saw what he was up against and lit off long ago. I'm bad, you know—always have been."

"You ain't bad. You've just had it bad. The Bible says that sometimes angels appear as strangers. That's why we need to be hospitable to folks, 'cause they might be angels—angels unawares."

"Don't they know who they is?"

"Of course, it's us that's unawares. That's one of the reasons we always fed men coming by, ones who was riding the grub line. My mother would watch them ride off and say that they just might be angels."

The line grew taut and Tipper hollered. He pulled hand over hand until he brought the struggling fish onto the bank. Reaching down, he held up the line with the flapping catch on the end of it. "Now here," he said, "this here's the grace of God, I reckon."

"I reckon it is."

Tipper continued to fish while Vonnie read the Bible to him. In an hour's time, they had five fish on the bank. Vonnie closed the book and lay back in the sun. She brushed her blond hair aside and watched the clouds drift overhead.

"You wanna go fer a swim?" Tipper asked.

She sat up, propped on her elbows. "Are you crazy? Girls don't swim with boys. It's an abomination."

"Sure is hot, though. Might be our last time to swim b'fore it turns cold and the snow flies."

She looked at the cool water and shook her head. "No, I ain't got nuthin' 'cept my dress and things. You go on ahead, though, I won't look."

Tipper jumped up and started stripping off his shirt. "All right. I shore got a hanker fer a swim. I ain't swum in quite a spell."

Vonnie picked up the Bible and walked to a spot behind the tree. She sat there for some time, reading and listening to Tipper splash. Then, lifting her gaze from the page, she spotted three men. She couldn't make out who they were, but they weren't from their group, she was certain of that. And they weren't Indians, because they were dressed like cowboys, chaps and all.

They were sitting on the crest of the hill and appeared to be content watching the two of them. She didn't know how long they'd been there, but she didn't like the looks of it. Somehow, she had to warn Tipper. She suddenly realized they'd been gone from the herd for a while and she wondered how far they might be.

Slowly, she got to her feet. She opened the Bible and pretended to read, but all the while she watched the men above her out of the corner of her eye. To call out to Tipper would be foolish. What would she say?

Holding the book in front of her face, she stepped carefully toward the pond. "Tipper," she spoke in a low half whisper. "Tipper, we got to go. We got to go now!"

"What? Put that book down."

Vonnie lowered the book slightly. "I said, we got to go!" she whispered.

"What? I caen't hear you."

She cupped a hand to her mouth and whispered more loudly. "There're some strangers behind us, and they're watching us."

Tipper's face brightened. "Are they angels? Do you reckon they'ze some a them angels unawares?"

"I don't reckon so. You better get out and get dressed so we can get back. I'm kinda scared."

"All right, git over to your tree, I'm comin' out." She passed by Tipper's clothes and unhitched the horse. Lifting the stirrup, she tightened the cinch. "Let's skedaddle on outta here. You get on up, and I'll get the fish."

After picking up the string of fish, she cast a glance up the hill. The men were gone! She hurried back to Tipper and handed up the fish. "They're gone. We better get moving fast."

Climbing up behind Tipper, she held on to the boy and the fish. Tipper sent the horse dashing around the pond and up over the hill to the far side of where Vonnie had spotted the strangers. They started out with a canter, and then Vonnie kicked the sides of the animal with her heels, sending them into a fast gallop. "I want to clear outta here as fast as we can," she said.

"Well then, hang on."

The two of them kept up a fast gait, then Tipper drew rein suddenly. "Wolf," he said. "Gotta slow down, that's old Wolf Macrae up ahead."

Wolf Macrae had always scared Vonnie, with his full black beard and eyes that reminded her of two lumps of coal. He could look right through a person. There was something about the man, a soulless quality. But now, just the thought of meeting up with someone they knew, anyone, even Wolf Macrae, was a strange comfort to her. She could tell by the tension in Tipper's muscles, however, that he didn't feel the same way."

As they rode up to him, Tipper began talking rapidly and apologetically. "Miss Barbara asked me to take Miss Vonnie here on a ride," he lied. "She said she'd tell Mr. Hammond and get his okay. We was all right, and we brung some fish for you and the others." He held up the string.

Macrae just stared at the two of them and grunted.

"Vonnie here spotted some strangers watchin' us back there. How many'd ya say they were?"

"Three, three strange-looking men. They were watching us for a long time, I think."

Macrae rumbled under his breath. "No count kids."

"We'll just head on back to the herd," Tipper said. "I'll ride night hawk tonight."

Without waiting for a reply, Tipper spurred the horse forward. Vonnie turned her head as they sprinted away and watched Macrae. He rode off in the direction they had come from.

The fish had been cleaned and were frying in the pan when Macrae rode back into camp. He stepped out of his saddle and took Hammond aside to talk. Vonnie could tell that Tipper was worried. There was something about Tipper. He always felt to blame for anything that went wrong. He usually felt lost and out of place too. Vonnie studied his pained look as he watched the two men talk.

They were all finishing supper when they heard the strange voice from the darkness outside the camp. "Ho the camp!"

Hammond got to his feet. "Come on in. Light and set, but keep your hands empty."

Three men walked into the firelight, each leading a horse. "We was hoping for some grub, if you can spare some."

"And a job, if you're shorthanded," a second man said.

Tipper and Vonnie exchanged glances.

"We can give you some food; we'll have to see about the job,"

Hammond said. He turned to Randolph, who had been seated on the tongue of the chuck wagon. "Get yerself up and give these boys a perch."

Randolph put on his large Texas hat and pulled it down. Standing up, he walked around the fire with his half-eaten dinner.

"What about it, Miss Barbara?" Hammond asked. "We are a mite shy on the help, and these fellers seem to be a likely match."

Vonnie watched as Hammond and Macrae exchanged quick glances. Something was not quite right about these men, and she could feel it in her bones. Did Hammond and Macrae know them? She could also plainly see that Barb was none too happy about being placed on the spot in front of everyone.

Barb shifted on the barrel she was sitting on. "We seem to be doing just fine the way we are. Vonnie, could you please get these men some food? They'll want to eat and be on their way."

Vonnie dished up three plates of beef and beans and handed two plates to the men on the wagon tongue. The final plate she gave to a younger, but hard-looking man. He wore a tan drover shirt that she thought she recognized. He took the plate and gave her a smile and a knowing wink.

It was plain to see by the way their spoons hit the food that none of them had been eating well. They talked very little. When they finished, one of the men, who had fire-red mutton-chop whiskers, spoke up.

"These here are dangerous parts for ladies to be traveling in with so light a bunch to watch out for 'em. There be Comanches and rustlers crawling all over out yonder, and it don't appear to me you got the men to handle such."

Randolph walked over to get another plate of beans. It was obvious he was still fuming about having to give up his seat. He shifted the frying pan and spooned the beans onto his plate. "Could be we got some rustlers crawling in here tonight too," he said.

The man with the red whiskers dropped his plate and shot to his feet. "You calling us rustlers?"

Randolph stepped toward him. "I said 'could be.' You're the one jumping at the notion."

"Now just settle down," Hammond interjected. "I just said in my judgment that we need the help, and maybe you boys riding in here tonight could solve a problem for me. You appear to be very capable fellers"—he paused and gave Barb a long look—"if my opinion counts for anything 'round here. After all, I am the trail boss of this here outfit."

The tension in the air was thick. It had been building between Barb and Hammond since the very first day, and Vonnie wanted to say something to Barb just about then. The thought of those three men frightened her, and if there was ever a time when she didn't want to see her sister back down, it was now. She had always tried to fight her fears, however, and continued to stand beside the strangers.

One man didn't sit down. It was plain that he was talking to Barb, but he was looking straight at Randolph.

"Ma'am, we've cut the trail of some dangerous types out here, and a Comanche war party the day before yesterday. I wouldn't want to see all that pretty hair of yourn sportin' some brave's lodge pole. Yer gonna need some men who can fight on this here trip. I just wouldn't go to placing much stock in fellers like this one. I mean, look at him—that little touch a snow over his ears. He needs to be snuggled up next to some warm fire, not out here living the hard life. That's for men like me and my friends here."

The remains of the fish continued to fry on the fire, and Randolph was giving a good imitation of the sizzle himself. "The trouble with you and your friends here," he said, "is we just wouldn't rightly know in which direction to shoot."

With that, the whiskered man took a swing at Randolph. For a man schooled in the law, Randolph was quick. He backed away from the swing and, dropping his plate of beans, removed his hat. As the man moved forward and threw a left, Randolph swatted him with the big hat.

The look on the man's face was a mixture of pain and astonishment. He swung again and Randolph deftly stepped aside and bounced the hat off the back of the man's head, sending him to his knees. He slowly got to his feet. "Fight fair, man, use your hands."

"I use my hands for work, and I won't be breaking any bones on the face of the likes of you."

The man danced toward Randolph and, without throwing another blow, received a wicked blow from the hat squarely in the face.

"Stop this!" Barb yelled at Hammond. "Stop this right now."

Hammond's only response was to stand up and move aside.

Randolph circled around the angry man, with his back toward the fire. He signaled the man, daring him to continue.

The man charged him and hit him head on in the stomach, sending both of them wrestling toward the flame. He straightened Randolph up and began to squeeze his rib cage, hard.

Pushing back on the man's chin with his left hand, Randolph took the hat in his right hand and reached for the flaming grate. He picked up the sizzling skillet and sent it crashing into the man's forehead, crumpling him to the ground.

Randolph stood there with his hand matted around the hot skillet. "You two want any of this?"

The other two strangers merely stared, first at Hammond, and then at Macrae. Looking at Randolph, they shook their heads.

Randolph turned the man over with the toe of his boot. "You two cart your friend on out of here. And don't let us cut your trail again."

"I'll see 'em out," Hammond said.

Barb grabbed his sleeve. "Mr. Hammond, you and Macrae can ride out with them, if you've a mind to. We'll make do."

"No, ma'am. We're in this thing. I may work for you out here, but I'm responsible to Frank Emmy."

The man with the tan drover shirt brushed up against Vonnie as he got up to leave. He stopped and smiled at her. "You sure are a pretty little thing. Maybe I'll see you again sometime, you never can tell."

A chill went up Vonnie's spine.

CHAPTER 18

+ + + + + + +

THE MORNING WIND ripped over the grass, and the campfire popped with each gust. Over the past several days, it was plain to see that the fall was slipping by fast, and early winter was coming on. Joe had positioned a coffeepot over two stones beside the fire. Using his bandanna to handle the hot metal, he poured two cups.

"You going to take some to Car?" Poor Soul asked.

"Yeah, got to find some way to get the kid up and blinkin' his eyes."

"You know the boy hasn't been carrying his sidearm for the last three days."

"Saw that."

"Seems to me like, when a man has something heavy weighing on him, he turns to sleep. Either that or the bottle—deadens the mind that way."

"Well, there ain't no forty-rod rye within a day's ride, and we just don't have the time for too much sleep 'round here. Besides, I been seeing them drifters off to the west of us for the last two days, and he just might need to pack that iron of his, like it or not."

Joe took a sip on the cup he was holding. "The kid can shoot!" he said. "I saw him bring that rustler down with a snap shot offa the hip—one shot"—he jerked his thumb next to his shirt pocket"—clean into the middle of the man's pocket. Darn good shootin', and I've seen good shootin'."

"You're pretty good with a .45 yourself."

163

"Well, I ain't near as fast as you," Joe said, "but I do hit what I point at. The kid's got instinct, nervous instinct I'd call it. Takes practice to boot, to do what he did."

Joe stood up and started toward the sleeping Karen.

"Go gentle on him," Poor Soul said. "Killing somebody never goes down easy with a man that has heart."

Joe walked over beside Karen and, placing his boot toe to her side, gave her a slight shove.

She murmured and waved her hand up near her head. "Leave me be," she said.

He knelt down beside her. "It's time to roll and thunder, kid. These horses won't be saddling their ownselves. Poor Soul and me has been holding up our own end—you gotta do the same. Here, I brung you some coffee."

"Just set it down and leave me be." She was hesitant to part company with her bedroll until she had a chance to tie the bindings on her chest.

"Car, there's times in a man's life when he needs folks to let him be, but there's other times when he just needs folks. I'd say this here is one of them times."

Karen rolled over, careful to keep the bedding under her chin. "What do you mean?" She blinked at him with her sky blue eyes. He was staring into them. His look worried her. Was her femininity showing through the dirt she kept on her face? What made it harder was the fact that she really wanted him to see her as a woman.

"I mean gettin' through havin' killed a man. I know you been thinking about it." He handed her the cup and watched her take a sip. "You better sit up now, you'll spill that hot jamoke all over you."

"I'll be all right." She craned her neck and took another sip.

"I'm sure you will, but it'll take some gettin' used to. It's one thing to kill an animal. Even that's hard for some, but killin' a man. . . ."

Karen dropped her eyes to the coffee and took another strained sip. "I never thought it would be this way," she said.

"Few men ever do, and the ones who don't think about it are

folks that ain't worth spit. You had yerself some practice with that .45 of yourn, but I'm sure all you ever worried about was doing what you needed to do, and how to shave time off the doing of it. Nobody practices on how to live with himself when it's all over."

Karen spoke softly. "The way I was raised . . . what I did was considered a sin. No two ways about it. My people didn't even fight in the war, and we caught terrible scorn for that in Texas. People 'round us figured us to be Yankee lovers."

"Somehow, Car, I don't take you to be a feller that's used to going the way he's been taught. I had you figured to be a man who has to find out for himself. Learning things that way is mighty hard, but when you learn a thing, it sticks."

"Maybe I'm learning that what my folks practiced and taught had a rightness to it that I just can't shake free of. My father was murdered. I thought when it happened that if he had prepared himself to shoot first instead of offering a helping hand, he might still be alive. I'd practiced a lot with a gun before he died, and I knew I could use one, but it was his death that made me want to use one."

"You have to put the thing behind you for a while, kid. Things are touchy out there. Those men Randolph sent off the other night are still shadowing us. I wouldn't want them to steal the horses while you have nothing to defend yourself with but a cuss word."

"I wouldn't do that."

"Maybe not, but there's not much else you could do without a gun."

"How can someone be cold enough to just go on killing?"

"It's a mighty hard thing for a decent man to do. War is one thing, but killing a man when there's any other choice is another."

Joe sipped on his coffee. "I've known very few men who could do it without some deep feeling. I'm ashamed to say that one of them was my brother."

"Your brother?"

"Yeah, Julian. We both killed Yankees during the war, but

on our way home after we got outta the prison camp, I saw him kill two others—for no reason. Makes me feel cold inside to think about it."

"He's the one with only one arm?"

"Yeah. A right arm and a right eye, but I fear if he's still alive that he's carrying around wounds that go a whole lot deeper. Killing will do that to a man."

Karen's hand began to tremble as she lifted the cup to her lips.

"It's bad business, have to or not. It's up to you, kid. You can carry that shootin' iron of yours and be ready to use it, or I'll swap you with one of the fellers riding drag with the herd. We won't hold it against you, either way. The problem is that these horses of ours are prime targets for them rustlers, and we're separated from the herd from time to time, as you know."

She gulped the rest of her coffee and dropped her head in thought. "Okay . . . give me a coupla minutes. I'll get the gun and be back."

Joe got to his feet. "Yer decision, Car. But if yer gonna wear the thing, you better be braced to use it."

+ + + + +

The line of cattle moved into the wind. They followed the red steer by the sound of the clanging bell. Cattle would normally turn their backs to weather, but by now the march had taught them to stay with the line and seek the shelter of the animal in front of them.

The men on the flanks of the herd whistled and whirled their riatas. Several men twirled poppers in the air, making a crisp cracking noise in the brisk breeze.

Crossy and Yanni rode swing. Staying near the front of the herd kept Yanni away from Dorothy, and he still made sure their eyes never met when he saw her. He cranked his popper over his head and swung it out over the lead steers, keeping them tightly wound in behind Big Red. Occasionally, he would pull aside and turn his gaze along the line, all the way back to the drag. He could see Dorothy in the wagon with Barb, but as long as he didn't come close, he didn't have to worry about meeting up with her eyes.

Dorothy had made little more than small talk since the herd moved north from San Antonio. Both Barb and Vonnie noticed it, but neither tried to pry out of her what the problem was. It was unusual for the sisters. They were normally very close.

Barb noticed Yanni turn aside up ahead and look back in their direction. Dorothy noticed it too, but looked down, so as not to catch his glance, wringing her hands on an extra bandanna she was carrying.

"You haven't said much for weeks now," Barb finally ventured. "That's not like you . . ."

"Well, maybe I just decided I talk too much," Dorothy snapped.

Normally, that kind of response would turn Barb away, but not today. "That's beside the point. Talking to your sisters, to the people who love you, is one of the things you do best. Is the work getting you down?"

"No, I'll do my part the same as the rest."

Barb looked ahead at the man in the distance. "Is it that man friend of yours?"

Dorothy shot out her lower lip. "He's no friend of mine! And I wouldn't go so far as to call him a man, either."

"Well, what brought that on?"

Dorothy turned her head and glared at her sister. "It's just not enough for you, is it? You want me to say that you and Karen have been right all along, and I was wrong. That's what you want, isn't it?"

Barb drove the team in silence. She had learned long ago not to respond to Dorothy's anger. Moments of silence ticked by, until it seemed like hours. "I don't need to be right . . ." Barb spoke up. "I just want my sister back, that's all."

"Well, you were right about him and I was wrong. There . . . does that make you feel better?"

"I'll feel better when you're back to your old self, Dorothy. I love you . . . I've missed you."

Tears began streaking Dorothy's dusty cheeks. She quickly

wiped them away with the bandanna. "I guess I'm not a very good judge of men . . . just like you've always told me. I see one that makes me feel pretty, and I lose my head. You and Karen have told me that so many times, it just makes me sick to think about it."

"You already are pretty. You don't need a man to make you feel like you are. Besides, there's more to choosing a man than knowing how he makes you feel at the moment. It's being sure of how you'll feel about him, and yourself . . . ten, twenty years down the road."

"And how is that? How do I know how I'll feel in ten years?"

"I guess you don't, really, but certainly a woman wants to feel more than loved for the moment. She wants to feel safe. She wants to feel cared for. And she wants to know the man she marries is one she can continue to respect, and one who deserves the respect of her children."

"Do you feel that way about Randolph?" Dorothy asked.

"Lance is a good man. He's still trying to prove himself, though, long after he should have settled down, in my estimation. I suppose growing up pampered in the East could do that to a person."

"He was a little hotheaded the other night."

Barb smiled. Randolph was riding flank and she watched him whistle at the cattle and slap his lariat. "Oh, he knew exactly what he was doing. Hammond put me in a terrible position with those men that night, and everybody was watching. Lance just stepped in to make things easier for me."

+ + + + +

Crossy was the first to spot the four men up ahead. He yelled out at Hammond and galloped forward. As the men came closer, they could make out the two boys who had ridden up to them earlier from the XL. Only now they had two older men riding in with them. Hammond and Macrae turned aside and Crossy joined them, followed by Yanni. Macrae spoke in low tones to Hammond. "We better handle this our ownselves, while we got the boss lady back there in the rear. Won't 'zackly do to have her cross you again in front of the men."

The men rode up to them. "My sons here tell me you got XL cattle in that bunch of yours." The older man had a weathered appearance. His face was wrinkled, and he sat his horse like a man who had been used to living on the quarter-deck of a cow pony all his life.

"I don't rightly know," Hammond lied.

"Well, then, you won't mind if we cut our steers out of that herd of yours.'"

"Didn't say that. Fact is, I do mind."

The man squinted, his eyes narrowing into two tiny BBs set deep inside his weather-beaten face. "I got work goin' on, otherwise I'da been here earlier myself. It's taken us quite a spell to catch up with you. Fact is, I got a dozen riders working my spread. If we have to, we'll be back here in four or five days. We'll scatter that bunch of yours to kingdom come, and then pick and choose to our liking. Your call."

Hammond leaned forward in his saddle. "No, you won't do that."

"Who's to stop me?"

"We will. It'll be your funeral . . . or them sons of yours. Your call."

The man dropped his hand to his side, but before he could touch his six-gun, Macrae and Yanni had drawn theirs and had them leveled at the man, whose face had turned crimson.

Crossy stepped his horse forward. "Look," he said, "I don't know if we got some of your cattle or not. But even if we may have picked up a few of your strays, it ain't worth killin' and dyin' over."

The man moved his hand up from his side and rested it on his saddle horn. "Everything I got's worth killin' and dyin' over. If it weren't, there wouldn't be no XL to talk about, just a bunch a rustlers and Comanches roaming 'round. I let you drift on with them steers of mine and I might just as well put a sign out over my place, 'Thieves and Rustlers Welcome.' "

"We seem to have got us a situation here, then," Macrae offered. His gun was still leveled on the men and he circled around to their left. "We can't have you trailing us all the way to Kansas with that pride of yours, and you don't seem to want to go on peacefulike and tend to your ownselves."

The old man jerked his reins and moved to go around them. "Like I said, we'll cut your herd. Just stand aside."

Hammond drew his revolver and grabbed the man by his shirt with his left hand, pointing the gun at his temple. "Nobody cuts any herd of mine. Any cow joins up with us, belongs to us. Any place we walk across is free range, as far as I'm concerned."

The old man pulled his shirt free from Hammond's grasp and backed his horse up.

"Now, old man," Hammond continued, "we're just gonna make sure here that we don't have you pesterin' us none till we get to where we're goin'."

The man glared at him. "That ain't about to happen."

"Oh, yes it will. Yanni, pick out one of them youngsters, take his gun, and ride him on back to the herd. Mister, we're just gonna keep one of these boys of yours till we're plumb outta Texas. You come after us, and you don't know what might happen to your boy."

CHAPTER 19

+ + + + + + +

BARB STOOD ALONE at the edge of the evening campfire, her face against the wind. She bowed her head and shook it.

Randolph walked up behind her with a plate of hot food. "Barbara, you'd better eat something."

She kept her back to him. "I'm not hungry." She looked up at the dying twilight. "How could he do something like that? Kidnapping! Taking a mere boy away from his father, and now I'm a party to it." Her shoulders shook, but it had little to do with the cool wind.

"Here, Barb, eat your beans. You'll think better with something hot in you."

"There's nothing to think about. I've got to take that boy back in the morning and offer my apologies. After all, a man has a right to keep his own cattle. We're driving the Circle R stock to market, not every cow we can pick up along the way."

"We did start out with almost four thousand head, and I'd put us over that now. Part of it is how late in the season we are. Every herd that comes through here loses steers. They're like anything else when they're lost. They seek out the company of their own. I don't know how many XL cows we have, maybe a hundred or better."

"It just doesn't make sense. All the fuss for so few." She turned around to Randolph and took the plate.

"I don't think the number of cows has anything to do with it. The problem is between you and Hammond—it has nothing to do with the XL. The way I see it, he doesn't want anybody to tell him what to do. He wants to show any and all that he's the boss."

"Why are men like that? Like a pack of dogs, having to show off who's stronger, who has the biggest bite. I don't think I'll ever understand them as long as I live."

Randolph dropped his head. "We're not all like that. Don't think that anything I did the other night had anything to do with my pride. If ego was what prodded me in life, I'd be practicing law in Philadelphia."

"Oh, I don't think pride entered into your thinking at all, Lance. I know why you did what you did, and I appreciate it. I don't think arrogance motivates you. You have a great deal of self-respect, and I admire that in a man."

"Thank you."

Barb ate a spoonful of beans. "I do think I'm going to have to remedy the problem with Pete Hammond."

"You better take care, Barb. If he leaves us, he'll take Macrae and Yanni with him, maybe Crossy too. With those three hombres that have been shadowing us, they just might be able to take the herd. I'll back you, of course, along with Earl. I think Greener will throw in with us, and I don't have any doubts about the three with the remuda. But it's gonna make us real shorthanded with this many cattle to move, and those six or seven would be doggin' us all the way to Dodge City."

"It has to be done. I just don't see any other way."

"Barb, if I was you, I'd do just what you plan to do—take that boy back in the morning. I'll go along with you, if you tell Hammond you want me to accompany you. But then I'd get back here and fight shy of the man for a while. Let him get us up close to Red River country. We just might be able to take on a few more men up there. Then you can make your move. That'll give me more time to work on Crossy too."

The two of them walked back to the fire. It was plain to see by the look on Hammond's face that he didn't like the idea of Randolph getting too chummy with the boss lady. He watched the two of them and glared at Randolph.

Tipper had brought food to the boy, and he and Vonnie were making talk with him around the chuck wagon with Joe, Greener, and Karen.

"Here, kids," Pera said. "I made some dried apple pie for you. You can have a piece too." He held the pie plate out to Joe. "The crust is something I spend lotsa time with, so you young folks eat it all. Old Bobby Pera here isn't about to let children go without."

Barb walked over and stooped down in front of the boy. The child didn't appear to be much more than twelve. "I'm sorry about this," she said.

The boy shifted nervously.

"I'll take you back to your father tomorrow, and then I'll tell him to look for those cattle of yours and take whatever he can find."

The boy nodded. "My pa can't be very far," he said. "He wouldn't just leave me and go back."

Barb put her hand on his shoulder. "No, I don't expect he would."

Tipper rolled a cigarette and slicked the paper together with his mouth. He leaned it into his lips and felt in his pocket for a match.

Joe jerked the cigarette out of the boy's mouth. "That stuff's poison, kid. If it don't kill you, it'll take yer wind clean away. Where'd you get that?"

"Yanni give it to me. Said it would keep me warm riding night herd."

Joe flicked the cigarette into the fire. "That man ain't got nuthin' you need. If you get chilly tonight out riding night hawk, then you jest blow on your hands. I'll tell you somethin', boy, the way a man starts out in life and the people he runs with has a whole lot to do with how he ends up."

"Me and Tipper here has the midnight run tonight," Greener said. "Mr. Hammond said we're to ride it, just Tipper and me."

"Then you just watch it, I'm with the remuda then my ownself, and I don't like the look of the herd. That wind has 'em all unsettled-like. See 'em out there all millin' about?"

"Yeah."

"Well, they're not even bedding down. You just watch yer-self, you two boys. Keep 'em tightly circled and sing real soft-like." Joe turned to Karen and spoke under his breath. "I don't know why that man has them two riding night herd together, not on a night like this. Usually the kid rides it with Crossy or Randolph."

The cool wind continued to blow, turning cold. Crossy and Earl had ridden the first shift. They stepped out of their saddles at the picket line and poured a cup of hot coffee. Crossy woke up the boys. "Okay, you two," he said, "it's your turn. Be real gentle, and don't make much noise. They're kinda spooky to-night. That spotted steer we picked up with the one bad eye has got 'em going 'round. Big Red's 'bout the only one down, so you just be real easylike, ya hear?"

Greener was up first, stuffing his shirttail into his pants and shuffling his mismatched boots on.

Tipper pushed his oversized hat down low over his ears. "Okay, Jim, we'll be mighty careful. We'll hum and sing a little bit to 'em, that ought to settle 'em down."

"Don't those things ever sleep?" Greener asked. "I'm sure sleepy, why ain't they?"

"Had a dry camp last night, so their bellies ain't full. That and the wind has got 'em all raring to go. You watch that pinto steer though, boy. He's shakin' them horns of his and pawin' at every rider he sees."

The boys mounted up and pulled their collars up against the wind. Hammond and Macrae were wide awake as they sepa-rated and rode out, watching the boys ride away.

On the bluff overlooking the herd, the three men who had been shadowing them also watched the two boys ride off. The man in the tan drover shirt poured what remained of the coffee over the glowing coals, and then returned to where the two oth-ers were sitting.

"You got them shakers?" the red-whiskered man asked.

"Got 'em right here." He produced a fistful of large rattle-snake rattles.

"Well, they sure ought to do the trick on a night like this. Them Longhorns look mighty spooky tonight."

"Yeah," the man grinned.

"The wind's coming out of the north. I'd say that was the best place for us to start. We'll get the bunch running south a here and leave the leaders where they stand."

"You don't reckon they'll go through the camp, do you?"

"They just might, some of 'em at least. But Hammond knows to look out. He won't be sleepin' none, not tonight."

"You see him today?"

"Yeah, he said he'd have his young'uns riding night herd at midnight. We don't want anybody that can settle 'em down, or throw a shot at us riding 'round out there."

The man in the tan shirt smiled. "That's got to be a little downheartening to you, I'll wager. I figured you'd want the gent with the hat out there."

"I'll take care of him later. I can get him chasing a steer sometime. Then there'll be just him, me, and my long gun. To-night, Hammond just wants us to scatter 'em some, make them folks lose sleep and maybe a bit of the herd to boot. We keep 'em on edge for a spell, and then maybe some of that starch will just wash right out of them folks."

"Do we take the horses?"

"No, not just yet. Hammond sorta misfigured on that one. Says them boys with the remuda are tougher'n grit. They ride well, and they shoot somethin' fierce. We was supposed to be with those horses before that woman hired those other three, but we better keep a wide circle from them tonight. Maybe once this herd gets spooky enough, Hammond can draw one of them off to watch the herd. That might make it a bit easier. We ain't in no rush, you know. Once we get this bunch to market, we'll all be rich men."

"Well, speaking for my ownself, I'd just as soon ride down and take up with that little girl."

"You just get that thought out of your head. We got work to do yet. There's plenty of time left and Dodge City will have lots of women just waiting for a man like you, somebody with his pockets fulla money."

"Maybe so, but she sure is a pretty little filly."

"Let's mount up. We got us a herd to scatter."

The men wound their way down the darkened bluff. Below them, the sound of the cattle bawling was mixed with the sound of a song.

Greener and Tipper passed each other in the darkness and pulled their horses up. "You riding that white horse tonight?"

"Yeah," Greener said, "but I ain't scared a no haunts and ghostly stories. You're doing some fine singing," he went on. "I can hear you clear across to the other side of the herd."

"Thanks, it's a song Vonnie done taught me," Tipper said. " 'Amazing Grace.' It shore is pretty. She said it was writ up by a man who used to be a slave runner. Now how'd a man who done that write a song so prettylike?"

"Don't rightly know. Sometimes I guess the way a man starts out don't mean he's gonna end up in such a way."

"I hope you is right then and Joe is wrong, 'cause I ain't started out so good. I reckon I had about as bad a start outta the gate as any feller I know. You reckon I'll end up straight?"

"All depends."

"All depends on what?"

"Well fer me, my wife April was what it took to straighten me out. When I saw her and found out what a nice girl was all about, then I just wanted to be the best person I could be. Couldn't have a racehorse hitched up with a mule."

"No, I don't suppose that would work none too good at that. You s'pose I'm too young to think about gettin' hitched yet?"

"Well, maybe just yet. A feller's got to shave regular first, even if there ain't that much to take off. Then a feller's got to be ready to make a place for a woman."

"You think Vonnie is gonna want to wait around that long for a kid like me?"

"I don't see why not. She seems to like you something fierce. She slid some of her apple pie onto your plate tonight. I'd say that was likin' you a powerful lot. And she taught you that pretty song."

"Yep, it's the grace a God sure 'nuff. She says that's when God gives us what we don't deserve. Just 'cause He loves us."

Greener scratched his chin. "Well, I 'speck that takes us both in."

Suddenly the quietness of the night was broken by the sound of what seemed like a hundred rattlers in the bushes. The cattle heard it as soon as the boys did, because they began to stir up and then run in every direction.

"Whoa!" Greener yelled. "You better ride back to camp. I'll try to turn 'em." The young man took out his rain slicker and, spinning it around his head, began to gallop full speed in the direction of the running herd. He swatted his horse with the slicker and ran forward into the blackness and the sound of the thundering hooves.

As he rode toward the camp, the sound of clacking horns all around him, Tipper could see the brutes running—over half a mile wide, many of them headed straight for the camp. A sense of panic swept through him. He had to find Vonnie, had to make sure she was safe. He knew any minute he'd come into the camp and face panicked cowboys, each running for their lives without boots, horses, or guns. The sound of the flying hooves was like thunder, each animal tearing up dirt and sending it back in a cloudy spray that blacked out the campfire up ahead.

Over the backs of the running cattle, he saw the flames stab out through the dust from the end of the revolvers. Tipper figured some of the cowboys were putting up a last ditch effort to turn the herd away from the camp and the precious supplies that the chuck wagon carried. What might be left if they were unsuccessful wouldn't be much to look at, let alone eat.

The cattle were headed south, and as far as Tipper was concerned, that was definitely in the wrong direction. Before they could get them stopped, he was sure the beasts would cover all of the ground they had made in the last day. The earth literally shook; trees and brush along the side of the bluff were being torn up like stalks of corn. Up ahead, he could see the faint outline of Greener waving his slicker in the air, trying to turn the herd.

He skidded his horse up to the wagon under which Vonnie and the women were hiding. "Here, take my horse," he shouted.

All around him, men in various stages of dress were firing their guns in the air and waving blankets to keep the Longhorns away from the wagons. Randolph had picked up a flaming brand from the fire and was waving it back and forth in front of the running cattle and shooting into the air with his revolver.

Crossy was wearing his red long johns, six-gun, boots, and hat. He grabbed Tipper's horse. "Here, kid, gotta turn that bunch around." With that he got on in a running mount and blended into the running cattle that were still streaking through the camp. Several other men had now found their mounts. They were up and away in a matter of seconds.

Tipper looked around to see if he could find Hammond or Macrae, but they were nowhere to be seen. He bent low under the wagon, where Barb, Dorothy, and Vonnie lay quaking in their bedrolls. "You folks all right?"

"Yes," Barb said, "we're fine. But I don't know where that boy from the XL is. Can you see him out there?"

Tipper straightened up. He looked back in the direction of what remained of the oncoming cattle. "No, ma'am, I can't see him nowheres." Drawing his gun, he stood in front of the wagon, directly in the path of the oncoming cattle. He began to wave his hat and fire round after round into the air.

The sound of the pots and pans clanking in the night told them the running animals had reached the chuck wagon. Pera stood on the seat of the Conestoga and banged away on a pot with a large spoon. One side of the wagon collapsed, accompanied by the bellows of frightened steers.

Then, almost as quickly as it had begun, the stampede was over. In the distance, Tipper and the women could hear the thunderous sound die down and then stop completely. He and the women walked out into the middle of what was left of the camp.

"They broke a wheel," Pera shouted, "but it coulda been mucha worse. The food's still here, at least, and not all over the ground. I think I lost a sack a flour, though." He pointed over to where the torn up dirt seemed to be plastered over with a white substance.

Vonnie took Tipper's arm. "You saved our lives, standing out there like you did, and you could have been killed."

"The grace of God," he said. "He give me something I didn't deserve, when I didn't know no better."

"Yes, the grace of God."

Hammond trotted his horse up to the small group. "You seen that XL boy?"

"No, we haven't," Barb said. "He's not in the camp, and if anything has happened to him, you alone are responsible."

CHAPTER 20

+ + + + + + +

PERA STOOD beside the morning fire and sliced bacon into the sizzling pan. Barb lifted the lid from the Dutch oven and began to pile biscuits onto the bent tin plate, one at a time. "I think after such a bad night, the men will like a big breakfast," he said.

"Have you seen all the men come in this morning?" Barb asked.

"I seen some of them."

Tipper had saddled a horse when things settled down and rode out to lend a hand in driving back the herd. They watched him slowly ride back in, leading the white horse. His eyes were a blank stare. Vonnie and Barb walked out to him.

"You seen Greener walking back in here?" he asked.

"No," Barb said, "but he's bound to turn up. Why don't you climb down and get something to eat?"

"No, I gots to find Greener. Him and me was together when this thing started."

He turned the two horses around and walked them out of the camp. Vonnie walked along beside him. "You can't blame yourself," she said.

"I reckon I can. I was on night hawk when it all happened. I should have been singing to them and calming them down. But I was talking to Greener when they ran. I'm just no good, I guess. Never have been, never will. It's like my pap says, I'm bad." With that, he kicked his horse and trotted off, leaving Vonnie to watch him ride away.

Crossy rode in, still wearing his red long johns. Never being a modest man, he tipped his hat to the women and smiled.

"Have you seen Greener?" Barb asked. "He's on foot. Tipper just brought his horse in."

Crossy's shoulders slumped. "No, ma'am, I ain't. But if he was on foot out there last night, I'd say he's a goner. That was a mess out there. I did see that white spook horse of his when I turned the herd, but I shore ain't seen him none."

Barb wrung her hands slightly. "Then why don't you get your pants on and come get some hot food. You look tired and wore out."

"That I am, ma'am, that I am."

She started to turn away.

"I did find that XL boy, though."

"Where is he?"

Crossy jerked his thumb over his shoulder. "Back there, what's left of him."

Barb turned to walk in the direction Crossy had pointed, but he danced his horse back in front of her. "Ma'am, don't do that. It ain't a pretty sight. Probably tried to get clean away when he heard the cattle start to run."

Barb hung her head. She was worn out, too tired to cry and too angry to speak. She wiped the back of her hand across her face and walked back shakily toward the fire.

One by one the tired men straggled back into camp. Karen and Joe had left Poor Soul with the horses, and they too had gotten involved with finding scattered cattle. Barb could see them in the distance driving a group of several hundred steers.

When Earl came riding into camp, he stepped out of his saddle and picked up a cup. "Pour me some of that black Yank sludge," he sighed. "I'm going to need a large amount to survive the day, I do believe." He held the cup with both hands and, peering over the edge of it, slurped it. "Ah, nothing ever tasted so bitter, or so sweet."

"Have you seen Hammond or Macrae?" Barb asked.

"Why, no. I did find someone, but I don't believe it to be either one of them." He drank the rest of his coffee down.

"Who then? Is it Greener?"

"I believe so, miss. It is hard to tell, but whoever it is wears two left boots."

Barb sank to the ground in a heap and put her head in her hands, emotionally and physically exhausted. Pera waved the men away as she cried silently.

Hammond and Macrae rode down from the bluffs near the camp. Aside from the night's growth of beard on their faces, each of them looked to be in the best shape of the lot. Crossy approached them as they rode in. "We lost Greener," he said, "and that there boy from the XL. Somebody's gonna pay for that."

The two honchos stepped down from their horses and poured themselves some coffee. Randolph inched up next to Barb and gently laid his hand on her arm.

"Well, we'll have to bury them before the buzzards and critters get to them," Hammond said. "How many head did we lose?"

"I'd guess about two hundred," Yanni offered. "It might take us all day looking to find them."

"Don't think we can afford to do that," Hammond said. "With that XL boy gone, I think we better put all the distance we can 'tween us and this place, and right fast. Two hundred head you say?"

"Yes," Barb broke in. "Two hundred head. About the same number of cattle you refused to give back to that man and his sons."

"Well, then, that's about the extra number we needed, I guess."

Barb pulled away from Randolph and stepped toward Hammond. He held up his hand to her. "That's far enough, Miss Barbara. You and I can have this discussion tonight when we camp. Right now we all got ourselves a passel of work to do."

Poor Soul turned from the group and picked up a shovel by the fire. "Right now, I'd say we have graves to dig."

He walked past Dorothy, who was shaking her head. "Why did it have to be ones so young?"

Poor Soul stopped and, leaning on the shovel, looked her in the eye. "Missy, I read once in Cervantes' *Don Quixote*, 'Death eats up all things, both the young lamb and the old sheep.' That boy Greener was doing what he could to care for his family. And the other one was just tryin' to get back to his. There's no higher callin' than caring for family."

✦　✦　✦　✦　✦

In Dodge City, Zac dressed himself in the only suit he had left and straightened his string tie. He hated the things, but he knew he'd more than likely have to buy another before the week was over. Skip was at school. Zac felt the remaining stitches on the top of his head. They were painful to the touch. It had been weeks since the beating he had taken, weeks in bed dealing with the aches that slowly subsided in his body. Even though he still looked a bit pale and his ribs were sore, he had to get to the stockyards.

He picked up his short .45 and crammed it down into his shoulder holster. Opening the top drawer of his dresser, he pulled out the short-barreled twelve-gauge he always favored. He was bound and determined not to be outmatched again. There was something about the business end of a twelve-gauge that always intimidated the worst of would-be gunmen. It was a weapon he had used many times before and, if necessary, wouldn't hesitate to use again. He wrapped it carefully in his overcoat.

There was a knock at the door. "Mr. Adams, it's me, Laura."

Zac opened the door.

The woman lowered her eyelids coyly. "My, you do look nice. It's so good to see you all dressed up and out of that bed." She glanced down the stairs. "There's a policeman here to see you, Mr. Adams. I think he'd like to ask you a few questions. You can use the parlor. I'll see that you're not disturbed."

Zac picked up the carefully wrapped equalizer and headed down to the bottom of the sweeping staircase, where a man in a dark suit was waiting for him. The man had a sweeping, thick black mustache and eyes that seemed to look right through a man. He carried himself erect and held his hat in his left hand. On the lapel of his black suit was a bronze badge: Dodge City Police.

"Good morning, officer, what can I do for you?"

The man didn't offer his hand in greeting. "I have some questions to ask you."

"Of course," Zac responded, motioning toward the open parlor door. "We can use this room."

The policeman insisted that Zac go first. He stepped through the door, and then closed it behind them.

"To what do I owe the pleasure of this visit?" Zac asked.

"Name's Earp," the man said, "and there's been a complaint about you from Quirt Muldoon."

Zac forced a smile. "More'n likely complaining that I ain't dead yet."

"No, complaining that you entered his home unlawfully. Now, he doesn't live in Dodge, and I can't exactly arrest you for what he said you did, but I want you out of Dodge City anyway."

Zac carefully reached for his pocket. He could see the tension in the man's eyes. "You mind if I smoke?" he asked.

"No, go right ahead."

Zac pulled out his briar pipe and stuffed it with tobacco. He motioned toward the chairs. "Mind if we sit down? That beating Muldoon's men gave me left me a little worse for wear."

The two of them sat down facing each other. Zac struck the match and held it over the bowl of his pipe, puffing the mixture to life. "Now, where were we?"

"We were talking about your leaving Dodge City. Now I don't exactly know who you are. I know what you call yourself, and I know you're here with your son, but I don't know who you are. And I can tell you one thing, Mr. Adams, you've muddied the water 'round here considerably since you got off the train."

"Sounds like you've done some work on me."

"That I have, and you don't appear to be a man who's well liked."

"Well, I must admit I didn't make too many friends with the tinhorns at the Longbranch several weeks back. They played me for a pigeon, but they were wrong."

"Short told me all about it. No, you didn't pick the right people to expose."

"I would think, Mr. Earp, that you would appreciate a man who exposes people who want to cold deck a stranger."

"Normally I would, but you seem to have stirred up more than that, what with going into Muldoon's home and all. I'd a shot you if it had been my place, and we wouldn't be having this conversation."

"Well, now, I am sorry about that. But you must know that I'm here to buy cattle, and since Muldoon deals in cattle, I was just trying to get the jump on any competition by looking him up. I was hoping we could patch up our little difficulty. I need to do business here, and having a man that owns so many head of cattle piqued at me just didn't seem the way to start."

"He owns more than just many head of cattle. Trouble for you is, right now he's doing a whole lot of buying and very little selling."

"Buying, is it? And have you seen his bills of sale? Do you know many men who have sold to him?"

"No, but he has a spread that goes on for miles, and a herd that keeps growing by the month. He says he's buying."

Zac puffed on his pipe. "And he told me he was playing honest cards, too."

"All the same, I want you out of Dodge City, the sooner the better."

"Now, Mr. Earp, I'm a respectable businessman with money to spend in your city. I've broken no laws that I can tell, and I don't plan to either."

"The problem is, Adams, you're going to be leaving here sooner or later, and Muldoon's staying. He'll be here and I'll be here. So if it comes down to who I'm gonna cross, it'll be you, not him. Do you understand where I'm coming from?"

"I understand." Zac got to his feet. "You no doubt are aware of the robberies that have taken place in regard to payrolls for these trail herds?"

"I'm aware, and we're working on that."

"Well, I don't have to tell you then that if somebody doesn't put a stop to them, this town will have a far sight less money to spend on anything, including the police department."

"What are you saying?"

"I'm just saying that if you have a man that has lots of cattle and no bills of sale, a man that seems to have a small army of desperadoes working for him, then I'd do whatever it took to turn that rock over, not be at his beck and call."

The man blew a short breath through his lips, rifling his mustache. "I'm at no man's beck and call, including yours. Now you ain't broke any law here, and I can't arrest you, but this is not a healthy place for you to be. Speaking for myself, I'm gonna be watching you. You so much as spit on one of our sidewalks, and I'm gonna come down on you like a ton a bricks. Have I made myself clear?"

"Perfectly."

"Then one way or the other, I don't want to see much of you from now on."

Zac walked him to the door. "Mr. Earp, I'm sorry you and me have got off on the wrong foot. I have a feeling that we'd like each other in other circumstances. Now, you may be looking to do me harm, but I can assure you that I'm gonna do my dead level best to make your job a whole lot easier."

"The only way you could make my job easier would be to cause me to see that backside of yours climbing the steps of the next train."

"Well, we'll have to see about that, won't we?"

Zac began a brisk walk in the direction of the stockyards. They weren't easy to miss, even if you didn't know where you were going.

The conversation with Earp bothered him. It was bad enough to have the bad element in town dead set against him, but having the police to fight too was playing once again into a cold deck. He'd tried to stay cool and not let on that he was much more than he advertised himself to be, but every day that passed brought greater risk that someone would recognize him. That made what he was doing even more dangerous, not just to himself but to Skip as well.

Reaching the stockyard pens, they looked to be only half full. But to a buyer, any cattle at all was a welcome sight. Stopping at the pens, Zac put his foot up on the rail and made small talk with the men who were sitting there. "Where would I find the buyer office?" he asked.

"Up them stairs, mister, but you won't find many buyers in there."

"Why not?"

"Most of these steers are already spoken for, and a number of the buyers have already fanned out south of town to strike a deal before the herds get here."

Zac walked up the stairs and straight into the office of the stockyard superintendent. Standing beside the window was Charlie Harrow, the man he had met at the rooming house. Seated on a leather sofa was the massive red-haired man that had taken part in his beating at Muldoon's.

"Why, Mr. Adams, how nice to see you up and around," Harrow said. "Let me introduce you. This here is Jock O'Connor. He works for one of the biggest cattle operations in the territory."

"Mr. O'Connor and I have met. Spent a splendid day together, right, O'Connor?"

The big man got to his feet and grinned. "That we did, me bucko, that we did. Fact is, I was kinda lookin' forward to more of the same."

"Well, Adams," Harrow said, "I can see you're an eager beaver indeed. Being here such a short time, laid up and all, and already you know the people that you ought to know." He patted Zac on the back. "You're a go-getter, boy. I admire that in a man."

"Do you mind?" Zac said. "Mr. O'Connor and I have some words we need to speak in private, about a business matter." Zac carefully placed the overcoat-wrapped shotgun on the table.

Harrow laughed. "No indeed. You are a man who's all business. You'll do right well here in Dodge City." Harrow walked to the door. "I'll just go down to the yard for a spell. Got to ask around about what might be expected to come in this week."

As the door closed, O'Connor hitched up his pants. "You learn mighty hard there, fella. I didn't expect to see you again."

"And I can see you're a man who likes to have other people do his fighting for him. First, you use six of your friends, and then you sic the law on me. You must be right proud of yourself."

"Oh, I'm just here to make sure that when Quirt Muldoon teaches a lesson, people learn it real good, that's all."

Zac gave a crooked smile. "Well, you and him are sure the teachers, aren't you? No, I'd like to shake your hand and tell you how well I learn my lessons."

The big man stuck out his right paw, and Zac took it with both hands. Suddenly, his left hand was around the man's wrist and he twisted it backward. O'Connor gasped in pain and sank to his knees, sweat beading up on his forehead.

"Now you listen to me, you oversized gofer. If you ever cross my path again, I'm gonna take this fat arm right off. You ain't man enough to take me by yourself. You showed me that at Muldoon's place. And that's fittin' 'cause that boss man you work for never gets his hands dirty. That's 'cause he's got children like you to do the dishes for him."

"Let go a me. Let me up." The man tried to wrest his hand from Zac's grasp and get to his feet, but Zac bent the hand back farther, drawing out a plaintive cry of pain.

"Not till you learn your lesson. Now I'm the teacher. You just better think twice before that man sends you up against me again, 'cause I may bend, but I don't break. You tell that man that I know exactly what he's doing 'round here and it ain't gonna wash no more. You tell him that I'm the Seventh Cavalry come back from the dead, and that I can ride through him like he was a village full of squaws."

O'Connor nodded his head rapidly.

"You tell him that if he continues to operate in these parts, that I'm gonna see him behind bars, or strung up to some two-by-four out there in the street. You got that?"

The big man quivered and nodded.

CHAPTER 21

+ + + + + + +

Late that same afternoon, Zac found himself in the uncomfortable position of sitting under a lamp in the office of Dr. Horace Renshaw. The visit was made all the worse by the doctor's appearance. The gray-headed man with the salt-and-pepper beard wore a torn and bloodied white shirt, most of which hung out of his pants. Red suspenders bulged over his ample belly.

"I seen cleaner looking uniforms worn by doctors during the war," Zac said. "And I fought for the stars and bars."

The old man knocked the ash off his stubby cigar. "What I got to do to you, Adams, don't require no spotless operatin' table. We ain't got no New York hospital here. 'Sides, since that last outfit from Texas brought their cows into town, I've had shootin's and stabbin's constantlike. Shoulda had these stitches pulled two weeks ago. I ain't hardly sat down in two days, though, let alone changed clothes."

The old man bent over him and grabbed the first stitch with a small—and Zac suspected tainted—gleaming instrument. He yanked out the first of the sutures. "There, that hurt, didn't it?"

Zac was silent, he'd said too much already.

"Good, it was supposed to."

"What makes this such an unfriendly town?" Zac asked.

The old man leaned back and pushed his suspenders forward. "Well, I tell you, mister, the word about you is all over town. We don't like folks snooping about in Dodge City. Anybody who done what you done ought to have some pain. You had some pain putting these gashes into yer head, it's only right for you to suffer some taking 'em out."

As the old man smiled and bent over to take out another stitch, his door flew open. It was Wyatt Earp.

"Why, Deacon Earp!" the doctor said. "What brings you here?"

"Doc, we got us a man out here, and he's hurt mighty bad. He's got arrows in him and he's been scalped. They just brought him in from south a ways. How he's still alive, I'll never know."

Earp caught sight of Zac and frowned. He then leaned out the door and waved for the men outside. "Doc's in, boys. Bring him on in."

Moments later, four men carrying the dirty and badly injured cowboy scooted through the door with their package of pain.

"Here," the doctor said, "lay him right over here."

The men stood by momentarily while Earp thanked them, and then left, one by one. The doctor picked up a cloth and began to wipe the man's face. The arrows had been cut to a shorter length to allow transport, but an inch or more of the clipped arrow shafts protruded from his shirt. Taking a knife, the doctor began to cut the shirt away.

The man groaned and his eyes opened. Earp remained, hovering over the doctor's work. "Was it Kiowa?" Earp asked.

"We drove 'em up from south Texas," the man croaked.

"Drove what up, son?"

"The herd. Fifteen hundred prime steers."

The doctor looked up. "Injuns don't take cattle. They might take a few, but not that many. They'll take the horses all right, but not all them cows."

Earp bent down low over the cowboy. "Was it Kiowa that did this to you?"

The boy gulped. "I'm thirsty."

The doctor reached for a glass and held it to the man's lips. The boy slowly sipped it. "B-B-Bar-W," he stammered, "fifteen hundred head a Bar-W beef. That was all we had in the world." He took another sip. "Was white men that done it, claimed to be stock inspectors looking out for tics. There was eight of us."

Earp nodded at the doctor. "They brought the other seven in on another wagon. They're over to Johnson's Funeral Parlor."

"This boy's been scalped," the doctor said. "Durn poor job of it for an Injun, I'd say, but what would a white man want with a scalp?"

"Did you see the men who did this?" Earp asked.

The boy gasped out the words. "One of 'em had silver-handled guns. He's the one that took off my hair. Silver guns and silver conches, and a scar on his forehead."

"You know who that is," Zac spoke up. "Fact is, I put that scar there myself."

Earp lifted his head and glared at Zac. "You are trouble."

"He was lying in ambush for me after that poker game."

The doctor pulled Earp away and took him over to the table where Zac was still seated. "This boy ain't got more than an hour left, I'll wager."

Earp continued to glare at Zac while the doctor spoke.

"Anything you might want to know, you better find out now, 'cause I'm gonna deaden him up some to make his passin' a mite easier."

"Deacon," Zac said with more than a touch of sarcasm, "you and I both know who did this, and we both know that if we took a ride over there and looked into that man's ranch, we'd find fifteen hundred head of Bar-W beef."

"We don't know anything of the sort for sure."

"All you got is my word on it," Zac said, "and the word of a dying cowboy that ain't got no reason to lie."

Earp looked over at Zac's hat. "I got the word of a Johnny Reb who ain't what he claims to be, and that of a driftin' cowboy from Texas who's more'n likely outta his head."

"Suit yerself. You can decide to be a man who upholds the law, or one who just protects the chosen few who happen to have power and money. When you're in church on Sunday passin' that collection plate, that idea will give you a lot to ponder."

"Are you finished with this man?" Earp asked, glaring at Zac.

"Nah, I still got me some painful stitches to pull outta his hot head." A smile creased the doctor's mouth.

"Well, when you're done with him, make sure he knows the way to the railroad depot."

✦ ✦ ✦ ✦ ✦

The memory of the stampede lingered for the next two days. It took that long for the settled march north to put them ahead of the old camp. Even the most experienced drover was spooked by sudden death and destruction.

Karen, Poor Soul, and Joe were still into the routine of bringing the fresh mounts to the line of drovers and snapping the jump out of the new additions to the remuda. And the occasional glimpse of the three men who shadowed them still brought an uneasy feeling.

Poor Soul and Karen were riding drag on the remuda, while Joe circled up ahead, turning the herd.

"Just saw those three riders," Karen said. "Why are they following us, do you reckon?"

"I suspect they believe us to be an easy target for their greed," Poor Soul responded.

"I don't think we are."

"Well, right now I'm afraid it's what they think that matters." He lifted his hand and signaled for Joe. "Perhaps we should discourage them a mite."

Joe rode back and reined his horse up next to the two of them. "What seems to be the trouble?" he asked.

"Car just spotted our three shadows again, up there on the bluffs."

Joe studied the high ridge. "Well, they're gone now."

"Yes," Karen said, "but they'll be back."

"More than likely," Joe replied.

"Do you think it was them that stampeded the herd?"

"I think it's the same men who rode into camp looking for jobs. Maybe Randolph got 'em so riled up they want to get even. Some men just never leave well enough alone."

"Perhaps I should just ride up there and persuade them to

find work elsewhere," Poor Soul said.

"Don't let him fool you, Car, he can be mighty persuasive when he puts his mind to it. He cuts a trail with the best of 'em. I've seen him put the fear of God in a man. When he's had enough of a feller, he doesn't have to kill him, he just makes him so all-fired scared of dying, he hunts out greener pastures."

"When the hunter becomes the hunted, he soon tires of the sport."

"Now who said that?" Joe asked.

"I just said that," Poor Soul grinned. "You see, Car, old Joe and me play games with each other's minds. We was both educated by the same woman—his mother, but I do believe that I was the better student."

"And he never lets me live it down," Joe responded.

"I do think young Car here is right, though. We have an accounting to do with those men." He showed a broad white smile. "He who dies pays all debts."

Joe pointed at him. "Shakespeare's *Hamlet*."

Poor Soul slapped spurs to his horse and galloped away laughing. "Noooo. . . . *The Tempest*, Joe boy, *The Tempest*."

"Maybe he was the better student."

Hammond had sent Crossy on up ahead to scout for a place to water the cattle for the night. They'd try to set their pace and get the herd satisfied in the late afternoon.

The sun was high overhead when Hammond and the men up front spotted Crossy racing back toward them. A trail of smoke rose from the heels of his horse, and he was still slapping the animal with his leather quirt.

"They got over three hundred head of ours in a draw up yonder."

"Who has?" Hammond asked.

"XL riders. That old man from the XL, and what looks to me like a dozen of his hands. More'n likely they want to make a swap."

"Only thing is," Macrae joined in, "we ain't got the kid to swap."

"You better ride back and tell the boss lady. She wants to

make all the decisions 'round here, we'll let her make this one."

Moments later, after Crossy had delivered his report, Barb mounted a spare line horse and rode to the front with Randolph.

"Jim has explained the situation to me. I think I should ride out with Randolph here and tell the man the news about his boy."

"What about the cattle?" Hammond asked.

"I will let the man do as he chooses when it comes to the cattle. He can keep what he's found, or he can cut our herd and look for his own. It will be his decision."

"You better durn well hope that's all the man wants to do," Randolph said, glaring at Hammond. "If it was my son, I'd come cutting to find you."

Hammond's muscles tensed, but he made no response.

"Where are these people?" Barb asked.

Crossy stuck out his hand and directed them. " 'Bout six miles on north and a shade east of direct north. You can't miss 'em. There's a lot a men, armed to the teeth."

Barb gave Hammond one more withering look and kicked the sides of her horse.

+ + + + +

The three shadow riders had separated at midday. Two of them had sent Buster, the young man in the tan shirt, on ahead to try to spot where the herd might settle down for the night. They knew it wouldn't be long before Hammond made his move. They stretched out on the grass and passed a plug of tobacco back and forth.

"What you reckon all them cows are gonna bring in Dodge City?"

The man with the red muttonchop whiskers sliced off a piece of chaw and slipped it between his lips. "I figure forty dollars a head, maybe forty-two."

"You realize what that might come to, Potter, not counting the horses?"

"I got it figured at about a hunert' an' fifty thousand, if you mix the horses in with it. Here, Tar," he added, passing the plug of tobacco to his companion.

"Whew . . . eee. Countin' the four down there and us three, that's . . ." He paused to use his fingers and figure in his head. "That's more'n twenty thousand dollars each."

Potter shook his head. "Not hardly. Hammond says half of it gots to go to the man back in Texas that set this here thing all up. 'Course, Hammond gets a triple share of what's left after that's all gone. But he said, especially if'n they don't lose too many cattle, that our share ought to be 'round seven, maybe eight thousand."

"Why not just keep the money and leave that Texas feller clear out of it?"

"Hammond says that would be killin' the goose that's gonna lay our golden eggs. He's got it all figured, that man in Texas. Says if this works well, he's gonna put us with some other herds moving north and do the same thing. Only difference is, we'll more'n likely be riding with the herd. We won't have no cranky woman in charge to keep us out. Ought to make the taking of the thing a whole lot easier."

"S'pose Buster's gonna be riding back here pretty soon?"

"I reckon. There ain't too many places they can light this time a day that has enough water."

"Good afternoon, gentlemen."

They cranked their heads around, surprised to see the black cowboy they had often spotted with the remuda. He was wearing a pair of moccasins that had allowed him to walk up on them unnoticed. His coat was open and his six-gun gleamed in his holster. A broad smile on his face showed a set of pearly white teeth. They were in no position to draw, being sprawled out on the ground. Little did they realize that even if they had been ready, they wouldn't have stood a chance.

CHAPTER 22

+ + + + + + +

"ARE YOU FRIGHTENED?" Randolph asked. "You know, I'd be just as happy to do this all by myself and send you on back to the herd."

"I know you would, and I appreciate that, but this is my responsibility," said Barb.

"Hammond's the one who dug this hole."

"Yes, that may be, but would you really trust him to ride out here and not get us into a shooting war? Besides, my father used to say that when he had a man working for him that did something wrong, ultimately it was his to pay. He said that when you gave a man a job, the work still belonged to you. My problem was in allowing this Pete Hammond to be in charge in the first place. Had I only known. You would have done a much better job, and I would have been able to sleep."

"Don't forget, it was Hammond who brought me along. I think he was amused at my education and the fact that I was a lawyer. I also think he thought he could bully me around into doing just what he wanted."

"There you are, then. I didn't know what I was doing when I hired him, and he didn't know what he was doing when he hired you. Either way you slice it, it was the sovereignty of God."

They both spotted the men on the rim of a draw and pulled rein. The cattle were bunched below them, spilling out onto the open ground.

"If we're going to die," Randolph said, "I couldn't think of a

199

prettier or nicer lady to go down with."

They rode to the bunched-up cattle and pulled their horses to a stop in front of several men. Looking up, they could see others with rifles dotting the sides of the depression.

The old man stepped forward, a rifle in his hand. "You here for your cattle?"

"No, we're not," Barb said. They both stepped down from their horses. Randolph held both sets of reins. "I'm here to see you."

The old man laid the rifle in his arms. "I don't have no business with a lady. My business is with the big fella in front of that herd back there."

"No, I'm afraid your business is with me. You see, those cattle are all my sisters and I have left of our father's ranch. I can only apologize deeply for not knowing what my trail boss had done, until it was too late. We had no right to any of your cattle that we picked up along our way."

The man grunted. His eyes narrowed. "Where's my youngest boy, then?"

Without hesitation, Barb spoke the words she had been dreading to say. "I'm sorry to say that your boy died in a stampede that we had two nights ago. I had planned on returning him alive to you myself the morning after he was taken." Tears welled in her eyes.

The old man's knuckles turned white. He gripped the rifle. He silently looked both Barb and Randolph up and down. Barb knew she had said all she could say at the moment. Anything else that came out of her mouth would only pour oil on the fire burning inside of the man.

"Why are you telling me this?"

"Because, even though what happened to your son was a terrible accident, I am ultimately responsible. We lost another man in that stampede also, a man who was only a few years older than your son, a man with a wife and a child soon to be born, and I am responsible for his death as well."

"Why isn't that trail boss of yours here telling me this?"

Barb hesitated. It grated on her not to tell the man that Hammond wasn't here because he was a coward.

"Because I insisted on doing this myself," she said. "Nothing can repay what you've lost, but all that my sisters and I have are at your disposal. What you choose to do won't change the sorrow I feel at the loss of your son. He was a fine boy. You did yourself proud bringing him into this world and raising him as you did. Now he sleeps in the arms of our Lord Jesus."

A slight glistening in the old man's eye gave way to the trickle of a tear. It slid down his wrinkled face and onto his lip. He turned away and walked back to his horse. He spoke to a few of his men, each of them registering expressions that ranged from rage to pure bewilderment. It was easy to see from the looks of the men which of them were the boy's brothers. Barb and Randolph waited in silence.

The old man mounted his horse and rode off quietly. One of his men walked over to where Barb and Randolph stood. "Mr. Larimer said we're to leave the cattle here. Three of us will ride out to that herd of yours and cut our cattle out."

Barb and Randolph both nodded and mounted their horses. They turned and walked the animals south, back in the direction of the herd. Minutes passed in silence between the two of them. They were in no hurry. There was too much thinking to do.

Randolph broke the quietness of the ride. "Barbara, I need to tell you something. I believe that's about the bravest thing I ever saw a body do, man or woman. I came out West to get away from my responsibilities, and you—well, you just stood where God put you and faced yours."

+ + + + +

Poor Soul's confidence was not lost on either of the men lying on the ground, and his smile was unnerving. "How lucky do you boys feel about now? I hope you're feeling your oats and are at peace with your God, because all those plans of yours will go into the ground with you. And all that money you're talking about can go to somebody else, maybe even to the people it rightfully belongs to."

"How long you been behind us?" the red-whiskered man asked.

"Potter, is it? I just need to know for your marker. Long enough, Potter."

"Look, we can go. We can just get up and clear outta here."

"But I doubt that you will. No, I heard a lot. You see, I sneak up on folks real good. 'Specially noisy gents like you. You're just fortunate I didn't come up on you at night." He produced a broad smirk. "You see, a body can't even see me at night. I could crawl right into your camp and you'd never know it."

Potter turned over and began to get to his knees. He held his hands up. "We'll just ride outta here and you'll never see us again."

"You know something, Potter, I don't believe a word you're saying. Fact is, I wouldn't believe you if you said I was black. Oh, you're gonna ride out of here all right, but it's going to be down in the direction of the herd. I'm going to bring you into camp myself."

"You can't do that. They'll hang us."

"Your old friend Pete Hammond hang you? I doubt that. Besides, what would he want to go and hang two dead men for? See, I'm gonna bring you into camp, but it won't be sitting in your saddles."

"He ain't even got his gun out, Potter. We can take him."

There was something about the look of confidence on Poor Soul's face and the gleam in his eye that would have been enough to caution Bill Hickok not to draw. Potter could see it. His life passed before him, and he mindlessly went for his gun.

As quick as the wag on a puppy dog's tail, Poor Soul filled his hand with iron. His first shot at Potter needed no follow-up; it slammed directly into the man's forehead, spinning him backward. He followed the shot with two tightly placed rounds into the second man, who was still struggling to draw his revolver.

Minutes later, he had done exactly what he had promised. The whole camp stopped in its tracks as Poor Soul led the two horses with the men's bodies draped over them directly into the center of the camp.

+ + + + +

Zac had decided to spend the evening gambling. He still wanted to find out how many men Muldoon had at his command. He also needed to discover what he could about the stolen Wells Fargo cattle payrolls. Rustling and murder were none of his business. If he couldn't interest the law in finding out what was going on, then doing the law's work for them made little sense. But the payrolls were another matter. They *were* his concern. It was likely that Muldoon had a hand in that as well, but he didn't know for sure. The only thing he knew he could get Muldoon on was something the local authorities seemed to care little about.

The table was full around him. Zac had found out that he did have a reputation in town. People considered him a dangerous man to befriend, but they also saw him as an honest man and a person they could gamble with and not fear any fast dealing.

Seeing Zac from across the room, Luke Short walked over to the table. He put his hand on Zac's shoulder. "Wonderful to have you at the Longbranch again, Mr. Adams. From what I've been hearing, I wasn't quite sure if I'd ever see you again."

"I guess I just keep turning up like a bad penny."

"Well, you can turn up in my place anytime you want. You were good for my gambling business. By the way, I have a friend who's coming into town tomorrow, and I'd sure like to introduce you to him."

"Happy to meet any friend of yours."

"Well, he's been known as quite a gambler himself, and he handles a gun well too. "

"Men who gamble often need to know that skill. You seem to know everyone in the territory. In fact, when we're done here, I'd like to buy you a drink and discuss some particular gentlemen with you."

The Longbranch had more than its usual share of bedlam that evening. The new group of drovers that had just come in from Texas were into their second night of blowing off steam. The only thing different about them tonight was the fact that most of them had now had a bath, a shave, and a haircut. They smelled of lilac water mixed with whiskey.

Across the table, the man who had been the trail boss for one of the incoming herds held his cards and raised the bet. Beside him sat a freshly opened bottle of French brandy, an unusual indulgence in normal times, but not for a cowboy at the end of the trail.

Zac called the man's bet and asked, "You come up the trail partway with the Bar-W?"

"You bet I did! Them folks waited for us and these other herds to cross the Red before they come across it. I tell you, the news 'bout what happened to them boys shook our crew down to the toes. That's a hard way to make a living, coming up the Chisholm like that, and the way them boys cashed it in is a harder way to die."

"Did you see any sign of Indians?"

"Saw plenty Comanche in Texas. Old Shanghai Pierce over there," he motioned toward a large bearded man at the bar, "he cut 'em out some cattle and saved all our skins. Them people is gonna be plenty hungry when the snow flies." The man chuckled. "Old Pierce there wrote a note and gave it to old Gray Eagle to boot, trying to protect herds that come up after ours. Told Gray Eagle to just pass it on and he'd get plenty of 'wohaw.'"

"That was good of him."

"Well, I'da done it too, but Pierce over there can write good." The old cowboy laid down his cards. The spread-out pasteboards contained three queens. He slapped his hands together. "Whooo . . . weee, this is some fine day."

Gunfire erupted from the street. A cowboy rode his horse through the batwing doors, lowered his head under the crystal chandelier, and continued to fire his revolver into the ceiling. The acrid smoke floated past the table of card players. Shanghai Pierce bolted from his position by the bar. He swatted the man's horse aside and, grabbing the drunken cowboy by the shirt, dragged him out of the saddle and onto the floor.

"Wonder where our police force is tonight?" Zac asked.

"Oh, they're out there, but they got their hands full." The man held out his cards to see better and sipped his brandy. "I told my men to check their guns like they was supposed to, but some fellers never do learn."

Pierce hoisted the drunken cowboy to his feet and ran him out through the batwing doors, throwing him into the street. Walking back into the saloon, he took off his hat and slapped the horse's rump, sending him bolting through the doors in the direction of his former rider.

The shooting outside continued, and a number of the Texas cowboys raced their horses up and down the street, firing their revolvers into the air. Moments later, a man ran into the saloon. "Any other police in here?" he shouted. "Wyatt Earp's got a gun to his head down the alley."

Zac got to his feet in a shot and, picking up the overcoat he now carried, shook it loose from the shotgun. Springing out the door, he saw the gathering of horses up the street. Several of the mounted cowboys had their guns drawn. He ran toward the sound of the shouting.

"Shoot the Yankee down and have done with it." There was still a great deal of animosity between the cowboys from Texas and lawmen in Kansas. Former Confederate soldiers, many of whom still had a chip on their shoulder, saw these men as the enemy all over again.

As Zac rounded the corner, he could see one cowboy on the ground; a man who had evidently been cold-cocked by Earp, and four more Texans, each with guns drawn, pointed at the lawman. He pushed his way past the three cowboys mounted on horseback at the entrance of the alley and fired one barrel of the scatter-gun into the air.

The blast of the shotgun sent the horses to bucking and kicking. The riders, two of whom had dropped their revolvers with their horse's first leap, began to hang on for dear life as the mustangs danced into the street.

Zac leveled the gun at the four men. "All right, that's enough fun for tonight."

The men swung around, three of them pointing their guns at the new intruder. "You another Yankee law dog?" one of them asked.

"No, I fought with Moseby in the army of Northern Virginia, and I ain't no lawman."

The man with the gun next to Earp's neck pressed it closer. "Then why you want to bust up our party? This feller here done cold-cocked Jimmy." He nodded to the man on the ground who was moaning and trying to push himself up. "That right? You ain't no Kansas Yankee?"

One of the other men peered at Zac through the lamplight. "He's right, Zeek, he's got himself a gray cavalry hat, and it's got one a them officer cords tied onto it."

"Why you wanna go and stop us from killin' this here Yankee, then? What's he to you?"

"Like it or not," Zac said, "he's the law. You boys are guests in his town. These people 'round here pay the man to keep things from getting out of hand, and you boys ought to respect that, even if you don't have a likin' for him."

The man who had Earp backed up against the wall slowly lowered his gun.

"Besides," Zac went on, "you got more celebrating to do. You've had a hard time, and you shouldn't be cuttin' your hooraying down by spending time in jail, or on these good people's gallows."

"He's right there," another one of the men said with a grin.

"We'll go then. You just keep this Yank outta our hair."

Zac nodded. "Go and check your guns in at the saloon like the law says and everything will be just fine. He won't bother you none. Besides, you don't need a .45 to do what you do in there."

Moments later the men stumbled off and left their semiconscious friend in the alley along with Zac and Earp.

"You all right there?" Zac asked.

"I am now." Earp picked up the cowboy by the collar and brought him to his feet. Pushing the stumbling man along the wall past Zac, he held the man up and turned around. "That scatter-gun of yours, Adams. Better see about checking that too."

CHAPTER 23

+ + + + + + +

THE BANJO RANG OUT LOUDLY, competing with the pianos up the street. It was late in the afternoon. Dr. Marvin was in his glory, singing at the top of his lungs, his hands and fingers fairly flying over the strings. "Oh, Suzannah . . . don't you cry for me, for I come from Alabama with . . . a banjo on my knee."

Skip stood below, near the bottles of elixir, looking up at the doctor as he sang. The boy felt deep admiration for the man who was teaching him not only to speak, but also how to think. It made him feel safer to begin to feel close to another man. Nursing Zac's wounds had once again been a reminder to Skip of how fragile life was in the West, especially for a man like Zac, whose whole life seemed to revolve around stamping out evil.

This had made Skip feel closer to Zac. The nights spent together, the meals taken day after day, and even the nights when he sat up reading to Zac and tending to his wounds had all made him feel closer to the man who was caring for him. The problem for Skip was that the closer he felt drawn to Zac, the more he wanted to pull away. For Skip, to feel close to someone was to lose them forever. It was a curse he couldn't seem to shake. Dr. Marvin, more than anyone else, had tried to open up his heart and heal his soul.

The crowd had begun to gather outside the general store, along with the balding man wearing an apron who kept the store—a man who looked very unhappy at the notion of his customers walking out of the place with money still in their pockets.

The doctor put down his banjo and, pointing his finger in the air, raised his voice to a high pitch. He was in fine form today as he began his speech.

"I am Doctor Marvin. I am known from Saint Louis to Denver as the miracle worker of the plains. My elixir has been known to cure gout, rheumatism, punies, flea bites, and the dropsy, the infamous disease of the Bible that only the healing touch of Jesus himself could affect—until now, thanks to His wayward but humble child."

With those words the good doctor, as if once again on cue, placed his hat on his heart and bowed his head. He looked at Skip on the sidewalk below and passed a wink along with a slight smile. "I can also favor you with vanities direct from Saint Louis—corsets, tortoise shell combs, and a vast selection of beautiful bonnets from Paris, the plumes of which were plucked from savage ostriches in the heart of Africa, not more than one year ago to this very day."

He picked up a brown square bottle and held it high in the air. "In my days on the open prairie, I have seen women, made old before their time by the harsh elements, brought back to vitality with my potion. One bottle regularly taken will open the bowels of the most pent-up patrician of the plains, freeing them once again to enjoy health and vitality." He paused and grinned. "Along with good eating, of course."

The crowd had begun to press around the colorful wagon. Individuals seemed to be hanging on the words that reassured them that the pain they experienced could be cured by the doctor's little brown bottle of remedy. Several held back, their arms crossed as though daring Dr. Marvin or anyone else to make them feel good about anything ever again. A few were already sold on the magic of the medicine. They leaned forward, waiting for revelation of the price.

"Now, my good friends, I suppose you're wondering what this miracle of healing might cost. I can see the eagerness on faces out there." He pointed, his finger sweeping a semicircle over the heads of the crowd. "Some of you are willing to sell valuables to once again be able to enjoy life with unrestricted bowels."

There was a pause while Dr. Marvin allowed the value of his potion to settle in upon the crowd. "This precious tincture of the miraculous, this divine intervention into the maladies of mankind, would cost the crowded unwashed of the East over five dollars a bottle. Wise men in China would crawl hundreds of miles on their knees clutching precious pearls as payment. This, however, is merely my mission in life. I do what I do as a service to mankind."

Several of the men from Muldoon's ranch had walked out of the Busted Flush saloon. They noticed the wagon immediately and wandered over to listen and amuse themselves. One of the men, Nat Black, carried his bullwhip. All of them were more than a little drunk. And they still resented the memory of Zac's visit to spy on their lair, a visit that Dr. Marvin and his colorful wagon had facilitated.

Dr. Marvin watched them join the crowd at its edges. He continued. "Being a minister, I must accept a loss of love on each bottle I sell, but alas, my reward is to see the healthy skip for joy. Your price, the price that I am making available for today only . . ."

He removed his hat and, placing it over his heart, bowed his head. ". . . is done out of reverence for my dear mother who died of the dreaded dropsy ten years ago today. It is in her honor that I offer this special price."

He paused. "For six bits, three-fourths of a dollar, the price of a sack of nails, the price of a villainous dose of the poison known as whiskey, you can save yourself and those you love. Now step up. My supply is limited. Four bottles per family is all I can offer."

The crowd surged forward, each member waving a dollar bill. Skip passed the bottles from the case at his feet to the good doctor while he took the money and counted out the brown bottles.

+ + + + +

Rass Bodine and Jock O'Connor rode into the ranch. They wanted to be in town with Nat Black and the few men that had gone into Dodge hours ago. They felt good about the new herds added to the ranch. The hard work would begin shortly. Forging bills of sale wouldn't be a problem, but changing the brands to resemble the brands on the documents would require weeks at the end of a hot iron. It was a job they wanted to put off as long as possible. For whatever reason, Muldoon had wanted to see them right away.

When they rode up to the front door, they noticed a strange buggy tied up outside. It was one that belonged to the Golden Livery in town. They recognized it, and they recognized the two black mares hitched to it.

They both walked through the front door and down the narrow hallway that led to Muldoon's study. The big man sat with his back to the setting sun, framed in his oversized window. In front of him sat a man in a wingback chair. They couldn't see his face when they walked into the room, but they could see his polished boots, a silver-tipped cane leaning against his chair, and the derby hat sitting on Muldoon's desk.

"Come in, boys." Muldoon motioned to them. "I have someone you need to meet, a man who knows of our mysterious Mr. Ian Adams."

They both circled the desk and stood in front of Muldoon's cowhide sofa. Sitting in the wingback chair was a properly dressed man who looked like someone who might be visiting a fancy church—or sitting in a high-stakes poker game. With his impeccable pinstripe suit the man wore a white boiled shirt, red tie, and diamond stickpin. His mustache drooped down the sides of his mouth, and his eyes were set with a dull stare.

"Sit down, men, but before ye do, I'd like you to shake the hand of one of our more famous Kansas shootists, Mr. William Masterson, better known as Bat Masterson, a man I'd like to see as our sheriff next year."

They each leaned forward and shook the smallish man's hand, and then took seats on the couch, O'Connor sitting back into the large cushions, and Bodine nervously perched on the edge.

"You say you know Adams?" Bodine inquired.

Masterson smiled. "I know him. Yes, I do."

Muldoon leaned back in his oversized chair.

"When Mr. Muldoon described him to me, I thought of who it might be right away, and when I saw him," Masterson smiled, "I knew right away what you were up against."

"Just like you said, Rass," Muldoon interrupted, "this man is no cattle buyer."

"No, indeed," Masterson said. "He sells all right, but he sells big trouble everywhere he goes. I ran into him last year in Colorado, and I can tell you this: He's not someone you forget."

"It seems Ian Adams is an agent for Wells Fargo," Muldoon went on, "a man by the name of Zac Cobb, Zachary Taylor Cobb to be exact."

"I've heard of him," O'Connor said.

Bodine's eyes raged, but he said nothing.

"We've all heard of him," Muldoon joined in, "but we didn't know he operated this far east."

"The railroad I worked for when Zac Cobb showed himself," Masterson explained, "dug up plenty of information on the man. He lives in California. He doesn't involve himself in the day-to-day work of their agents—he's a special agent. Accepts an assignment only after Wells Fargo has run out of patience. And he can't be bought—not at any price."

"Shame," Muldoon interjected.

"Does he have help?" O'Connor asked.

"Doesn't need any," Masterson's eyes twinkled. "He usually works alone, likes it better that way."

Muldoon sat back and smiled at the exchange. The men before him were those he trusted to run his illegal empire, they and Mr. Nat Black. How they responded to events that happened and the questions they asked were important to him, even amusing at times.

"Is he quick?" Bodine asked, finally entering the conversation.

Muldoon sat forward, a knowing grin on his face. "You see, Bat, Rass here is mighty fast with those silver-handled Remingtons of his. And the scars you see on his noggin were put there by Mr. Zac Cobb."

"No, he's not a gunslinger," Masterson said, "not that you'd think of in the classic sense. But he's more'n likely killed more men than Bill Longley or Ben Thompson. He just doesn't like to talk that up. It's part of his job, but something he seems to take no pride in. No, but I'd say he's the type of man gunslicks fear the most."

"And what type would that be?" Muldoon's curiosity was aroused.

"The type of man who hits what he aims at—the first time. He's cold as a snake about to strike, but doesn't waste the effort on anything foolish. He has little fear, and take it from me, he doesn't back down. He'll keep coming after you until he's dead, or more'n likely, you are."

Muldoon got to his feet and walked around his desk. "We do thank ye for your trouble, Bat. Are you sure you won't reconsider my offer? Not even if ye were alongside these men of mine?" He knew Masterson would refuse, but he also knew something about men who craved power—if they refused a first offer, they might be more apt to accept a second. Men of power intrigued him because he was like them. He gathered politicians around him the same as he did other men, but they took longer to develop.

Masterson got to his feet and shook his head. "No, indeed. There's no amount of money I would take to face Mr. Cobb again. I do admire watching him work, but I never want to be the 'job' he's working on." He picked up his derby and cocked it on his head. "My plans include living a long life and dying at my desk."

"Gentlemen, stay seated," Muldoon said. "I'll walk our guest to the door."

When Muldoon returned from showing Masterson out, the jovial face he had worn for the famous guest had disappeared. He walked around his desk and sat down.

"We can take this feller," O'Connor said.

"The Wells Fargo man isn't the least bit interested in our cattle operation," Muldoon announced.

"He ain't?" O'Connor look surprised.

"No, man. It's the payroll shipments he's here to stop. Of course those robberies have kept our business afloat while we wait to sell the cattle we've acquired."

"What about Nat?" O'Connor asked. "He's takin' one of them shipments this evenin'. It's comin' in on the train."

"To be sure," Muldoon mused.

"He ought to be just fine," Bodine chimed in. "He's got some men with him to create a scuffle somewhere. When that happens, he'll grab the strongbox."

"I think after tonight," Muldoon cautioned, "we'd be best served by leaving Wells Fargo alone. We'll double our efforts with the cattle, perhaps try to sell a few. A fellow named Buster rode in here today looking for a job. He and a couple of Texicans had been trailing a herd from Texas. It seems they were in cahoots with the trail boss and a banker down in Texas that I know. Well, his partners were killed, but he thinks that bunch will be easy to take, especially since the trail boss is being paid not to bring them in."

His red eyes flashed in the lamplight, blending in with the setting sun. "Aye, then we will make careful plans for this man Cobb—careful, thorough plans."

✦ ✦ ✦ ✦ ✦

Zac sat down to eat at the boardinghouse, and for the first time the place beside him was empty. So was Dr. Marvin's chair. He looked at his watch and snapped the lid shut.

"Skip is still with Dr. Marvin," Laura said. "I have food saved for them in the kitchen, so you needn't worry."

"That's nice of you, ma'am, but I wasn't worried about them. I have a friend coming in on the train tonight. He's the one I asked you to reserve the room for."

"Oh, Mr. Peterson. Well, you needn't worry about him either. There will be enough chicken for him as well."

They had almost finished their dinner when Skip burst through the door. He was out of breath and panting, the excitement putting the stammer in his speech again.

"C-c-come quick. You gotta c-c-come real quick. They're 'bout to hang Dr. Marvin. Some m-m-men got him down by the livery."

CHAPTER 24

+ + + + + + +

ZAC REACHED for his wrapped shotgun and, shucking it free of the overcoat, ran out the door, followed by Skip. He didn't slow down or even think twice about how he was going to do what needed to be done; his only thought was to get to the livery before the old man who had befriended them began his dance of death.

As he ran out onto Front Street, Zac could see the westbound train pulling out of the station. He also saw the wagon parked out in front of the livery. The doctor stood high up on the top of the wagon with the rope attached to the overhead beam and looped around his neck. Men had gathered around the vehicle; some of them Zac recognized as belonging to Muldoon, others were merely Texas drovers looking for a good time. The law was nowhere to be seen from where Zac stood.

Even with the noose around his neck, the doctor continued to talk. "Gentlemen, you are mixing my blood with the blood of the martyrs, a man who only meant good for you. You see no fear in me for my soul, my only fear is for you. You will have to approach your Maker with this sin upon your conscience. By doing the deed you now contemplate, you only show that your names are not written in the Lamb's Book of Life."

"Oh, hush him up!" someone shouted. "Whip that team and let's have done with the man."

"You can destroy the messenger, gentlemen, but the message will never perish."

From the other side of the wagon, Zac heard a man shouting.

215

"Pull that man down, and do it now." It was Wyatt Earp. "You don't hang a man for no reason at all."

It's about time I saw the law work in Dodge City, Zac thought.

"We got plenty of reasons," one of the men said. "Nat Black says the man's a sneak thief. Says he'll be comin' 'round our places like he done his, creeping in on us." The man swiveled his head around. "Where is Nat, anyhow?" he asked. Several of Muldoon's men and one of the storekeepers began a litany of complaints about the doctor and his method of sales.

"That ain't no reason to hang a man!" Earp yelled. "What's got into you people? Every day men do things against the law that this man never dreamed of, and I never hear your voice of complaint."

It didn't make sense to Zac either. Why form a mob around a man who simply tried to make a living on the streets of Dodge City?

He glanced across the street, and the answers he needed flashed before him all at once. Several men rode off from the train depot at a gallop. They wore dark dusters and appeared to have masks on their faces. Zac sprinted across to the depot.

Several people milled about the well-lighted passenger area, but the door to the baggage compartment was ajar and dark. Zac pushed open the door with the muzzle of his shotgun. The room was black except for the glint of moonlight through a small window. Zac felt into his vest pocket and removed a match. As his eyes adjusted to the dark, he could make out the globe of a lantern. He raked the match against a post and sizzled the lamp to life. Then he saw the man on the floor. It was Duff Worcester, an agent for the company. There was a knife in his chest, and he lay bleeding beside an open Wells Fargo green strongbox.

Zac knelt beside the fallen agent.

"Zac," the man croaked, "I fear I'm done for, and they got the payroll to boot."

"Just rest easy, Duff. We got a good doctor here in town, mean as a stepped-on snake, but a decent sawbones."

The man grabbed hold of Zac's jacket. "They knew I was

coming, and nobody was s'posed to know but you."

"We got us a two-timer somewheres, Duff. We'll find him, but first we got to take care of you."

The man's eyes widened, and Zac cranked his head toward the door. They were no longer alone. The telegraph operator darkened the doorway, Nat Black next to him, a whip uncurled in his hand.

Zac brought up the shotgun, but Black's whip flagged out and jerked the scatter-gun from his hands.

"I'll keep a lookout," the telegraph operator nervously said. He stepped outside and closed the door.

Black grinned, his eyes dancing in the flickering lamplight. "So, it's you and me."

Zac reached under his arm and, cocking his revolver, swung it free.

Once again Black lashed out with his whip, curling it around Zac's wrist. When he pulled it back, it tore at Zac's flesh, flipping the gun from his grasp and across the floor.

Zac got to his feet, stunned. Pulling off his coat, he wrapped it around his bleeding arm, forgetting that without his coat his underarm holster and the band concealing the knife he carried down his back were exposed.

"Don't think that bit of cotton will keep you from what I got here. I only wish I had the time to do you up right."

Zac moved toward the open storage room. As the man drew back his whip, Zac picked up a box and threw it. Black ducked aside and laughed. "I'm very good with this thing. Not even you can be quick enough to dodge me for long." Seeing that Zac had positioned himself close to the fallen revolver, Black flicked his wrist, sending the singing snake across the room. It flipped the revolver toward the door where he stood.

"Your time is just about up, Black," Zac warned. "You and everything you're doing is well-known. You'd do best to save your own hide and clear out."

Ignoring his words, the man cracked the whip again, raking the steel barbs across Zac's left shoulder. Then drawing the whip back, he circled closer. Planting his left foot in front of him, he uncoiled a wicked lash.

Zac held up his wrapped arm. The ends of the whip bit chunks of cloth from the tightly wrapped coat, sending the scraps whirling through the air like a Kansas tornado, but only scratching Zac's arm.

Scattering the whip across the floor, the metal barbs sounded like a cat on a tin roof. Then he raised it, sending several bursts popping over Zac's head in rapid-fire succession.

He seemed to enjoy his skill with the whip, his smile betraying not an ounce of doubt. "This is the fun part, before I kill my prey," he explained.

Beads of sweat began to form on Zac's forehead. It wouldn't be his best day to take on a man with a whip. Weeks in bed and bruised ribs had made his movement less than fluid.

"For a cattle buyer," Black said, "you are troublesome. But we're going to make sure all the trouble you've made is put behind us. You won't be asking any more questions, and you won't be turning up places where you ain't invited." Unexpectedly, the man crouched low and swept the whip along the floor, wrapping it around one of Zac's ankles and pulling him down.

Zac tucked himself into a continuous roll to avoid the man's aim. Black, however, began a round of quick blows, sailing the bullsnake leather through the air and into Zac's legs and backside. Several strikes glanced off the knife and holster strapped to his back.

Zac's mind raced. He made it a point to learn the tactics of every man he faced. In a fist fight, it meant taking a few blows in order to discover a weakness. Up against a gunman, he noted which side of his body the holster rested on, how he looked or moved before he grabbed for it. But right now, he was reaching his limit. He rolled over on all fours and rested on his knees.

"You are a bit of sport for me," the man taunted. "I like to think of myself as an artist—only thing is, I use a whip instead of a brush."

Zac laboriously got to his feet. He could see that Duff was still breathing, but he knew every second counted. He thought about the knife in the holster down his back. He would need to distract his opponent in order to use it.

When the whip was once again searing through the air, Zac

scrambled toward the agent, extracted the knife from his chest, and flung it. Black used the whip to parry off the thrown knife, sending it crashing to the floor. It was the instant of vulnerability Zac had been waiting for.

In the time the man had used to blunt the knife with the whip, Zac had produced his own keen edge. He sent it flying through the air. Black's whip was open, and at the very instant he turned his head back toward Zac, the second knife buried itself deep into his shoulder with a thump.

The total shock made the man let go of his whip. His teeth gnashed as he reached for the knife and dropped it to the floor. Zac used the seconds to separate the burning lamp from the wall. The hot metal singed his hand as he threw it, but it exploded into a fireball as it reached its mark.

Zac ran toward the flaming man, knocking him to the floor. Then, feeling for the knife, his fingers closed around it and he brought it up, rapping the fallen desperado hard on the skull with the hilt of the shining weapon, putting the would-be killer momentarily out of his pain.

The following minutes seemed like hours. Zac could barely remember Wyatt Earp helping him and Duff into a wagon and driving them to the doctor's office.

"These here wounds ain't deep," the doctor was saying, "but there's sure a bunch of 'em. When're you gonna learn to quit stirrin' things up 'round here?"

Zac blinked at Earp while the doctor applied ointment and dressings to his stripes. "Is Duff okay?"

"The Wells Fargo man?"

"That's the one."

"He's in the back room."

"It'll be touch and go fer a while," the doctor said.

"Do you know the man?" Earp asked.

"Yes, I do. It might help if I told you who I really am. I'd appreciate it if you men would keep it to yourselves, though."

Earp nodded and the doctor's face softened. "Doctors is like priests. We get paid to keep our traps shut."

"My name is Zac Cobb, and I work for Wells Fargo."

"Well, that explains a lot," Earp said. "You're like no cattle buyer I've ever seen."

"I'm here to work on the payroll robberies we've been seeing from Newton to Abilene, most of 'em right here in Dodge City. I think I've already done most of what they're paying me for in that regard."

"Son," the doctor said, "whatever them people is payin' you ain't near enough."

"Just arrest that telegraph operator and hold him for questioning. He's how those people know when the shipments are coming down the rails. How's the rattlesnake with the whip doing?"

"Nat Black?" the doctor asked. "I'd say he's doing pretty poorly. He's got burns over most of his body and a goose egg on his thick head."

"I probably should have done him in," Zac said, "but I figured if he lived, you might just want to question him."

"Lookin' at what the man tried to do to you," the doctor said, "I shoulda thought you'd a finished him off."

"There's many a time when I've held off doing what I wanted to do."

"If you're suggesting Quirt Muldoon's been in on those robberies, there's not much I can do about it," Earp said. "My jurisdiction is strictly Dodge City. We'll have to send for the U.S. Marshal, or catch him red-handed."

"I suppose that's where I come in, until we can find the U.S. Marshal. That's what Wells Fargo pays me to do. They don't rightly care if these people are alive to prosecute, they just want the holdups stopped."

"Well, I can tell you right now, Mister Cobb," Earp said, "if you try to do what that company's hired you to do here in Dodge City, I'm going to have to arrest you."

"Fair enough," Zac said. "What happened to the medicine man?"

"Doctor Marvin? Well, I didn't let those men hang him. But I did tell him to leave town. I want as little trouble in Dodge as I can find."

"That's too bad. My boy's gonna be heartsick."

CHAPTER 25

✦ ✦ ✦ ✦ ✦ ✦ ✦

"DOAN'S CROSSING, UP AHEAD," Macrae called as he rode back to the herd. They had crossed many rivers before, but they knew that in all likelihood, this would be the big one—the Red River. It meant that, like so many before them, they were leaving Texas and moving the herd into the Indian territories.

The grasslands were flat, with scattered cottonwoods and oaks bunched up near the riverbank. The ground was wet. Almost two weeks of rain, some of it hard, had cut the dust down on the trail, but had made the river crossings difficult.

Hammond and Macrae rode ahead of the herd and pulled up near an adobe. Under a large oak tree stood a man, his wife, and their three children. The man waved the cowboys at the front of the herd closer. The group talked, and then Randolph peeled off and rode to the rear where Barb and the girls were waiting in the wagon.

"The man's called Corwin Doan. He and his wife, Lide, have invited you ladies to come to their house and bathe if you've a mind. Says he's got a tub and plenty of hot water."

"Oh, that would be heaven!" Barb enthused. "Tell him we'd be delighted. Right, girls?"

Dorothy and Vonnie nodded.

"Doan says the river's high," Randolph added, "so we can't expect to cross till morning."

✦ ✦ ✦ ✦ ✦

Pera made a special meal that evening, along with fresh-baked bread. Tarps were spread between the branches of several trees, and under the shelter of the overhang, the men ate heartily.

"By Jove," Earl said, "this, my good man, is a blessed confectionery! You should be baking it for Windsor Castle."

Pera smiled and bowed low at the waist.

Crossy munched on the bread and waved the heel of a small loaf at the Italian. "It's good all right, but being on the trail makes it seem a whole lot better. These boys are used to eating beans, beans, and more beans. Maybe a bit of beef now and then." He tore off another hunk of bread. "If I was in Windsor Castle, though, I reckon I'd be just looking over everything inside and be too busy to eat."

"Trying to find something to steal, more'n likely," Yanni said.

Crossy grinned around a mouthful of bread at the remark.

Tipper sat with the girls, next to Earl. "That river kinda scares me a mite," he said. "Ain't never learned to swim."

"My boy," Earl said, "should you fall in, take my advice and hang on to your horse. Hold to the pommel of the saddle, and it'll keep your head above water."

"Can you swim, Englishman?"

"But of course I can."

"How'd you learn yerself to do that?"

"My father taught me when I was just a lad, a mere stripling."

Tipper swirled his bread around on his plate. His face was long.

"Does the notion of having a father teach you things bother you?" Vonnie asked.

"I reckon so. I knowed only guilt and punishment from my pap. The type a father who'd teach his son anything is a type I only heard about." He took a bite of his bread. "I s'pose the notion of family makes me feel like an orphan in a candy store."

Tipper turned his attention back to Earl. "How'd he teach you?"

Earl shrugged his shoulders. "What can I say? How do I describe the means of my tutelage? I suppose it will do me no good to sweeten it for you. He took me out on the river in a boat and threw me overboard." Earl paused to take a bite. "Then he proceeded to laugh and move the vessel away from me."

"Were you scared?"

"I was much too busy staying alive to be frightened. I paddled and spit water something awful."

"What would he a done if you started to go down? Would he a saved you?"

"Mercy no. My father couldn't swim a lick, which was why he wanted me to learn."

"Don't seem right to me," Tipper said, "making a feller do something you can't do yerself."

"Quite the contrary. My father has always insisted that I do what he would never dream of doing."

"Why's that?"

"He's always said it is the duty of every father to make his son a better man than himself—standing on the previous generation's shoulders, he called it."

Tipper paused and munched on his bread. "Well, at least he was teachin' you somethin'. I guess a body can be thankful fer that."

The Englishman laid some beef on his piece of bread and bit down, mulling the thought over as he chewed. "Frankly, I've always believed he did it for the same reason he's done so much else in life—for his own amusement, to have something to pass on to the men at his supper club. I also believe it's the principle reason he sent me to America. That way he can sit in his overstuffed chair with a brandy snifter and a cigar and boast about what a stern disciplinarian he is, thereby gaining the dubious respect of his meager-minded chums."

"Don't sound like you respect him very much."

"No, can't say as I do. I grew up as a member of the idle rich, but as each year passes I've learned to revere the landed gentry less and less. They are all ne'er-do-wells that live at the expense of other people's misery, never contributing a wit to society except their cynicism, and fodder for their own gossip mills."

"I ain't sure what that all means," Tipper said, "but it don't sound good, no way."

"Believe me, my young friend, there is little in my social circle for an honorable man to admire."

"Then yer glad to be out here, being a cowboy?"

Earl grinned widely. "I adore this work."

"Ain't you ever gonna go back?"

"Oh yes, I am due to return next year. My father has me a position as an officer in a large London bank, but I think I will wind up with a career of my own choosing."

"Whatcha gonna do?"

Earl reached into his saddlebags and produced a stack of written papers. He dropped the pile into Tipper's lap. "I compose poetry, and I've been somewhat successful in writing stories for the English press." His eyes sparkled. "The genteel British society cannot get enough of the wild and woolly tales of the American frontier, it would seem."

Tipper stared at the stack of papers, then handed it back. "I sure got 'nuff of it, my ownself. 'Sides, I caen't read a lick."

+ + + + +

The rain had stopped before the sun rose the following morning. After downing some fresh fried eggs, purchased from the Doans, and several pots of coffee, the men felt full and fortified for the deep crossing. If the river was as high as Corwin Doan said it was, they'd get a chance to test the bottoms of the wagons. The caulk and pitch would have to hold if they were to keep the supplies and bedding dry.

Tipper rode drag next to the wagons. Vonnie passed him a fresh biscuit and a broad smile.

The line of cattle moved slowly to the river, which now overflowed its banks. The drifting stream meandered through the trees, and the morning mist made it difficult to see the opposite side of the river.

"We'll be swimming today," Crossy yelled.

"Watch out for the snakes," Randolph bellowed. "The rain

will keep the quicksand down, but the snakes will be out of their holes."

The men whistled and slapped their lariats, moving the cattle into the river. They could see the remuda swimming the stream; Poor Soul, Karen, and Joe keeping them moving in a steady tide of horseflesh. Barb and Dorothy rode in the front of the chuck wagon with Pera; and Vonnie bounced along in the back, first craning her neck around the three of them in order to watch the sight, then moving occasionally to the rear of the wagon to watch the water flow underneath the wheels.

The leaders of the herd began to swim, head-deep in the stream. They craned their necks up and strained, fighting the fast-moving current. "Do you think we'll float free?" Barb asked.

"That bottom oughta be pretty tight," Pera said. "I made sure of it myself."

"Will the river carry us?"

"Just a bit, I think. The horses will keep us from floatin' too far off."

Crossy was swimming with his horse, holding on to the pommel of the saddle and allowing the animal to drag him through the moving stream.

Looking upstream, the women gasped as Tipper's horse slipped into the deepest part of the river, and Tipper floated out of the saddle, kicking and screaming while straining to maintain his grip.

"Tipper's in the river!" Vonnie hollered.

Hand over hand, Tipper grasped at the wet leather to no avail. The water surged over the riderless horse, sending a rooster-tail stream over the saddle and onto the grappling cowboy. Having difficulty himself fighting against the tide, the horse finally slipped completely away from the boy.

"Somebody, get him!" Vonnie called. "He can't swim!" Then she quickly moved to the back of the floating chuck wagon. Tipper was heading that way, fast. If she could reach him in time, she might be able to haul him into the wagon. Dorothy rolled back off her seat to follow.

Vonnie held her hand out for the boy. "Grab on to me!" Dorothy screamed. "You hang on and I'll get him." Vonnie scrambled onto the top of the cook box as the wagon bobbed in the river. She could see Tipper still floating and kicking, but his heavy clothing and leather chaps were sending him deeper into the stream.

Dorothy grabbed her sister's dress. "Be careful," she said. "I don't want you in there too."

"But what about Tipper? I can't let him die." Vonnie could see the boy's panicked face as he tried to keep his head above the surface and fight against the swelling river. She leaned out over the tailgate and opened her fingers, straining to get the best reach she could.

Tipper went under for a few seconds. As his face broke the surface he whipped at the air wildly with his arms. Vonnie leaned out from the wagon. There would only be one chance and she had to make it count. She'd grab on to him and hang on for all she was worth.

As he came closer, Vonnie reached too far, slipping and falling into the water. She grabbed on to the floating wagon with one hand and latched on to Tipper with the other.

Dorothy screamed, "Vonnie's in the water!" She climbed onto the cook box and reached for her sister, but she toppled in headfirst herself.

When Vonnie grabbed Tipper, the force was enough to pull them both out into the middle of the current. Now all three of them were at the mercy of the raging river.

Several of the cowboys spotted the three young people, and Yanni and Earl rode back into the river. The horses hit the stream galloping and surged into the deep, rust-colored water. Yanni splashed his horse in Dorothy's direction, and Earl rode for the two younger ones.

As his horse swam toward the girl, Yanni reached out from his saddle as far as he dared and clutched the collar of Dorothy's dress. She grabbed his wrist and hung on.

Earl reached Tipper and Vonnie, who were hand in hand, their heads still above water. He seized Vonnie's arm and pulled her toward the horse. "Here," he said, "hold on now. I'll take the boy." Vonnie released Tipper's hand and grabbed for the saddle. Earl let go of her and caught the boy.

Earl's hand held fast to Tipper's shirt collar while he tried to haul Vonnie up onto the saddle with his left hand. Momentarily losing his grip on the boy, Earl reached out and gripped him once again. He struggled and pulled, finally able to take the boy's hand and place it onto the saddle. Reaching low, he heaved and scooted Tipper onto the horse. Earl slid his leg over the saddle and pushed Vonnie higher. As he lifted her up, he suddenly lost his grip and slipped into the stream.

Vonnie and Tipper held fast to the horse as it swam for the shore. Moments later, they both dropped into the shallow stream bed. Panting and sputtering water, they rolled over and staggered to their knees. Tipper stumbled to his feet and helped Vonnie up.

"Thanks," he gasped. "You okay?"

She fell into his arms and held him tight. They both turned and looked at the fast-moving river. They could see Earl's head bobbing on the surface and moving downstream at a rapid rate.

"Will he be all right?" Vonnie asked.

"'Course he will. His pap taught him to swim."

+ + + + +

Hours later, the men gathered near the chuck wagon. They were drinking some of the new black coffee from Doan's trading post, when Randolph came walking back into camp leading his horse. Lying across the animal's back was Earl's body. "I'm afraid he didn't make it," he said sadly.

Vonnie burst into tears. "He saved our lives! Both me and Tipper." Barb took her younger sister into her arms and held her close.

Within the hour the subdued group was gathered around a hastily dug grave. Earl's body, wrapped in a blanket, was lowered into the fresh dirt.

Tipper turned to Barb. "I don't know any religious songs, but I think I know an English one."

"That would be fine," Barb said. "I'm sure Earl would approve."

Tipper removed his hat and sang out clearly: "O where and O where has your highland laddie gone? Where and O where has your highland laddie gone?" The boy's voice rose on the air, a sweet high tenor. "He's gone to fight the war for King George upon the throne, and it's all in my heart that I wish him safe at home."

Joe read from his Bible, and the men turned the soil.

Dorothy edged her way over to Yanni. "I'd just like to thank you for what you did—saving my life, that is."

Yanni's eyes were still fixed on the ground. He couldn't bring himself to look Dorothy in the eye. "Oh, it weren't much, nothing another man wouldn't have done."

"I don't think that's entirely true. You may think you've turned your back on everything your mother and father taught you, but I don't think you have. I don't think anybody ever shakes their roots completely, or for long."

Yanni lifted his eyes at Dorothy's gentle words and looked at her directly.

CHAPTER 26

✛   ✛   ✛   ✛   ✛   ✛   ✛

THE WIND POURED OUT of Colorado and onto the Kansas plains, scattering a number of the leaves that had fallen. The darkened sky reflected the feelings of Skip and Zac. The two of them walked briskly, Skip with a pencil and writing book. "Mm-m-m . . . I don't understand why he had to go," Skip said.

"Like I told you, Skipper, the men who planned that holdup needed something to distract everyone. Doctor Marvin just happened to be there."

"Mm-m-m . . . but then why did they have to send him away?"

"The police thought it was the doctor who was causing all the trouble. By the time they found out, it was too late. He'd already lit out of town."

"Why didn't he at least stop and say goodbye to me? He coulda done that, I reckon."

"You're getting better at your talkin', boy, a whole lot better."

"Mm-m-m . . . he teached me."

Zac put his hand on the boy's shoulder while they walked. "Looks to me like he taught you mighty fine."

"Mm-m-m. . . . he said that stammer was like a clock inside me that I didn't need no longer, and I reckon he was right 'bout that."

"I reckon he was."

"Why you s'pose God takes everybody away from me that matters?"

"Many was the time I thought that myself, son."

"You? You done had thoughts like that too?"

Zac nodded. "Straight as a wagon's tongue, I did. Had brothers and sisters die young, and when I came back from the war, I came back to just graves. Ain't seen my brothers since they went off to fight. So near as I can figure, they're all buried somewheres that nobody knows, nobody but God."

"I'm glad I know where my ma and pa is buried."

"It's knowin' where they're living that counts most, I s'pose."

"You mean heaven?"

"Well, yeah, but I was thinkin' how people leave tracks across your life, tracks a body can't never shake. It's like they leave a part of themselves in you. They teach you the important things about everything that counts. They teach you who you are, what the world is like, how to bring out what's best in you while you're down here in this world, and who God is. After that, I reckon, there ain't much else a body has to learn."

"Then why am I going off to school?"

Zac smiled and mussed the boy's hair. " 'Cause those books are full of the lives and learning of other people. A body who don't learn from other folks is prone to repeat his mistakes and miss all the good there is to know. Anybody who tries to learn on their own is gonna get a powerful lot of scrapes, bumps, and bruises that just ain't necessary."

"Mm-m-m . . . then I reckon you ain't read enough yet."

Zac let out a slight chuckle. "You're right about that. I sure got more than my share of bruises and bumps."

"Mm-m-m . . . you s'pose Dr. Marvin left tracks in me by teachin' me how to talk?"

"I think so. But the first thing seems like he did was teach you how to think. Things go wrong in folks' lives because of the way they think about those things I mentioned that are so important."

"You mean 'bout the world, and God, and themselves?"

"That's right. You learn quick, Skip."

They continued to walk on in silence, each with his own

thoughts. Zac knew that it was for times just like this that he had brought Skip with him. The gaps in the boy's life would remain unfilled if he didn't take some responsibility for caulking the cracks.

"Mm-m-m . . . you reckon those people that tracked across yer life and then left suddenly are what make you stand off—like, to yerself?"

"Uh . . . you maybe got something there, son."

They continued to march on. "I-I sure hope that don't happen to me."

The boy's words hit Zac like a dagger. He'd always thought what he showed the boy would be the things he wanted Skip to imitate. The thought that he was showing Skip what to avoid had never occurred to him.

"You think I'm standoffish?"

"Well, Jenny likes you, but you never stay around her much. I just figured maybe you was afraid of losing her. I kinda feel that way too."

Skip's insight caught him off guard. But he knew one thing—truth was truth no matter where a body learned it.

+ + + + +

Joe, Poor Soul, and Karen rode ahead with the remuda. They had already tethered a fresh string of mounts to the wagon in the drag and were using the time to make some distance while they could. They'd find a likely spot now that they were well out of Texas and into Indian territory. Breaking in some new mounts was what they had in mind now. Even if all the horses weren't used like they should be, a well-broke horse would be more valuable when they got to Dodge than a green-broke one. As it was, some of the more skittish animals were taking to the hackamores well, but a bit and bridle was something else.

Karen and Joe circled back and forth to the rear of the horses, moving them on. The grass was good, and if the horses had their own way they would stop and eat. "You ain't said much about your folks," Joe said out of the blue.

"What does that matter?" Karen asked.

In the West, men didn't normally pry into another person's personal life. Seldom did a man even ask for another man's name if it wasn't offered. But for whatever reason, Joe persisted.

"Well, anything you got inside is yer own business, I reckon. I s'pose I'm just taken to thinking of you as a friend. A man don't fall far from the tree that sprung him, so I just figured it might help me to know you better."

"I appreciate the fact you'd even want to. There really ain't much to tell. My folks were like lots of others that put roots in Texas, hard-working Christian folks who believed in God and lots of hard work."

"That's the best kind. The type of folks that first stepped down offa Plymouth Rock. That type tends to teach a body what's important in life."

"They never did want me to be a cowboy, though. I reckon I was quite the disappointment to them, sorta the black sheep of the family."

"Well, I s'pose it's those type of sheep that shows what a shepherd's really made of. Folks never really give up on their young'uns. Sometimes I can feel mine looking right down on me. There's times when I lie out here and look at the stars and just imagine my folks on one of them, peering down to get a better look at me."

"You're a strange type."

"How's that?"

"Well, I've seen you handle horses, and you're about the best I've ever seen. You look rough and ready, but you got a mind like some kind of poet."

Joe laughed. There was a genuineness to his laugh that showed many things about him. Karen had seen that right away. He laughed best when the joke was on him too, showing plainly that he had a clear conscience.

"I think that's about the nicest thing anybody's ever said about me. I don't s'pose you can tell everything about a man by what he does in life. With some you can. But with others, what they do with their hands is only part of what goes on in their heads."

"Since we're asking questions about our insides, let me ask you one," Karen said.

"Ask ahead, I got little to hide from anybody, let alone somebody I ride with."

"You ever think much about women?"

Joe blushed. "I s'pose I do a mite; dream, mostly."

"Well, what type of woman do you dream about?"

Joe clawed the back of his head, pushing his hat forward slightly as he scratched. "I don't really think much about women in general, but I think a lot about the girl that I oughta marry, if I was to marry."

Karen tried to sound casual. "About what she should be like?"

"Yes. I think the woman in my head is one that's as soft and pink as a nursery. I'd like a woman to smell of cologne, with a pretty gardenia planted in her silky hair, to have the grace of an angel when she moves. And when she smiles—I'd like it to be a smile that melts me like butter on the inside."

"Don't you think you'd do better with a strong woman, especially out here in the West?"

"Oh, I don't think women who are graceful and full of beauty have to be weak. Fact is, the women who appeal to me most are the ones that have their own mind—they know what they want and they know who they are."

Poor Soul had ridden on ahead, and when Karen and Joe brought the remuda up over the rise, they spotted him stooping over some debris on the ground. He signaled them to join him, so they stopped the remuda and rode over.

Reining up their horses, they could see the bodies—what appeared to be six men in a bad state of decomposition.

"We're gonna need to bury these fellas," Poor Soul said. "'Course they're long past caring. Looks like the buzzards and coyotes done left 'em long ago too."

"Pilgrims?" Karen asked.

"No, I'd say they was drovers, same as us."

Joe and Karen stepped down from their saddles and led their horses forward. The smell of death made the horses skittish.

"Indians, you reckon?" Karen asked.

"I wouldn't say so," Joe said. "These boys got arrows in 'em, but I don't reckon it to have been Injuns."

Poor Soul walked over to his horse and pulled out a small spade from his bedroll.

"Why not?" Karen continued to be inquisitive.

Joe pointed to their pistol belts. "These boys still got ammunition. Injuns wouldn't leave that. And that one's got some beads and such hanging off his vest." He pointed to a third body, and a small mirror by the man's pocket. "The looking glass over there's a good one, no cracks or nothing." He got to his feet. "Now what Injun would leave beads and a mirror out here when he could take them back to his squaw? Besides, these days the fiercest Injuns in these parts is the ones we got herding them cattle back yonder."

"Rawhiders," Poor Soul added, "half-breeds and renegade white men. They come up on you and take most anything that ain't tied down." He began to dig.

"More'n likely Texicans," Joe said. "They're the lowest form a white men there is. No offense, Car."

Karen swung her head around, as if she were trying to spot where the murderers had ridden off to, or as if she expected at any moment to see the same men who had done the deed come swooping down the hills right for them. She shivered.

"I'd say there's been some wolves working these bodies over too," Poor Soul said.

"We ain't seen nor heard any wolves so far on this drive," Joe said. "We better be plenty careful with the remuda. Horses panic something fierce at the scent of a wolf."

Karen continued to hold the horses, even though the animals were fighting shy.

+ + + + +

Around the campfire that evening, the three told the others about the bodies they had buried in the afternoon. Pera had butchered the pinto steer, the one the men thought had been

234

making the herd skittish. A sizable portion was roasting over the fire on an iron spit.

In the distance, lightning crackled across the sky, without the accompanying sound of thunder. The men nervously eyed the flashes. The sky had turned dark prematurely, casting a pall across their conversation. "Let's hope he goes down better than he kept to the herd," Crossy said. "I seen them spook steers keep a herd on the prod for months on end, half cow, half haunt."

Yanni rode into camp carrying a gunnysack. "Do you believe in ghosts?" he asked.

"Shore do," Crossy said. "I seen many a spook in my time. Time was when I was out riding night hawk . . ."—he paused, sweeping his eyes around the fire until he was sure he had the full attention of the young people—". . . and I seen the rider on the range. When you're out there all alone with them cows and see that—well, I tell you, it's a sight a body never forgets."

"What's that?" Tipper asked, eyeballing both the man and the distant lightning.

Crossy scooted forward on his knees, chewing on a piece of meat. He raised his right hand, meat and all, and swept it toward the darkness. "The rider on the range is a cowboy that's had his head cut clean off ropin' a steer." Crossy held his hand up to his neck. "Caught a loop 'round his bony neck and the durn thing snapped it clean off."

Tipper's and Vonnie's eyes widened.

"Now he rides these parts lookin' fer that head a his, downright refusing to be buried till he finds it."

He held the piece of meat to his mouth and tore off a hunk. He chewed and swallowed it, allowing the silence of the moment to make his point. "Only thing is," he went on, his eyes narrowed for effect, "if'n he can't find his own, he'll come lookin' fer yours. I guess he figures any old head will do. Now take yers"—he pointed at the boy—"it may be small, but I'm sure he figures it'll do right well."

"Now stop that," Barb said. "You'll have the boy so he won't get a wink of sleep tonight."

"He ain't supposed to sleep tonight," Yanni said. "He's suppose to ride night hawk."

Crossy looked at the boy and arched his eyebrows. "Then let's stop this kind of talk altogether. With that sky, this could be a bad night, and I won't have the boy missing what little sleep he ought to have."

Barb turned to the men as they ate. "Don't any of you know any good poetry, or even a comedy piece of writing? You make the worst campfire conversation imaginable."

"They're just talking like ordinary men on the range," Dorothy said. "They can't be depended on to tell the truth."

Poor Soul set his plate down and got to his feet.

"Uh-oh," Joe said, "now you've done it."

Poor Soul straightened his vest and took off his hat. He grinned, showing his set of pearly white teeth. Holding up both hands, he swept them dramatically at the darkness. " 'Sigh no more ladies, sigh no more. Men were deceivers ever, one foot on sea and one on shore, to one thing constant never.' " He bowed low from the waist.

"Where'd you get that stuff?" Yanni asked.

"Shakespeare," Joe answered. "One of the Englishman's worst, but one of Poor Soul's favorites—from *Much Ado About Nothing*."

Dorothy clapped her hands. "It was wonderful!" She cast a glance at Yanni. "And it sounds like Mr. Shakespeare knew his cowboys."

"Much ado about nonsense, if you ask me," Joe said. "But he sure does delight in prodding my hide with that section of verse."

Hammond rose and put his plate away. "Let's get at it. Time to send the first two out there. If what those horse jinglers say is right," he said, sweeping his eyes over the three who had reported the bodies they found, "we don't won't want no wolves or rawhiders creeping up on the herd."

"To say nothing about the rider on the range," Crossy added and smiled. He edged his way up to Yanni and whispered, "What you got in the sack?"

Yanni looked around slyly and, taking Crossy aside, opened the bag. He looked over the campfire at Karen. "Yer sleepin' here tonight, kid. We got you riding the second go-'round and I ain't goin' over to them horses to wake you up."

CHAPTER 27

+ + + + + + +

As THE HOURS PASSED, the storm moved closer to the herd. Randolph and Tipper, who were riding night hawk, knew the cattle had sensed the storm in the air because the brutes were standing and moving about, too nervous to settle down and relax.

The men in camp sat up drinking coffee and watching the approaching but silent storm flash in the distant sky. Yanni signaled Hammond and Macrae over to the fire. He and Crossy had been making plans, that was plain to see. They kept looking at Karen's bedroll, where the woman had drifted off to sleep.

Yanni grinned and opened the bag. A hissing sound erupted from the bottom of the gunnysack.

"What you got in there?" Macrae asked.

"I got me one of the meanest-looking snakes you ever did see in all your born days."

"What do you aim to do with it?"

Crossy joined in. "Yanni here wants to put him to bed with the kid over yonder. Then we can all see what happens. You game for it?"

Hammond and Macrae blinked at each other. Little by little, they had been thinning out the men they couldn't rely on, and this just might be another chance to do just that. Hammond nodded.

Yanni took a large stick and the sack over to where Karen was sleeping. Picking up the corner of the sack, he gently slid the rattling reptile onto the cool ground. The snake hissed and, coiling into a tight loop, began to rattle.

"How we gonna get him in with the kid?" Crossy asked.

"Don't you worry none about that. You men just back off to where he can't crawl past you. These things like dark places, dark and warm places—like a bedroll."

The men backed off, standing between the snake and the outer edges of the camp. Karen continued to sleep, and the reptile uncoiled and slid toward the bedding. Yanni balled his fists and shook them in the air, then grinned with delight as the snake probed the foot of the bedroll.

"What you reckon'll happen if the kid wakes up?" Crossy asked.

"He just better lay real still, that's all I got to say."

A crackle of thunder was the first sound of the approaching storm. Hammond and Macrae swung their heads around as the cattle bellowed. Fire danced in the sky in the not-too-distant prairie. They knew they should all be mounted and with the herd, but nobody wanted to miss the show.

The reptile poked his head under the foot of the bedroll and slithered in. The men began clapping and circled the bed, closing in, afraid to miss the slightest expression on the boy's face when he woke up.

The lightning crackled closer to the herd as Joe rode into camp for coffee. He poured a cup. Crossy signaled him over to where they had surrounded Karen's bed.

"What are you boys up to?" he asked.

Crossy pointed to Karen. "Yanni's got a rattler in bed with the boy."

"You *what?*" he said, spitting out a mouthful of coffee.

All of the men's eyes were fixed on the sleeping time bomb. Crossy nodded. "Yeah, this oughta be real good."

"Oughta make this drive something to remember," Yanni added.

Joe stared at him. "That kid gets bit and I'm gonna make sure it's a drive *you* never forget. I'll take one of them running irons and get it glowing onto your backside."

It was no idle threat. Joe Cobb was not given to exaggeration.

Karen knew she was going to night hawk later, so she had gone to bed fully clothed, minus the binding around her chest. She was in a deep sleep when the faintest movement on her leg disturbed her.

Her eyes fluttered, and when the reptile slid forward onto her right leg she knew instinctively what it was. Blinking her eyes open, she saw the men standing around her.

Joe spoke softly. "Car, don't move a muscle. Keep your breathing steadylike."

Karen's mind raced as the men moved in closer. *What on earth are they doing here?*

Yanni smiled. "That critter might jest decide to spend the night with you."

Inside, Karen boiled. There was nothing she'd have liked better than at that moment than to use the gun she'd tried to put away on this particular cowboy.

"That kid's more man than you are, Yanni," Joe said.

Crossy chuckled. "Yeah, right 'bout now you'd be soakin' yer britches, I reckon."

Yanni frowned. "We'll just see what happens here."

The thunder was closer now, and they could all make out the distinct shape of the lightning darting down on the range. A number of the cattle had begun to bawl nervously.

Barb and Dorothy awoke and, peering out of the wagon, noticed the gathering of men around Karen's bedroll. Wrapping themselves in blankets, they headed toward the circle. Joe watched the two approach and held up his hand. "Don't come any closer. There's a snake in there with Car."

"Oh, dear Lord . . ." Dorothy put her hand to her mouth.

Joe pointed toward the wagon. "You best wake your sister, and then Pera. Have him hitch the team and get your horses ready to ride. That sky looks bad, and we just may have 'em run on us tonight." He looked over at Yanni. "But we got us this to deal with first, thanks to a feller who can't figure out how to prove he's a man."

Barb put her arm around Dorothy and pulled her away. They hurried back to the wagon, whispering their fears to each other.

Karen lay as still as she possibly could. Her biggest fear was just what Yanni had said. If the snake decided to settle in for the night where it was warm and dark, she had a long wait. As long as it continued to move, she had hope.

Joe's voice was insistent. He pushed his hands in the air. "You men back up to the foot of the boy. I won't have that thing sticking his head out and catching sight of y'all."

"Now see here," Hammond said. "I'll do as I durn well please. I'm the boss."

"If you were really the boss, instead of just callin' yourself one, this wouldn't have happened," Joe said firmly. "And if you don't do as I say right now, and that buddy a mine gets hisself bit, you're gonna be a dead boss man real quick."

Macrae pulled on his sleeve. "Our time's coming," he said. "We'll let the Reb hang himself for now."

The men did exactly as Joe instructed, and Joe inched his way clear of Karen's bed. He looked her straight in the eye. "Just keep real still, Car. Make your mind go somewheres else. Get to fishin' b'side a shady pond with the bright sun overhead. Or, if you've a mind, say the Lord's Prayer. Yer gonna be all right, boy. Yer gonna be fine."

Karen closed her eyes as the creature slid into the crook of her arm.

Barb and the girls nervously saddled their horses, constantly craning their necks to watch the gathering. Pera had begun to hitch the team. The lightning danced closer to the herd, and the thunder grew louder.

Joe looked at the men. "You men better get mounted and get out to them cows. All 'cept you, Yanni. I want you right here when that snake comes outta there."

The men grumbled, but they could see the approaching storm and knew they had to get out to the herd. They slowly walked to their horses and mounted. Hammond walked his horse back to where Joe stood.

"When this is over, Reb, you and me is gonna have more than words."

Joe glared at him, then turned his attention back to Karen.

The snake was sliding forward now, up from her arm and onto her chest. She held her breath, could feel the pounding of her heart. The tongue of the serpent flicked at the warm air rising from the ever-increasing heat of Karen's body. It continued to slide, now toward her neck.

Joe stepped back and slowly drew his revolver, pointing it at Karen. He spoke softly, steadily, "I ain't about to shoot, what with the cattle out there. I'm just gonna be ready though, Car, and I don't miss."

Karen slowly exhaled. She could feel the serpent on her neck putting pressure on her throbbing jugular vein.

The thunder boomed closer and the accompanying lightning lit up the sky around them. They could hear the noise of the nervous animals' hooves as the herd milled around.

Karen clinched her right hand into a fist. When it came time to move, she wanted to be ready. She had to be faster than she ever had before, and right now she felt too paralyzed with fear to move a muscle. She had never grabbed a snake with her bare hands, but she'd seen her father do it when one had come too close to Vonnie's cradle. She remembered how he'd seized it suddenly just behind its head and walked it outside the door of their ranch house.

The snake's tongue touched her chin, then, slipping over her left shoulder, it slithered back under the blanket.

Seeing her chance, with lightning-quick movement, Karen clutched the beast just behind its head, immobilizing it. Throwing off her covers, she scrambled to her feet and flung the reptile in the direction of the startled Yanni. Instinctively, he drew his revolver and began to shoot.

Joe was more shocked at the sight of Karen, standing there looking like the fragile, innocent woman she was.

Yanni continued to fire until the snake was dead.

Then the three of them stood blinking at one another, almost unable to comprehend what had happened, until the thunder of the herd mixed with the booming of the skies brought them back to reality.

Without a word, Karen tucked in her shirt and ran for her

saddled mount. Joe and Yanni stared at each other blankly before holstering their guns and running for their horses.

The horns of the running cattle clacked as the lightning above them struck down again and again, casting an eery glow around them. The herd streamed toward the camp like a thousand angry bees stirred from their nest, their hooves biting into the rock-strewn terrain.

For the three recently mounted cowboys, the women, and the chuck wagon, the only chance of survival was to stay well in front of the deadly, mindless mass. Joe waved his arm forward. "Get outta their way. There ain't no turning 'em now, not by a country mile."

Pera put the whip to the chuck wagon mules and they lurched their burden out of camp as though the devil were behind them. Vonnie hung on behind Dorothy in the saddle. Barb had positioned herself in the chuck wagon. She had a revolver in her hand, but it was apparent to all that this stampede was not about to be stopped by mere gunfire.

Dorothy and Vonnie both kicked at the sides of the bay gelding they rode. The animal was a fast one, but he was carrying double through the darkness and over ground they could barely see themselves, followed closely by the wildly running cattle. They both stared ahead as his white-stocking feet shot out over the dark ground.

Behind them, they could hear the herd ripping through the deserted camp. The noise of the iron spiders, tin pots and pans could be heard in the thundering darkness. Vonnie clutched Dorothy closely. If they were going to die, she wanted desperately to die with her sister.

Barb stubbornly fired the revolver as the cattle got closer, scraping the sides of the bouncing wagon. Pera continued to apply the whip. The only thing more cruel than whipping the mules he had grown to love was allowing them to be crushed to death in their tracks. He whistled and yelled as he spun the whip overhead and sent it popping off of the mules' backs.

"Oh, Lord," Barb said under her breath, "are we all going to die?"

"You'd better go to praying," Pera yelled back at her, "real hard."

Barb continued to fire the revolver out the side of the wagon as she muttered a prayer.

Yanni, Joe, and Karen had fanned out in front of the herd. Joe and Karen had taken their bright yellow slickers out and were waving them over their heads as they rode. They looked for all the world like soulless spooks from the netherworld, angels of death leading a great charge of mass destruction.

Joe pulled his hat down tight and continued to spur his horse forward, jumping stumps and rocks that littered the hilly ground. One slip, one misstep, and he was a dead man, and he knew it. But for some reason, he could not take his eyes off Karen. She had pulled off a very convincing disguise all along the trail. But now he knew. *She's a woman!* he thought. *My word, she's a woman!*

He dashed down a gully, followed by hundreds of rampaging steers. The lightning flashed overhead, and all of a sudden he lost her. She was nowhere in sight!

Reining his horse hard, he headed up the slope of the gully. Rounding the hill, he saw her again. She continued her blistering pace in front of the cattle, whipping the sides of her horse with her unfurled rain slicker. Then, without warning, the animal suddenly dropped out from under her, and she tumbled to the ground.

Joe jerked on his horse's reins. The animal's mouth was foaming. They had run hard and far. He had broken the mare himself, and now it was time for the payoff. Galloping over the dark ground, Joe saw Karen get to her feet and begin to fire her sidearm in the air. Reaching down, he jerked her off her feet in front of the stomping cattle and, draping her over the front of his saddle, he spurred the mare forward.

The horses were tiring quickly, but with the thunder booming and the lightning continuing to flash overhead, the stampeding herd showed no sign of letting up.

In the distance he saw the faint shape of a scraggly tree and made a run for it. It could be the worst place to be in a lightning storm, but right now it offered them their only hope. He ran the mare toward it, now surrounded by the storming cattle.

"Grab for the tree, Car, it's our only chance."

Reaching out for the thorny branches, she wrapped her arm around one as the mare scraped by it. Joe felt her weight leave his grasp as he surged past the tree. Briefly looking back, he saw her crawling up the sparse branches.

In front of the main body of the herd, Vonnie clung tightly to Dorothy's waist, shouting in her ear, "Are we gonna make it?"

The cattle were coming up fast behind the two girls; their hooves seemed to be pounding in their ears. "We gotta make it," Dorothy said. "Just hang on tight."

The horse faltered. Vonnie's grip tightened. The ground dipped beneath them into a shallow draw, and the animal stumbled and fell. Vonnie and Dorothy hit the ground hard. The hooves of the cattle flashed around them. Vonnie reached over to Dorothy and shook her hard. "Dorothy, get up! We gotta get up!"

Dorothy groaned. "I can't. I think my arm's broken."

Vonnie looked around. The cattle were flying past her face. "Dorothy, the horse's in the ditch. Let's get under him. It's our only hope."

Dorothy groaned again, and Vonnie slipped her arm under her and dragged her toward the ditch. Just as they both managed to wedge themselves under the fallen horse, the cattle raced over them, hooves flashing and horns clicking with mindless rage.

CHAPTER 28

+ + + + + + +

ZAC WALKED DOWN Front Street and pushed open the door to the Alamo Saloon. The room was full of Texas cowboys drinking everything from milk and lime juice to forty-rod rye whiskey. Three bartenders were working overtime pouring drinks just as fast as they could bend their elbows. Zac pushed his way past several cowboys hanging on the arms of the women who worked the Texas cowboy bars.

Wyatt Earp sat in the corner of the saloon, gambling at a table alongside several other lawmen who were occasionally eyeballing the crowd. He saw Zac walk up to the table, and he put down his cards.

"Sorry, gentlemen, you're gonna have to excuse me." He passed Zac a glance. "I need to go with our cattle buyer here and see to something."

Earp swept up his winnings and stuffed them into his pocket. Picking up his hat, he straightened it on his head and smoothed his long mustache.

Zac walked with him outside the bar to where their horses were tied. "I hope this ain't no wild goose chase," Earp said as they mounted their horses. "Normally, I wouldn't think a doing such a thing, but I ain't about to go and make a fool of myself by wiring the U.S. Marshal or even talking to the sheriff until I can be sure."

"My interest is in the payrolls, but a thief's a thief, and I figure that where there's smoke, there's fire."

They both turned their horses to a trot down the busy street.

Music poured out from the open doors, and a drunken cowboy was thrown out one of them, causing Earp's and Zac's horses to bolt slightly away from the sidewalk as the man reached it.

"Quiet night," Zac said.

"I've seen a lot worse," Earp said. "We've had three herds pull in here since yesterday, and these boys haven't smelled liquor in a couple of months."

"For as much as that stuff is flowing here, I'd reckon they've been able to smell it on the trail since day before yesterday."

Earp smiled and they both began to canter their horses when they hit the edge of town. The sun had long set as they turned and rode north into a cold wind that appeared to be carrying a storm with it. They had ridden several miles when the dark clouds overhead began to spit snow. Arriving at the fence line, Earp dismounted, took out a set of wire cutters from his saddlebags, and snipped open a wide gap. He mounted again and they rode through.

"I imagine he'd put the cattle somewhere away from the house," Zac said. "I'm sure he's already heard about the cowboy that was carried in."

"Maybe," Earp said. "But he don't know the man was from the Bar-W, so he just might not be too cautious."

Minutes later, the two men began to ride through scattered cattle. The brands seemed to be mixed, but they didn't spot any Bar-W steers.

The deep grass waved in the growing wind. From the crest of the hill, they could see the Arkansas River winding below and the glowing lights through the windows of the log ranch house. Trees pockmarked the landscape around the house, springing up in the swelling darkness like bony fingers. Downwind from the house, a large holding pen held thousands of cattle. Wooden shoots ran alongside the holding pen.

Zac pointed toward the pen. "If that's where they do the branding, you can bet that's where they're keeping those Bar-W steers."

"Let's picket the horses here, then," Earp said. "We'll make the rest of the way on foot. I don't much like being gone too long, with the sheriff out of town."

"Where'd he go off to?"

"He went to tracking that payroll of yours."

"That's a wild goose chase. The money's right here."

They moved quickly to the pens, taking care not to come near the house. Moving quietly next to the shoots, Zac's hand shot out and he grasped Earp's sleeve. The lawman turned and Zac pointed to the far corner of the corral, where a cigar glowed in the dark. Earp drew his revolver and stooped low. The two of them moved around the corner of the pen, coming as close as they dared.

Zac nudged Earp. The man had his back to the fence, facing out into the dark grassland. Zac stepped forward, out from the protection of the shadows. "Howdy," he said. "You got yerself a match?"

The man drew his gun. "Who are you?" He stepped forward.

Zac held out his hands. "Take it easy there. I'm just a guest. I came out for a smoke."

The man took several steps toward Zac. "I didn't hear about no guests tonight."

Earp brought his revolver down hard on the man's head, sending him to the ground.

The two of them climbed over the wooden shoot, moving close to several of the penned-in cattle. It didn't take long to discover that they carried the Bar-W brand. As they moved around the herd, it was the only discernible brand either of them could make out.

"All right, I've had enough," Earp said.

They climbed out of the pen. "I'll meet you up at the horses," Zac said. "I got to see one more thing."

Earp gave him a second look, but then walked back up the hill as Zac ran quietly over to the big log house. The curtains were drawn back on the big window and Zac crept toward the edge and looked inside. On the desk were several empty sacks clearly marked "Wells Fargo." It was just as he expected.

+ + + + +

Pera had established a new camp near where they'd been the night before. A number of the pots had somehow survived the brutal beating, and the iron spiders that formed the frames of his cooking fires suffered no damage at all. He stood stooped beside the fire and stirred the pot. Randolph rode up, got down from his horse, and picked up a cup of coffee.

"I have some soup here. It willa warm you up." He looked at the darkening sky. "You're a gonna need something hot in you."

"Right now I just need to find some missing people and about a thousand head of cattle."

"That many?"

Randolph nodded his head. "It's the missing men that worry me most, though."

"I saw Hammond and that Wolf man ride through here about an hour ago."

"Those are the people we could stand to lose." Randolph slung what was left of his coffee onto the ground and walked to his horse. "The remuda came through this thing in fair shape. We may have lost about twenty head. If we had more men like that Poor Soul fella, we'd have come out of this thing with a lot less dirt on our faces."

Barb walked up from behind the wagon. "Have you seen my sisters?"

"No, I haven't, but I'm sure they'll drift in shortly. I saw them out there in the stampede—they had a good mount under them."

Randolph swung up onto his horse and looked up at the sky. "Just when I thought it couldn't get any worse. . . . Will you look at that." He cocked his head and looked up. "We're going to get us some kind of a snowstorm." He shivered. "You were right, Pera, it's turning plenty cold."

Over an hour later, Randolph spotted the two women. Dorothy's right arm was wrapped around her sister; her left hung useless at her side. As soon as she spotted their rescuer, Dorothy began to cry.

He galloped up to them, bounded out of his saddle, and gathered them both in his arms. "Thank God, you're safe," he said. "Let me get you onto my horse and I'll walk you back to camp. There ain't no hurry now that I've found you."

The remainder of the herd had been chewing grass since dawn. They had their backs to the wind and snow and continued to graze as Joe rode by. He felt like a man who was lost, lost in the middle of the thing he was supposed to find. The cattle would be no good if he couldn't find Car. He wove his horse through the milling herd and searched the hilly gray horizon with his eyes, looking for the tree, if it was still there. Riding to the top of the slope, he looked in the direction of the plowed-up ground. *There's somebody*, he thought.

He kicked the mare into a canter in the direction of the stumbling figure. Minutes later he was sure it was Car. "Car!" he called out. Urging the mare on, he rode up to where she stood, looking up at him like a lost kitten. He got out of the saddle. "Here, you take her. I can walk."

He helped her up onto the back of the big black and pointed toward the northeast. "The camp's up yonder. I'll make it fine if you just want to ride on."

She shook her head.

He held on to the saddle and looked up at her. "You sure had me spooked. It's been quite a spell since I lost a man."

Her face fell. "You know, don't you, Joe. I'm not who I pretended to be."

He raked his hand over his mouth and mumbled, "Well, yes, and . . . no, you are not a man, but you're one of the best I've ever ridden with." He swung easily up into the saddle behind her and tugged on the reins. "You know, I don't even want to know why you done what you did."

"I just didn't want to be treated like some china doll on the trail." She wiped the dampness from her eyes. "I didn't want to have to stay with the wagon and just be smiled at like some weak female."

"Oh, but, Car . . ."

"Karen. My name is Karen."

"K-Karen, I don't care what you are. You're mighty good with horses. You can be proud of that. You're some kind a woman to be doing the things you do."

"I just want to be respected for my work. . . ."

The snow was falling harder now. It began to swirl, and the wind blew in their faces, the sky taking on the color of slate.

After a time of silence, Joe said, "We got some day ahead of us. Some of the herd's back where I left them, but the rest is probably scattered all over creation. I 'spect they'll be looking for low ground, probably down back by the Canadian River by now. There's lotsa brakes and maybe even a little grass offa the slopes. 'Course them dumb animals are too stupid to dig for grass. If it ain't staring them in the face, they'll plumb starve to death."

Tipper and Crossy rode over the next hill, slapping their lariats and moving about three hundred steers in front of them. Tipper took off his hat and waved it.

"Ain't that a fine sight," Joe said. "That boy ain't got much sense, otherwise he'd be in school instead of out here proving he's a man. But I sure do like the kid. He's full of vinegar, I'll say that for him."

"It takes a lot to prove you're a man, doesn't it?" Karen said.

"I guess. It starts with an act of God, creatin' that boy child in the first place. Ain't sure where it quits. There's a lot of living out what God puts in a body."

"Maybe that was my problem," Karen said. "I was trying to live out what God didn't put in me."

"Well, be that as it may, I'll say one thing: you did a far sight better than many men I know." She looked back at him and he said, "You musta had a good teacher."

"One of the best."

"I gotta say, though, I do like you better as a woman."

The thought brought a blush to Karen's face and she was glad Joe couldn't see it. "Why do you say that?" she asked.

"I suppose I operate with the notion that a person does best with what God gave 'em. You got a lotta good inside you, girl, things that don't belong in no man."

A short distance from camp, Barb ran to meet them. "Am I

glad to see you! Come on down, we've got hot food ready for you. She held out her arms and helped Karen dismount. "Everyone's accounted for. Dorothy broke her arm, but otherwise we're all okay."

She looked up at Joe. "Thanks." Then, "Poor Soul's got a fresh string of horses by the wagon. He says we're missing about a dozen head from the remuda."

"That's not bad," Joe said. "We'll make it just fine."

"Tipper came in with some of the cattle. He, Randolph, and Poor Soul are looking for the rest of the horses before the snow gets to be a problem."

Joe looked up at the sky. The flakes were flying faster now. "By the looks of that weather, we'd better get every man that's able to ride in the saddle pretty quick. There's lots to be done and we ain't got much time to do it."

"Everybody's all done in," Barb said.

"That don't matter," Joe replied. "The work's got to be done."

Karen stretched her back and rolled her shoulders. "I'll go get another horse," she said.

Joe wanted to stop her, but didn't say anything.

"Get something hot inside you first," Barb said. "I won't have you out there freezing to death. We've come too far."

Joe kept the reins of the mare, and Karen walked off toward the fire. "She's something else," he said.

Barb watched her walk away. "Yes, she is. She's my sister. As bullheaded as our father, but with the heart of our mother—although, I'll admit, sometimes I'm hard pressed to find it."

Joe took his soup and looked across the campfire at Yanni. "You still here? I'da thought you wouldn't have come back without bringin' with you all them cattle you scattered."

Yanni dropped his chin. He was just too tired to be angry. "I reckon I'm sorry about that."

"You durn near got us all killed," Joe shot back. "And besides, you owe Karen here one big apology for yer foolishness."

Yanni found it hard to look her full in the face, not only because of what he'd done, but because he couldn't adjust to the fact that she was a woman. "I-I am sorry, ma'am."

Hammond drank down the rest of his coffee and stood up. "No sense goin' on about it," he said. "We got us work to do, before we lose half that herd."

Macrae mounted his horse and began barking out orders. "Crossy, you zigzag to the north."

Joe murmured into his cup, "Ain't no sense to that."

Macrae's eyes flashed. "What did you say, Reb?"

Joe lifted his mouth from his cup. "I said, there ain't no sense to that. With that wind and snow blowing in from the north, those cattle will be putting their rear ends into it. We'd do better to fan out east and west and work our way back south. More'n likely, though, we'll find them scattered all along that Canadian River we crossed the other day."

"He's right," Hammond said, lifting his hand up to the angry ramrod.

"Maybe I'm just a little tired of him being so right," Macrae shot back. He spurred his horse out of camp and rode off to the east.

CHAPTER 29

+ + + + + + +

THE WIND CURLED around the rocky hills. Each area appeared to be a huge pile of stones, each one carefully balanced on the other, frozen like some molten mound of bubbles the fingers of God had formed long ago.

The snow had been blowing for some time. Tipper had found groups of the scattered cattle and sent them scurrying in what he thought was the right direction. The snow was getting deeper, but he knew there was more of the herd to find. He circled the rocks and saw the first wolf. The beast was picking his way through the rocks, stopped, and stared at him from a distance of some forty yards.

He reined his horse and turned it back. He'd get behind the few cattle he'd driven back if he could find them.

The snow came heavier now and swirled around him. He squinted through the falling flakes and could still make out the dark outline of the rocky hills. He rode on slowly, the horse stepping carefully through the fast-forming drifts. He pulled his hat lower and scooted up the collar on his threadbare jacket.

Dark shapes moved through the snow. Wolves, several of them now, were keeping pace with him and the horse, walking slowly and cocking their heads in his direction. The sight of the animals made his blood run cold.

He had lost sight now of the rocky mounds, and the thought worried him. In the storm, it would be easy to inadvertently turn in the wrong direction. He wasn't even sure if giving his horse his own head would be enough for the animal to find his own way back.

Tipper's mind raced. He had ridden northeast from the herd and passed the rocky mounds off to his left. Now, he believed the hills to be on his right, but just how far, he couldn't say. Had the wolves come from the rocks? He didn't know. Would they stray far from their den just to follow him? He didn't know, but he supposed it depended on how hungry the animals were. He knew he was getting hungry. He hadn't eaten since the night before, the night of the thunderstorm and the stampede.

The herd had run before, probably more than a dozen times since leaving south Texas, but never on the night before a snowstorm. The thought of the cattle wandering off into a blizzard worried him. The Reddiger girls needed all the cattle they could bring to market, and they were depending on him, him and the other cowboys, to find them. The thought of being depended on made him feel proud.

Peering through the swirling snow, he found it harder and harder to see where he was going. His mind wandered. Did he really have a guardian angel? Or was he too old? Maybe his had packed up and left. Maybe God figured he was a man now and didn't need any angel to keep watch over him.

Of course he hadn't started to shave yet. Maybe that was the sign for when a feller's angel could take leave. If that was the case, he knew he'd stay clear of a razor, at least until the drive was over. He didn't know. All he knew was that he needed someone or something to tell him he was going in the right direction.

The sound of the wind and the biting feeling he got when the snow blew into his bare face was beginning to make him feel lonely. It was as if he were the only person left on this part of the earth—just him, his horse, and the wolves.

He turned his head, hoping the wolves had given up. But they were closer now, keeping him in sight, and there were more than a few. He urged the horse ahead faster.

The wolves padded alongside him in a way that seemed unnatural to him. Like ghosts in the mist, they skimmed the white surface, their eyes shining in his direction. His horse was having a hard time maintaining a trot. The ride had taken it out of him, and it worried Tipper. Tired horses make mistakes and this was no time for one—not now.

Through the blowing snow, Tipper thought one of the wolves' eyes flashed at him. It seemed like an angel of the devil, come to track him down.

The thought was unnerving. If his angel was gone and the devil's angel was on his trail—it just didn't seem right. His heart beat faster and he again urged his horse to pick up the pace. Maybe he could outlast the predators.

But the pack seemed to have no worries about where they were. They were confident. Tipper knew he should be confident—after all, he was the man. They were just dogs—big dogs, but just dogs all the same. The thought struck him first as humorous, but it didn't make him feel any better.

He drew up his horse. The animal was breathing heavy now, tired just like he was. He stared at the circling wolves. "Hey!" he yelled, waving his arms. "You get outta here!"

The sound of his voice took them by surprise. They stopped and backed up, but the move was temporary. The bold one, the one he thought he had seen up close earlier, moved in, his eyes glowing.

Tipper turned the horse and kicked hard at his sides, sending both of them on a slow gallop into the howling wind. Wait . . . hadn't the wind been coming out of the north? Why was he riding into it? The thought of going in the opposite direction of the camp worried him. Maybe he was all alone . . . maybe no one would even find his body. He'd been alone all his life, but meeting Vonnie and getting this job had changed all that. Now he was alone again, alone with the wolves.

Tipper, you is in trouble, he thought to himself. *Yer in bad trouble, son, and there ain't nobody 'round to pull yer fat outta the fire. Yer gonna have to do what you gotta do all by yerself.* The voice inside his head sounded a whole lot like his father's, except it wasn't slurred. It sounded sober, and it sounded serious.

The horse was breathing hard now. He could see the steam pouring out its nostrils, and he wasn't losing the wolves. They kept pace with him. It seemed to be a game. He'd heard stories about wolves, but had never seen one. He'd heard how they preyed on young and helpless cattle, taking the weak ones out. Folks said it was nature's way of thinning out the herd.

The thought made him shake inside. Maybe he was one of them weak one's God had in mind. Maybe he was one of the worst of the herd, just spoiling the feed for people that deserved more than he did. He pulled up one the horse's reins and stopped, once again allowing his tormentors to form a semi-circle around him.

He yelled again. "I ain't tellin' you again. You git!"

The wolves moved their heads from side to side, but they didn't run. They had heard his voice before.

He fumbled for the rifle he carried in his saddle. Drawing it out, he jacked home a round in the chamber. *That's it!* he thought. *If they won't listen to me, they'll listen to this.*

Trying to hold the rifle steady, he sighted down the barrel and put the sights on the bold one that seemed to be leading the others. He squeezed his finger and the gun's muzzle exploded.

The wolf leaped in the air when the shot was fired and Tipper's horse staggered and began to run. Behind him, he could hear the sound of the snarling wolves. *Maybe they got something else to eat now*, he thought. *Maybe that'll learn 'em to leave this feller plumb alone. I ain't as easy as they thought.* He slowed the horse and stuffed the rifle back in its boot. Turning, he put the wind on his right side. If he couldn't see the sun, maybe he could use the force of the storm to give him direction. He couldn't be that far away. Maybe the men looking for the cattle had heard the rifle. Of course, chances were, none of them were foolish enough to be out in this storm like he was. They'd more than likely seen the snow coming and turned around right away, like he should have done.

He plowed ahead, the storm dropping a deep blanket of snow all around him. Urging his horse to pull through the deeper drifts, he kicked its sides. It seemed now he had to do that just to make the animal walk, let alone run. Besides, there was no reason to run. He was lost. There was no place to run to.

Minutes later, he saw the wolf pack again. How could they

find him in this snow, when no one else could? They ran toward him now, seemingly more determined than ever.

He kept kicking the sides of the horse, spurring him now in an effort to keep ahead of the wolves. If they nipped at the horse's hind legs, they just might bring him down, and he couldn't have that.

The wolves ran along beside him now, growling and baring their teeth. Apparently the spilt blood of their comrade hadn't slowed them down a bit. If anything, it had whetted their appetite for the main course.

He scooted down in the saddle and urged the horse to plunge ahead through the deep snow.

Then, without warning, his horse went to its knees, pitching him headlong into the snow and falling on top of him. The breath knocked out of him, Tipper lay pinned beneath the struggling animal. All around him, he could hear the sound of the snarling wolves, their jaws snapping. He shivered at their fierceness and the noise of their frenzied hunger.

+ + + + +

"I ain't about to go out in that storm for no lousy kid," Hammond said. "And I sure as blazes don't figger on sending any a my men out there. We're shorthanded as it is without risking good men to go out and find some fool kid that don't know enough to come in out of the cold."

Vonnie stood beside Barb, gripping her hand tightly, wordlessly begging her to do something.

"We have to find that boy," Barb said. "If he stays out there all night, he'll freeze to death, and you know it."

Macrae sucked on a cigarette. He sneered slightly. "The kid ain't got no folks to speak of. There ain't nobody you got to go and jaw with about him when you get back to Texas."

"He has us. We're his family," she stated flatly.

Karen rode her horse into camp, having overheard her sister's and Hammond's exchange. She dismounted and beat the snow from her coat. "Joe and Randolph are out there looking for Tipper right now. Poor Soul's with the horses. I said I'd bring him some hot coffee in one of those pails."

"There," Hammond said, "you got your Reb friend out lookin' for the kid—your Reb friend, and that highfalutin lawyer of yourn to boot. Can't expect much better than that, now can you?" He swung his head from side to side, first looking at Crossy, then at Yanni. "You sure don't expect everybody to go?"

"Time was out here when if one man was in trouble, everybody'd come a runnin'," Barb chided. "We'd do the same for you."

Crossy beat his arms together. "Dag nab it, I'll go. Beats sittin' 'round here and turnin' into a frozen post."

"You see that you don't go far," Macrae said. "We don't have another man to lose. And don't be gone long."

+ + + + +

Joe had ridden an ever wider circle for what seemed like over an hour. Occasionally, he would stop and call out the kid's name, but he knew in this wind and snow, the sound wouldn't carry far. After a while, he just gave up the yelling.

The biting wind lashed against his face like a flurry of tiny bullets. The snow seemed to be coming out of the north at an angle that suggested the fury of the storm was increasing, not letting up. The flakes sailed past his face in ripples of frozen lace—banking, whirling, and then dashing to the accumulation on the ground. A time like this made him wish he wore a full beard like most of the other men did.

He cocked his head to the side, thinking he heard something. But it was not the sound of a man's voice, it was something like the faint murmur of the wind itself, yet somehow different. He stepped his horse forward. It was coming clearer now—the sound of a group of feasting wolves.

He turned his horse aside. More than likely, the wolves had found one of the stray yearlings from the herd. A meal for them meant one less beef to sell in Dodge City. And moving in on a kill could put him into considerable difficulty.

He reined his horse and moved off slowly to the west, but nagging thoughts swirled in his brain. Then, *What if they've got*

Tipper? That distinct thought caused him to break out in a cold sweat. *But what chance would the youngster have with a pack of hungry wolves?* Whatever the chances, whatever the danger to himself, he couldn't ride on without knowing. He drew his rifle from the saddle boot and turned his horse back in the direction of the low growl.

The noise became more pronounced as he neared the scene. His mount began to shy away from the sounds and smells. *Blamed animal*, Joe thought. *He's more'n likely got a heap more sense than I do.*

Peering through the swirling snow, Joe could make out the fuzzy shapes of the pack of wolves, each straining and snarling to get his share of the meat from the large carcass lying in the bloodstained snow. He slowly dismounted from the horse and, holding the animal's reins, fired his rifle into the air.

The wolves backed up at the sight of the new intruder, but it was plain to see they had no intention of beating a retreat. This was likely their principal supply of food for many days to come, and they would not be denied.

As Joe inched closer, his horse reared and tugged violently on the reins in his hand. He could identify the carcass now. It was not a cow after all, but a horse—a saddled horse. Tipper was nowhere to be seen. It had to be his horse, but where was he? Could he have beaten a timely retreat somewhere?

The wolves were clearly not backing down, and Joe held the rifle to his cheek, squeezing off another round. One animal leaped with a chilling death cry.

The sound of the rifle and the howl of the wolf were too much for Joe's horse. The animal jerked the reins from Joe's distracted grip and bounded off in the direction of the camp.

Joe watched his mount gallop away, and then turned back to the snarling pack. He took aim and fired again, dropping a second wolf.

The second shot seemed to surprise the beasts. They bolted off for a few paces, and then began to menacingly circle the man on foot.

Joe aimed and fired again, wounding a yelping animal.

When it looked as if the wolves would charge, Joe counted seven or eight of them. A rapid calculation told him he was two or three bullets short, and that was only if he could hit them with what he had.

He fired off several snap shots at the charging animals, pitching first one, then another, in rapid succession into the swirling snow. Taking careful aim, he shot a third just before it was about to make a leap at him. Taking the hot barrel of the rifle in his hand, he began to swing the thing like a club. With one crack and thud after another into the snapping jaws, he finally sent the wolves scurrying back into the cloak of the blinding storm, back to lick their wounds and find easier game.

Without wasting another second, he ran toward the fallen horse. It was Tipper's all right. It had the boy's old Texas kack saddle on it. When he reached the half-eaten animal, he heard the faint cry, "Hel-lp, hel-l-p-p me."

Scrambling to his knees, Joe pushed at the carcass to reveal the young boy trapped beneath the animal, half buried in the deep snow. Joe began to dig frantically. Seeing his face, he shouted, "C'mon, boy, we'll get you outta here." Thrusting his frozen hands under the boy's arms, he leaned back and pulled with all his strength. Digging in his heels and giving another good tug, he slid Tipper out from his prison, stood him up, and brushed off his face. Shrugging out of his own jacket, he wrapped it around the kid and lifted him up into his arms to begin the slow trudge through the snow, back toward the camp.

CHAPTER 30

+ + + + + + +

THE SNOW HAD BEEN GONE for a week in Dodge City and the sun shone brightly overhead. Zac was seated at the Longbranch drinking a pot of coffee. He wanted to find out as much as he could about the Muldoon operation, and so far one of the friendlier faces he'd seen was that of Luke Short.

"He's got quite the operation up there. I hear he sells more than a little beef to all the army forts in Kansas and the territories. Don't know how he got all the contracts, but they got to bring in quite a bit. He undercuts the prices of every other meat company around. The army's got to be more than a little grateful, but I can't figure out how he keeps the beef flowing."

Outside the saloon on Front Street, a band had struck up a dirge. Brass instruments played loudly, accompanied by drums.

"What in the world is that?" Short asked. He got up from the table and, pushing one of the batwing doors open, looked down the street. "Appears to be a funeral," he said. "From the looks of things, I'd say somebody important died."

Zac rose from his chair and walked to the door. All along Front Street, men stood by with their hats in their hands. Several blocks away the Odd Fellows band continued to play. They didn't play well, but they played loud. The hearse was being pulled by a matched pair of black horses, each with a mountain of red and gold plumes spouting from the harness that went over the tops of their heads.

"Fine horses," Zac said.

"Yep, that they are. Old Mortimer keeps them animals in

fine shape. Hades and Purgatory he calls them. They got this job studied down to a pin."

As the matched team drew the hearse up the spectator-lined street, the men could see the curtains in the ornately designed case had been drawn back, revealing an equally beautiful casket. Across the glass, the funeral director had plastered golden paper letters that sparkled in the bright sunlight. The words read, "Zachary Cobb, Rest in Peace."

"Zachary Cobb," Short said, scratching his head, "now who in blazes is that?"

Zac buttoned up his jacket and pulled his hat low. "Well, I'll be. I reckon that's one funeral I shouldn't be missing. I'm Zachary Cobb."

Short's mouth dropped open but no words came out.

Walking down the street, Wyatt Earp was keeping pace with the slow-moving cortege. Zac stepped out to join him, and the two of them fell into place behind the hearse.

"Ain't often a man gets to attend his own burial," Earp said.

"It's been my experience that a man is always at his own funeral, just not on his feet," Zac replied.

Earp smiled. "It ought to be real interesting."

Zac slowly nodded.

The procession turned up the hill and the horses slowed down just a mite, allowing the band to play while they climbed the slope. Wheeling around in front of the gate, Mortimer got down from the front seat and opened the back of the hearse. He pointed to the tuba player, a trumpet player, Wyatt, and Zac. "Here, you men help me out with this thing."

"With pleasure," Wyatt said.

Zac shot him a quick glance. "Pleasure?"

They both smiled at the thought and grabbed the brass handle on the end of the casket, sliding it from the velvet floor of the ornate death wagon. The funeral director signaled to two other men, and together the six of them lifted the heavy box and followed the man in black up the hill. On arriving at the freshly dug hole, they placed the casket on top of the grave and stepped back under the awning that had been erected.

Mortimer signaled to one of the men in the band, who stepped forward armed with a Bible. "Lord, we confess we don't rightly know who this feller was. We do know he musta been somebody real important. We're also confident that you knowed him, and even if he couldn't have afforded this ceremony today, he'd a been just as important to you. That's enough for us, I'd say." The man proceeded to open his Bible and read the Twenty-third Psalm.

After the service was completed, the men from the Odd Fellows all began to walk down the hill. Zac and Earp stood by to ask the all-too-obvious questions.

"Who's buried in that thing?" Earp asked the man.

"Why, Mr. Zachary Cobb," Mortimer replied. "Didn't you read the sign?"

Earp ran his hand under his mustache. "Yes, Mortimer, but who or what is really in that casket?"

The director pointed to his driver, who snapped a weighted leach to the horses and proceeded to shovel the dirt onto the coffin. "Why do you ask?" he inquired.

Earp summoned Zac forward. "'Cause this feller here is Mr. Zachary Cobb, and as you can see, he's very much alive."

Mortimer appeared flustered, but kept his ramrod straight posture. "This was none of my idea," he said. "But when people pay me to do something, I ask no questions. And for this I was paid very well—five hundred dollars, to be exact, a top-of-the-line funeral, if I do say so myself."

"And you did a first-rate job too," Earp said, "even if it was a mite premature."

"Like I said, I do what I'm instructed to do."

"What's in the coffin?" Zac inquired.

"Rocks, Mr. Cobb, nothing but rocks."

"More importantly, Mortimer," Earp joined in, "who paid you all that money just to bury rocks?"

The man in black turned his head, as if afraid of being overheard. He leaned toward the two men. "Quirt Muldoon paid me, paid me in fresh cash bank notes."

Earp tipped his hat. "Thanks, Mortimer. Spend the money wisely."

"Yes, thanks," Zac added, "it was a fine service, even if it was mine."

The two of them strode down the hill. "Now what do you make of that?" Earp asked.

"It appears that our Mr. Muldoon is sending me a message. He's sending it out loud and clear and using Wells Fargo money to do it."

"If you ask me, I don't think our rancher friend knows you very well."

"Our rustler friend," Zac corrected him, "hasn't even started to find out what I'm really like."

✦   ✦   ✦   ✦   ✦

On the second story of the stockman's exchange, the three men who had watched the funeral procession roll by stood drinking. O'Connor's eyes glistened from the whiskey. He hoisted his glass. "Well, lads, here's a toast to our recently departed Zachary Cobb."

"Only thing is," Bodine joined in, "the boy weren't there to see it pass by. The kid's in school."

"Somehow, gentlemen," Muldoon said, "I think you're underestimatin' our man from Wells Fargo. I don't see him as the type who will haul himself away from a fight. Why should he? He's already taken down Nat Black, and he didn't fare so badly with the likes of you there, Jock O'Connor."

The notion brought blood to the big Irishman's face, to the great delight of Quirt Muldoon. The Scotsman took pleasure in needling other people, especially the ones he had control over.

O'Connor had never before experienced being bested physically by a man. To hear the Irishman tell it, the quickness of the attack had taken him totally by surprise. Muldoon knew it had shamed him, made him boil with resolve to break the man in half when he had the chance. Muldoon's design was to manipulate men by the use of shame, anger, and hatred.

"The man's got the kid," Bodine said. "He's got the kid to

watch out for. That there's what they call his Achilles' heel. We get that kid of his, and we got him in the bargain."

"Harmin' a child would bring the wrath of the law down on us so quick, it would make yer heads spin." Muldoon's statement was obviously designed to show up Bodine.

"I didn't say anything about harming the boy. I'm just a sayin' that we ought to give Cobb there somethin' else to think about besides how to stop us. We get him thinkin' more about protectin' what's his own, then he won't have the time, nor much of the inclination to bother us none."

"Rass could be right about that," O'Connor interjected. "What do you think, Quirt?" O'Connor had learned long ago that it was best not to come down too hard on an issue until he had learned exactly where Quirt Muldoon stood. After all, he made his living by backing Muldoon's play, not sticking out his own neck.

The snow-white mountain of a man continued to stare out the window and down Front Street. He could see Cobb walking back from Boot Hill with Earp. He studied the man's movement. Reaching into his coat pocket, he extracted a pair of gold-framed eyeglasses, with oval-shaped, green lenses. Hooking one bow around his left ear, he pulled the lenses across his broad face, and anchored the right bow to his other ear. Sipping his whiskey, he never took his eyes off Cobb.

"However you choose to do it," he said evenly, "I expect you men to find some way to get our walking corpse into that box of his. Get him back on our property without Earp." He knew his second-guessing of the men's ability would pry out their best effort, a thought he calculated with great amusement.

Bodine put his face to the window. "We'll watch him. We gonna find us a way, some way that don't involve Wells Fargo business."

Muldoon took his eyes off the street for the first time. He looked at Rass Bodine through the green lenses and his lower lip protruded. "You just do that."

+ + + + +

Zac and Wyatt Earp walked back into the Longbranch Saloon and pulled up chairs around a green velvet-covered table. Earp signaled the bartender. The man rounded the corner with a cup, a pot of coffee, and a mug overflowing with buttermilk. By this time, Zac's choice of libation had become common knowledge. Earp poured himself a cup of the coffee. He looked up at Zac. "I see you're a teetotaler."

"Bad liquor's killed more men than bullets," Zac said.

Earp sipped his coffee. "I'm a deacon over at the church, as you know," he said. "People would sure enough start talkin' if I was to take alcohol before the sun went down." He blew on the steaming brew. "Five hundred dollars is a lot of money to pay, just to deliver a message somebody already knows."

"The man's got style," Zac said. "It's just his way of telling me that he's thinking on me. He also wanted to tell the both of us that he knew we were out at his place the other night, and that that's the last time he's going to allow that to happen."

Zac sipped his buttermilk, then licked the underside of his dark brown mustache.

"You seem to take special pleasure in getting between the ears of the men you face, Cobb."

"I do what is necessary, but I don't take any pleasure in it, none at all."

He reached into his coat pocket and took out his briar pipe. Taking out a penknife, he scratched the inside of the bowl. Then, tapping the pipe on the table, he emptied it of the burnt ash. "The people I generally go up against are not the everyday sort. They think, they plan, they cipher."

He produced his leather pouch with its dwindling supply of tobacco and dipped the bowl of the pipe into it, tamping down the mixture. "Over the years I've learned that if I can think one step ahead of them, then I can be there waiting, when they least expect it."

He reached over and took a match from the shot glass in the middle of the table, striking it on a stone next to the glass. He ran the flame over the pipe, sending a cloud into the already smoky room. "If a feller can't outgun the opposition, he'd best outthink it."

"Muldoon's been here since shortly before the Santa Fe laid their track out there," Earp said. "In that short a time, he's managed to corner everything that has a dollar sign attached to it. He's got the politicians in his pocket too. My own speculation is that once he has the biggest herd of cattle that can be found in Kansas, he'll find a way to seal Kansas off from the cattle coming in from Texas. Then he'll have all the cattle in Kansas that's fit to sell."

"How's he gonna do that?" Zac asked.

"Tics," Earp said. "Tics and Texas fever. He'll breed his cattle with the eastern Shorthorns, and then find a way to outlaw all them Texas Longhorns."

Zac puffed on his pipe. "That would just about do it. He'll need cash if he wants to do it quickly, and he's getting that by way of Wells Fargo."

"He's buying—or stealing—lots of cattle. He ain't shipping much, neither. Keeping the prices high for now. A body gets the feeling he's a spider making his web and waiting for just the right time. Then he'll make his political moves and make sure all the cows that are sold belong to him."

"Most of the thieves I run up against," Zac said, "are the type of people who just want to make some money the easy way. They plan for a robbery, but few take the time or have the wherewithal to plan for an empire."

"Muldoon's an empire builder. He's a thinker and a plotter, and right now most of what he's got to worry about is seated right here at this table."

Zac smiled and sent another cloud of smoke toward the chandelier. "Men who plan on the mountains often stumble into gopher holes."

"And you count yourself as the gopher, I take it."

Zac smiled. "I keep digging."

Minutes later, when Earp had taken leave in order to make his rounds, Zac took out a pencil and paper. *Dear Jenny*, he wrote. *I'm not quite sure when I'll get another chance to write,* but I need to tell you that I'm still kicking. Skip's making out just fine. He's in school, and his talking is getting better, thanks to an older gentleman who took the time and had the learning to do what I never could. I suppose something important that a body plans to do generally gets done in a way that takes him by surprise. Wonder why it is that the things that last are oftentimes the stuff that you can't take credit for. I don't mind it none, though. I just want what's done in the boy's life to be what'll make him the best man he can be.

You need to know too, Jenny, as surprising as it may seem, that the times I'm away from you are the times I feel the closest to your spirit. My mind drifts off, I guess, and it always goes to you.

Your humble servant,
ZTC

CHAPTER 31

✦ ✦ ✦ ✦ ✦ ✦ ✦

MULDOON HAD USED the line shack near the Cimarron many times before. It offered little in the way of comfort, but the lamp did allow him to read and keep up with the latest papers he'd been able to get in Dodge. Cattle prices were something he had to know. A sudden swing in prices could instantly move his wealth far beyond the ability of anyone to touch him. He knew that the more cattle he could prevent from coming on the market from Texas, the better price he could get for beef he now called his own. He took great pride in manipulating everything around him, including the price of beef.

It was getting late in the year for a drive from Texas, but when one of the men he had riding for him reported a lone herd nearby, he had to come out himself. He shuffled through the *Kansas City Star*, but couldn't fail to overhear the conversation between O'Connor and Bodine.

"I think you're getting soft, Jock. Time was you'd a killed that old man too quick to even talk about."

"Yer too impatient, my good man. Things and people die of their own accord. Death is an act of God the same as life."

"People die when I say so." The angry purple scar on Bodine's forehead had kept the man on the prod for some time now. He ran his finger over it, then, reaching for the bottle, poured himself a shot.

The big red-haired man took the bottle out of Bodine's hand and poured another glass of the amber liquid for himself. "That type of crooked spirit will only get you killed. One of these days you will not be able to wait. You'll draw down on a man who's just a mite faster."

"Ain't likely," Bodine shot back.

"Everything is likely given enough time, bucko, and it will happen to you just as sure as I sit here. After all, who'd a thought Nat Black could be done in?"

Bodine pulled one of the Remington revolvers out from his holster. The solid silver grips of the guns shone like icicles on a winter morning. He spun the cylinder and squinted down the barrel.

"Never saw it coming myself," O'Connor said. "Never had any idea. Before I knew it, he had my hand cranked back and me on my knees."

Bodine touched his forehead again. Muldoon watched and listened, thinking the scar had taken on the idea of a cattle brand in Bodine's brain. As long as he wore the scar, he would belong to Zac Cobb, and the only way he'd be free would be when the Wells Fargo agent met his end.

Bodine gingerly pressed on the scar. "He come up on me in the dark," he said. "The man's a spook. But if he is a ghost, then I'm gonna to be the first one to make somebody die twice."

A slight smile curled Muldoon's lip. He figured the men were like fighting cocks; if he could keep them stirred up, they'd do better in the ring. They'd kill or be killed, if for no other reason than to show up the other. It helped to play with the men a mite before a fight. Muldoon put down his papers and picked up the brass telescope. He raised his voice to them. "Enough of the palaver. Let's be on our way to that herd. I want it, but we gotta make sure it's the bunch this Buster told us about."

+ + + + +

The sun was breaking in the east when Muldoon and the two men walked over the crest of the hill that overlooked the campsite below. Buster joined them and Muldoon slid open the telescope and squinted into it.

O'Connor pointed to the west. "Glory be, will ya have a look at those horses. Must be nigh on to a hundred or more."

"Yeah," Buster said, "we trailed them things a bunch of days. They are mighty handsome animals."

Muldoon swung the telescope in the direction O'Connor was pointing. "I count one, two, might be three men. That many horses, it would take three or four to handle them well."

"Not with them fellers," Buster replied. "We watched them work. Those horses are well broke by now, ought to fetch a pretty penny."

Muldoon slid the telescope shut. "I count ten to twelve drovers with the cattle, but with the size of that herd, I might have expected more."

"Too risky to take on a group that size," O'Connor said. "We'd best go back to the spread and get some more men."

"Not necessarily," Muldoon said. "What's wrong with you? That little showing up by Cobb make you shy of trouble?" He watched the big man's anger rise. "If what Buster here says is right, then we just need to find an excuse to talk to that trail boss and the men he has with him, but we won't take the cattle here, not just yet. Let's ride down there and take their measure."

"I can't go with you," Buster said. "I'll just stay up here on the hill."

"And why not?" Bodine asked. "A man gets his share, he's gotta take risks same as the rest."

"They all done seen me. Like I told you, we all had coffee with them one night. I'll say one thing, though," he said to Muldoon, "I got my eye on the youngest girl in that camp."

+   +   +   +   +

Hammond's men broke camp on the banks of the Cimarron. Scores of other herds had camped there before them. The remains of burned-out campfires dotted the bare ground and scrub wood was scarce.

All night long, Pera had been dragging wood out from the possum belly stretched underneath the chuck wagon. He poured the last of the coffee for the men before they mounted up and threw the leavings into the smoldering coals. "You'll be drinking forty-rod rye before long," he yelled.

The men whooped and hollered at the notion of the end of the long drive. Crossy grinned. "I ain't stayin' long for this Kansas rotgut. I'll be off to Kansas City. I'm gonna see the elephant up there. I'll be on that train quicker than a snake can pounce on a rat." The men grinned as the cowboy whipped the sides of his horse with his hat and bounded to the front of the line.

Within the hour, the herd had begun crossing. They sank belly deep in the slow-moving stream and silently ambled through the muddy water. The gathering after the last stampede had been slow and painstaking. Literally hundreds of the cattle they once claimed as their own had been lost, but now the Longhorns had been totaled for the last big push. They numbered over three thousand, more than that if the new calves were counted. At thirty to thirty-four dollars a head, the beasts would fetch a small fortune, more than enough to pay the hands and save what the girls still considered the Reddiger ranch, with enough left over to stock the place and then some.

Joe and Poor Soul had the remuda fanning out to the west of the slower cattle. The horses had been well worked and their numbers had diminished only slightly during the drive.

Already, both of the men had chosen several of the horses they would ask for in exchange for part of their wages. Early on, both of them had been planning on taking good cow horses north to sell in the horse-poor area of the Dakotas. But Joe had become distracted. The more he saw of the new Karen, the more he thought about going back to Texas.

Karen, Dorothy, and Barb were riding drag with Tipper while the chuck wagon pulled out of line to try to make camp ahead. "You seem pretty distant," Dorothy said to Karen. "Like your head is a thousand miles away or something."

Karen swung her horse back and forth, occasionally slapping at a slow-moving steer. "No, that's just the trouble," she said. "I wish it was a thousand miles away." She looked off at the distance, toward the remuda.

"You thinking about that cowboy?"

The words braced the woman in her saddle. She spurred her horse away from Dorothy and down the line to the rear of the cattle. She yelled, and slapped her lariat at the flanks of the Longhorned brutes.

Dorothy watched her sister's deliberate busyness. Somehow the idea of wanting a man seemed a foreign thing to attach to Karen. To want something was close to needing something, and Dorothy knew Karen well enough to know how she loved her independence above anything else.

Dorothy never dreamed of being anything other than a wife and mother, but she was sure the thought had never entered Karen's mind—that is, until she rode with Joe Cobb. There was a magnetic quality about the man that attracted Karen. The sisters had talked about it. He had an innocence about him that was mixed with maturity. He was competent but didn't flaunt it.

"What did you say to her?" Barb yelled.

"I just asked her if she was thinking about that cowboy, and she lit outta here like a scalded dog."

The last of the herd crossed the Cimarron more than an hour later. Barb and Dorothy swatted the stragglers out of the stream. They formed their horses at the rear when they spotted the surrey and the riders up ahead. The strangers had fanned out on either side of the rig and sat waiting.

Hammond, Macrae, and Yanni rode up the hill to talk to the men. As they pulled up in front of the line of desperate-looking gunmen, it was plain to see that this was a dangerous situation. The look of the man in the surrey was what caught their attention first. They'd seen plenty of big men, but this one was bigger, and his milky white hair and skin made their blood run cold.

The man spoke. "Welcome to Kansas, gentlemen. We're here to inspect your cattle for tics."

Poor Soul and Joe had spotted the riders, and Poor Soul rode out to lend a hand should it become necessary. He pulled his horse up next to Yanni.

"What do you take us for, mister?" Hammond asked. "Them horns of ours ain't nobody's business but our own." The men from the herd had taken the straps off their holsters, prepared to draw at a moment's notice. The report of the bodies found on the trail had been more than enough to alert them to the possibility of rawhiders in the area.

Muldoon moved forward in the seat of the surrey. "I own an extensive ranch north of Dodge City. If I allow those Texas beasts of yours to contaminate my herd, I'll be ruined."

"That's nonsense," Hammond fired back. "We're taking these cattle into Dodge City, and they'll be heading east quicker'n you can talk about."

Poor Soul noticed the strangers begin to fidget, twisting ever so slightly in their saddles. The white-haired man seemed surprisingly calm, but the man in front of him with the silver-handled guns had begun to flex his fingers. His hands drifted down to his sides and hung there loosely. It was obvious from the look of the character, and the fact that he carried two guns, both tied down, that he considered himself somewhat of a shootist.

Poor Soul looked into Bodine's eyes and flashed him a pearly-white grin, a move that caught the man off guard. Poor Soul had gone through enough in his life to be able to keep what he was feeling on the inside separated from what showed on the outside. It was the way of a slave in the South, even though his slaving days were very different from what was common, because of the fact that he belonged to the Cobbs.

"What you lookin' at, darky?" Bodine asked.

Poor Soul's expression never changed. He wasn't about to give the man the satisfaction of showing hatred. The smile that remained on Poor Soul's face irritated Bodine something fierce, a fact that was obvious to all.

Bodine showed his contempt for the man when he asked, "What's wrong with you? Can't you talk?"

"As the fool in *King Lear* says, 'Have more than thou showest; speak less than thou knowest; lend less than thou owest.' I'd say those were thoughts, my man, that you could profit from. Often the fools in Shakespeare's writings show the most wisdom."

"You calling me a fool?" Bodine's right hand dropped lower.

"No, I'm suggesting that you'd have much to learn from this particular fool."

Bodine went for his gun, but before he could extract it, he found himself staring down the business end of Poor Soul's .45. The former slave was quick—perhaps the fastest any of the men present had ever seen. And the sight of Rass Bodine a split second from death stopped the group cold in its tracks. "Ignorance with a gun fairly cries out to be corrected," Poor Soul added.

"Easy there, good fellows," Muldoon said. They were looking for a deal with the trail boss, not a shoot-out, especially against a man so quick with a gun. He tried to smooth things over: "Aye, I can see we've underestimated you men. There's no cause for a shooting here." Lowering his eyebrows, he cast Bodine a look of contempt.

Hammond marveled at the drawn revolver in Poor Soul's hand and the coolness with which he held it. He hadn't forgotten the day the black man had brought the bodies of two rawhiders into camp strapped to the saddles of their horses. Obviously, in addition to being quick to draw, he was quite capable of getting off the first shot. The thought gave Hammond pause.

"All right," Hammond spoke to Poor Soul, "you can put your shooter away." Then he looked to Muldoon. "I think we can work out our grievances without spilling blood."

Poor Soul's smile disappeared and his eyes narrowed on Bodine. He slowly lowered his .45 and placed it back in his holster.

"Maybe next time," Bodine said quietly.

The soft smile creased Poor Soul's face once again. "Just remember the words of the fool: 'have more than thou showest.' And I think I've already seen what you got."

Bodine's face flushed as his temper raged inside. But what he saw was enough to warn him that to give into that temper right then would mean certain death.

Muldoon caught the look. Rass Bodine had been stirred up like this before. It was an attitude Muldoon liked to see in his men, provided they knew how to bide their time and not do anything rash. He also knew that up to a few minutes ago, Bodine had placed every bit of his confidence in a face-to-face fight with any man. But today he'd faced someone that could put up an equal fight, if not a better one.

Muldoon tried to lighten up the moment: "Mister, you have to be kind of careful of Bodine here. He's got himself a temper and he's a scrapper. Got himself a good scar too."

"I would think the man to be careful of would be the one who gave him the scar," Poor Soul retorted.

The exchange brought a smile to Muldoon's face. "Oh, I'm not sure Cobb will still be in Dodge City when you get there, but if he is, I'd suggest you fight shy of him."

"Cobb, you say?" Poor Soul's eyebrows shot up. "Julian Cobb? A one-armed man that wears an eye patch?" He looked at Bodine. "If it was Julian Cobb you were up against, you're lucky to be alive."

The fact that the black knew a Cobb made Muldoon curious. "No . . . this fella has two arms and two eyes . . . calls himself Zac Cobb. You know of him?"

"That I might. From a long while back. I grew up with a Zac Cobb—hot-headed kid and plenty tough, but more like a brother to me. With a name like that, they're probably one and the same."

The thought that this fellow might be associated with the Wells Fargo man in any way put Muldoon's mind to calculating. Maybe there was a way to take the herd and draw Cobb back out of town. He glanced at the still simmering Rass Bodine. His fists were tightly clinched at the very mention of Cobb's name.

Hammond studied Muldoon and his men. He and Macrae exchanged words under their breath, and Hammond spoke up. "Poor Soul, why don't you head on back to the remuda. You can leave these men to us. I'm sure we can reach an understanding here."

Poor Soul nodded. The information that Zac might be in Dodge City, the brother that all the rest of them thought had died in the war, made him anxious to get back to Joe with the news.

He took one more sharp look at Bodine and then spoke to

Muldoon. "Mister, I'd suggest you teach your dog here to watch which bull he chases across the field. Some of them have horns." With that, he clapped his spurs to the sides of his horse and took off like a shot.

Riding up to Joe at a full gallop, he skidded to a halt, his face beaming.

Joe was looking past him at the continued conference on the top of the hill. "I don't like it," Joe said. "All them rawhiders and Hammond, Macrae, and Yanni to boot. They're like a bunch of cats talkin' 'bout all them fat mice in the barn."

CHAPTER 32

+ + + + + + +

HOURS LATER, as the sun hovered high in the western sky, Joe and Poor Soul spotted an airborne swarm of vultures. Close to ten of the big birds swung lazily in the sky, their wings dipping, sending them into ever narrowing circles over something they had spotted either dead or dying. Neither man was quick to move and inspect the spot. The number of birds indicated that whatever the birds had their eyes on was indeed large. It might have been a dead or dying horse, or some cow that had long since wandered too far and gotten into trouble.

Joe and Poor Soul continued to move the horses, swinging their lariats and whistling to the milling mustangs. Karen was riding with them now. She had brought the used-up string back to the remuda after she supplied the men with fresh mounts. "What you reckon it is?" Joe asked.

"Normally I'd suspect it to be some critter that got a leg broke," Poor Soul replied. "But with those rawhiders we come upon this morning, I s'pose it don't pay to take much for granted."

"Grass is good here," Joe said. "You just hold 'em here and I'll go take a look. If it is a horse or cow, I'll just put the thing down."

"I'll ride with you," Karen said.

"Good, I'll be glad for the company."

The two of them rode off toward the circle of buzzards, trotting their mounts in leisurely fashion.

"You haven't said much these past few days," Joe said. It

seemed obvious to him that she had something to say, or she wouldn't have volunteered to ride with him.

"I feel a little silly about what I did," Karen said matter-of-factly. "The disguise, I mean. I suppose I should explain."

"Karen, here in the West a fella takes what comes. There's no need to explain, or to ask questions. I figure you had good reason. If it was right for you at the time, that's all I need to know."

"You really trust people, don't you?"

"Until they give me reason not to."

"That's why I need to explain. I let on I was something I wasn't, and your trust is important to me."

Joe pulled up rein and stopped. "Karen, I trust you. You did what was required. Far as I'm concerned, I'd ride with you any day."

"Even though I'm a woman?" She pulled up beside him.

"You're a durn good hand, no matter what. And now that you quit wearin' that dirt on your face and dressing more like the woman you are," he said, looking at her admiringly, "I must admit you're a mite more pleasin' to the eyes."

Her face flushed, sending the roses to her cheeks. "I just wanted to be noticed for the work I did, that's all. I figured I could do the job same as any man. Now, I guess, I want to be seen for what I really am . . . especially by you."

She slapped the rawhide thong to the rump of her horse and bolted ahead, leaving him to watch her as she rode. There was an audacity to Karen that would catch any man's eye, a boldness and a beauty in everything she did. She was a woman of purpose. A blind man could see it. Joe shook his head. It would take a bit of getting used to—Car . . . as a woman—but it was an adjustment Joe was more than willing to make. He spurred his horse forward and took a lope behind her in the direction of the birds.

As they crested a hill moments later, they both caught sight of a brightly colored wagon. Whatever had been pulling the rig had been driven off, but the buzzards were circling for another reason. Stretched out beside the wagon was a man, stripped almost bare. His gray head was moving from side to side, showing signs of life and keeping the buzzards in the air. His hands and legs were secured by rawhide tethers attached to stakes driven into the ground.

Karen skidded her gelding to a stop near the man, and Joe brought his horse to a halt nearby. Their movement sent several buzzards flapping into the air after a short landing.

Joe unstrapped a blanket from behind his saddle and took out his wooden canteen. After laying the bright green wool over the man, he drew his knife and cut the leather shackles.

The old man's eyelids drooped, and Joe took off his bright red bandanna and moistened it. Kneeling beside the man, still without speaking, he gently sponged his face with the cool cloth.

The man moaned and moved his mouth, as though craving the moisture. Joe held the canteen to his lips and allowed a few sips.

"Take it slow, pardner, I got plenty."

Karen stood over him. "Indians do this to you?" she asked.

He shook his head and with great effort croaked out the name: "Mul . . . doon."

Joe looked up at Karen. "Find the chuck wagon, will you?" he said. "We can't move him till we get a travois rigged to pull him. Get a couple of them long tent poles Pera's been hauling, and bring some extra blankets and piggin' strings."

Without another word, Karen swung back onto her mount and galloped off toward the herd.

Joe gave the old man more sips of cool water, then pulled back the blanket to inspect for any further damage. His ribs were tender, but nothing was broken. Someone had given the poor fellow quite a beating. The sun was setting when Karen rode back with Barb. They were leading a spare horse and carrying the equipment Joe had asked for.

Joe rigged the travois to the extra horse and laced two of the blankets to the poles to support the injured man. Gingerly lifting him, Joe at the head, the women at his feet, they placed him on the sagging carrier. He tucked his blanket around him and tied him down. "We need to ride back real gentlelike," he said. "This man's gonna need some careful nursin'."

"Who did it?" Barb asked.

"Near as I can figure from what the old gent was able to say, it was white men. More'n likely that same bunch that came a callin' on us this morning."

"Mr. Hammond said those men would be no problem to us," Barb said.

Joe mounted his horse and shot her a look. "If Hammond says that bunch is no problem, then I reckon we got us something else to worry about—that trail boss of ours."

"I've been worried about him since we were branding cattle in War Eagle."

Joe gently urged his horse forward, leading the horse with the travois. "Why'd you pick a man you can't trust?"

Karen spoke up. "Women sometimes find themselves at the mercy of men they can't trust." Her emotions simmered and threatened to spill over. Joe could tell by the sound of her voice. "Barb has placed herself at the risk of marriage . . . to a man she doesn't love . . . if we can't sell the herd."

"Why would you strike a deal like that?" Joe asked.

Barb looked straight ahead. Karen wouldn't let the issue go. "She did it to save the ranch, Joe. She signed papers and everything, agreeing to marry the man."

Barb's eyes narrowed. "A family's life has to count for something. My mother and father gave everything they had to build that place, and I'll not see it pass over to the man that had my father murdered," she said sternly.

"You're right there," Joe agreed. "A family's life has to count for something, but—excuse me for saying so—it counts for the *people* in the family, not the dirt they live on. Your ma and pa gave their lives for their daughters, not their cows. If you give up the life and dignity they gave themselves for in order to keep the place they lived on, you will have missed what they was aimin' at by a far sight."

Both Barb and Karen were subdued by Joe's reasoning. It made sense. "Joe," Barb began, "you know, if anyone else called me to task for what we're doing, I might be angry, but my sisters and I respect you."

"How can you understand what we've gone through, what we're facing now?" Karen asked Joe.

"Well, my pa wasn't murdered, but I can sure respect your feelin's on that score. The war did take away everything we ever built, though, and scattered us boys like a bunch a flushed quails. Poor Soul just told me that a brother a mine might be up ahead in Dodge, one I ain't seen since '63. Sure hope it's true. My folks gave us something no bluebellies, carpetbaggers, or scalawags can ever take away. They gave us love: love for people, love for each other, and a love for God. That's what they built in us, and nobody can take that away."

"You're right," Barb said, nodding her head slowly.

"I do know a lawyer who'd be happy to take a look at them papers you signed." He smiled. "He's a Yale lawman."

"I'm sure he would," Karen grinned.

Barb quickly changed the subject. "Aren't we too close to Dodge for those men to attack us?"

"More'n likely that bunch holds up in Dodge. Where are we camped?"

"Some farmers practically begged us to use their land over east of here."

Joe kept up the gentle tug on the horse that carried the travois. "I shouldn't wonder why. Considering all the fertilizer left behind by that many head a cattle, them folks'd be set for some time to come. With the buffalo long gone, Texas cattle passin' through is the next best thing, to a farmer's way a thinkin'."

"Sod busters and cowmen," Barb mused. "They sure are two different types of people."

+ + + + +

It was noon the following day before the herd moved down Front Street, Zac was seated in the Longbranch Saloon. Keeping himself in a public place whenever possible seemed to be in his best interest, at least until the gang made another move on Wells Fargo money. Wyatt Earp walked through the swinging doors and stood beside Zac.

"It may be time for the ball to open up 'round here," he said.

Zac looked up, pushing back his hat.

"There's been a bank robbery over in Cimarron. The sheriff is getting up a posse for what could be a long chase, and I'm elected to go with him. Seems like a strange thing for him to want me to do, with that herd coming in and all. It's probably one of the last drives of the season."

"You think it's a wild goose chase?"

"No, that bank was hit all right, but I think you and I both know where we could ride out to and find the loot. The sheriff lives too well for earning only a hundred and twenty-five a month. Where he gets the rest of what he spends only time will tell. One thing's for sure, though, he don't want nothing to do with riding out to Muldoon's."

Zac nodded his head.

"I just wanted to come over and tell you that you'd better be carrying that short scatter-gun of yours when I ride outta here, 'cause it's the only help you're gonna get."

Zac smiled. "But that's against the law."

"I don't care. Let's just hope that what them people don't know won't hurt them, until it's too late to make a difference. Those short little cannons can be quite a surprise."

"Yes, they can."

"The one thing I would tell you, Cobb, is to stay in town. Those people would like nothing better than to find a way to get you out of Dodge, even for a little bit. They might even try to pull something off to get you out of here. They got their people out in the street," he lifted his head and swung his gaze around the room, "even two people in here. They watch everything you do, and everyone you talk to."

"I've put you in danger, then."

"I put myself in danger when I pinned on this badge and swore to uphold the law."

People were crowding to the door and out onto the boardwalk to watch the herd move through the street. Charlie Harrow got up from his seat and moved to the door. "It seems we finally got some cattle to buy. You wanna take a look?"

Zac got up from his chair and he and Earp joined Harrow on

the boardwalk. The cattle were flanked on either side by cow-boys trying to hold them in as narrow a line as possible. "This is a sight that won't be seen for much longer," Harrow said. "The days of the wild and woolly Texas drives are coming to an end I'm afeared."

The cowboys couldn't keep from gawking at the windows on the street. This was the place they'd all be spending their hard-earned money, a place that held fancies they'd only dreamed about up till now. From the balconies above the street, ladies of the night whistled and waved long scarves at the men passing below. Respectable women on the sidewalks shook their heads and spoke in subdued tones.

Down the street, Zac spotted the remuda, a black cowboy leading them. His hat thrown back from his head, he waved to the ladies on the balconies, laughing as he did so. The face was somewhat familiar to Zac, but the laugh was a dead giveaway. He stepped out into the street and called out, "Poor Soul!"

The cowboy jerked his head forward and stared, then hol-lered across the horses at a dusty-haired cowboy riding on the other side of the street. "It's Zac!" he yelled. "That's him up yonder, bolder than brass."

Joe wove his way through the remuda and pulled up to the saloon. Jumping from his horse, he threw back his hat, and Zac ran to embrace him.

"You . . . in Dodge City of all places." Joe pushed Zac back at arm's length, then touched his face with one hand. "I never thought I'd see you again, brother."

Zac gripped Joe's arms tightly. "After the surrender I walked home, but no one was there, only Ma and Pa's graves. I waited around till the place had to be taken for taxes."

Poor Soul ambled up, having given the brothers a few min-utes to themselves. He looped his reins around the hitching rail and took hold of Zac's arm. "You sure are a sight to behold, boy, a mighty good sight to behold."

Zac shook his hand and embraced him with his other arm. Looking at Joe, he asked, "He still spoutin' Shakespeare?"

"Can't shut him up. Likes to show off Momma's education."

"Well, I reckon one of us should," Zac replied.

"Look, little brother, we got to get this herd penned up over at the stockyards. Where can we find you after we're done? I got some people I'd like you to meet."

"He's got a woman," Poor Soul confided. "A fine Texas woman."

"Why doesn't that surprise me?" Zac said with a smile. "And I got a boy I want you to meet."

"A boy? You married, Zac?"

"No, no. It's a long story, but I'll fill you in soon enough." Zac knew Muldoon's men were eyeballing the reunion. "We can't talk here, though, too many eyes and ears. I'll get us a big table over at the Bon Ton. Maybe you can finally eat some of that beef you been movin'."

"Now you're talkin'," Poor Soul said. "We're gonna say the finest grace ever said west of the Mississippi."

CHAPTER 33

+ + + + + + +

RANDOLPH AND CROSSY HELD open the large
gates that surrounded the cattle pens, forming a shoot that allowed the herd to march in behind Big Red and his clanging bell.
Yanni and Tipper stood their horses close to the gate, preventing
any independent-minded sorts from milling back into the herd
or continuing on past the gate. Dorothy and Vonnie were bringing up the drag, slapping their lariats to the rumps of the plod-
ding beasts and keeping them in line.

The march down Front Street had gone off without a hitch.
As tired as everybody was, there was an exhilaration in each
drover at the prospect of ending the drive. Barb, Hammond, and
Charlie Harrow stood at the gate, each one making an inde-
pendent count of the number as they passed. With each count
of a hundred, Harrow gave a wide grin.

Karen, Joe, and Poor Soul put the horses into a corral. Then
they stripped the ones they'd been riding of their saddles and
slapped them into the wooden pen to join the rest of the remuda. "Feels good, don't it?" Joe said.

Karen nodded and smiled. "Real good," she said.

"Desire fulfilled is sweet to the soul. There just ain't nothing
like starting out to do something, and then seein' it done."

The stockyards were on the edge of town next to the tracks.
The three lifted their saddles and gear and began to walk back
down the street. Joe knew enough not to offer to carry Karen's,
even though he wanted to. Lately he found himself thinking
about her and what she wanted all of the time. It was a strange

feeling, one that he wasn't accustomed to.

"After we get cleaned up, I want you to join me and Poor Soul over at the Bon Ton Restaurant we just passed. Though I'll miss Pera's fresh bread, meals on real plates will be real pleasurable."

She smiled. "I'd love to."

"I'll pass on the invite to your sisters too."

She nodded.

The three of them stopped by the stockyards and watched the last of the tabulations. Charlie Harrow scratched out the last of his figures. "I count three thousand, four hundred and sixty-five yearlings or better, and another eight hundred and forty-six young ones."

"Mine's pretty close to that." Hammond leaned over and showed his numbers.

Randolph helped Barb down from the platform that had been built on the side of the wooden pen fence. "I reckon we ought to go and discuss the sale," he said.

"We can go up to the office," Harrow added. "I'll make you a mighty fine offer."

Joe set down his saddle. "Miss Barbara, I want you and your sisters to join Poor Soul and me over at the Bon Ton for a meal after you get yerselves settled here. I want you to meet my brother."

"That would be lovely, Joe. We'd be delighted to."

"Oh, and bring that lawyer cowboy with you."

"Thanks, Reb," Randolph said. "You pay and I'll eat. Got no problem there."

Minutes later, Barb, Randolph, Hammond, and Macrae settled down in the cowhide chairs and couches scattered about the stockyard office. Hammond and Macrae looked tense, while the rest of the group were the picture of instant satisfaction.

Charlie Harrow poured liquor for the men, and offered Barb a glass of ice water. "We ain't had much to buy since that first fall snow. I can pay top dollar for your herd—thirty-two dollars a piece for the yearlings, and nine for the calves. That's a tidy sum by anybody's standards—over one hundred and ten thousand dollars."

"One hundred and eighteen thousand, six hundred and twenty-six, to be exact," Randolph said.

"That's mighty quick cipherin' there, fella," Harrow said.

Hammond glared at him. "We got ourselves some quick cowboys. You'd be plumb amazed."

"I'll have to think it over, Mr. Harrow," Barb said. "I'll need to entertain other offers and talk them over with my sisters."

"You won't get better offers than this one. Some might quote you a slightly higher price, but then they'll inspect the herd and start chippin' away."

"The men will want to be paid right now," Hammond interjected. "They'll need drinkin' and spendin' money. It's been a long, hard drive, and they won't be wantin' to wait for some decision from you tomorrow or the next day."

"That won't be a problem," said Harrow. "I can advance you five thousand dollars to pay your drovers and then we can settle accounts when you're ready. You won't have to sell to me, if you choose to go elsewhere; you can just repay me. I don't keep all the money here, but I got enough to do that."

Barb looked at Randolph and he nodded in agreement.

Harrow walked over to the desk and took a piece of paper, scratching figures into the blanks provided by the boiler-plate agreement. He opened the safe and extracted a stack of bills, counting them out as Randolph looked over the agreement.

"Seems all right," Randolph said.

Barb scratched her signature onto the document and placed the money in her purse. "Mr. Hammond," she said, "have the men meet me downstairs. I'll pay them there and they can sign for the money."

Hammond and Macrae grinned.

Thirty minutes later, the men had all been paid and Barb and Randolph walked toward the hotel to find rooms and clean up. "It always makes me nervous to sign papers," she said.

"Well, right now you owe Charlie Harrow five thousand dollars, but you're good for it, you and those cattle back there. We haven't even started to think about the sale of the horses yet, but they ought to bring a pretty penny up here."

Over two hours later, the Reddiger women, accompanied by Lance Randolph and Tipper, entered the Bon Ton Restaurant. Zac, Poor Soul, and Joe had been there at an oversized table with Skip for an hour or better, talking about home and what had happened to their lives since they had last seen each other. Skip's head bounced from man to man as they spoke, soaking in all he could of what it meant to belong to the Cobb family. They spotted the women, now in dresses, and got to their feet, scooting back empty chairs.

Joe held a chair for Karen, unable to wipe the grin off his face. Seeing her in a dress that brought out the blue of her eyes, and her short hair adorned with a ribbon was almost more than he could handle.

Joe made introductions as each took a seat.

"You boys are looking at some rich women," Randolph smiled, holding out Barb's chair.

"I wouldn't exactly say rich," Barb corrected. "Over half the money will go to pay off the ranch; the rest will buy stock for the place."

"But it will all belong to you Reddigers."

Steaks were served around quickly, and a waiter stood by to ensure that everyone was satisfied with the preparation of their meal. Joe led them in a short word of grace, and then put his knife to the tender beef.

Skip noticed that Poor Soul had not been served. "Mm-m-m . . . what about him?" he asked.

Zac motioned to the waiter. "You forgot to serve our friend here," he said.

The waiter looked anxiously toward the back room. "I'm sorry, sir, but we don't serve buffalo skins here at the Bon Ton. He'll have to eat in the back with the help."

Zac started to get to his feet, but Joe reached over and put his hand on his brother's arm. "What seems to be the problem? Isn't our money any good?" Joe asked.

"Yes, sir, your money is fine. But the cook will not prepare food for a darky."

Once again Joe had to hold Zac in his chair. "Little brother, you've always been a bit quick on the scrap. Just settle down. Me and Poor Soul here have been traveling together since the war. We've widened more narrow heads than I can recollect."

Joe got to his feet and took the napkin from around his neck, dropping it on the table. "Now, why don't you just show me this stove of yours. I'll cook my friend his steak. Besides, I know how he likes it, and more than likely your man would burn it."

"I don't know . . . I don't know if we can do that."

Joe smiled an innocent smile. His calm expression was in sharp contrast to every other one around the table. "Believe me, mister, you don't want my little brother Zac to go back there. When he's all het up it ain't a pretty sight. He's an unreconstructed Rebel, you know."

The waiter reluctantly led Joe back to the kitchen. Within a matter of minutes, Joe returned to the dining room with a rare steak that was larger than the plate he carried it on. He placed the meat in front of Poor Soul, took a napkin and flung it open on the black man's lap. "Now, sir, will there be anything else while I'm up?"

Poor Soul laughed, and Joe held his hand up. "I ask only one thing of you, my friend."

"What's that?" Poor Soul asked.

"That you keep Shakespeare from the dinner table."

"Fair enough. Why would I want to waste my education on the likes of you anyway? That would be casting my pearls before swine."

Joe sat down and picked up his napkin. "Hungry swine," he said.

They continued to eat, and Joe looked over at the boy and said. "Son, I'm curious about your use of 'mm-m-m' before your words."

"Mm-m-m . . . Dr. Marvin taught me. It keeps me from stuttering."

"They ran the man out of town a short time ago," Zac explained, "a medicine drummer—medicine, sundries, and clocks."

"The man who has Jesus' healing waters for the dropsy?" Poor Soul asked.

"Yes," Zac said. "That's the one. Do you know him?"

"We picked him up two days north of here," Joe said. "He was all staked out for the buzzards, Injunlike, only weren't no Injuns that done it."

"Where is he?" Skip asked excitedly.

"Pera took him over to the doc's. From the way the man looked, I'd say he'd be there for a while—days more'n likely."

Skip looked excitedly at Zac. "C-c-can I go? Can I go see Dr. Marvin?"

Zac nodded, and the boy pushed back his chair and scampered out the door before anyone could change his mind.

"The kid's all right," Joe said.

"He's more than all right," Zac added. "He's all I got in this world."

When they finished the meal, Randolph got to his feet. He put his hand on Vonnie's and Tipper's shoulders. "I ain't much for drinking and smoking. You mind if I take the youngsters down to the stockyards? It'll give us a chance to say goodbye to all those cattle we've been sleeping with on the trail. I'll stop by the doc's place and pick up your boy too."

Zac and Barb nodded their approval.

After the three left, Joe turned to Karen. "Would you care to take a walk? We could look at some city houses up on the hill, see how folks in town live."

"That would be nice," Karen responded.

Dorothy and Barb smiled at each other.

+ + + + +

Dusk settled on Dodge City as Joe and Karen walked up the hill. Dim lights glowed from the houses, making them look cozy and happily occupied.

Joe and Karen paused in front of one. Through the large window they could see candles burning at a dinner table, a family seated around it. The man at the head, presumably the father, was carving a large roast. Turning away, Joe said sheepishly,

"Funny, I never thought much about such things."

"You mean families gathered for dinner?"

He looked at her from the corner of his eye. She was looking straight at him. "Yes . . . I guess that's what I mean."

They began their leisurely walk back. Joe took Karen's hand gently in his. It had been so long since he held a pretty girl's hand—any girl's, for that matter. It felt so natural, so relaxed, Karen's hand in his. Warm, comforting. "You look beautiful, Karen."

She smiled. "Thank you, Joe. I feel beautiful tonight. Can't remember when that even mattered to me."

"Do you remember the night on the range when I babbled on about the kind of woman I dreamed of marrying?"

"Yes, I do recall something of the sort. You rambled on, 'course not knowing I was a woman. If you'd known me as a woman from the beginning, you probably wouldn't have had anything to do with me . . . would you?"

"No, I guess not. I tend to fight shy of womenfolk."

"And if I hadn't been trying to be a man, I wouldn't have let you get close to me, even if you'd wanted to."

They continued to walk on hand in hand through the growing darkness. The music from the saloons blared down Front Street, but everything around them seemed strangely serene and quiet. Karen asked coyly, "Am I soft and pink like a nursery?"

Joe stopped, turned to face her. He took her other hand and, holding the two up close to his chest, said, "Yes, ma'am, you are at that. And I'm here to tell you that I could have no fonder dream of a woman than I'm seeing right now."

Karen blinked back a tear, afraid to speak. Afraid if she did, the moment would spin off into the darkness never to be retrieved again. It was like a flash of magic, a wink of time that each wanted to savor forever.

Joe swallowed hard. "Since I already stepped out on a limb here, would you permit me to go ahead and make a complete fool of myself?"

"Why don't you let me be the judge of that?"

He swallowed hard once more. "Well, you're a woman of means now, and I'm just a no-count cowboy. There's no cause for a pretty lady like you to settle for someone like me." He stopped and shook his head.

"Are you saying you love me, Joe?"

His eyes widened. "I-I'm not exactly sure what that means, but I do know that I'll never be able to look on another woman."

"Well, truth is, I won't always smell of cologne, or wear a gardenia in my hair. After breaking a horse, I won't have the grace of an angel. But I'd like you to think all those things about me just the same, Joe."

She put her hands on his shoulders and looked straight into his eyes. "I've never in my life done what I was supposed to do, what was expected of a proper woman, but I know one thing, Joseph Cobb. I do love you."

"And . . . I love you, Karen. I want you to be my wife more than anything else I've ever wanted in my whole life."

"Good," she smiled.

"Is that a yes?"

"Yes." She wound her arms around his neck and their lips met, gently at first.

Several hours later, when they seemed to have talked for only moments of their dreams and plans, the two started back to Front Street.

"When Father read the Bible," Karen went on, "he'd always tell us that the plans of God were so much better than our own."

"I know, my pa used to say the same thing. I can almost hear him now: 'Son, God's way is better.' You know, for the life of me I could never figure out how that would be possible. I've always placed a whole lot of stock in my own thinking. But now I know how right my pa was. This morning I was a simple cowboy ready for payday, and now I've got plans to marry the woman I've always dreamed of, and found a brother I ain't seen in fifteen years. This sure has been some day."

"Karen! Joe!" They pulled their heads up and saw Dorothy running up the hill. Her skirts were hiked above her knees and she was out of breath when she reached them.

"They're gone! They're gone!"

"Who's gone?" Joe asked. "What's gone?"

Dorothy began to sob. "Randolph and Tipper are hurt real bad, and Vonnie and Skip are gone, along with the herd."

CHAPTER 34

+ + + + + + +

ZAC WAS AWAKENED by a pounding on his door. He'd waited for Skip to return, but figuring the boy had taken to sitting up with the old drummer, he'd drifted off to sleep.

"Zac, open up. It's me, Joe."

Zac opened the door to the look of panic in his brother's eyes.

"Your boy's gone, been taken along with the youngest Reddiger girl. The herd's gone too. They must have been with it when the rustlers struck." Joe shook his head. "It beats all. What kind a place is this that rustlers will steal a herd of cattle right out of the stock pens? Where could they hope to sell them?"

Zac buckled on his gun belt. He tossed the big rifle to Joe and slipped an ammo cartridge belt over his shoulder. "It's just the kind of place I told you about before dinner. Those men want me, and now they're gonna get me. How many of your men can we count on?"

"They've all been paid. Randolph and Tipper are with the doc—they won't be able to go nowhere. They've been stoved in pretty bad. Crossy took the eastbound for Kansas City, and Macrae and Hammond are nowhere to be found. Dorothy's out looking for Yanni. He may be in on it along with them other two for all I know. I'm afraid all we got is you, me, Poor Soul, the cook Pera, and the Reddigers."

Zac scooped up shotgun shells and put them into a saddlebag. "We won't be takin' no women."

"Little brother, you don't know these women. It's their sister and it's their cattle, and as much as I'd like to back your play on this, you couldn't keep 'em away if you tied them up. Those rustlers couldn't have gotten very far. Near as we can figure, they only got about a three- or four-hour lead at best."

"I know where they are. It's not more than an hour away, a place owned by the flower of the Dodge City community."

+ + + + +

At the same time Joe was finding Zac, Dorothy had gone upstairs at the Alamo Saloon, the place where Yanni had last been spotted. She felt out of place in the smoke-filled, stale-smelling hall. From behind the doors drifted the smell of cheap perfume, the laughter of giddy women, and the voices of men with too much liquor under their belts. Why she'd volunteered to find the man, she would never know. But they needed him bad, and they needed his gun.

She stood in front of a door with a number 9 scrawled in charcoal on the dirty white paint. The man behind the bar, who seemed surprised to see her in the saloon at this hour, had told her the young cowboy was in number 9 with a woman called Tiger Tooth. Dorothy paused, summoning up every ounce of courage inside her. She rapped on the door loudly. "Yanni! Are you in there, Yanni?"

"Who is it?" he yelled.

"It's me, Dorothy."

There was silence, and her heart sunk.

The door to room number 11 opened and a man in red long johns stuck his head out, rubbing his eyes and blinking at her.

"Please, Yanni," she tried again. "Something terrible has happened. We need you to come and help. Please don't make me stand out here."

"Come on in, darlin'. The door's open."

Hating the thought of entering the dingy room, Dorothy turned the white knob and slowly pushed the door open. A flickering red Tiffany lamp cast moving shadows about the small, cramped room. There was a brass bed in the middle of it. Her eyes adjusted to the dim light and fell on Yanni. "Yanni, we need your help . . . right away."

The woman next to him pushed back her hair. "Who's this?"

"It's one of them women I worked for."

The woman grunted. "For a minute I thought it was your wife."

Dorothy averted her eyes from the woman. "Vonnie and a young boy have been kidnapped. Randolph and Tipper were badly beaten. The herd's been stolen too. Please, help us go after Vonnie and the boy."

Yanni scratched his head. "Well, I ain't exactly working for you no more."

"I know that, I just thought maybe you'd help. Crossy's already left on the train, and we need every man we can get."

"Why should I? I done pulled your fat outta the fire once; that oughta square myself with you."

"You don't owe me anything, Yanni. I just thought you'd want to help."

"You got me pegged for somebody else. I might fish you outta the water, but I ain't likely to get into no shootin' war for somebody else's cattle."

"It's not for the cattle. It's Vonnie we need to find."

Yanni ignored her plea. "You really got me misfigured. That Hammond and Macrae joined up with them rawhiders. I was there when they talked about it. Those men are rough; they shoot to kill. No, ma'am, I ain't gettin' up from my comfort here till noon tomorrow."

"You knew about this?"

"I knew they was gonna take the herd, but I didn't know nothing about your sister and all. Don't take it out on me—after all, I didn't go with 'em. They gave me an invite with plenty of money in it, but I didn't go."

The blood rose in Dorothy's face, and she stomped over to the bed. "You miserable cowboy! You knew they were going to do this, and you said nothing?" Without warning she slapped Yanni soundly, rocking him back on the pillows. "Your father was right about you. Whatever soul you have left is nothing more than a rusted corkscrew."

She turned and walked to the door. Holding it open, she shot him a withering look. "For a while I thought better of you, but I guess I really am ignorant about men. If anything happens to my sister, you better not be within fifty miles of this place when we get back."

+ + + + +

Quirt Muldoon stirred the fire in his massive stone fireplace. The shiny floor was cluttered with the skins of cattle, sheep, goats, and bears. He squatted near the jaws of a large black bear and used a steel rod to probe the licking flames.

He had wrapped a shawl around his shoulders. No one could get a true indication of the weather by what Muldoon wore. He might be out in a snowstorm in his shirtsleeves, or be hugging the fire in a fireplace in the middle of summer.

The weather of late had been unpredictable. Dark clouds might bring hail and snow as easily as warm rain. The blizzard that had swept through the plains several weeks back had been followed by warm rains and then blue skies.

What had looked to be the start of an early winter had become one of the warmest, wettest falls anyone could recall. The wind started to howl sometime after midnight, and when Muldoon stepped outside to survey the sky, he could see the fast-moving clouds covering the moon and stars. It was then that he decided to build a fire.

Hours later, Muldoon was stirred awake by the sound of thunder. He had fallen asleep at his desk. Lightning flashed outside the large window behind his desk, and the door down the hall flew open. It was Jock O'Connor, followed by the newest business partners, Pete Hammond and Wolf Macrae.

"It went better than any of us expected," O'Connor said when he entered the room. "There was no gunplay at all, although Hammond and Macrae here did take down a couple of those cowboys who might have wanted to interfere."

"Where are the cattle?"

"Just north of here."

Muldoon pulled his shawl closer. "Keep them cattle off of my place, at least for now. I don't expect the sheriff and that posse of his back for another four or five days, but until we get this matter of Zac Cobb taken care of, I don't want any of them things traced to me."

"When do we get paid?" Hammond asked. "Macrae and me is gonna want to get back down to War Eagle just as fast as we can. We got things to settle up down there too."

"That we do," Macrae added. Wolf Macrae was normally a man of few words. "I got me some money to collect on my own."

Hammond smirked a half smile. "This whole thing started with Wolf," Hammond said, "and it should have ended right there too. The man who hired us down in Texas never thought this drive would happen when he hired Wolf here to put a bullet into the old man who owned the herd. Then, when the man's daughters decided the drive was still on, he made sure we'd be well paid if these cattle didn't get sold."

Muldoon knelt beside the safe and twisted the tumblers. Opening the door, he took out two stacks of bills, each wrapped with a band marked "Wells Fargo." He closed the safe and spun the dial. "There you are, gentlemen. One thousand dollars each, as promised."

Hammond stuffed the stack into his pocket at once, but Macrae carefully fingered through the bills, silently counting.

"You are going to be wealthy men when you get home, collecting from me, and then from your Texas benefactor as well." Muldoon smiled. "I'm sure those women paid you too."

"Oh yes," Hammond said, "I made sure of that. And with the cattle gone, they'll be owing the man who put up the finances to pay the men. That ought to fix their wagon for good."

"Aye, there's nothing like the smell of cold cash, is there, Jock?"

The big Irishman gave a grin.

"You men had better get back to those cattle. We will need your guns when those people get here, it's part of what I just paid you for. You do your work well, and I'll always be here for any new herd you bring up the trail."

Hammond and Macrae nodded. They turned and shuffled back through the door. Muldoon pulled O'Connor aside. "Make sure you finish those dudes off. I know the man they're working for. He'll thank me by sending more business. I can't have any loose ends to what we're about here. Besides, those men are carrying your bonus in their pockets. Make sure you take care of that Buster fella as well."

The door opened and Rass Bodine pushed Skip into the room, followed by Buster and Vonnie. Muldoon's mouth dropped open. "What did you bring them here for?"

"Weather's bad out there," Bodine answered. "Storm clouds comin' on somethin' fierce."

Muldoon lashed out at the man with the back of his hand, rocking him with a slap. "You fool!" he shouted.

Bodine's right hand quickly pulled out one of his revolvers.

Muldoon was unfazed. "Put that thing away, you snake. You ever pull a gun on me again and I'll kill you where you stand."

O'Connor had drawn his own revolver and had it pointed at the gunman. He cocked the six-shooter, and the sound of the hammer moving into place froze Bodine. Muldoon looked at the boy. "This wasn't necessary. He'd have come anyway. I know that man. Where there's women involved, and a brother too, wild horses couldn't have kept him in Dodge City. Your problem"—he leaned into Bodine—"is that there's so much hatred in you for the beating you took, it clouds yer thinking. There's no need to get Cobb killing mad, and there certainly isn't any call to have us arrested for kidnapping a child."

Bodine quietly holstered his gun. "You said Buster could have the girl."

"That's his business. You've brought these kids here, and we can't have that."

CHAPTER 35

+ + + + + + +

IT WAS ALMOST DAWN when Bodine and Buster returned to the draw with Skip. O'Connor had stayed behind with the girl. The cattle had been taken to a flat area behind them, and the men had started fires to give off the appearance of a camp. Bodine tied Skip up next to a tree, with a length of rope wrapped around the narrow scrub oak.

"Mm-m-m . . . you gonna kill me now?" Skip asked.

"I ain't gonna kill you, kid. In spite of what that white freak mighta said, I ain't no baby killer. I want that man who's comin' after you."

The rain was pelting Skip's face. He blinked it out of his eyes. "There's been lotsa men tried to do that, I seen it myself a time or two. But ain't none of 'em done it, and you ain't a gonna do it neither."

"Bold talk for a little kid." Bodine tightened the cords around Skip's wrists.

"Mm-m-m . . . It ain't just talk. I seen him up against better men than you. 'Sides, if'n I die, I know where I'm a goin', and it's a better place. I know where you're goin', too, and you could be goin' there today."

The thought sent a shiver up Bodine's spine, but he said nothing. He took out a handkerchief and clamped it into the boy's mouth, tying it into a knot behind his head. "There, that oughta shut you up."

He signaled to Hammond and Macrae, pointing to a knoll off to the left. "You two take your long guns and get up that rise.

Anybody rides down here, shoot to kill."

The men nodded and rode their horses up the rise with Buster. They picketed the animals behind the small hill and took their position. Below them, they could see the tree with the boy tethered to it. A shallow creek ran the length of the draw, and behind the boy was the low ground that they had taken the cattle through. They watched Bodine take his position with seven or eight other men on another small rise the other side of the boy.

Now all they had to do was endure the driving rain out in the open and wait. They pulled their hats low and turned up the collars of their jackets. The wind was blowing hard, and overhead they could see dark clouds continuing to form. They had hoped the sunrise behind them would give them the advantage of the sun in the faces of the men who were coming, but now that wouldn't be possible.

"Those men over there have got more staked out than that boy," Hammond said.

"Durn right," Macrae shot back. "Eight of them over yonder, and they got just the three of us up here."

And the three were mighty uncomfortable. They felt isolated in the wind and rain. Men who were uncomfortable had little motivation to stay put.

"We got the money we came for," Hammond said. "When the shooting commences, if we don't get them people on the first pass, I'm lightin' out for Texas. We'll let the old white man take the heat for this."

Macrae nodded his agreement.

"I still got to get the girl I come for," Buster shouted over the wind. "I ain't a goin' nowhere without her."

"You're on your own, then," Hammond replied. "Suit yourself. A dead man ain't no good for nothing."

Macrae stifled a sly smile. In all the time he had known him, Pete Hammond could always be counted on to make sure he was well protected. He took no chances when it came to saving his own skin. It was why Macrae had been picked to kill Will Reddiger and not Hammond.

A few miles to the west, Zac rode the horse he'd gotten from the livery. Behind him, Joe rode with Poor Soul, Pera, and the Reddiger sisters. The trail of a large herd of cattle was easy to follow, even in driving rain and semidarkness. But Zac didn't like the look of the clouds. Yesterday had been unusually warm, and now the sudden storm, accompanied by wind, spelled danger.

He looped his bandanna over the top of his hat and knotted it securely under his chin. The rain poured from the brim of the beaten gray hat. It should have been well past dawn, but the sky was still in total darkness. Fires glimmered in the distance. Dismounting, Zac held the horse securely as the animal shied from the storm.

The group rode up to him. "Why are we stopping?" Joe asked.

"We'd be better off on foot for a ways. They can't be much farther, and I don't cotton to riding up on 'em, gives them too good a target. In weather like this they can't see too well to shoot nohow, and I don't plan on making it any easier for 'em. We got women here."

"Don't do anything different on our account," Karen said. "We can take care of ourselves."

"Ma'am, I ain't about to let this brother of mine become a widower before he's a groom. Now you and the rest of you folks just get off them horses and hold 'em fast. When the shooting starts, they just might take off." He pointed off to the south. "That high cloud in particular has me worried."

Joe stepped out of his saddle and signaled for the rest to join them. "Zac, I guess you know we're putting you in charge. From what we heard last night, you've had a bit more experience with these types than the rest of us."

Poor Soul checked the loads in his revolver and placed a sixth round under the hammer.

Zac turned to him. "That's the idea. You'd all best be fully loaded, rifles and all. And take extra ammunition out of those saddlebags. When the shooting starts and this storm kicks up, we don't want these horses running back to Dodge City with our munitions."

"You will see that Poor Soul here has become quite good with a gun," Joe said.

"I can tell that from the cut of him," Zac replied.

"In fact, he's about the fastest, best I've ever seen with a short gun," Joe said.

"Being a man of color," Poor Soul said, "I've had to put up with a lot. Knowing I can defend myself in a tight spot gives me confidence, and confidence does something for a man."

"I can'ta be shooting with one of them short guns," Pera said. "To be honest, I'm nota much good with anything short of a spoon."

"Just use the rifle then," Zac said. "When we tell you, you can lay down fire in their direction. It will keep their heads down at the very least. Now let's all move forward real slowlike. Keep your eyes open on the tops of those ridges over yonder, and stay low, real low."

Zac slung the big rifle over his shoulder and handed the shotgun to Dorothy. "You hang on to this. Anybody comes at you women, just wait till they get close, point it, and pull back both triggers. It'll do the rest."

They all moved slowly on foot into the gloom. The sky was getting even darker now, with little or no hint of the sunlight behind it, and the wind had become strong—it flattened the prairie grass—and the rain stung their faces.

Suddenly several shots rang out. The lead buzzed over their heads. "Get down!" Zac yelled. "Let them horses go and get down."

The horses stampeded in the direction of Dodge City. Zac pulled his people together. "The shooting came from the direction of those two hills over yonder, the ones behind that tree. We're gonna break up into two groups—I don't want them concentrating their fire to one spot. Joe, you take the women and Pera here and move south. Keep those people on that hill occupied. Poor Soul and me will slip north. If you see a chance to get behind them, take it. But keep an eye on that high cloud. If it touches down, it'll tear up the ground. I've seen it happen.

And if it comes down, flatten out and don't move. Don't raise your heads for nothing."

"There's somebody tied to that tree," Joe said, pointing.

Zac turned and squinted through the wind. "It's Skip. . . . They got him staked out, waiting for me."

"You be careful!" Joe shouted. "Wait till we get to the place where we can give you some cover."

"You'd better hurry!" Zac shouted back. "I can't leave Skip there. You start shooting first. We'll stay quiet for a while and get them looking your way. And do something for me. . . . Keep them women low."

Joe led his group to the right, directly into the teeth of the whistling wind. They kept low to the ground, almost in a crawl, bracing themselves against the storm.

Zac and Poor Soul moved off to the left. "I can't leave that boy down there," he said.

"You best do what that big brother of yours said. You wait just a bit and give them a chance to get into place."

Minutes later, Zac and Poor Soul were hugging the ground above the flowing creek. They could see Skip clearly, struggling against the ropes that held him to the tree. Lightning had begun to flash in the clouds overhead, and the wind howled in their ears like a thousand hungry wolves. Ahead of them, they could see the hillside dotted with gunmen.

Zac took off the hat and stuffed it down his shirt. "I'm going to crawl down this hill when they start shooting. I'll get as close as I can, and when you see me get up and run, then you cut loose."

Poor Soul nodded. He put his hand on Zac's shoulder. "Boy, if I let anything happen to you, I'm a gonna have to face that momma of yours when I get to heaven. Don't you go puttin' me in a spot like that."

They crept closer and waited. In a matter of minutes, the gunfire from Joe and Pera started. Zac began his crawl down the slope of the shallow draw. He crawled quickly on his elbows, his Sharps rifle nestled in his arms. It puzzled him how men could take a child and put him at such terrible risk, no matter what Muldoon was paying them. There was no way that man was out here in this storm, of that he was sure.

He continued to crawl as the flashes of gunfire started in front of him. They weren't shooting at him. They were returning Joe's fire. If anything happened to Joe or any of the others, he'd have another thing on his conscience. It worried him, but at the same time he was somewhat comforted to know that the men in front of him didn't know he was coming. They would think he was with Joe, returning their fire.

He counted three rifle blasts at Joe's party from the knoll behind the tree. That was another group he'd have to take care of. He continued to crawl forward. He was almost to the creek now, only yards from Skip. The creek bed would give him cover.

Joe kept the women down. They were prone on the ground and firing at the flashes of gunfire on the hill opposite them. Pera pointed his rifle and squinted down the barrel of the gun. He continued to squeeze off round after round, jacking shells into the chamber after each shot.

Dorothy looked off to the right. She could see the high cloud building. "Look at that!" she shouted. A wall of darkness seemed to drop out of the bottom of the towering, menacing funnel. In front of it, she could see a man on horseback. He was whipping his horse, galloping like the devil himself was behind him.

Joe swung his gun around.

"Don't shoot!" Dorothy yelled. "It's Yanni!"

The man rode past them and toward the sound of the popping gunfire on the hill opposite them.

Joe turned back to face the gunfire. "Let's just hope he ain't gonna join 'em."

On the knoll in front of them, Hammond, Buster, and Macrae could see the man approach. "Who's that?" Buster asked.

"It ain't one of them," Hammond shouted. "That there's Yanni."

Yanni scampered his horse up the hill. He jumped down and swatted the rump of the pony, sending him running off from the gathering storm.

Hammond stood up. "Keep yer rifle, you idiot. We'll need it."

"You ain't gonna need nothin' no more!" With that, Yanni jerked his .45 out of his holster. He fired into Hammond's mid-section, jolting him backward. Cocking the pistol, he fired again. The bullet drove itself home, right through the breast pocket of the trail boss, dropping him to his knees, and then face first to the ground.

Macrae leveled his saddle rifle at Yanni and fired a shot that pitched him backward, sprawling him onto the wet ground.

On hearing the shots, Dorothy got up and began to run. "Stop her!" Joe yelled.

"Too late!" Pera shouted. "She's gone."

Joe watched the woman run in the direction of the creek. He turned to her panicked sisters. "Start shooting, and keep it up."

Macrae turned and saw the woman running. Behind them, the horses were pulling at their picket pins. The intensity of the wind coming from the direction of the black wall was sending them into panic. "I'm gettin'!" he yelled. "I'm headin' back to Texas."

"I'm goin' for the gal!" Buster shouted.

The two of them ran down the backside of the hill. Jerking their horses free, they rode off in different directions.

Dorothy ran up the hill. She was out of breath when she found Yanni, and she fell on top of him. Wiping the fresh blood off her hands, she smoothed back his hair. "Yanni, Yanni, you didn't have to come."

His eyes fluttered open. "Yes, I did. I ain't done nothing worthwhile in a long time." He spat up blood. "Would you forgive me?"

"Oh yes! Yes!" She hovered over his face, protecting him from the fierce wind.

"Do you think God will forgive me? Can He remember who I used to be? Before I turned out so wrong?"

"Yes, oh yes, Yanni. God remembers and He knows your heart right now. I will never forget your bravery."

He smiled, and closed his eyes forever.

Zac had watched the woman run up the hillside. The guns had been silenced on the knoll, but in front of him, the main group continued to shoot in the direction of Joe, Pera, and the women. He got up and ran for the tree. From behind him, he could hear Poor Soul cut loose with his rifle. One of the men on the hill above him pitched forward.

When he reached Skip, Zac pulled down the bandanna from the boy's mouth. He took Skip's face in his hands. "Skipper, it's me," he yelled into the wind. "I ain't gonna let nothing happen to you."

Pulling the knife from the sheath between his shoulder blades, Zac cut the ropes. He pulled Skip from the tree and severed the bindings on his wrists, freeing the boy.

The wind bent the tree almost to the ground. The black wall of cloud came closer, and for the first time they could see the funnel dip toward the earth, sending debris into the air. The rumble of the wind was deafening and was heading right toward them.

Zac grabbed Skip's hand. "Run for the creek!" he yelled. They both began a dead run in the direction of the small stream. Throwing themselves over the bank, they lay in the water, Zac holding on tightly to the boy.

CHAPTER 36

✦ ✦ ✦ ✦ ✦ ✦ ✦

THE SEMI-NIGHT that had once passed for daylight turned into total darkness. Overhead the noise of the blast roared like a freight train, drowning out every sound but the beating of Zac's heart. He held Skip down, lifting the boy's face, but pressing him into the shallow water. The world around them was a blur. There was no herd of cattle, no kidnappers, no killers with bullets meant for him. For Zac, there was only Skip, the boy who had become his responsibility. Skip could help him to become a man like his father, a man that could be trusted with the responsibility of another human being.

Lying in the shallow water, they could feel the swirl of the tempest all around them. The tunnel of wind was very close to them. Zac knew any gunmen who remained on the hill were absolute fools. They would be dead men. Nothing could stand in the way of a twister and survive the deadly holocaust. Even bits of debris could become deadly missiles in the hand of the storm.

Zac had seen the aftermath of a tornado before—straw driven into trees like nails, trees uprooted and tossed about like sticks. It was his desperate hope that Poor Soul, Joe, and the others had possessed the good sense to seek low ground, or at the very least to cling to the earth where they lay.

For Zac, there was something about the calm serenity of sure death that made fear disappear. Facing his Maker, knowing he had done everything he could have done in life was a feeling he was well acquainted with. He didn't exactly know where he stood with God, though. From early boyhood, he'd thought himself to be a Christian. He looked at the faith of his folks and thought he took it as his own. But was that enough? He wasn't sure. All he knew for sure was that he continued to break one of God's sacred laws. He killed men for what he considered to be good reasons, but the men were dead all the same, an act that belonged to God alone.

He felt like praying now. Not so much for himself, but for Skip and the others he had led out there. These were lives that he truly valued. He hadn't cared much about his own life the last ten years or so, at least not until Jenny and Skip stepped into it. Now, for the first time in a long while, he felt he really had something to live for: Skip here, and the woman in California. Joe showing up in Dodge City had reminded him about what it meant to be a part of a family, one he could see and remember.

✦ ✦ ✦ ✦ ✦

Buster burst into Muldoon's house only slightly ahead of what he knew was the worst of the storm. "There's a twister headed this way!" he yelled.

Muldoon and O'Connor were in the oversized great room. The fire was out and both of the men were huddled near the wall with Vonnie between them, listening to the sounds of the creaking woodwork and overhead beams.

Buster's look told them they had more to fear than a posse. He took Vonnie's hand and pulled her to her feet. "And if that twister passes us by, you got a lot more to worry about than the wind."

The men blinked, their hands pressed to the wall behind them. "What do you mean?" Muldoon shouted above the noise.

"That man you sent us to kill. If he and his people survive the storm, he's gonna light into you worse'n this wind."

Muldoon got to his feet and turned to O'Connor. "Jock, you stay up here and take him if he comes in. I'm going down to the root cellar."

Muldoon retreated down the hall while Buster watched him,

shaking his head. Holding fast to Vonnie, he asked the cowering O'Connor, "You got somewheres else we can hide?"

"There's a gun vault under the stairs, just as you come in. You'll be safe there." He looked at the struggling girl. "The rifles are all unloaded."

Pulling Vonnie behind him, the young cowboy inched his way along the trembling wall toward the entrance of the big house. He spotted the heavy door under the stairs. Pulling it open, he shoved Vonnie into the darkness and jumped in behind her.

O'Connor stood and moved toward the big white man's study. The thought that Muldoon hadn't even thought of anyone's safety but his own made O'Connor angry. He wasn't about to be treated like an ox, hitched to a wagon for Muldoon to ride. He'd had enough. He thought of a way to get Muldoon and teach the man he wasn't so dumb and easy to control after all. Muldoon had played him off Bodine and Nat Black for years. No more. Black was in jail and would likely be hanged. Before that happened, the man was sure to tell all. There was no way of knowing where Bodine was by now, but if the man was out there with the storm and Zac Cobb to boot, O'Connor doubted he'd ever see him again.

He squatted in front of the safe and began to turn the dials. In all the times he'd watched Muldoon open the big safe, he'd pretended not to look, but he knew the combination like he knew his own name. He cranked the brass handle and jerked the heavy door open. Reaching into it, he drew out a cloth sack. Opening the drawstrings, he began to stuff the bag with greenbacks. He'd leave the coins; they were too heavy. He knew he'd be able to live high on the hog for quite some time with this cash. Maybe he'd even go to Europe.

Pulling the drawstrings closed, he slammed the door to the safe and spun the dial. Then he opened the first few buttons on his shirt and stuffed down the bulging bag.

+ + + + +

Vonnie had pressed herself into the corner of the gun vault.

It was pitch black and all she could hear was the sound of Buster's breathing. Then she heard him slide toward her on the floor.

"Little girl," he said. "It's just me, honey. I'm gonna be real nice to you, if you're nice to me."

+   +   +   +   +

The worst of the storm had passed over Zac and Skip, but the wind persisted like something out of a Gothic tale. Debris continued to swirl around them, making them keep their heads down.

"Get up!"

Zac recognized the voice without looking up.

"I don't want my shots passin' through you and hittin' the boy, so get yerself up and face me like a man."

Zac lifted himself off of Skip and got to his knees. Bodine stood in the swirling wind and darkness and gleamed a bright smile, pointing both silver-handled Remingtons straight at Zac.

"I don't care whatever else happens today," Bodine said. "This is gonna make it all worth it, worth it and then some."

Zac squinted his eyes. Walking forward out of the swirling storm like a spirit out of the mist was Poor Soul. The noise of the wind made it impossible to hear the man's footsteps, and Zac pretended not to see him.

"Stand still!" Poor Soul shouted. "You ain't man enough to face either him, or me, for that matter."

Bodine whirled around and began shooting both guns in the direction of the voice behind him. Zac quickly covered Skip again and drew his own revolver. Poor Soul had leveled his gun and taken careful aim. He fired one shot, a well-placed one that slammed into Bodine's forehead, jerking him backward and onto the ground beside Zac. The man was dead before he hit the ground.

Zac got to his feet and pulled Skip up beside him, covering the boy's eyes from view of the fallen cowboy.

Poor Soul continued to brace himself against the wind, moving forward out of the whirling dust and rocks. "You all right,

Zac?" he asked. "You and the boy?"

"We're just fine, thanks to you. What made you walk down here with that twister in the air?"

"Just foolishness, I reckon. But fools are sometimes the wisest of the bunch."

The dark-walled cloud had moved north of them, straight toward Muldoon's ranch. It was like the finger of God digging a deep swath in the Kansas dirt.

Zac saw Poor Soul's eyes brighten and then he turned around to see what the man had seen. There, walking through the swirling dust, were Barb, Karen, Pera, and Joe. Joe was leading a saddled horse. "I don't know who this animal belongs to, but he was plumb loco when I got hold of him," he called above the wind.

Then Dorothy walked down the hill toward the others and, spotting her sisters, ran toward them. The three women embraced, shaking their heads over their good fortune to still be alive.

"Where d'ya think them fellers went to that was ona that hill?" Pera asked.

"That twister cut right through here and over that rise," Zac said. "If they stayed on the hill, they're miles away by now."

He took the shotgun from Dorothy, who looked stunned. "You all right?" he asked.

She nodded, but said nothing.

"I'm gonna take that animal and ride for Muldoon's place," Zac said. "The storm's headed thataway."

"Is that where Vonnie is?" Barb asked. "You don't think she was up on that hill with those men, do you?"

"N-no," Skip answered. "She's at the ranch. They left her there and took me here."

"Then she's right in the path of the twister," Joe stated flatly.

+ + + + +

Vonnie kicked hard in the direction of the man's voice. She felt her heel jolt his head back and spill him onto the floor. Reaching for one of the rifles she had felt standing next to her, she pushed open the door slightly, sending a narrow beam of light into the vault. Then moving back into the corner, she crouched low.

"Girl, that weren't nice. Now I'm gonna have to hurt you. I come all the way back for you when I coulda ridden on outta here, and just because I had a fondness for you. I been looking at you ever since that pond in Texas."

He leaned his head into the light and Vonnie swung the rifle. It caught the man's head with a snap, collapsing him onto the floor.

Vonnie scrambled to her feet. She could see that the man on the floor was still. The sound of the wind had become more intense, and she thought the roof was being torn away.

Opening the door the rest of the way, she looked for ammunition. On a top shelf, she spotted a box of Winchester shells. She fumbled for the box, got it out the door with the rifle, then stumbled and dropped the box. Collecting as many shells from the floor as she could, she crammed them into the action of the gun. She'd used one of these firearms plenty of times.

The house was dark because of the storm except for the flickering lamplight. Vonnie thought of the fires that followed such storms, often doing more damage than the wind.

She clung to the inside wall and moved toward the front door of the mansion. Somehow being out in the storm seemed a better prospect than being in the house. The walls swayed and buckled; window shutters first slammed against the windows and then flew off all together. Then she heard popping sounds, and small explosions, like glass breaking.

She rounded a corner and ran directly into Jock O'Connor. He grabbed for the rifle, pulling it easily from her hands. There was a look of wild panic in his eyes as Vonnie backed away from him. "We're all gonna die in here!" He grabbed for her, but she fell backward onto the floor. And as she scrambled to her feet, the man lurched forward and ran back into the great room.

Before he got there, O'Connor's feet hit the scattered cartridges. He swung his arms wildly, then crashed to the floor.

Vonnie ran past the prone man, seized the rifle, and went for the entrance. But the sound of debris bashing against the front door caused her to back up, all the way down the hallway, until she was at the door of Muldoon's study. Pictures on the wall had fallen and the tapestries were flapping like giant birds in flight. Looking back from where she'd come, she saw the huge red-haired man coming straight for her. She aimed the rifle above his head and fired.

The man darted back and Vonnie searched frantically for someplace to hide. On either side of the room were massive bookshelves with doors beside them. A heavy desk stood in front of the massive window. She moved quickly to one of the doors beside the bookshelves.

An explosion rocked the house. It felt like the whole place was breaking up, and Vonnie sank to her knees, dropping the rifle. Her hand touched the side of the shelf as it swayed, dumping books onto the floor.

As she lifted her head, the big Irishman was over her with a drawn revolver. "I can't just leave you here, lass," he said.

Vonnie closed her eyes. The room was shaking, and all at once the wall-length shelf beside her began to topple. She stole a peek just as O'Connor reeled backward in horror. The shelf pitched forward and fell directly onto the man, crushing him beneath the pile of heavy oak boards and hundreds of volumes of hard-backed books.

Vonnie began to tremble. Her teeth chattered and her skin became cold and prickly. The air felt electrified. Even the floor beneath her seemed to move and groan as if in the throes of death. Why did it all have to end this way? In a place of strangers, away from her family and loved ones.

Down the hallway, she heard the front door finally give way. The loud crash was followed by a roaring wind that literally tore through the house.

Then, just when she thought her life was over, Vonnie looked up to see the man with the bleach-white skin standing in the doorway of the room, his long, snowy hair whipping around his head. She blinked and stared, unable to move. The man's red eyes looked like flames to her as he reached for a gleaming knife from a sheath at his side.

As he circled the big desk, another explosion rocked the study as the colossal windowpane blew into thousands of glimmering daggers that were launched into the room in every direction. Vonnie covered her eyes.

When she lowered her hands, she saw to her horror that a slender shard of glass had driven itself through the man's throat. He stood there in shock for seconds, which to Vonnie seemed like hours, unable to move, apparently unable to comprehend what had happened. He mouthed words the girl could not make out, and then, he dropped to the floor.

CHAPTER 37

+ + + + + + +

THE DAY OF KAREN AND JOE'S wedding marked the highlight of what had been a rather late and unusual Indian summer. It came one week after the cattle were gathered and sold to a happy Charlie Harrow. Only seventy some-odd head were missing from the original count, but Harrow was so happy to have an end to the rustling, he gave his full quoted price to the family as a wedding gift.

It hadn't taken Pera long to find a way to make money in his newfound restaurant. He had rented the large storage area next to the depot and was soon busy serving the best bread and veal west of Kansas City, even when there wasn't a passenger train at the Dodge City stop. The wedding reception was held at Pera's restaurant, and he put out the best spread many of them had ever seen.

"You lika my ravioli?"

Joe smiled and nodded, his mouth as full as the mouth of a groom in a new suit was permitted to be. Zac sat next to him, along with Skip. Next to Skip was Dr. Marvin. The man was recovering nicely and selling more clocks than he had ever imagined possible.

"It's a shame James and Julian couldn't have been here," Zac said to Joe.

"Yeah. It would have been great to have shared this day with them, all right. James's wife wired back to say he was in Europe on business."

"He always was able to help me with my ciphering," Zac

replied. "Glad he's able to use his talents building bridges."

Joe nodded. "Did I tell you the last time I ran into Julian was in El Paso, shortly after the war? He'd come up in the world quite a bit by then, working for the Emperor of Mexico—that Austrian fella the French got goin' down in Mexico. Julian was part of the man's personal guard, recruitin' an army of gringos."

Zac stuck a fork into the meat-filled pastry and chewed it with apprehension. "Sure would be something to run in to him again."

"I couldn't see the sense of going off and fighting for someone that didn't even belong there," Joe continued his train of thought, "but you know Julian."

"Yes, I know Julian," Zac smiled.

"He never needed much of a reason to fight. To him, war was what made life worthwhile, and he's got the scars to prove it. I think when that Maximilian fella was shot, Julian took himself to Russia. At least that's what I heard."

Karen was circulating among the guests, and Joe watched her with admiration. The woman was a constant surprise to him. The last thing he expected of her was to be sociable like this. It seemed she could be or do most anything she put her mind to. Zac and Skip were leaving for California on the morning train, and Joe was thankful for these moments of conversation with his long lost brother.

"I always held out hope that I would meet up with you somewhere," Zac told Joe. "You know, I brushed shoulders with the man that was your and Julian's prison commander during the war."

"Wretched man," Joe exclaimed.

"Then I don't reckon he'd changed much since you knew him."

"It don't look like you've put the war behind you, either," Joe said.

"It does seem that the curse of killing follows me wherever I go. I don't look for it, mind you, I'm just sent out by Wells Fargo to end the robberies. They pay me to do it, and they don't much care how it's done."

"I would think that now you've got the boy to look after," Joe said, "and the woman whose picture you carry with you, that you'd be looking to build something that lasts—like a family."

"I plan to do just that. It'll be hard for me to leave my line of work, but someday soon I do plan to settle down. I don't rightly know when that will be, but I do say no to Wells Fargo from time to time already."

"Well, little brother, when you get down our way in Texas, you know where to find Karen and me. We'd like a visit."

"I sure do plan on that," Zac smiled, "and I expect you'll have a passel of kids by the time I make it there."

CHAPTER 38

+ + + + + + +

SEVERAL WEEKS LATER, when the group rolled into War Eagle, Randolph and Barb had already cemented an agreement to marry, and Joe and Karen had enjoyed honeymooning on the trail back from Dodge City. It hadn't seemed to bother them that they couldn't be off somewhere alone. The two were lost in each other. Karen's sisters were extremely happy for Karen, and seeing her with her new husband sent constant giggles through Vonnie. Dorothy was back to her old self. Poor Soul and Tipper had ridden along with the small caravan, Poor Soul to lend a hand wherever needed, and Tipper, if for no other reason, to show his father that he had grown up and become a man.

The winter ground was hard and brown, but it looked beautiful to the Reddiger women. Overhead, whispers of clouds traced a sketchy scrawl across the blue sky, and the chill was barely noticeable.

Barb had debts to pay, and an agreement that she was looking forward to breaking. They pulled their two wagons up outside of Bickerstaff's General Store. "I'll just pay our debt," Barb said, "and then pick up a few supplies for the ranch. I doubt there's a stitch of anything to eat there but rattlesnakes."

"Good," Joe said. "Karen and I have a little shopping to do while you and Randolph handle the business."

Karen squeezed Joe's arm and smiled.

Bickerstaff was sweeping the store when the group walked in. "Sure an' to God be the glory!" he yelled. "I knew you'd be back, I just knew it. No matter what dem people told me, I knew

325

ve hadn't seen the last of you Reddiger women."

Barb gave the man a hug and introduced him to the others.

He looked Randolph over. "A lawyer, you say. Lord knows ve need some legal law 'round here. Mosta the time, whatever Blev Henry says is the law."

"Well, that's gonna change," Randolph replied, "starting today."

"I'm here to settle our accounts, Mr. Bickerstaff." Barb pulled out a wad of fresh bills. "We'll need some supplies as well, and we're paying for them with cash."

The balding man scooted around the counter. He rifled through a stack of papers that he kept in a well-worn cigar box. "The missus vill be plenty happy to see some cash money, but we always knew you girls was good for anything you took."

"I won't forget you stocking us with those supplies, Mr. Bickerstaff, and the wagon."

"It worked well for you, did it? And how'd that Italian fella do?"

"He was a godsend. He's set up a fine eating place up in Dodge City, serving hot bread night and day."

"By golly, I sure do miss dat bread of his, and de fancy stuff he fixed for us last Christmas, land sakes alive."

They paid their bill, and Bickerstaff helped to load the new supplies into the wagons. He wiped his hand on his flour-covered apron. "Dat Blev Henry's over to the bank," he said. "Emmy's over there, and they got another fella with them—a gunslinger type, I think."

"A man with a black beard?" Karen asked.

"Dat's him. Goes by the name a Wolf. He rode into town a week ago. From the looks of the animal he was riding, I'd say he had hisself a mighty hard trail."

Karen turned rigid. She cinched her hat string tight and, reaching into the wagon, pulled out her .45 and buckled it on.

"What's that thing for?" Joe asked.

She tied the holster to her leg. "This is Reddiger business," she said.

"You're a Cobb now, and that makes it my business too."

Poor Soul had taken out his six-gun and was dropping a sixth round under the hammer.

Karen looked over at him. "I appreciate all you can do with that," she said, "but like I mentioned, this is Reddiger business."

Barb took hold of her arm. "Karen, you're a married woman now. You've got your own life to think about. We'll settle up the ranch's affairs here and start over again. That's the way Father would have wanted it to be. We have things to do to build the place back up, and we need you to help with that."

"I don't want my sister-in-law as my first client in this town," Randolph added. "We'll make these people pay, and pay dearly before we're through."

"Henry's got his cattle grazing on your place," Bickerstaff added. "He's calling all of dat bottom property Bar-H land."

"That will all change," Randolph said. "Those men will see a new lay of the land in just about five minutes."

He turned to Dorothy. "You, Vonnie, and Tipper can wait right here—the rest of us will deal with the bank." Looking at Karen he added, "It's best if you leave that gun out here. If you don't have the temptation close to hand, it'll make it all the better for the rest of us."

Karen looked at him and then pulled the .45 from her holster. She opened the door to the revolver and, pulling a round from a loop in the gun belt, slid it into the empty chamber. Spinning the cylinder, she planted it back in the holster. "Let's go," she said.

The five of them started across the street, and Joe put his hand on Karen's arm. "I'm not about to try and stop you," he said. "But I want you to remember how you felt on the trail when those men tried to take the horses. Any hatred you feel now isn't going to change how you'll feel when this thing is all over. The guilt will be deep, and anger isn't going to change it, no matter what you think now."

She kept her eyes straight ahead and continued to walk, keeping pace with Barb and the others. Joe had seen the look on Karen's face before on the trail, so it came as no surprise. And he'd already decided to love her no matter what—the tenderness about her as well as the tough.

When Barb entered the bank, she spoke to the teller. "Can you tell Frank Emmy that the Reddigers are here to see him?"

"He's in there with Mr. Henry," the teller replied.

"Good," she said, "we have business with both of them."

Moments later, when the teller came out of the corner office, he motioned the group in.

As they entered the office, Emmy rose from his desk, but Blev Henry remained seated in a leather chair beside the window. Standing beside him was Wolf Macrae. Barb ignored the two of them and placed the stack of bills on Emmy's desk. "That should cover what's owed on the Circle R."

Emmy smiled and came around his desk. "That ranch was to be a wedding gift, Barbara."

"If you'd like it to be, I'd be happy to accept it. But first, let me introduce you to the man I'm about to marry. He's my fiancé and my lawyer, Mr. Lance Randolph."

Randolph stepped forward. "I will be opening an office here in War Eagle, and handling the affairs of the Circle R, along with other business." He looked over at Blev Henry, still seated in the chair. "I'm given to understand you have cattle grazing on our property, Henry. We will take a count of them and invoice you fifty cents a head for the grazing. For as long as they remain on the property, we will bill you at the rate of two bits a day, per head."

The statement brought Blev Henry to his feet. His rumpled brown suit hung loosely on his bloated body. The man's gray eyes glared in the direction of the challenge. "I won't pay it."

Macrae spoke up. "Yer just a no-count cowboy, Randolph. That's all you was, and that's all you'll ever be."

Ignoring the remarks, Lance replied, "Oh, you will pay, Henry. We will collect a number of steers equal to the market value of what you owe. I'll draw up legal papers to that effect and have the sheriff here serve them on you tomorrow. This is business, sir, nothing personal."

He looked at Macrae, then. "I may have been a cowboy, and

a better one than you, I might add, because unlike you I always rode for the brand. But now I'm returning to the legal profession. I think all of you gentlemen will soon discover that I am a very good attorney-at-law. I've already sent word to the bank examiner in Austin. He will be here tomorrow to check over your books. We'll see if this bank is handling its affairs in an even-handed manner."

He glared at Emmy. "Now, you just draw us up a receipt for these funds and find the paper you are carrying on the Circle R. We will soon be buying stock, and before you know it, we'll have a right smart operation up and running."

"We'll just see about that," Henry replied.

"Yes, we will," Randolph shot back. "I think you'll find that you've thrown your loop much too widely in these parts. You're welcome to be an honest rancher here, but the thievery has come to an end."

Macrae put his hand to his chin and pulled slightly on his beard. He and Blev Henry exchanged glances. Macrae moved to the door, leaving the group to talk.

Karen watched him carefully as he left the room. Turning back to Henry she said, "We want a ranch my mother and father would have been proud to call their own."

"I think you'll find that there's more than one way to deal with hard heads," Henry said. "Men like the one that just left teach their own brand of Texas wisdom. Your father discovered that."

Karen wheeled around and bolted for the door, followed by Joe. Moving out onto the sidewalk, she saw Macrae. "Wolf," she yelled. "Turn around and go for your gun."

It happened so fast Joe had no time to react. The man called Wolf whirled around and went for his gun, while Karen's fairly leapt into her hand. She fired, hitting the man in the leg and sending him to the ground in shock. His shot slammed into the boardwalk, and then he allowed his gun to dangle loosely in his hand.

Karen marched forward and fired a second time, sending a hot round searing into the arm that held the weapon. Her eyes blazed as she approached the wounded man and cocked her gun.

Pressing the steel rod to his forehead, she spoke low and deliberately. "Who told you to kill my father? Was it Blev Henry?"

"Why . . . Why should I tell you? You're gonna kill me anyway!" Intense fear was written on his face.

"It's different facing someone when you can't bushwhack him like you did my father, isn't it? Why should I kill you? You're just a tramp with a gun—one who won't even be able to pick one up for a while. And you're a killer—a killer that's been beaten by a woman. There's plenty of men in Texas that'd be happy to put your lights out. I will tell you one thing, though," she continued, still pressing the steel to his head, "if you don't tell me the truth right now, I might just be the one to take your head off."

The man held up his good arm. "Okay, Henry gave me the order. Emmy paid me the money, but it was Henry that gave out the order."

Joe pushed the gun away and pulled the man to his feet. "Let's go back into the bank. We have a new officer of the court hereabouts and I'm sure he'd love to hear your story."

EPILOGUE

+ + + + + + +

VONNIE STOOPED DOWN to lay fresh flowers on the side-by-side graves. She paused for a moment and, close to the ground, her lips moved silently. Tipper looked on. The group had assembled at the small plot that day as if to give an updated report on the ranch to its original owners. There was little to be said, but everyone gathered knew that much was being said in the hearts of each of the Reddiger sisters. Barb slipped her arm around Randolph, and Karen stood alone as Joe watched. Dorothy had a bucket of water in her hand and proceeded to moisten the soil on the graves with a tin ladle that had been punctured with a nail.

Vonnie stood up and walked over to Barb. "Do you think they know?" she asked.

"They've always known," Barb said. "From the day each of us was born, they knew what we would be like and they knew what we would do, if we had to."

"Should we be putting stones here to mark their graves?" Vonnie wondered aloud.

"I don't think so." Barb looked around at the congregated group. "I believe we are the only stones they would have wanted. Do you remember what Father said to us when we asked about a stone for Mother's grave?"

"Yes," Vonnie said. "He looked us each in the eye and said that when he looked at us, he saw Mother. And that was all he needed to see, the look of Mother in our eyes."

"That's right," Barb said. "They never came here to build a

331

ranch, or anything else made from wood or stone. They came out here to build a family, people who would love each other and make a difference for all time. And when I see us all standing here, I can't help but see them too."

NOTE

+ + + + + + +

A BEST TOLD STORY is a story that's been lived. As a
writer of historical fiction, I believe it best to experience what
is written. There are many ways to do just that. The areas I
write about are places I've walked over, land I've slept on, and
rivers I've crossed. *The Rawhiders* is centered around the cattle
trade of the late 1870s. I've worked with and branded cattle myself, and know it to be a hard, dirty, and thankless job, with
many bruises to keep a cowboy company long after the round-
up's done. I also read extensively about the people and events
from any era I write about.

I use what I learn from a study of the time and people as I
develop my stories and create the characters that live them.
Some of the people in this book are historical and presented ac-
curately; others are representations dressed in different names.

The people who lived in the West had dreams and lives that
are reflected by our own. Their values, however, were more distinct. To read deeply into the lives of men and women of the
West is to see a time when a distinct line existed between black
and white, right and wrong. Often the worst of men possessed
a definite sense of it, and made little attempt to justify wrong-
doing. Many acknowledged a hereafter of righteous judgment,
and the great majority were marked by a sense of Christian
training and Judeo-Christian values.

I have borrowed from the diaries of people who lived in the
West in order to capture their thinking and the values that made
up their way of life. I thought you might be interested in a few

of the historical facts I learned and incorporated into *The Raw-hiders*:

The early salesmen of the plains had many techniques designed to generate sales among the farmers. For example, they would place clocks on loan in prominent positions in the sod cabins. After several weeks, they returned to take the clocks back. But by then the farmers were hesitant to part with what seemed to be an unnecessary purchase only weeks before.

The overland cattle trade from Texas to the Kansas cow towns reached its peak in the late 1870s and early 1880s, with close to 400,000 cattle brought to market by means of the cattle drive.

By 1876 Dodge City was known as the "Cowboy Capital of the West." For almost fifteen years, Texas herds were trailed there. Quarantines of Texas cattle with the dreaded Texas fever, brought north by tics the Longhorns seem impervious to, signaled the death of the trail drive.

Able "Shanghai" Pierce was a Texas cattle baron and trail boss known for his bravado. At one point he controlled 50,000 head of cattle while owning only eleven acres of land, which he later turned into a property of over one million acres.

Bat Masterson became Sheriff of Ford County, Kansas. After serving as a U.S. marshal, appointed by President Theodore Roosevelt, he became a well-known New York sportswriter and died at his desk in 1921.

Wyatt Earp became a policeman in Dodge City in May of 1876. In 1878 he assumed the position of assistant marshall of Dodge, also acting as deacon of the Union Church. Rumor has it that during his time there, Doc Holliday saved his life from several Texas cowboys who resented being ordered about by the slender "Yankee lawman."